Ro~

~ ~otland's great Romantic. Ther~ ~s a pas~ ~al
~eir courtship is drawn gorgeously. *The Jewel* finally
~oice to Jeany Armour, the girl who sang as sweetly as the
nightingale, who was muse, mother, wife and lover to Scotland's
national poet. This is her song.' SUNDAY MAIL

'Uplifting…does much to put right the wrongs of historians.
The characters come to life beautifully on the page…Serves as a
superbly researched biography of a deeply admirable woman who
until now has been…unjustly neglected.' UNDISCOVERED SCOTLAND

'Beguiling and enchanting…Czerkawska is an excellent
storyteller… Full of suspense…and lush sensuality, so you can
almost feel the grass brushing against your skin, and smell the
honeysuckle in summer evenings.' SCOTTISH REVIEW

'A beautiful historical novel.' EDINBURGH CITY OF LITERATURE

PRAISE FOR CATHERINE CZERKAWSKA'S PREVIOUS NOVELS:

'Czerkawska tells her tale in a restrained, elegant prose that only
adds to its poignancy.' SUNDAY TIMES (SEASON'S BEST HISTORICAL FICTION)

'A powerful story about love and obligation…a persuasive novel,
very well written.' JOHN BURNSIDE

'Moving, poetic and quietly provocative.' THE INDEPENDENT

'Take any aspect of the novelist's art and you'll find it
exemplified here to perfection.' BILL KIRTON, BOOKSQUAWK

'Heart-warming, realistic and page-turning.' LORRAINE KELLY

'Beautiful – lyrical and sensual by turns.' HILARY ELY

'A compelling read, with a satisfying blend of history, nature and
romance.' AMANDA BOOTH, THE SCOTS MAGAZINE

'Czerkawska's script is blisteringly eloquent. She is particularly
brilliant on ~

MACMILLAN

The Jewel

A novel of the life of Jean Armour
and her husband, Robert Burns

Catherine Czerkawska

Saraband

Published by Saraband
Suite 202, 98 Woodlands Road
Glasgow, G3 6HB, Scotland
www.saraband.net

ISBN: 9781910192238
ebook: 9781910192245

Printed and bound in Great Britain by Clays Ltd, St Ives plc.

Publication of this book has been supported by Creative Scotland.

3 5 7 9 10 8 6 4

The Belles of Mauchline

In Mauchline there dwells six proper young belles,
The pride of the place and its neighbourhood a';
Their carriage and dress, a stranger would guess,
In Lon'on or Paris, they'd gotten it a':

Miss Miller is fine, Miss Markland's divine,
Miss Smith she has wit, and Miss Betty is braw:
There's beauty and fortune to get wi' Miss Morton,
But Armour's the jewel for me o' them a'.

Robert Burns

Chapter One

Jeany

There was a lass, and she was fair,
At kirk or market to be seen;
When a' our fairest maids were met,
The fairest maid was bonnie Jean.

The first time Jean Armour spoke to Rab Burns of Mossgiel, she was spreading linen on the bleach green. It was a fine day, but cold: one of those sharp, sunny days of early spring. There were catkins on the willows, buds on the trees, and the grass was greening up, but nothing was in leaf yet. You could see the light growing and feel the push of it in the ground. There was already a scattering of golden blossoms on the whins, like a promise of something to come. Later the hedgerows would be ablaze with it.

'When the whins are in bloom, kissing's in season,' the lads would chant, trying to catch her around her neat waist as she passed them by.

Jean had been spreading out the linen: sheets and shirts and tablecloths, including the big cloth that her mother kept for best, draping some of them over small shrubs and bushes so that the twigs would keep them in place. The frost was as good as the sunlight for bleaching linen. You would put it through the mangle to smooth the fibres and then spread it out for the frost or the sunlight or both, one following the other, to do their work, hoping that the birds wouldn't do theirs on the newly washed sheets. Sometimes a lad could be persuaded to scare them away for a bawbee or even a piece of bread and cheese, just held in his hand, if he was hungry enough. But all lads were hungry all the time. Her

1

father, James Armour, liked his shirts well laundered for the kirk, although it was hard when the house was so full of the stone dust that he brought indoors with him every evening.

Jean had begun later than usual, and the other lassies had already gone home. It was one of those days when the fire had refused to blaze up properly to heat the water, so she and her mother and sister had started the laundry late. Her mother blamed the chimney although her father said it was only when the wind blew a certain way. Now everything was late and like to get later. She was working alone on the green, spreading the linen over bushes and smoothing out the sheets on the grass, hoping that the weather wouldn't turn, that she hadn't missed the best of the day. As usual, she was singing to speed the work.

That was when Rab Mossgiel came walking along on his way to visit his landlord, or that's what she assumed, because he seemed to be heading in the direction of Gavin Hamilton's house. A young dog was at his heels, a collie, more black than white, half grown and skittish. Jean recollected that somebody had killed Rab's much loved dog, Luath, the night before his father died. That had been at Lochlea, the place where they had farmed before moving to Mossgiel, just outside the town of Mauchline. Somebody had killed the poor animal while Rab's father, William, lay at death's door, with his family gathered around his bedside.

She supposed this must be a replacement for Luath. Although Rab was careful to avoid the sheets and shirts, the dog, little more than a puppy, was not so cautious and ran over the linen after his master, leaving muddy paw-marks in its wake. The work involved in washing those sheets! She thought of her aching arms and the pride her mother took in the wash and her father's complaints about marks on his Sabbath shirts. What would he make of paw prints? Especially Rab Mossgiel's dog's paw prints.

'Away you go!' she shouted.

She picked up a pebble and threw it at the dog. Her aim was true, and the stone hit the dog on his rump, not really injuring him, but stinging him, so that he sat down suddenly, turned around and bit repeatedly at himself as though a flea had nipped him there. Then he gazed at her, panting, one ear up and one ear down. He looked so comical that she couldn't help but laugh.

'Lassie, lassie!' said the young man with a sort of mock indignation. 'If you thought ought of me, you wadnae hurt my dog!'

His eyes were full of mischief. He was laughing and she was laughing and she raised her eyebrows and said, 'I wadnae think much of you at any rate, Rab Mossgiel!'

At the time she said it, it may even have been the truth. She couldn't have cared less about him, even though he made her laugh.

'That's me tellt then,' he said, pulling a rueful face.

She gazed at him, the sheet in her hand. He wore a light blue wool coat, home-spun and homemade too, she thought, but smart for all that. Long black hair, tied back and curling down over his collar. And a book in his hand. Well they were right about that. He aye had a book in his hand.

He'd moved to Mossgiel earlier that year. Most of them didn't yet call him Rab Mossgiel in the town because it was too soon, although she'd heard that's what he called himself, proud of his new farm. Rab's father, William, had used the old north-eastern family name of Burness, and Rab still spelled his name that way, although he was about to change it to plain Burns for reasons best known to himself. James Armour clearly thought that was just another affectation.

'Who does he think he is with his tied hair and his fancy plaid and his fancy manners?' he said, scathingly, when Jean mentioned the incident at home later that day.

Her mother had laughed and sung a few lines of a song:

'Oh they gaed to Kirk and Fair,
Wi' their ribbons round their hair,
And their stumpie drugget coats,
Quite the dandy O!'

3

James had already made up his mind to dislike Rab, although there were many people of whom her father did not approve, so there was little wonder in that. The 'fancy plaid' was a yellowy brown colour that put you in mind of autumn leaves. He was wearing it now. Rab fastened it around his shoulders in a peculiar way, taking time and trouble to get it just right. The lad's reputation as something of a dandy had come to the town before him, so said Mr Auld the minister. He was known as Daddie Auld because he was practically built in with the stones of the kirk. Every town and village had its 'faither', the oldest and wisest man, but although Mr Auld was perhaps not the oldest, he was certainly deemed wisest. Rab did not have a very good reputation with the kirk elders, even though his new landlord, Mr Hamilton, seemed to like him well enough. But as her father said, that was no recommendation either, for Gavin Hamilton was not a God-fearing man. Jean was nineteen when the Burns family moved to Mossgiel, and she already knew all about the eldest son – that he was a lad best avoided by a lass like her, a lass with a good reputation to maintain.

* * *

She had been a February baby, a dangerous time to be born, when the days were dark and sickness was rife. Spring and summer babies fared better as a rule. She was named for her mother's mother: Jean. Wee Jeany, her father called her, even when she was grown and not that wee any more. But she was strong and she thrived. They told her later that she sang before she spoke. Or rather sang and spoke at the same time, jigging up and down on her mother's knee in time to the rhythm of the song. She was the apple of her father's eye. Stern and strict as he was, he softened whenever he gazed at her. Couldn't help himself.

'My lass,' he would call her, patting her head. 'My bonnie lass.'

Whenever anyone asked her what her father did for a living, she would say, 'He builds bridges,' which was, in a way, quite true. But it made him smile to hear her say it. James Armour was a master mason in the parish of Mauchline, and he did build bridges and houses too – the fine houses of the gentry, Skeldon House and Dumfries House – but not always with his own two hands and not always the whole building. He contracted much of the work out to others, overseeing, supervising, but not above getting his hands dirty himself when occasion demanded it. The men he worked with feared him but always respected him. He had the hands of a working man, the stony dirt of years engrained there, the nails ragged and grimy, however much he washed them of an evening. When she thought about him, she remembered chiefly his big hand in hers, the roughness of it beneath her small fingers.

There were plenty of children in the Armour house on the busy Cowgate, and there was plenty of sickness too. She had lost five siblings, some when she was too young to feel more than a pang of sadness at the passing of the new baby sister or brother, an absence coupled with a mild sense of panic, mostly caused by her mother's misery and sudden silences. But all the while, whatever troubles came to their door, her father was steady, a beacon of good sense, trusting in his God through all his sorrows. She was sure of his love at least.

They were not exactly a rich household, but there was no shortage of money. When any of the children were really sick, the doctor came. But more often than not, his medicine was inadequate and the infants died anyway. Perhaps it made the survivors, Jean especially, all the more precious in their father's eyes. The more tragedy struck the family, the more he seemed to want to shield this dearly loved daughter from harm. She learned that lesson herself and never forgot it. But as a child, she took his love for granted.

They lived decently in a certain amount of comfort, with fuel for their fires, blankets and clean linen for their beds, and they always ate well, even at the lean and hungry times of year. They were no more cramped than any other house in the town and considerably warmer, far better off than most. James even paid for a good family pew in the body of the kirk, more than anyone else in the town, ten shillings and eight pence every single year, even when times were hard. He paid for shawls and warm cloaks for winter; bought silks and cottons for best dresses for the women of the family, woollen coats for the men. The cobbler made leather shoes for Sundays so that nobody need be ashamed of being seen shoeless in the kirk.

The Mauchline folk knew who she was, Armour's eldest daughter who could sing like a lintie and dance too. Fleet of foot, whether shod or not, and light of heart.

'Jeany, can ye no be still?' her father would say in loving exasperation, but even then, he couldn't seem to help smiling at her. Looking back on her childhood, she could see that it had mostly been happy. She could picture herself running about the green with her friends. It was always summer in her mind's eye, and she seemed to be free from care. She had been a small person of some consequence in the town, with well made clothes to cover her back and, once past the commonplace dangers of infancy, the robust good health that came from the blessings of good food and a warm, dry home.

She had always loved to have nice things about her. Back then, of course, she accepted it as her due, but only later did she come to appreciate what a good provider James Armour must have been, never leaving her mother without the wherewithal to feed and clothe the family, always putting himself last, even though he was as fond of his dram as the next man. When his day's work was over, he would often take a drink with Johnnie Dow who owned the Whitefoord Arms along the road. But she had never seen her father the worse for drink. He knew when to stop. He was a canny man, a man of sound business sense.

'A good provider is worth a very great deal. A hungry care's an unco care,' as her mother was fond of saying.

Jean learned that lesson too, although she didn't always heed it as perhaps she should. Not once she had fallen acquainted with Rab. The first time Jean spoke to him rather than about him, that time at the bleach green, she had been singing while she worked. Her mother knew all the old songs, and from the moment when her lips could utter recognisable words, Jean had been singing. She knew so many songs that she could hardly remember what she did know: songs for all seasons and none. They just came into her mind when she wanted them. Jean often found it easier to sing than to speak. Like many dark-haired people, she always found herself blushing easily, the crimson spreading upwards from her breast to her cheeks, impossible to disguise. It was hard to say what she thought or felt. The words would not come. But she could sing it all, and there was a song for every occasion. There were songs to speed the work, where the rhythm helped the hands and feet. There were songs to send a wean to sleep. There were songs to celebrate a birth and songs to mourn a death. There were songs to curse and songs to bless. Jean had never been able to count the songs she knew. But whenever they were needed, the words came easily off her tongue and the notes soared to the heavens.

It was a gift, this singing. Sometimes, on a winter's night, when the younger children were asleep, the house seemed too quiet, and it was then that James Armour would take down his old fiddle and play, telling Jean to sing for him, and she always did. She was pleased and proud, knowing that the good Lord had given her the gift of song and it was something to treasure and nothing of which she needed to be ashamed.

But there were some songs she didn't sing for her father.

These were the songs women sang, about the joys and sorrows of love and lovers and bonnie boys and birds in briar bushes and whaups in nests. These were what women sang when they were working together, perhaps in the dairy, or weaving and spinning, cooking or washing, especially when they were out of earshot of the men. There were songs about false lovers, men who slipped away from you at time of need like knotless threads, and songs to mock those same men, mercilessly. Jean knew that these were not songs for men, even though they were sometimes songs to heal a broken heart. They would bring a blush to her cheek if she sang them to a man. But she knew them all the same. And she sang them in the

7

company of other women or when she was alone.

She was singing as she was spreading her linen on the bleach green, an old song about a ploughman. '*The ploughman he's a bonnie lad, and a' his wark's at leisure, and when that he comes hame at e'en, he kisses me wi' pleasure!*'

She was singing when the dog ran over her fresh linen and she threw a chuckie stone and Rab stopped to remonstrate with her. The song died on her lips. She found herself blushing.

'If ye thought ought of me, ye wadnae hurt my dog!' he said.

And she answered him boldly enough, 'I wadnae think much of you at any rate, Rab Mossgiel,' but she could feel herself blushing even as she said it.

'That's me tellt,' he said. And then, 'But it would be a singular pleasure for this ploughman to kiss *you* for sure!' He bowed to her suddenly, mock gallant. 'My apologies for my dog and your linen, madam!'

And he was gone, striding onwards in the direction of Gavin Hamilton's house with the dog at his heels. He was whistling jauntily, not once pausing to look behind him. Oh, a fine conceit of himself that one.

The young man seemed to be full of self-love, a besetting sin for which James Armour could see no justification whatsoever; a young man whose reputation preceded him. Nobody in authority approved, although the lassies might admire from a distance as lassies always will admire such young men. As Jean found herself gazing after him now, and admiring this dangerous young man with jet black hair, snowy white wool stockings and a fine plaid, the colour of the woods in autumn.

The words of the song came unbidden into her head: '*When my ploughman comes hame at e'en, he's often wet and wearie. Cast aff the wet, put on the dry, and gae to bed my dearie.*'

She shook the sheet, impatient with herself as much as with him.

It meant nothing. He would have said as much to any young woman.

8

Chapter Two

Fancy Plaid
and Fancy Manners

Snaw-white stockings on his legs
And siller buckles glancin,
A guid blue bonnet on his head
And O! But he was handsome.

She had heard her father and mother talking about the Burns family, talking about the farm, how for all that Robert Burns was friendly with the nabbery, no good would come of the move because Mossgiel lay high up on a ridge of land. Winters and summers alike had been cold and wet of late, and the two lads would struggle with the clay. Although Gavin Hamilton was supposed to be a friend to the poor, he was not above renting out his land to be improved by the toil of others. Daddie Auld was right when he said it was 'aye the poor who maintained the poor' in his parish. A good judge of men, James Armour had also heard that the eldest of the Mossgiel brothers suffered intermittent ill health, even though he looked like a strapping lad: fainting fits, aches and pains and all manner of other ailments that James had no patience with in a man.

'Women's ailments,' he said. 'He's no farmer, no farmer at all. An idler and a ne'er-do-weel with nothing at all to recommend him.'

Jean was forced to agree with her parents. Even if she had wanted to say something kindly about Rab Mossgiel – and perhaps she did – she didn't dare. Her father was softer with her than with anyone else in the house, including her mother. All the same, and though she wouldn't say so, Jean thought that Rab may have something to recommend him. It was mostly to do with his appearance. You couldn't help but notice him. He seemed to make an effort to stand out, and that was not well received in a town where an observance of all the conventions, as well as a careful avoidance of anything that might be labelled scandal, was considered praiseworthy and prudent. Tall poppies were ruthlessly cut down, and Rab was a very tall poppy. He wore his black hair longer than most. Her father was right about that, although it didn't infuriate Jean as it clearly infuriated James. Rab tied it behind with a ribbon, as nobody else in the parish did, an Edinburgh fashion and one that James thought was more fit for a lassie. As far as James Armour was concerned these signs betokened a young man with a high opinion of himself for no good cause that he himself could see. Too clever for his own good, thought James.

It seemed that there were gentlemen, some of them very fine gentlemen indeed, who *did* value the lad's company and that mostly because he had come to the parish with a reputation as something of a poet. It was not unusual. There were other lads and old men too who fancied themselves as poets. One of them, Saunders Tait, a Tarbolton tailor and a man of some means, disapproved of Rab and indeed his whole family, whom he seemed determined to tar with the same brush as the son. In fact, Tait disapproved of them so violently and so jealously that he had written and circulated more than one piece of insulting verse. In Tait's eyes the family could do nothing right, and when he heard of it, this was one more thing to make Jean's father disapprove of the incomer.

'Too clever by half,' said James Armour. 'See what happens when you draw attention to yourself?'

Rab's reputation with the lassies had also come before him, and that did him no credit either. The truth was that James and Mary had their hearts set on a good marriage for Jean. A weaver, perhaps. The weavers did well for themselves and, although being the wife of a weaver meant hard work and long hours, the families were generally very comfortably off. Weavers were good providers too: independent, well educated men. They made good husbands. There was a lad called Rab Wilson whom James seemed to approve of, as much as he could bring himself to approve of any potential suitor for his darling ewe lamb. Wilson was a sober, clean living, kind hearted man. He'd gone to Paisley to make his fortune at the loom, learning new ways of working from the more experienced men there. He had a good head on his shoulders, and Jean's father would be pleased if Rab Wilson might decide to come courting her. Maybe he would, one day. Maybe she wouldn't object. She liked him well enough, but she was in no hurry, and for the present, out of sight was very much out of mind.

The lassies, meanwhile, had talked about the newcomer among themselves, but their conversations were quite different from those Jean listened to at home. Jean's friend, Helen Miller, fancied that Rab Mossgiel favoured her and maybe he did. But there were those who said that he favoured any lass at all who was half-way pretty and besides, he was still seeing buxom Betty Paton.

'He's a lad who can make you laugh,' Helen Miller said, blushing as she said it. 'And there's something fine about a lad who can make you laugh.'

Jean agreed with her. She had long ago reached the conclusion that Rab Wilson, the weaver, whatever his excellent qualities, was not a man to make anybody laugh very much. He had been known to chide her for singing on the Sabbath day. In the most gentle way possible, of course, and perhaps he was right. Still, Jean sang as the birds sing, and couldn't help but think that her maker, having created the voice as well as the lass, would not be offended to hear it on His special day. She had a feeling that Rab Mossgiel would chide nobody for singing on the Sabbath. In fact he looked like a man who might do a wee bit of singing on the Sabbath himself, and it might not just be the psalms in the kirk either.

He was taller than many a lad in the village and handsome enough, although not just as handsome as Rab Wilson. All the lassies said as much whenever they spoke of him, and they spoke of him often, intrigued by the stranger, the interlowper in their midst. They were forced to admit that he had the look of what he was: a tenant farmer, with broad shoulders and coarse hands and a ploughman's slight stoop. He was a wee thing coarse about the face too, although Helen Miller was quick to say that his manners, when he chose, could be as close to those of a gentleman as made no difference. The others did not entirely believe her, wondering just how much conversation she might really have had with him. But even though Rab was mourning his father, he had already made his presence felt in the town.

It was known that he was still walking out with Betty Paton of Largieside from time to time, and nobody could say that walking out was the whole of it with a lad like Rab Burns. Betty was big and bonnie, and she was as strong as two young men put together, so she would make a good wife for a farmer. Jean and her friends had laughed about it, giggling about Rab Mossgiel and Betty Paton, wondering what they got up to, and where they did it, *if* they were doing it – behind which hedgerow or under which hayrick? They all wondered what would happen now that Rab was his own man, with a farm to mind and a family to keep, but with no stern father to keep him in check. It was well known even in Mauchline that Rab's mother, Agnes Broun, was very fond of Betty Paton. Incautiously, she had confessed as much to one of the gossips, wishing that her son would marry the lass. But that being the case, thought Jean, why had Betty not come to work at Mossgiel, now that the family had moved in? Jean could only assume that Rab didn't want what his mother wanted and that would surely be the end of it. By reputation at least, Rab Mossgiel was not a man to do as he was told. Not by anyone.

In point of fact, Jean knew Betty, although they were not friends. Everyone knew everybody else, knew their business, their faults and failings. There were few secrets in the parish but Betty and Jean were not at all the same and never had been. Jean's father had a position to maintain in the town. Betty was a dairymaid. There was no shame in being a dairymaid, of course; Rab's mother and sisters worked in the dairy at Mossgiel. His younger brother, Gilbert, was noted for the sweet milk cheese he had learned how to make, instructing his mother and his sisters in the art. But Betty had a voice and a laugh that you could hear halfway across the town and maybe even the parish. There were no airs and graces with Betty. Whatever she was thinking, she would open her mouth and out it would come. She would say what she felt. If she liked you, she would let you know. If she disliked you, she would let you know, but even more loudly and crudely, laughing to drive the point home. And her laughter would raise the dead to join in the fun.

When Rab's younger sisters could be persuaded to say anything at all about her, which was not often, they said that she was 'still half demented with love for oor Rab'. Poor Betty, thought Jean, although she was not sure why that word came so readily into her mind. It never had done until now with regard to Betty Paton, of whom Jean was always a bit afraid on account of the caustic tongue and the loud voice. Poor Betty. Half demented with love for Rab Burns of Mossgiel. Who would ever want to find herself in that position, with, maybe, a baby on the way, a whaup in the nest, which was what the gossips were whispering. But that was all hearsay, and Betty was just the same as she had ever been, a big sonsie lassie, but certainly no plumper than she had been, so per- haps it was just talk. All the same, Jean found herself wondering if a lad who aye had his nose in a book would be contented to be married to a lassie who had never even learned her letters.

Not that there were many books in the Armour household, either. It was Jean's father who had first taught her to read and write. Her mother had taught her to sing and to dance her first steps, but her father had taught her her first letters when she was too small even for the school. Later, clutching her penny in her hand and a piece of peat or wood for the fire, she had gone to the

Mauchline school with the other children, where Andrew Noble, the session clerk, attempted to improve on what her father had begun. She had never taken to that very much. The schoolroom was chilly and bleak, in spite of the fire for which there were never enough peats or coals. Not all fathers were such good providers as James, and Andrew never turned anyone away, with or without penny or peat. The room smelled of unclean clothes and unwashed bodies. The damp rose from the flagstones, summer and winter alike. And the fire smoked. Once, she came back with flea bites on her legs and her father had words with Noble. After that, they sat her elsewhere, not next to the lass that had carried the fleas in with her. Her mother would cover her dark curls with a linen cap and tell her to keep her head away from the other children. But once or twice she brought lice home with her anyway and had to suffer the indignity of the fine-tooth comb tugging through her curls, making her cry.

'Here,' her father had said. 'Give it to me, Mary. I'll do it.'

He was always very gentle with her, back then.

Andrew Noble was a good man but a stern one. She preferred the lessons from her father. James Armour was more than content to sit with his Jeany in the evenings and teach her to read some of her bible, first and foremost, and then to form letters for herself. They would use a big piece of Ballachulish slate of which there was no shortage in his line of work, and a bit of chalk, so that everything could be rubbed out and you could begin again. Mistakes didn't matter.

'See,' he would say to her when she began to cry because she couldn't get it right. 'You just rub it all away, Jeany, and you're left with a clean slate so that you can start over again!'

She had a memory of sitting with him by the light of the fire, all cooried in – she must have been only four or five – and his hand enfolding hers, the slate resting on his knee. She was fidgeting as usual and the sharp edge of the slate was digging into her leg.

'Sit at peace, hen!' he said. 'Can ye no sit at peace?'

He moved the slate to make her comfortable and planted a kiss on the top of her head lest she should think he was really cross with her. 'Now, let's begin again,' he said. And then he was forming the letter J with its curly top and bottom and saying, 'Here we go, making the wee piggy's tail. J for my Jeany.'

Once she had a rudimentary grasp of the mysteries of letters and words from her father and later on from the school, bills of sale from the business were pressed into service. James Armour had an office in the low thatched house next door. When she was a child, there were lodgers in the rest of this cottage, but later it was where Jean's elder brother John and his wife lived, along with two of her other brothers, James and young Adam. All the brothers worked for their father as soon as they were old enough. It was there too that James Armour kept his business papers in a heavy wooden desk, one that he could keep locked, keeping his affairs safe from prying eyes. He would bring a few goose feather quills, a pot of ink and some old bills through to their kitchen in the bigger house, so that Jean could practise on the back of them by the light of the fire. This was how she learned her letters, not without a certain amount of trouble, but she didn't remember any great difficulty either. Perhaps it was just that he was patient with her mistakes. Gruffly patient, almost ashamed of his partiality. Like most of the fathers in the town, it did not come easily to him.

There were few books in the house beyond the heavy family bible and the bonnie Old and New Testaments her mother took to the kirk, a gift from James upon their marriage. But when Jean grew older, some of the lassies managed to acquire novels. From where, she was always unsure and she would never enquire too closely for fear that the supply might dry up. Betty and Helen Miller were the daughters of an innkeeper, and Christina Morton's father also kept an inn on the Back Causeway, behind the kirk. These lassies saw more strangers than Jean, for the town was a great crossroads for travellers. The change houses were well patronised. These intriguing little books with their tales of forbidden love, romantic trials and tribulations, might be left behind or, so Christina said with a grin, might mysteriously disappear, never to be found again, when some guest had imbibed too freely of the excellent ale on offer. The cadger too would bring tattered copies with him from time to time, picked up along the way from heaven knows where. Some of these tales were written by women. They were not new even then, but they were books of which she knew fine her father would not approve, had he known or guessed what they were about. But he did not know or guess. Such works were beyond the limited compass of his imagination.

Worldly wise in so many ways, James Armour could scarcely comprehend that any woman could or would write such words and put them out for all to read. The girls would pass the books around, the well thumbed copies practically falling to pieces. Each prized volume would be concealed in a pocket, well out of sight of disapproving elder eyes and then kept under the mattress for a while. Jean remembered sliding the leather bound volumes out, stealthily, late on a summer's night or early in the morning when a deafening chorus of birds had woken her, and peering at the pages by the light filtering through the casement window, anxious not to wake her sisters who could never be trusted not to give the game away. They were much too young to keep secrets.

Chapter Three

The Dancing

O leave novels, ye Mauchline belles,
Ye're safer at your spinning-wheel;
Such witching books are baited hooks
For rakish rooks, like Rob Mossgiel.

Some months passed before Jean had occasion to speak to Rab
Mossgiel again. She would see him sometimes and would be
intrigued by the gossip that clung to him like peat smoke to a woollen coat. It was inevitable in a place as close-knit as this one. As
the summer progressed, she saw him in the town and she saw him
in the kirk. She even saw him in Morton's Ballroom from time to
time, where she regularly attended the dancing classes organised
by Christina's father so that the young people could assemble and
enjoy themselves under supervision. Her father tolerated rather
than approved of it. In reality, these were country dances rather than
regular classes, although occasionally some visiting master would
teach them new steps or a whole new dance. Morton would ply
him with whisky and the dancers would pay him a few coins. There
were always older ladies, widow women for the most part, happy to
sit and chaperone the dancing while eating and drinking whatever
was on offer. They were supposed to make sure that nobody over-
stepped the bounds of propriety, although the place was so crowded
that it was impossible for them to observe everything that went
on. Hands might wander when occasion arose and lips might meet,
briefly, in the middle of a dance.

Jean was good at the dancing. She had been light on her feet
from early childhood, loving to jig about the kitchen of the house

in the Cowgate, and now she had a great memory for the figures of the dance. The ballroom was a busy place, with a wooden floor that magnified the sound of their shoes and the heavy boots of the men as they jumped and spun. You had to wear shoes or boots or your toes might be flattened by over-enthusiastic neighbours and partners. The young people were crushed together in there like so many peas in a pod. In summer it was hot, and everyone was beaded with a fine layer of sweat. The girls had it easier in their cotton or muslin gowns, although even they had damp patches under their arms and around their breasts, but the young men in their best or second best linen shirts, their woollen coats and breeches, had a hard time of it. Morton would try to disguise the smell of the place with sweet herbs, but it didn't always help to mask the scent of perspiring bodies, damp linen and wool, and dirty feet. Morton would engage a couple of fiddlers; one would take over when another became weary and they would be paid a penny a reel, or whatever dance was popular at the time.

Sometimes, as Jean and her partner went down the line, Rab Mossgiel would birl her around and cast her away from him again, and their eyes would meet. Once or twice, she caught him gazing at her, then shaking himself like a dog and turning his attention elsewhere. There wasn't time for conversation and they could hardly hear each other above the din of fiddles anyway. The more she saw of him, the more she was forced to admit that he was a handsome man with fine dark eyes and long lashes like a girl, but she still thought that he was somebody to be avoided, not to be trusted with the lassies.

By November of that year, the whole town was buzzing with the news that a whaup truly was in the nest. Betty Paton was with child and the father was Robert Burns in Mossgiel. There were those who avowed they had been right all along, their neighbour Johnnie Dow's wife for one, although this made Jean smile, since if she had been right all along, Betty's confinement must have been a prodigiously long one. As it was, the lass was barely showing her shame.

In fact Helen Miller refused to believe the rumours for a long while.

'And even if it is true that she's having a wean, it's likely somebody else's,' she said, robustly. But they all knew that this was because Helen still rather fancied Rab herself. They all did, if the truth be told: the sisters, Helen and Elizabeth Miller, Christina Morton too. The Mauchline belles, Rab called them, well aware of their interest in him. Jean thought it was like setting down a peacock in the middle of a hen coop: so much fuss and consternation. But perhaps he was a fox in peacock feathers. So the fuss and consternation might be justified, although the lasses were too confident, too sure of themselves to feel really threatened.

Once or twice the gentry would deign to look in when there was dancing in Morton's Ballroom: generally Gavin Hamilton and his friends. They always arrived late and left early and they would look around them with that expression they so frequently had: one of smiling condescension as though they should be congratulated for being there at all. Jean had heard that Rab Mossgiel was good friends with his landlord, and he certainly seemed at ease in his company. But it was different for the lassies. The nabbery, especially the young men, would be eyeing up the girls in the ballroom, looking not just for the prettiest but for the most compliant, the bold lassie who would return their stare. Which Jean did not. When she was very young, fifteen or so, she had been allowed to go to the dancing with her mother or one of her aunts to supervise. Once, one of the gentlemen had brought his sister and a friend, enviably decked out in the latest fashions, and they had giggled behind their hands all evening, pulling faces at the dancers. The joy had gone out of the dance for Jean, although she couldn't have explained why she should have been so hurt by the antics of a pair of daft lassies who seemed to lack the sense they were born with.

One evening, she was in Morton's Ballroom with her friends when Rab Mossgiel came to the dancing, although he wasn't in her set. All the folk in his set were laughing uproariously. She wondered what he was saying to them to make them laugh so much. The thought occurred to her that even fashionable ladies would not laugh behind their hands at Rab. They wouldn't dare. His tongue was his weapon, but so was his verse. He could pin a body to the page. Words were powerful things. But they might laugh with him. Who could help laughing with him?

This time, though, it was not Rab's mischief that was causing the laughter. A bat had found its way into the room and was flying back and forth in a panic. It was this, and the reactions of the lassies in particular, as the creature grew weary and swept lower and lower, that was causing so much hilarity. The poor bat was in danger of scorching itself on the lamps, and the lassies were shrieking and trying to protect their heads. The fiddler was resolute and kept on playing although all the sets had become haphazard with arbitrary extra steps and evasions. A few of the lads opened a window and tried to encourage the creature to fly in that direction. Rab fetched his plaid that he had set aside while he danced, and eventually he and John Blane, the Mossgiel farmhand, managed to leap up in concert, brandishing it. The bat, momentarily disorientated by the sudden barrier, veered out of the window. The dancing resumed. Jean thought how light on his feet he was. She regretted that she wasn't in his set this time. Who could help being curious about such an intriguing lad?

Later on in the evening, Morton opened the door to let in some air, because the place was stifling and Rab was heard to remark that even wee flying mice were preferable to suffocation. The older ladies sitting around the walls, watching proceedings, were fanning themselves with whatever was to hand. Not all of them had fans and those who had were passing them along the row, or fanning their friends ferociously and wishing they could have worn muslin. One or two had brought posies of dried lavender flowers from their gardens and were holding them up to their noses to counteract the smell of unwashed clothes and rank sweat on leather boots.

Suddenly there was a commotion. Rab Mossgiel's dog had come in through the open door, the same dog that had run over Jean's sheets. Everyone knew he followed his master about like a shadow now, the replacement for poor, poisoned Luath. Everyone knew about that too, and speculation had been rife about the culprit, even here in Mauchline, with some saying it was a rejected suitor of Betty Paton, and some saying it was the jealous would-be poet, Sauny Tait. The new pup had grown over the summer. He was one of those animals with a smiling face. His pink tongue was hanging out, and when the dog saw Rab, he grinned even more widely and rushed towards him, showing all his teeth in an ingratiating smile, the very picture of delight. Rab was dancing, and for a few moments the collie was following the figures of the dance, his plume of a tail waving. He was almost tripping up the dancers, but most of all, he was almost tripping Rab Mossgiel, doing what collies do and staying close to his heel, weaving in and out. Just then the fiddler stopped, the dance ended and Rab bent down to fuss the dog, scratching behind its ears. You could see that a few of the lassies were wishing they were that dog. Jean saw that Rab was glancing over. She could see the line of his gaze and thought that he might be looking at her friend, but Christina turned her head away, deliberately putting her nose in the air. He pushed through the press of people and the dog followed him, panting in the heat.

'He's aye following me,' he said to Jean and Christina. 'I wish I could get a lassie to follow me that way!'

'There'd be no lassie daft enough,' said Christina, forthright as ever. 'Well, no lassie that I ken.'

'Do you not? That's a pity. But I think I might ken one!' He caught Jean's gaze and, greatly to her embarrassment, winked at her. 'Enjoy your dancing, lassies!'

Then he was off through the door, taking his dog with him.

'I thought he *had* a lassie to follow him that way,' said Jean.

'You mean Betty Paton? But he'll never marry her, not even with the wean.'

'No. I don't think he will. He'd rather face the cutty stool and the kirk session than marry her. But he's no denyin' he's the father, and he's looking after the wean. He's doing that at least.'

'Aye, and that's better than many a lad.'

'Maybe he fancies *you*, Chrissie.'

'It was you he winked at, Jean.'

'Aye. Well, a cat may look at a king and even wink at him. But it disnae mean he'll be wearing the crown any day soon.'

Chapter Four

The Rocking

O, clappin's guid in Febarwar,
An kissin's sweet in May
But what signifies a young man's love
An't dinna last for ay?

The Mauchline belles, the witty, well dressed lassies that Rab flirted with and courted light-heartedly by turns, had become friendly with the Mossgiel sisters, which was why they were invited to a 'rocking' out at the farmhouse, very early in 1785, not long after Jean's twentieth birthday. It was that harsh time of year when the ailing tended to die and when all entertainments that involved light and warmth were welcome. Jean's father disapproved of the party and would have probably forbidden his daughter from attending if the Miller sisters, Helen and Betty, ably assisted by Christina Morton, had not managed to persuade him. Helen and Betty were well practised at wheedling, and James was as susceptible as the next man. They didn't mention Rab at all, but spoke of Gilbert Burns in glowing terms. Gilbert was a plain, douce, grave young man, without the obvious charm of his elder brother, as self effacing as Rab was spirited. He seemed to disapprove of the Mauchline belles, but James wasn't to know that.

Rockings were intimate celebrations for families and a few friends. Folk would bring a contribution to the feast if they could, especially at this lean time of year, and perhaps a candle too, to add to the light. They would gather beside the kitchen fire, eat and drink, chat, tell tales, sing songs. Each woman would bring her rock, her distaff, with a bundle of flax, and her spindle, so that she could pass the time productively. That way the light wouldn't be wasted either. There might even be a fiddler. Rab fancied himself as a fiddler although there were better in the village, and probably better even at the Mossgiel rockings. There were most certainly better singers. Rab could just about carry a tune, but that was all.

The previous autumn, Johnnie Dow, at the Whitefoord Arms, had decided that a singing school might bring in a few extra pennies. He always had an eye to a profit. Morton's dancing school had done well, and Johnnie 'Pigeon' Dow had long been pondering a way of competing with him. In an inspired moment he had engaged the services of a fashionable singing master from Ayr, and some of the young people from the town were quick to take advantage of the classes, held in an upstairs room at the Whitefoord Arms.

Jean was an enthusiastic pupil. Her father thought it much more respectable than the dancing and had encouraged her to go. She lived so close that attending meant going across the alleyway at the side of her house and in at the back door of the Arms. Singing was a perfectly respectable pastime for any young lady, but all the same it was a relief to be able to avoid the prying eyes of the Cowgate. It wasn't that folk disapproved, so much as that they liked to know everything that was going on, had an insatiable curiosity about everyone. And the old men were just as bad as the old wives, talking behind their hands and exaggerating everything as the tale was passed on. One day they had had one of her father's workers, Hugh Rodger, 'Big Shug' they called him, sick, dying, stone dead and on the way to his funeral, all in the space of one day, when he had taken nothing more than a chill that had kept him indoors. Even her father had been forced to laugh at that one.

'It was a gey close-run thing!' he said to them that night. 'I was on the way to offer my condolences to the widow when I met Mr Auld and he told me the true tale!'

Jean soon became the acknowledged star of the singing class. She had a fine memory for all the old ballads her mother and grandmother had taught her, words and music both. She even knew the names of most of the tunes. There was nobody to match her and the tall, slender singing master seemed half in love with his star pupil, although she did nothing to encourage him. Far from it. She and the other lassies would giggle over his blushes and cow's eyes, the way he stammered whenever he had occasion to speak to her, but he was by no means a handsome man. It was rumoured that he had a wife and five children in Ayr, with another one on the way, and that the wife had to take in sewing because the singing didn't pay too well. His shirts were always threadbare, and they supposed that his wife was too busy to attend to her husband's linen. John Blane, one of the farm servants at Mossgiel, had a decent tenor voice that he was never shy of using, and he also attended these classes whenever his duties at the farm permitted.

At the Mossgiel rocking there was another singer, a visiting cousin of the Burns family who was said to have a fine tenor voice and well he knew it. He would not sing unless the company had fallen silent, and then he stood with his hands folded together, gazing into the distance. Rab hated pretension of any sort and was inclined to chuckle over his cousin's absurd solemnity, but had to acknowledge that the man had a good voice. Still, he moved to the back of the room so that nobody would notice if he started to laugh.

It was when the cousin had finished his latest dignified performance that John Blane shouted out, 'Miss Armour! Will you not give us a song?'

Jean was not particularly shy of singing, but the room was crowded and the previous singer had been so sure of himself that she shook her head, suddenly diffident. 'I'm not sure what to sing!' she said.

'Perhaps the lassie is shy,' said the cousin, patronisingly.

Blane persisted. 'Miss Armour, you have the voice of a lintie, so you do. Sing whatever you like!'

'Give us an auld ballad,' came from the gloom at the back of the room. 'D'you ken Tam Lin, Miss Armour?'

She recognised the voice as Rab's. 'Aye, I do.'

'Then sing Tam Lin for us.'

She put down her spindle, stood, gathering herself together, summoning her breath along with the words and the story, gazing across the assembled faces to where Rab leaned lazily against the wall, arms folded, half smiling at her.

She sang:

> '*O I forbid ye, maidens a'*
> *That wear gold on your hair*
> *To come or gae by Carterhaugh,*
> *For young Tam Lin is there.'*

It was an ancient ballad, one that Jean seemed to have known her whole life, perhaps because her mother had sung it to her in her cradle. It was a song full of mystery and magic and unanswered questions, about Janet, who finds herself with child, and then bravely rescues her lover from the Queen of Faery.

> '*First she let the black pass by,*
> *And syne she let the brown;*
> *But quickly she ran to the milk-white steed,*
> *And pu'd the rider down.'*

His eyes never left her face the whole time. When she emerged from the world of the song, he was still gazing at her, still with that half smile.

'Miss Armour,' he said, from the back of the room. 'I think you have the finest and purest wood-note wild I have ever heard in all my born days.'

He turned away to spare her blushes, but later in the evening, when the air in the parlour had become as stuffy and smoky as Morton's Ballroom in the middle of a dance, she slipped on her shawl and stepped outside the back door for a moment, only to find him standing right beside her, wrapped in his plaid. The contrast between the warm room and the chilly night was remarkable.

'What a fright you gave me!' she said. 'What are you standing out here for?'

'The same as you, I suppose, Miss Armour,' he said, quietly. 'It's gey smoky in there. But we could go round by the stack and sit in the fause-house for a bit. If you have a mind.'

She looked at him doubtfully by the subdued light of the moon, not yet at the full. When the corn was too green or too wet at harvest time – and when was it ever not too wet, here in Ayrshire? – the stack builder would construct a kind of apartment in the stack, propping it up with timbers, so that the wind could get in and dry the corn out. It was known as the fause-house or false house, and was a great resort of courting couples.

'You needn't worry. I'd just like to talk to you, Miss Armour. I never seem to get the opportunity to talk to you without a wheen of other lassies, twittering and giggling.'

It had been a chilly day, and was growing colder by the hour. They could already smell the frost in the air. When she did not object, he took her by the hand, and led her round to the haystack, where they crept into the fause-house 'like a pair of daft weans' she said, much inclined to giggle. He seemed determined to be on his best behaviour, although when it was clear that her shawl was inadequate for the wintry night, and she could no longer stop her teeth from chattering, he untied his plaid and wrapped it around both of them. Still like a pair of daft weans and just as innocent. They spoke mostly about Rab's father because it had been the anniversary of his death only a week or two ago. Jean knew she had a face and a kindly demeanour that seemed to invite confidences, but she had never imagined Rab Mossgiel confiding in her like this.

'What a terrible winter that was!' he said. 'That last winter at Lochlea.'

There had been constant frosts and greyish yellow mists that made everyone cough uncontrollably. Even Jean, who was as robust as anyone, had found herself waking in the night, struggling to breathe.

'He hadn't been well for several years. The Tarbolton doctor came to see him, but nothing seemed to help him breathe more easily.'

'Do you miss him?' she asked. 'But of course you must miss him.'

She felt him shift uneasily in the darkness that smelled of smoke from the house, with just a hint of summer, the grassy scent of the stack surrounding them.

'Aye,' he said at last, with a little sigh. 'He was a stern man, but I do miss him. I can hardly believe a whole year has gone by.'

'Where was he from?' she asked. 'He was not a local man, was he?'

This had been a subject of much speculation among the belles. And since Rab seemed inclined to talk, she thought she might as well find out as much as she could.

'He came from the north-east to Edinburgh. Looking for his fortune I suppose. Times were hard.'

'Times are always hard.'

'They are so. He worked as a gardener there. Then, he travelled by a roundabout route to Alloway and set up as a nurseryman. He rented land, and even began building a house, but I think he found it desperately hard to make a living, so he took up a position as head gardener at the Doonholm Estate instead.'

'But your mammy's from Maybole?'

'Aye, she is. Well, there or thereabouts. He met her at the Maybole fair, and she says he proposed to her almost immediately and she accepted him without hesitation. Love at first sight.' He paused. 'I think it was the only time in his life he ever did anything on impulse.'

'And then you were born.'

'Aye.'

She could sense him grinning at her in the dark. She could feel

28

the warmth of him beside her, beneath the plaid. Like a good fire, she thought, vaguely, realising that she would be very happy just to lean against him, close her eyes and sleep. There was something oddly familiar about him. And safe, in spite of his reputation.

'Aye,' he said, again. 'Like a true hero, I was born on a wild January night, in a storm so fierce that the chimney blew down. My mammy had to wrap me up and take shelter with the neighbours while my father got help to rebuild the gable end. Maybe he wasnae as good a builder as he was a gardener. Not like your father, eh, Jean?'

'My father always says he builds to last. But then he's no gardener. So you moved from there to Mount Oliphant?'

'You ken all about me it seems.'

'There's been a lot of talk. Hard to avoid it in this place.'

'We flitted when I was six. That was the first farm. A bad bargain. And thence to Lochlea near Tarbolton. Which was the least fortunate of all.'

Jean knew that there had been a long-running legal dispute with the landlord. William had died a year ago, fretting over the fate of his wife and his children, but fretting most – so the gossips said – over his eldest boy, fearing for his future. Rab had been a trouble to him, for sure. It was whispered that William had said as much on his death bed, reducing his son to tears. If James Armour was stern, it seemed Rab's father had been obdurate, even in the face of death.

'Your poor father,' she said, choosing her words carefully. 'He seems to have been a good man, but life didnae treat him well.'

'No. He had nae luck for all that he was a good, God-fearing man. He aye thought I was feckless. I was off to Tarbolton with the lads, or at Masonic meetings. I went to the dancing even back then, but he thought dancing was the devil's work. I could not agree with him and I could not shut myself away to suit him. I needed my friends about me. I still do.'

'He would have had a lot in common with my father. He thinks the dancing is the devil's work too.' She chuckled, suddenly. 'My mother told me once that father danced Bab at the Bowster when they were courting, but all the kneeling down and kissing that went on mortified him completely. He was blushing and stammering and didn't know where to put himself and she had to kiss *him*!'

She fell silent, wondering if she should have mentioned kissing, but rather to her disappointment, Rab only tucked the plaid a little more tightly round the two of them.

'He thought me idle,' he said, and there was a sadness in his tone that wrung her tender heart. 'Well, he couldnae understand why I was always reading and writing. Why my nose was aye in a book.'

'I've noticed that about you, Rab. It's hard not to!'

Unconsciously, she had slipped into calling him Rab. But you couldn't sit wrapped up in a plaid with a lad and call him Mr Burns, could you?

He squeezed her hand. 'Your wee fingers are cold.'

'I'm fine. Tell me more about your father.'

'He was responsible for our education. He believed education to be a fine thing. I think he believed it till his dying day. But he was torn. He used to say, what good was reading, when there was hard work to be done and stony ground to improve? What good was reading, when there was a family to feed and clothe? How could a body waste money on books when poverty came knocking at the door?'

'Perhaps he just worried about you.'

'Perhaps he did. Me more than any of them. I could settle to no respectable occupation. That was his chief complaint. Maybe it's still true. My brother is by far the better farmer. He's cautious and sober in all his dealings. I've tried, and I still do try, but it's never enough. I've made too many mistakes. I ought to have settled to something by now.'

'What do you want to do?'

'Ach, Jeany, if I knew that, I might be able to set my mind to doing it. If I could spend my days reading and writing, I would. I was a disappointment to him. Even on his deathbed, I was a sore disappointment to him.'

She hesitated. But the truth seemed so clear to her that she had to put it into words. 'Rab, d'you not think...'

'What?'

'D'you not think that one of the reasons he was so hard on you, might have been because he loved you best?'

He paused, thinking about it.

She persisted. 'Sometimes fathers in particular are harder on the weans they love most. I should ken that! He must have worried himself sick about you, but it doesn't mean he loved you any less. I think it means he loved you more. Maybe he was more like you than you ever kent. He must have been an adventurous lad, once upon a time, to leave his home and head south the way he did.'

He sighed. 'You're a good, kind lass, Jeany Armour. And maybe you're right. But it still hurts me to think about him.'

'You should come to the singing school,' she said, in an effort to lighten his mood and her own. The pity she was feeling for him at this moment seemed perilously close to love.

'Ach, it's no for me. The dancing, aye. Singing? I don't think so.'

'You never know. You might enjoy it.'

'I'd enjoy the pleasure of your company,' he said, slyly.

'Well, we sing for pleasure more than ought else. We like to share songs and melodies.'

'I'm no singer, Jeany, though I like the old Scots songs fine, so I do. There's such a wealth of wisdom at the heart of them. But I like to hear them sung with simplicity. A good pure sound. None of your airs and graces. None of your twiddly bits and singing five notes where one will do.'

'I agree with you there.'

'Which is why I would not gie you and your wood-note wild for a score of my cousin, singing his heart out in there.'

She was glad of the darkness for she was blushing again.

'Besides, what would your father say, Miss Armour, if he found out you were inviting a rakish rook like Rab Mossgiel to the singing class? Or sittin cooried up in the fause-house in the dark with him for that matter.'

She knew all too well what her father would say, but she didn't respond.

He took her hand again, squeezed it, held onto it. 'Ach, I ken fine he hates me. If looks could kill, I would already be laid in my coffin in the kirkyard down there.'

'He worries about me. Like your father worried about you.'

'And who can blame him? I don't suppose the news about Betty Paton pleased him very much either.'

She had been avoiding the topic, but now he had named the lass himself.

'No. It was one more thing to upset him.'

'I'm very fond of her. And I'll no abandon the wean. I would never do that. But I'll not marry the lass either. We would not go a month without hating each other.'

She thought, but didn't say, that if he knew as much all along, he should not have made love to Betty, not have got her with child. But then mistakes were all too easy to make in the heat of the moment. She felt quite hot right now. Warmer than the night and the fause-house merited, even with the plaid.

'Then maybe you were right not to marry her.'

'They tell me in the toun that your father has got his heart set on a weaver for you, Jeany. Yon Rab Wilson. Off to Paisley to mak his fortune.'

'Is that what they're saying?'

'Aye, it is.'

'So you've been asking have you?'

'I have. And then they say he's to come back and marry you.'

'I'll tell you something, Rab.'

'What's that?'

She leaned over and planted a daring kiss on his prickly cheek.

'You shouldnae believe all you're tellt,' she whispered.

She slid out from under the plaid, jumped down from the fause-house and wrapped her shawl about her. The back door of the house was open again, light falling on the flagstones with smoke curling through it. He followed her and caught her arm.

'Wait,' he said. 'Listen to me. If I come to the Whitefoord Arms before the singing school, will you meet me there? You could bring your friend, Chrissie Morton.'

'Why? D'you fancy Chrissie as well?'

'No. But – for appearance's sake, just. I'll walk down with John Blane.'

'He comes to the singing whenever he can.'

'And he does fancy your friend Chrissie, although I suspect she has small interest in him. But then we could all have a wee chat together, before the singing. If you're agreeable. We could meet up in the snug, downstairs, the four of us. It would be respectable enough.'

'Aye, maybe it would.'

'So, you will?'

'I don't see why not.' She smiled up at him, their two breaths mingling in the frosty air. They went back into the house, taking care, by a sort of mutual but unspoken agreement, not to go in at the same time. Jean went first, sliding into the darkest part of the room so that she could pretend she had been there all along.

That night, a hard frost fell. The road back to Mauchline was treacherous, with ice filling all the deep winter ruts, so the visiting lassies elected to sleep over at the farm. Rab and Gilbert were sent to join the farm servants in the stable loft while Jean, Christina and the Miller sisters slept in the garret room. Jean lay awake for a long time, listening to the gentle snores of her companions, the sighs and mutterings, the rustle of chaff as they turned. It had occurred to her that she was quite probably lying in Rab's bed, although he was elsewhere. The thought made her smile, gave her a little thrill of excitement, banished sleep.

Chapter Five

Assignations

There's not a bonnie flower that springs
By fountain, shaw, or green,
There's not a bonnie bird that sings
But minds me o' my Jean.

The following week, a message came from Ayr to say that the singing teacher was indisposed, having contracted a fever of some kind and lost his voice entirely. Between that, and various more pressing engagements that had to be fulfilled as soon as he was well, it was well into spring before the singing school resumed, before Robert Burns and Jean Armour could do more than pass the time of day with one another.

Jean would not think of going alone to such an assignation, if assignation it could be called. It was one thing to sit in the dark of the fause-house with Rab Mossgiel where nobody could see them, but this was very public. It was supposed to be an innocent enough gathering, a conversation between friends, but it felt like something more, something illicit, and she had a tremor of excitement at the thought that Rab wanted to see her in particular. But Jean would have thought shame to go alone. There had to be a chaperone. And even then it was daring and somewhat inadvisable. The Miller sisters had given off fancying Rab altogether, the reason being that there was a new baby in the parish. Betty Paton had just given birth to a healthy girl child, Bess. She had named Robert Burns in Mossgiel as the father and Rab had admitted his culpability in the kirk. He had agreed to support mother and child, but he had also written a poem to celebrate the event, calling the infant *the sweet fruit o' mony a merry dint.* The kirk elders were outraged.

The belles had pretended shock and surprise at the bawdry of it, though they had all giggled over the tale when one or two of the lads had repeated the verses in their hearing. There still seemed to be no question of Rab marrying the lass, but he had offered to bring the child to Mossgiel as soon as she was weaned, to be brought up by his mother and his sisters, so that Betty Paton might not be encumbered with an unsought-for daughter and might be able to find a man willing to marry her.

'Aye,' said Jean's mother drily, when she heard the news. ' And it'll be the women of the family who'll have all the work of mind-ing the wean!'

But at least Rab had not denied his child or his fault, and there was, so Jean thought, something praiseworthy about a man who would admit to his own mistakes so readily. Too many lads were quick to blame the lass for 'getting herself with child' and would deny everything, branding the woman a whore and leaving her to suffer the consequences, unless the minister and his elders might be able to prove otherwise. Then the kirk would do everything possible to force a marriage or at least force some acknowledg-ment of fatherhood and responsibility. One man had staunchly refused to accept any responsibility for a second baby borne by the same woman, loudly proclaiming before the kirk session that he had lain with her more than nine and a half months previously, and that 'no woman gets more than nine months for the second child.' There might even have been some truth in it, as Jean's mother had knowingly observed. But for a lad to claim responsibility as readily as Rab seemed evidence of his good nature, if nothing else.

The way it went when a lad had his eye on a lass and wanted to know her better, was this: he would choose a public house, although it must be a respectable kind of a place such as the Whitefoord Arms, a place where a young woman might not be ashamed to be seen, and he must arrange a meeting there, just openly enough – perhaps in some quiet but visible snug – so that people could see without really eavesdropping upon the conversation. There was no use going into one of the back rooms, because everyone knew what that meant, and they would gossip endlessly about it, and that would be the girl's good name gone forever. Mostly a lad would take a crony with him, and the girl would always be accompanied by a close female friend. That way, the lads and the lasses could sit and converse two by two, so that no suspicion of improper behaviour could fall on them, the one pair chaperoning the other. It was a good way to start a respectable courtship. You could fall acquainted, slowly and carefully, and extricate yourself with your reputation still intact if all did not go as well as you hoped.

Jean sometimes wondered how it must be for the gentry who, in spite of their big houses, had no recourse to such kindly contrivances, but who barely seemed to know each other before embarking on a marriage that all too often was arranged by their parents, with scant regard for the feelings of the young people involved. More often than not it seemed to be a financial arrangement with the tocher – the dowry – of more importance than any mutual affection. But perhaps they found their own ways and means of circumventing supervision. Big houses and big gardens must afford some privacy. And after all, the protection afforded by sedate meetings only lasted for a short time.

The previous year, gossip had been rife about James Montgomerie of Coilsfield House that lay between the two towns of Mauchline and Tarbolton. He and his brother were close friends of Gavin Hamilton and acquaintances of Robert Burns as well. If folk loved to spread rumours about their neighbours, there was something even more enticing about scandal among the nabbery. James was a soldier, a big, handsome young man of great charm and energy. He was the youngest brother of Hugh Montgomerie of Coilsfield, also a military man – Sojer Hugh they called him. James had been brought up at Coilsfield. The house stood on the banks of the River Ayr, and when James was not engaged on his military activities, he would come home to Coilsfield where his sociable elder brother would indulge him and his friends with such balls and parties as he thought fit to host. Perhaps Hugh hoped to find a suitable wife for his young brother. Soon it was whispered, and then not even whispered but openly discussed in the streets and change houses of Mauchline and Tarbolton, that charming James had found himself a lovely young wife.

Unfortunately, she was the wife of another man.

Her name was Eleanora Maxwell Campbell of Skerrington House near Cumnock, not far from Mauchline – a pretty name for an accomplished young woman. Some six years previously, Eleanora had married Charles Maxwell, from Dumfries, but the marriage had proved to be unhappy. Jean had seen Eleanora occasionally in the town, visiting the clock-maker or the draper perhaps, or passing through on her way elsewhere, and had envied her fine clothes. But Eleanora seemed doomed to disappointment in life and in love. Her father was something of a spendthrift and so was her brother, who had died while still a young man. Both had been declared insolvent, living on promises and loans. Eleanora, with only a little money of her own from her mother, had inherited the Skerrington estate upon their deaths, but in desperation and in haste, she had then married Charles, believing that his declared income of £500 a year would help her to avoid penury. It was a lie, and she was left to repent her misjudgement at leisure. He had no such sum, but perhaps he had expected a bigger dowry. Perhaps, it was whispered in the town, they had misled each other as to the size of their respective fortunes. However it was, the estate was sequestrated and Charles proceeded to spend whatever small amounts he could get his hands on of what was left of his wife's inheritance and to treat her with casual disdain, gallivanting here and there while she cared for their two children. She had few protectors in the world other than Gavin Hamilton of Mauchline. He was a good friend to her and acted as factor on the Skerrington estate, attempting to save it from the worst of her husband's depredations and debts, while mediating as best he could between the perennially warring couple. Perhaps, thought Jean, it was easier to be at war with your spouse in a large house. At least escape would be possible.

While the unhappy couple were visiting Coilsfield House, Eleanora met and was instantly charmed by James Montgomerie. It happened, so it was reported by some of the servants, while her husband was slumbering in Hugh Montgomerie's library, having imbibed not wisely, but much too well, of his host's fine claret, and James came upon a weeping Eleanora in the garden. Foolishly, perhaps, James had managed to arrange a series of assignations with Eleanora. The affair had a not-unexpected conclusion when Eleanora fell pregnant with James's child and when Charles, who had not gone near his wife for some months, realised that he had been cuckolded. Fearing for his mistress's safety, for Charles was beyond enraged, James had arranged for her to take shelter with sympathetic friends in Paisley. It was here that she had given birth to a son, named James for his father, in November of 1784, while the Burns family were experiencing their first harsh winter in Mossgiel.

The denouement of the drama had been a nine days' wonder and the subject of intense speculation, not to say entertainment, in Mauchline and Tarbolton, with the Coilsfield servants reporting that Charlie Maxwell had ridden to Coilsfield and hammered on the big front door, shouting for James Montgomerie to come out and face him like a man. James, nothing if not brave, might even have obliged, and then there would have been 'wigs on the green' as they said, but he was not at home and the offended husband suspected, with good reason, that he was with Eleanora in Paisley. The servants had threatened to set the dogs on him but Sojer Hugh, a man of great presence and authority, had come out, sent his men away and spoken to Maxwell firmly but quietly, putting an arm round his shoulders, and eventually leading him inside, where he was persuaded to sit beside the fire, drink more claret and weep about the perfidy of women.

The fact of the matter was that Hugh – while despising Charlie Maxwell somewhat – was not particularly happy with James, who had got into this kind of scrape before and would probably do the same thing all over again. Hugh had succeeded in pouring oil on troubled waters and had persuaded Charles Maxwell to go back to Skerrington to await developments. Eleanora, meanwhile, had steadfastly refused to return to her husband, but had taken refuge with friends in Riccarton near Kilmarnock, along with her baby, a big, healthy boy.

While all this was taking place at Coilsfield and beyond, Robert Burns and John Blane had made much more conventional arrangements to meet up with Jean Armour and her friend Christina Morton before the singing school. For a few weeks they spent a pleasant hour, talking together in the snug at the Whitefoord Arms. Christina was more fond of Rab than she was of John, but by now it was clear to her that Rab had eyes only for her friend and there was nothing to be done about that. Since she was a smart and practical girl, not given to repining about what she could not change, she decided to give Jean every chance to get to know Rab better, although not without a pang of worry on her friend's behalf.

Jean still had an inkling that Rab might be a chancy young man who might slip away from a girl at time of need, for all that he had so readily acknowledged his first child. But there was all the difference in the world between giving a home to a sweet wee daughter when you had your mother and sisters to shoulder the burden of responsibility, and making hearth and home for wife and wean. But although Rab intrigued her, although she was undeniably attracted to him, she resolved that she would not be as easily persuaded as some.

The two by two meetings soon began to pall, however, mostly because Christina began to resent wasting the summer months in John Blane's company, even to please Jean and Rab. She had her eyes on a better match than a farm servant at Mossgiel. She had fancied Robert Paterson ever since they sat in the schoolroom together and he put burrs in her hair, to her pretended outrage. Paterson kept the draper and general merchant's shop in the town alongside his widowed mother, and the belles were frequent customers, although even more frequent browsers, who seldom had the wherewithal to buy all that they wanted.

The shop kept linens, everyday woollen fabrics and sometimes silks, although that was a luxury seldom seen in the town and must generally be sent for if wanted. There were pretty printed cottons or muslins, much favoured by the girls for summer gowns. There were common woollen shawls, although such items were mostly homemade; gorgeous stockings with clocks worked onto them at the ankle; and stays, which very intimate items of clothing were kept well hidden away by Mistress Paterson and only brought out when requested. Fine lace was expensive these days and so scarce as to be impossible to find, even if you could afford it, but you could sometimes get Cluny or Torchon in the shop if you were lucky. Good gloves were taxed out of existence or in the case of French gloves, utterly unattainable. But Paterson had haberdashery of all kinds, and you might find silk satin ribbons in a multitude of colours to trim a bonnet, or good, affordable worsted tape, or perhaps a yard or two of trim recovered from an old gown. Mistress Paterson herself was not above scavenging when times were hard, washing what she could and selling second or third hand trims in the shop. There were, besides, glass, brass and bone buttons, threads of all kinds and colours, needles and pins, thread winders and needle cases and a hundred other small necessities of everyday life.

'Things you could not bear to live without,' Christina called them. Among these things she numbered Robert Paterson.

She tried to persuade her reluctant beau to come to the Whitefoord Arms, but he said he was too busy in the shop, and besides, he could settle his heart on no woman. If he liked a lass, he would call her a 'grand cracker', but there were a number of grand crackers who seemed to be tenants of his heart and he was never quite able to make up his mind to attach himself to any single one of them.

'He's far too fond of the siller. If her tocher is good enough, he might fall in love with her on account of it.'

This was what Rab remarked privately to Jean, when they had arrived fortuitously early in the snug at the Whitefoord Arms. Christina was always late these days and John Blane had been finishing a job out at the farm, so Rab had left without him, hoping perhaps to get Jean to himself for a while.

'He seems fond enough of Chrissie. And I know she likes him fine. Besides, she'll have a tocher and a good one. Her parents are not short of money.'

'Well, maybe he is fond of her and maybe not, but tell your friend he's not a lad to be trusted.'

Jean laughed. 'And you *are?*'

'I'm as trustworthy as the next man, Jeany. And I suppose that's all that can be said about any of us.'

'I suppose it is.'

The way he said it made her feel suddenly sad. He must have seen her face fall, the way he seemed to notice everything about her.

'I'm sorry, Jeany. And who knows? If the right lass comes along…'

Chapter Six

The Black Fit

O whistle and I'll come to you, my lad.
O whistle and I'll come to you, my lad.
Though father and mother and a' should gae mad;
O whistle and I'll come to you my lad.

The truth was that Christina was disappointed in Paterson and his inability to make up his mind, but she thought that she knew him better than most and perhaps she was right. Certainly she had known him longest and thought that one day he might come round to realising what a treasure lay on his own doorstep, as it were, waiting to be discovered.

'And if,' Jean remarked to her friend one day as they were sighing over some splendid trim, newly come from Ayr and from Glasgow before that, 'If you were to marry Robert Paterson, all this would be yours and you could have whatever you liked from the shop!'

'I'm not sure his mother would be so accommodating. She watches us like a cat watching a dunnock. Have you noticed?'

'But even so, you would get to see everything first. It would be a fine thing to be married to a draper.' Jean sighed. Finer than being married to a weaver, she thought.

Christina's liking for Paterson was genuine and had very little to do with his trade. And so, after a few weeks of sedate conversation in the Whitefoord Arms, she left off even being late and instead took herself away to stay with relatives outside the town for the summer months, where Paterson might realise that he was missing her, and might visit her if he chose. He didn't choose to do so very often, just at first, but as the summer progressed, he seemed to be asking where she was and when she might be coming back and began sending her notes on the back of drapery receipts. This meant that the balance of any lawfully chaperoned courting for Jean Armour and Robert Burns was well and truly upset.

The fact of the matter was that there was nothing lawful about it.

Jean had been more or less deceiving her father and mother for the few weeks that she and Rab had been meeting. James Armour knew that she was going to the singing school, and his wife told him that there was no harm in it. Jean had a fine voice and the master was pleased with her, judging her the star of his school. What could he do but give his permission? Besides, he frequented the Whitefoord Arms himself in the evenings, and thought that the proprietor and his wife would keep an eye out for any untoward behaviour. But nobody had mentioned the meetings with Rab, not even Johnnie Dow, who made it a steadfast rule to keep all confidences and turn a blind eye wherever possible. Once Christina had given over coming, it was an easy matter for Rab to have a quiet word with John Blane, and suggest that perhaps work at Mossgiel might delay him. Which was how Jean and Rab spent a few more weeks deep in conversation, mostly by themselves in the snug, with Mistress Dow looking in occasionally to check that all was as it should be.

It was all feeling, all sensation and there was no denying it. Or, as it turned out, him. It was in the way he looked at her, the way he took her hand in his, the way he seized it across the table, raised it to his lips and kissed the palm, gazing into her eyes all the while, and she knew that she was lost. One way or another, sooner or later, she would be his, even though she snatched her fingers away, glancing around to see whether anyone had noticed, put her hands on her lap, blushed furiously, told him not to do it. Oh but she wanted him. She could do nothing to prevent her body from responding to him.

From time to time, he would recite his poetry for her, telling her what he was working on, telling her the ideas that were fermenting away in his head. One of his poems, about the kirk elder, Willie Fisher, shocked her to her core with the irreverence of it, even though he only whispered bits of it across the table, saying that some of it might not be fit for her ears. And yet it was true. Everyone knew that Fisher was a hypocrite, up to all kinds of fornication even while castigating others for it. But should such things be committed to paper? Wouldn't that bring trouble to your door? And what would it be like for a young woman to be publicly associated with a man who could write such things and circulate them around the town?

He said he was writing feverishly, every evening, by candlelight or by the uncertain glow of a single rushlight when his day's work was done, writing at the desk up in his garret chamber at Mossgiel while his brother slept. She remembered the room where she and the other lassies had slept on the night of the rocking. Remembered the bed she had slept in.

'I'm so glad of the early dawns. They give me light to work by, when the house is quiet and before the day's work has begun.'

'You need to sleep though, Rab!'

'Ach, time enough for sleep in the winter. I can do without sleep. But if I couldn't meet you, talk to you like this, steal a kiss now and then, I don't know what I'd do. You inspire me, Jeany!'

She knew he had said as much to other lassies, and was well aware that he could charm the birds out of the trees. Perhaps he only wove a web of words to seduce daft lassies like Betty Paton and herself, to entice them into making fools of themselves with him and worse, ruining the rest of their lives. Except that he hadn't done that with Betty, had he? No. She hadn't been ruined at all, really. Everyone said Betty had been a willing partner. He had taken the child and given it a home at Mossgiel, and even though he hadn't wanted to marry her, Betty herself said that he had made no promises, had been true to his word, or lack of it. But he hadn't left her in the lurch either. Not like some of the lads that needed to be practically dragged kicking and

44

screaming into the kirk and forced to admit their sins.

'Listen,' he said, a week later. 'Do you know Catherine Govan?'

Jean nodded. She did indeed know Katy Govan, the aunt of Rab's nine year old herd boy, Willie Patrick. Willie worked out at Mossgiel as a general servant, feeding the cattle, mucking the byre and running back and forth to Mauchline on various errands. He would often be entrusted with Rab's correspondence, being a trustworthy little lad. Sometimes, when John Blane was other-wise occupied, he was even allowed to work as gaudsman help-ing Rab with the four horses at the plough. His mother had died giving birth to him, but his father lived and worked as a shoe-maker on the Cowgate, alongside Willie's elder brother, George. Whenever Willie was in the town, being a wee thing homesick, he would seize the opportunity to call in and see his relatives. His aunt Catherine was a widow herself, living at the Cross, quite close to the Whitefoord Arms. The woman was sober and grave but kindly enough when you knew her well. She kept herself to herself and did fine sewing as a way of earning a living for herself and her surviving children, helped out by the charity of the parish and Mr Auld, the minister.

'What about her?' Jean said.

'I've been thinking that she might be persuaded to be our...' He hesitated, looked at her again, smiling ruefully. 'Och Jeany, I do not think your father approves of me yet, does he?'

The truth was that far from approving of him, James Armour still hated him like poison. Rab knew it. Jean knew it. There was no hiding the fact, although in public, Armour did his best to keep his feelings to himself, well aware that Rab Mossgiel had the ear of many of the gentry, and these same gentry might be the source of much needed work for him in the future.

'No.' She could do little but agree with him. 'He dislikes you, Rab. After your wee Bess was born...'

'What would he have had me do? Deny the wean? How could I do that?'

'No. And I admire you for it. But he would have had you *not* get Betty Paton with child at all.'

'We all make mistakes.'

'Was it a mistake?'

He grinned. 'It was a great pleasure, I'll allow.'

She shook her head, laughing in spite of herself. 'There you go! You see what I mean? What am I to say to that, Rab? Have you heard yourself?'

'Say you'll keep seeing me, Jeany. I'm not seeing Betty now, you ken that fine.'

'Are you not?'

'Only when she comes to visit Bess. We're not walking out together, if that's what you mean, although we are friends. I'll hate nobody if I can help it. So what do you say? Will you meet with me so that we can take a walk together? If I can arrange it?'

'Maybe aye, maybe no.'

'The trouble is, it's summer. The roses are blooming and the birds are singing and I'd rather be walking out with you, my Jeany, than sitting in here with the smell of spilled ale and smoke in the air. What do you think?'

It would be a perilous undertaking, to be sure. Walking out meant being alone with him, unsupervised, unchaperoned. There would be nobody to protect her, although she sensed that he was not a man to force himself on any woman. Not like some. But there would be nobody to dissuade her. And she certainly didn't trust herself to be alone with him.

'Word will get back to my father. Word that we're seeing each other, without any chaperone. And my mother's not much better, you know. She's no friend of yours, Rab. They take every chance they can to remind me how much they dislike you. How unsuitable they think you are.'

'That's where Katy Govan comes in.'

'What about her?'

'I thought she might act as black fit to us.'

'Black fit?'

'A go-between for us two.'

'Aye. I know fine what you mean.'

A black fit or black foot was somebody, often an older woman or man, whose help might be enlisted to carry messages back and forth between lovers. This was a more serious undertaking altogether, an admission that they were a couple, that a lad and lass might be something more than friends. Sometimes the black fit was needed where parental disapproval was a bar to meeting. Sometimes it simply meant that a respectable person would act as match-maker within a small and curious community like this one, easing the means of two young people getting to know each other, with marriage more often than not being the outcome. But either way, there was a gravity about the arrangement that could not be ignored.

'Have you spoken to her?' asked Jean with a mixture of anxiety and excitement. Suddenly, what had seemed like a mild flirtation was becoming very serious. She had not expected it, not of Rab Burns.

'Aye I have. I walked with Willie when he was going home to visit his father. We passed her house and I made sure he went in to see his Aunt Katy first, for it suited me that he should. I went in with him, took her a basket of eggs and some cheese from my mother.'

'That was kind of you.'

'Aye it was. She felt beholden to me and grateful. I thought it was a good time to speak to her, once I had sent Willie away to see his father, of course.'

'What did you say?'

'I said I was half mad with love for you, Jeany, and I might die of a broken heart if I could not get courting you properly, but your parents would not hear of it.'

'You didnae say that!'

'Why wouldn't I? It's the truth.'

'Well, even if it is, it's the first I've heard you say it.'

He leaned over the table that divided them. 'That I love you? But I do. I thought you would see it for yourself. I'm fair daft about you, Jeany. And I think you love me, or why else would you be here?'

'Hush!' She looked around. 'Don't speak so loud.'

The main room of the inn was busy and they could hear the buzz of conversation. Smoke drifted through. Somebody was tuning up a fiddle. Upstairs the singing school was about to begin. 'I have to go. The class is starting. They'll wonder where I am.'

'And that's another problem. You aye have to go. It's fair killing me.' He seized her hand again. 'If I don't kiss you properly and very soon, I'll go mad as a hare in March, and it's already coming on summer.'

She couldn't help but laugh at him. 'And what did she say to all this nonsense? Katy Govan?'

'She said she'd see what she could do. I was honest with her. I'm an honest man even though you and your friends seem to think I'm not. I said I wanted to court you properly, to become seriously acquainted with you, more than I could ever do in a snatched hour here in the Whitefoord Arms and so often under the keen eye of somebody else, of a great many curious people. I want to walk out with you, just you and me alone. Is that a sin?'

'No. It's not a sin. But...'

'She's a widow woman and she knows what it is to pine for a man, and it's the same for a man when he pines for a woman. She said she'd see if she could help and she had an idea. Well, I'll confess it was *my* idea, but she fell in with it immediately.'

'Did she?'

So many women fell in with Rab's ideas immediately. He had a bright eye and a coaxing tongue. Maybe that was the long and the short of it. He was charming. But what if that was the whole of it? Nothing more. It was a frightening thought and one that her mother and father would agree with.

'You could tell your mother that you're going round there to learn some fine sewing. A way of earning an honest shilling or two to add to your household income. Your father would approve of that, surely?'

'He might.'

'She's an excellent seamstress, and naebody would be any the wiser. She agreed that she would send me a message with her nephew. Willie's aye going back and forth between the farm and the town, with my letters, chiefly. But Katy is a fond aunt, and sometimes she sends Willie back with this or that sweetmeat of her ain making, or she's darning his stockings or mending his breeches or I don't know what else. His ain mother is dead, you ken.'

'So I could maybe let you know when I could get away.'

'You can write, surely?'

'Of course I can.'

'Then you could send me a note with Willie, who doesn't know his letters yet, although he's learning. But if you keep it to a scrawl, he'll be none the wiser. Aye, and then you could come out to meet me. Out by the back of Netherplace. Don't take the road. Too many prying eyes.'

'In the evening? You mean in the evening?'

'I do. When my day's work is done and yours too. They could have no objection to you keeping an honest widow woman like Katy Govan company for a few hours, could they?'

'No. They couldn't. But I wouldn't be keeping her company, would I? And they would find out. You know fine what this toun is like and how everybody kens fine what everyone else is doing.'

'They would suspect nothing. You're a good girl, Jeany. Who's to know that you're spending a scant half hour with her or maybe an hour, so that you have some sewing to show for your time, and then slipping out by the back way to spend another hour or so with me? The nights are light, you'd be back before dark and naebody in your house would ken where you've been or who with.'

The words brought her up short for a moment.

'I'm a good girl,' she said, quietly. 'Or I aye thought I was.'

She had not been tempted before, not even by Robert Wilson the weaver, although he would never have been less than courteous, a gentleman. More of a gentleman than Rab Burns. He would never have pressed her to have illicit meetings with him. He would have thought it immoral. And perhaps he would have been right. But then there would have been no need. Her father would have encouraged any meeting. Rab Wilson would have been made welcome in the Armour house. They would have given the young couple every opportunity to become more closely acquainted.

'It would be sic a risk,' she said, slowly. 'I think folk are already talking. We've been meeting in here, and do you think Johnnie Dow does not mention it to my father?'

'I think he does not. Johnnie is very close, very quiet on some matters. Men of his trade must be. And besides, what does he have to tell? That I sit here with you, all very proper, and we have an hour of polite conversation, and then I go on my way and you go to your singing school and there is no more to be said or done. Why? Has he asked you about it?'

'My mother has. Somebody must have said something to her.'

'What did she say?'

'She said, was it true that I was meeting with you here at the Whitefoord Arms and I said...' She hesitated.

'What?'

'I said John Blane the ploughman was sweet on Chrissie Morton and I had promised to accompany her, as you had John, but that nothing much would come of it because Chrissie's affections were inclined elsewhere and she was no fool.'

'You have more enterprise than I thought, Jeany.'

The lie had come so easily. She had surprised herself by how easy it had been to lie to her mother or at least to convince her with half truths.

'And did she believe you?' he pursued.

'I think she did. But she's no friend to you, Rab. Neither she nor my father. The more they hear of you, the less they like you.

Now there's your wean with Betty and all that scandal. And you're friends with Mr Hamilton. They hate Mr Hamilton.'

'Whatever have they got against Gavin?'

'They think he's shows small respect for the authority of the kirk.'

'That's true enough.'

'And they've heard things. They've heard all the gossip about Jamie Montgomerie and Eleanora Campbell.'

'What does Gavin Hamilton have to do with any of that?'

'You know fine what he has to do with that. A friend to both of them and to you too it seems.'

He looked uncomfortable, but he only said mildly, 'Well, what else could he do? Friendship demands no less. Gavin's a good man and a kind man and a friend in need to Eleanora Campbell.'

'Everything is cause for complaint with my parents. It frightens me.'

'They think me what I'm not – a ne'er do weel who will betray you. But perhaps if they knew me better they might like me more.'

'Perhaps they would. I'm not denying you're a kind man, Rab. But I'm not likely to find out what they might think, because they would turn you from the door.'

'Ach, Jeany, I'm wanting to court *you*, not your mother or your father. If I could, I would do it openly. I'm in want of a wife! There, it's said!'

'Wheesht!' She was thoroughly alarmed now. 'People will hear.'

'Let them.'

'I don't ken what to think of you, Rab!'

But she did know what to think. The words just came into her head. Am I in want of sic a husband? she thought.

'I may be a poet, but I'm a farmer too and I'm as good as a weaver any day.'

'You don't need to worry about Rab Wilson. I'll no be marrying Rab Wilson.'

That surprised her too, the way the words just popped out of her mouth, but she was suddenly as sure of it as she was of her own name.

'Then your mother and father will be sorely disappointed. Or that's what the town's saying. So make up your mind. Will you meet me, Jean? While the nights are light and sweet? Or will I go home to Mossgiel and never trouble you more?'

'Maybe I will meet you. If you're speaking the truth. If I can trust you.'

'You could trust me with more than this.'

'Then I'll do it. I'll go to Catherine Govan's. I'll take my needlework. And if I can, I'll slip out and meet with you.'

Chapter Seven

Stitches, Poems and Kisses

But blithe's the blink o' Robbie's e'e.
And weel I wat he lo'es me dear:
Ae blink o' him I wad nae gie
For Buskie-glen and a' his gear.

The truth was that, like Betty Paton before her, she was half daft with love for him. It had come upon her gradually, like a sickness, and there was no cure for it but to be close to him. Except that being close to him made it worse when they were apart. For a week or two she fended him off and he didn't press her, contented to bide his time and wait for her to be ready. She didn't entirely trust him, that was the problem. She saw the way he gazed at other lassies, the gleam in his dark eyes, and she saw the way they looked at him, and she thought that she might be storing up trouble for herself.

He was a fever in her blood.

She slept little during that summer. The nights were light and the days were long, and for most people the inclination for sleep lay in abeyance. Everyone here slept less in the summer than in the winter. But she would lie sleepless, while every waking thought was of him. Whatever it was that drew a woman to a man, it lay between them like a fine web. It wasn't that he had caught her, like the spiders that lurked in all the corners of the house on the Cowgate, because it was so clearly mutual. If she could not keep away from him, could barely help herself, he could not keep his hands off her either. But she managed to fend him off for a little while, afraid of the consequences, afraid of what her parents would say.

On a Saturday in June, she went to Catherine Govan's house at the Cross and spent a good hour stitching at a piece of needlework at Catherine's behest. It was a trim for a petticoat, white embroidery on white linen, and they were seated close to the small west-facing window to catch the light.

'Are you going to meet him, hen?' asked Catherine, eventually.

'D'you think I should?'

'Lassie, it's not for me to say.'

'Would *you* go?'

Catherine gazed at her. The room was already darkening, but there was plenty of light in the western sky. It would be much lighter outside than it was in this little room. A fine night for a walk.

'I think maybe I would. He's not a bad lad.'

'You think not?'

'Listen, Jeany. Mostly as we get older, we regret things undone. Unless the things we've done are very sinful.'

'Willie Fisher would say this was sinful.'

'Aye, well, he should ken! But seriously, why not go? Talk to the lad at least. He won't ask you for ought you're not willing to give. He isn't that kind of lad.'

'That's what worries me.'

'What?'

'What I might be more than willing to give him.'

'He's very fond of you. A fool could see that. He wouldn't have gone to so much trouble else. You ken fine he can have his pick of the lassies round here. But he seems to want you.'

Folding the piece of work away for next time, almost sick with a mixture of apprehension and anticipation, Jean set off across the fields in the summer gloaming, slipping carefully out of the village that was quiet at this time of the evening. Several times she almost turned around and went home, but the thought of how upset he would be deterred her. She had agreed to meet him by an ancient thorn, a gnarled fairy tree that he had described, standing at the furthest point of the drystane wall surrounding the old house called Netherplace. The estate, owned by William Campbell and his proud wife Lilias, was a large one, and the woods were beautiful in summer. The turnpike road passed the front of the house, with its massive old yew tree, but Jean slipped round the back, well away from the house, and through the woods on the outer fringes of the park. This was a sheltered place, with light still slanting between the leaves, and the branches alive with birdsong.

He was waiting for her there. She saw him before he saw her. He was standing with his back to her, leaning sideways against the gnarled thorn. She saw his homespun blue coat and his unmistakable black hair, and her heart gave a lurch of excitement. His head was bent and she wondered what he was looking at, and then she realised that he was reading, of course, because he always carried a book in his pocket. In any free moments he would be reading. Her friends despised him a little for that. But she admired it. It was one of the things that made him different: his defiant determination to find out everything he could about all kinds of things. He had once, in one of their conversations in the Whitefoord Arms, remarked that ignorance was a curse, but it was more of a curse for the poor than it was for the rich who could always buy ways to disguise their folly. She couldn't help but agree with him. Even her father, if he could have persuaded himself to talk to Rab, would have agreed with him. She had not thought about it before, but once he said it, it seemed self-evident. Knowledge was a blessing. The more you knew, the more you understood. And although it might be frustrating for a poor man to be a learned man, it was far better than ignorance.

'Rab?' she said.

He turned, slipped the book into his pocket and held out his arms to her. She took his hands and then he birled her round, just as if they were at the dancing again. But it was nothing like the dancing, because he pulled her close and kissed her full on the lips, as he had never done before. It came as shock. His coat smelled of peat smoke, but there was oil of cloves on his breath. Not only did he kiss her hard on the lips, but all unexpectedly he thrust his tongue into her mouth.

She drew back, frowning, rubbing her hand across her lips. And yet she couldn't say that she hadn't liked it, because there was something in her that had liked it very much. She was embarrassed that she liked it so much. It was all new, all surprising.

He hugged her, running his hands up and down her back, under her shawl, warm hands through the cotton of her gown, the light summer stays, but he didn't kiss her again. Not then.

'Ach, I'm sorry. You're that bonnie. Ye shouldnae be that bonnie.'

The cautious part of her, the sensible Mauchline girl, knew that she was no great beauty. She had a light heart and a light step, a sweet voice and a sweet face, but she was no goddess to be a muse to poets. But then maybe he was no great poet either. How could she tell? He fair fancied himself, as her father said often enough. But was that only self-love? Would his poems ever stand up to the scrutiny of the outside world? She didn't know. They said in the town that Rab was clever. Too clever by half. Too clever for his station in life. And what was he doing, striking up a friendship with Gavin Hamilton, and even with the Montgomerie family? He should stick to his peers, the young men of the town, the drapers and ploughmen, the weavers and clockmakers.

He seemed half mad with love for her and she doubted if he could dissemble to this extent. But she was far more certain of her own feelings than she was of his. Hadn't her mother drummed into her that young men were only after 'one thing', and when they had got that one thing without the surety of marriage they would be as likely to abandon a lass as not. There were no half measures with Rab. She already knew that much about him, and nothing since then had caused her to change her opinion. All the lassies knew it and laughed at it. He would fall in love and then the beloved was invested with every virtue known to men in general

and poets in particular since time immemorial. He was susceptible even when the lassie was quite plain and homely, far more
homely, if the truth be told, than Jean herself, with her dark curls
and hazel eyes. But how long would his love last? How long could
or would he remain faithful?

With an effort she moved away from him, but when he took her
hand, she didn't object. He threaded his fingers through her own
and swung her arm as they walked. A pathway wound along the
back wall of Netherplace and they took it. Above them, oaks and
elms reared their summer canopies. The long grasses beside the
wall were threaded with the flowers of midsummer: a tangle of
vetch, delicate wild roses clambering over shrubs and stones, rang-
ing from deep to palest pink, brambles in bloom – there would be
plenty of fruit later – and everywhere a froth of bishop weed.

These pathways had been familiar to her from childhood, as
they were to Rab who had roamed these woods and fields even
when he lived at Lochlea. When she thought of that place, she was
reminded of the other women Rab was supposed to have courted
while he was there – not just Betty Paton, but May Campbell who
worked as dairymaid for the Montgomerie family at Coilsfield
House. They called her Highland Mary in the town, but she was
not Mary at all, not really. She was May or Margaret frae Dunoon,
with a soft voice that sounded sweet and foreign. There were
rumours and counter rumours about May, mostly asserting that
the lass was 'no as good as she's cracked up to be.' But what that
might mean, and whether Rab was at fault in the matter, Jean
couldn't tell. Once or twice, back at the Whitefoord Arms, she
had attempted to broach the subject of other lassies with him, but
he had seemed reluctant to discuss May Campbell and his friendship with her in any way at all. Tonight, she hesitated to mention
her misgivings, very reluctant to break the spell that seemed to be
encompassing them, happy just to have him to herself for a while.

They wandered around the back of Netherplace and then
headed slowly south-west, towards Barskimming and the banks

57

of the River Ayr that negotiated these woods and fields in a series of slow meanders. Not far from the river, he spread out his plaid against the evening damp, and they sat down together. The sun was very low in the sky now, but the light lingered, as it always did at this magical time of the year. There was a breath of wind, a chill on the air that gave him an excuse, if any were needed, to slide his arm around her.

'Are you cold?'

'No. No, I'm fine.'

He kissed her again, more gently this time. Maybe he thought he had been too forward. Maybe he was adept at gauging her response to him, any lass's response to him. They lay back on the rough wool, side by side and then face to face. She had never been so close to any man except her father, and that only when she was a wee lass. Her breath mingled with his. He had unbuttoned his coat, and she slipped her hand daringly inside, feeling the cool linen of his shirt, his ribs underneath, his heart beating fiercely in response to her touch.

Time passed. If she could have slowed it down, she would, although they did no more than kiss, caress, talk of this and that. Daft, inconsequential things. What Willie Fisher would think if he could see them now. What Sauny Tait, the Tarbolton tailor poet, would make of it.

'Never mind Sauny Tait,' she said. 'What would my father make of it?'

'Are you feart of him, Jeany?'

She considered this, gazing into his eyes.

'No. Not exactly feart of him. He's never harmed me, never been anything but kind to me, never taken his strap to me like some fathers I could name. I just wish...'

'What must I do, Jeany? To mak him like me?'

'Be what you're not. And I cannae ask that.'

'So he'll just have to thole what I am. They both will, your mother and father. For I'll not give you up, my jewel, my Jeany. Not now.'

'Will you not?'

'Not for a king's ransom!'

She thought that there were two Mauchlines. One was the Mauchline of the kirk and Daddie Auld and her father: a little dour and dismal but kindly enough, as long as you obeyed the rules. It was like one of her father's buildings, with each stone carefully fixed in place: a shelter to be sure, but quite possibly a chilly prison too. And then there was the other Mauchline, a place where young folk might wander through the woods and fields, a place of flower scented days and nights, older, softer, enticing, a place at once perilous and inescapable. Perhaps that was why the elders of the kirk fought against it all the time, knowing that it could never quite be contained, but that a measure of restraint was necessary and even desirable.

He kissed her again, bracing himself above her, saw the alarm in her face, grinned, and suddenly got to his feet and pulled her up beside him.

'We have plenty of time. I'll not ask you to do anything you're not ready for. D'you hear me?'

'Aye, I do.'

'D'you trust me?'

'Aye. I think I do.'

'That's good then. And I'd best get you home. Your father will be fretting that the Sabbath is coming on and his wee ewe lamb not safe indoors. Wi' poets in the shape of wild beasts, prowling around outside.'

Chapter Eight

At Coilsfield

My heart is sair — I dare na tell,
My heart is sair for somebody;
I could wake a winter night
For the sake o' somebody.

That summer was the time of their first real courtship, during those long, light evenings and on the occasional even more illicit Sabbath afternoon, while she was meant to be learning embroidery in Catherine Govan's house. They would wander where they pleased when the weather was fine, or take shelter wherever they could when it was not. Even the frequent showers never deterred them. Instead, inclement weather was an excuse to draw even closer together, sheltering beneath the dripping trees or beneath his plaid, wrapped up close, the scent of wet wool, flowers and leaves all around them as they kissed and kissed, taking each other to the very edge of sensation. Sometimes they would forget the time and walk for miles, lost in the pleasure of each other's company, lost in conversation and the joy of proximity, hand in hand, or arm in arm. There was a kind of innocence about it and an intensity that she knew instinctively would never be repeated, and so she would try to hold onto it, cling to the moment. Later there would be a different intensity, the intensity of fulfilled desire that for a while feeds off itself and increases as it is fed. But the sharp, almost painful sweetness of those first caresses could never be recaptured, or only in memory. Often they would head south-west towards Coilsfield House, following the meandering Mauchline Burn to where it joined the River Ayr and then rambling along its banks towards Coilsfield and Montgomerie's woods.

Although they had done more than kiss, his hands ever more frequently fumbling to unlace her stays, or finding their way beneath her skirts, she was wary of giving herself to him completely, afraid of disastrous consequences, and so she resisted and he still seemed content to caress without forcing her to go further than she wanted. He was, in fact, a model of good behaviour and patience. One evening, when they were sitting on the banks of the Ayr, trying to avoid the midges that plagued them, she heard a rustling among the leaves behind them. Alarmed by the sudden disturbance, they both turned, half expecting some animal to come careering through the undergrowth, but instead a young woman burst into view, sobbing violently, distressed and clearly almost blinded by her own tears.

Jean instantly recognised May Campbell. Rab had said that her real name was Mairead – Margaret in the Gaelic tongue – which was hard for a Lowlander to say. She answered to all three: Margaret, May, Mary. Jean saw the girl in Mauchline from time to time and knew her as a friend of Rab's from his time at Lochlea, although whether they had been more than friends, she still didn't know. During these weeks of their serious courtship, she had always hesitated to mention her, perhaps fearful of whatever answer Rab might give. 'May Campbell frae Dunoon,' was how Jean and her friends always spoke of her, with a touch of scorn. She was one of those lassies that the lads liked well enough, with her soft, compliant ways, but the girls were less generous towards her. And yet you couldn't help but feel a measure of sympathy. She seemed one of life's victims. Too trusting by half.

Now, May looked distraught, with her long hair – the prettiest thing about her – unpinned and straggling out behind her, tangled with burrs and briars and a few stray petals, as though she had been pushing her way through the bushes, taking the shortest route to the river. Just as they saw her, she became aware of them and halted, her breast heaving with exertion. She was flushed, her face scarlet and shiny with tears. Her skirts were muddy, and she had a plain woollen shawl clutched about her.

'May!' Rab rose to his feet with a mixture of concern and dismay.

'Rab. Oh, and Jean!'

Jean didn't know how to respond. Sympathy for the girl vied with irritation at the interruption. Her time with Rab was dear bought, and she treasured the few hours in the week when they could be together. What was May Campbell doing here, and what was wrong with her?

'May, are you all right? What ails you? For God's sake, lass!'

'I don't know. I don't know what to do.'

Rab took her hand, made her sit down between them. She clutched her shawl even closer about her, although the evening was warm, and rubbed at her eyes and then at her nose with the back of her hand, like a child. She didn't look very bonnie tonight, thought Jean, instantly rebuking herself for her lack of charity, for her ill nature. Clearly something was very much amiss.

'What's wrong?'

'He's gone! He's gone away. He's off to Kilmarnock and she's there and...' She paused, her voice broken by sobs again. 'And she's having the baby baptised. Oh my God, what am I to do, Rab? What's to become of me?'

Rab glanced from Jean to the distressed girl and back again. He seemed both embarrassed and uncertain. It was not at all like him. He stretched out a tentative hand and patted the girl's bent back, looking sidelong at Jean, apologetically. She shook her head. What else could he do? The girl seemed so distressed. And she had been heading for the river, that much was plain. It was shallow and far from dangerous at this time of the year, but there were still deep pools called weels where it was possible for the unwary to drown. Besides, there were sandstone cliffs nearby, and if she had misjudged her route, she could easily have gone tumbling over. Perhaps that had been her intention all along. The horror of it seemed to strike both of them at the same time.

'Lass, this is no solution.' Rab seemed thoroughly alarmed now. 'Whatever you were planning, this is no way out.'

'Then what is, Rab? What is? There *is* no way out. Oh what's to *become* of me?'

May Campbell glanced up at Jean, seemed about to speak, changed her mind and buried her face in her hands again, her shoulders shaking with sobs.

'Jeany, I don't ken what to do,' Rab said suddenly over her bent head, his voice low and urgent. This was so unlike him that she was taken aback for a moment. He was usually so confident, so clearly in control.

'What ails her?'

He glanced down at the girl between them, absorbed in her own sorrow, weeping uncontrollably. He spoke in a low voice, hoping that she was crying too hard to hear him properly.

'It's not my secret to share, Jeany. Not here and not now. But you ken what's been happening at Coilsfield, don't you? I mean it's all over the town. How can you not ken?'

'You mean Jamie Montgomerie and Eleanora Campbell?'

'Aye, I do. She went off to Paisley late last year, and the wean was born there.'

'Her wean!' May Campbell looked up at them piteously. 'She cried him James after his daddy. Her wean and his, and now he's gone for the baptism. She's at Riccarton. And he's left me! Oh Rab, he's left me and I don't know what I'm to do!'

'We'll think of something.' He looked helplessly from one woman to the other. 'Listen. When you're calmer, we'll walk with you back to the house. Here.' He felt in his breeches-pocket and handed her a linen handkerchief, somewhat the worse for wear. He could never keep his handkerchiefs clean for more than a few hours together. They were aye covered in mud, Jean thought. 'Here, hen. You dry your eyes.'

Jean put her hand inside her skirts, where Rab's exploring

fingers had been just a little while ago, and took out her own, finer piece of cotton lawn that had been tucked into her pocket. 'Use this, May. God knows what Rab has been using his linen for. Wiping the coos' backsides, maybe.'

She knelt down and patted the girl's face gently, wiping the tears away, pleased to see that there was the beginnings of a smile on her face.

'Don't cry now. Tears won't mend things. Whatever it is, if Rab says he'll help you, then he will, you can be sure of that.'

When she seemed calmer, they walked her back to the house between them. Rab had his arm around her shoulders, but she took Jean's hand and held onto it all the way there, clinging so hard that her fingers were numb by the time they got to Coilsfield. They met nobody, which was fortuitous, only disturbing a few pigeons in the woods. The birds went crashing through the trees, shedding leaves as they went. As they walked, Rab spoke to May in a low voice, carefully and sympathetically, trying not to give away her secrets, very much aware of Jean's proximity and, no doubt, her suspicions. They took her to the dairy where they were met by one of the other dairymaids, obviously concerned about her. There was a low cottage to one side where the maids slept and she was quickly hurried inside, beginning to weep all over again. Then the young woman came back out to them.

'We'll tak good care of her. She needs to rest. But where was she?' the girl asked, her forehead creased with worry.

'By the river. What happened? Why is she so distraught?'

'Because Mr James has gone to Riccarton to be with Eleanora.'

'Aye. We heard that...'

'The wean was born in November, or so they say. Sojer Hugh got word. A fine big boy and they've called him James for his father. No shame. They have no shame, Rab.'

'And May?'

'Eleanora was away having the wean and hiding from her husband, and May was here, a daft wee lassie who couldn't say no, could she? She's been hiding it for months. I don't think she even knew what ailed her for a long time, she was that innocent.'

Jean drew in her breath, suddenly understanding, but saying nothing.

'Poor lass,' said Rab.

'Aye, well, she lost it. May, I mean. She lost her wean. Hers and Jamie's. Maybe just as well. But it was very late.'

'Does anybody else know?'

'No. I don't even ken what she did with it. She went out into the woods, and when she came back she was bleeding and in pain. We're all wondering if she even kent what was happening to her, she was in sic a panic. Up at the big house, they are too taken up with Jamie and the scandal. And there's Charlie Maxwell threatening lawsuits against the whole family, and violence and God knows what all. They've barely even noticed one wee dairymaid's absence from the dairy.'

'No. They wouldnae, would they?'

'She wouldnae be the first. But he kent fine she was with child, Jamie did. I'd believe nothing else. How could he not? Dear God, it must have been easy enough to see, for him at least. Even though she managed to conceal it from everyone else. It didnae show much. But she was more than seven months gone. And that's hard.'

'But the wean died?' said Jean.

The girl glanced uncertainly at Jean who, until that moment, had remained silent throughout the exchange. 'Och, this is not for public discussion. I wish you hadn't found out.'

'It couldnae be helped. She practically tripped over us. And you can speak in front of Jeany. I'll vouch for that. You can trust her. She knows when to keep her own counsel.'

Jean hoped that she looked as trustworthy as Rab seemed to think.

'I've tellt you. She lost it. All to the good as far as I can see. But she lost it, and Eleanora has a fine big boy, and…'

'No wonder she's distraught.'

'But you'll say nothing, you, Rab and you, Jean Armour?'

'I'll say nothing. I have my own secrets to keep,' said Jean.

Rab took Jean's hand, pulled her close. 'Listen. When she's feeling a wee bit better, tell May I'll do something for her. Maybe get her away from here. I cannae bear to see her so distressed. Do you think that would help? If she were away from this place?'

'It might. But what could she do? Where could she go?'

'Does she have milk? I mean has her milk come in?' he asked suddenly.

The lass blushed and Jean found herself colouring up too. How like Rab, to come straight to the point.

'Aye she does. She had milk before she had the wean, and that's hard on her as well. She thought he would look after her when the time came, but all he could think of was Eleanora. She's binding up her breasts, but it's hard.'

'Would she come to Mauchline do you think?'

'Where? You're not meaning Mossgiel are you?'

'No!' He shook his head. 'Are you mad? I may be a fool but I'm not that much of a fool, and they would all blame me for what is not my fault. As would the session. And then Jean's parents would hate me even more than they already do. No, not Mossgiel. But I hear that Gavin Hamilton's wee lad Alexander is in great need of a nursemaid. They say that Helen's milk has all but dried up, that she can no longer feed him herself and that the coo's milk is making him sick. May Campbell would be the answer to a prayer. And maybe a wean, even another woman's wean, might be the answer to hers.'

'Can you arrange it?'

'Maybe. We must be getting back to Mauchline. Jean's parents will be missing her, and I think there's been enough scandal for one day. Tell May to leave it with me. But only if she's agreeable. Tell her I think it'll work out fine.'

They set off through the gardens, taking the quickest way to town. The sun was setting, and Jean would be late home, that was for sure.

'I had no idea,' she said as they walked, her arm tucked in his. 'I thought ... well, I don't know what I thought. I thought she had her eye on you, Rab.'

'Maybe she did. I used to see her in the kirk when we were at Lochlea. She's worked at Coilsfield for years, from when she was very young.'

'She's very young now.'

'Older than you. By two years, I think. But I'll allow she has always looked very girlish. I used to have a fancy for her, and I used to think she might have a fancy for me. She's a sweet, good natured lass. Maybe she did fancy me for a while. But her heart was aye elsewhere.'

'With Jamie Montgomerie?'

'Aye. With Jamie Montgomerie. Who is certainly in love with Eleanora Maxwell Campbell. And she gave birth to his child. While poor May Campbell...'

'Has just lost his child. Does Eleanora know about May?'

'I doubt it. And even if she does know, if she hears the gossip, what can she do but ignore it?'

'What a sad and sorry business!'

'I said to her, to May, why? Why d'you continue to lie with him whenever it suits him? She told me he was kind to her when first she came here and she was homesick. He didn't force her. She said she couldn't help herself. That he crooks his pinkie at her and she's helpless.'

Jean sighed.

'You don't believe it?' he asked, pulling her closer.

'I do believe it, but I'd think shame to be so weak-willed.'

Those words were to come back to haunt her, as such things often do, but at that time she was still in possession of her senses. Just.

'Maybe she's faithful to him. Maybe having given herself to him she's reluctant to break the vows she made,' said Rab.

He would always give a woman the benefit of the doubt.

'But they must have been one-sided vows at best, Rab. It's a fine thing to keep your vows when both have sworn to be true, but this is different. Poor lassie. What a situation for her to find herself in!'

'You're right about that.'

'But if she goes to Gavin Hamilton's house - would they be discreet?' asked Jean. This had happened so suddenly that she had only just begun to add it all up in her head, only just realised the full implications of it.

'Oh aye, Gavin can be more than discreet and his wife will do as she's told. They're badly in need of a nursemaid, a wet nurse if possible, a good, clean lassie. And if Hamilton arranges it with Montgomerie, there will be no more questions asked, I can tell you that.'

'But there'll be gossip.'

'There's aye gossip, Jeany. I expect they're doing it right now, about you and me.'

'I expect they are.'

That night, she was very late home. It was dark by the time she stepped through the door, having first stopped by Catherine Govan's house, to pick up a piece of half finished needlework as proof that Jean had been industrious. Truth to tell, Catherine had generously done most of it for her, so that she would have something to show for her time.

'In for a penny, in for a pound,' was all she had said about the deception.

Jean's mother wondered that she had lingered so long at Catherine Govan's house and she prattled blithely on about this or that stitch and told tales about Willie who had been helping with the hay at Mossgiel and had been more of a hindrance than a help according to Catherine. But even this harmless mention of Mossgiel was wormwood to Mary Armour and she frowned, hoping that they didn't waste too much of their precious time gossiping about the Burns family, and what did Catherine Govan's brother think he was doing, sending his son to work for that good for nothing Rab Mossgiel anyway?

Chapter Nine

The Rocks at Ballochmyle

The Catrine woods were yellow seen,
The flowers decay'd on Catrine lea,
Nae lav'rock sang on hillock green,
But nature sicken'd on the e'e.

A few days later, May Campbell left Coilsfield to take up the position of nursemaid to Gavin Hamilton's baby son, Alexander. Only a few of those most closely involved knew that she was not just a nursemaid, but a wet nurse, and those household servants who had to know were well warned, on pain of dismissal, to keep the matter strictly secret. There was no guarantee of privacy in a place like Mauchline, but Hamilton and his wife were well liked, and the immediate household respected his wishes, realising that the good name of a young woman who had done nobody any harm was at stake. It was well known that Hamilton's wife was finding the new baby something of a trial and that an extra pair of hands in the nursery would be no bad thing, so few people from the wider population thought to enquire further. Besides, May Campbell had been nursemaid to a minister on the Isle of Arran before coming to Coilsfield. What more natural, then, than that she should be sent from Coilsfield to help out with Hamilton's youngest? If Rab Mossgiel had a hand in the matter, it was never common knowledge, and Jean said nothing to anybody about it.

All the same, the girl's presence in the town made Jean uneasy. Much of the time she was hidden away in the nursery with the baby, but the house was in the very centre of Mauchline, and May was made so comfortable there that she blossomed. Jean, living close by, couldn't help but see her from time to time. She found the improvement in the girl's appearance faintly disturbing too: the bloom on her cheek was obvious. They were looking after her well in that household, even though Jean fancied it was more out of consideration for the baby than out of any great care for May Campbell. But the girl was obliging, good natured and pleasing. Her breasts were still swollen, but her figure was shapely, her fair hair thick and shining. It was her best feature, giving her rather bland face a distinction it would never have possessed without it. She lacked animation, thought Jean. There was a sweet vacuousness about her that men seemed to love. She would always be biddable, would always do as she was told, would try very hard not to give anyone trouble on her account, apologising for things that were not even her fault. What was there to dislike in this? Rab had said. She was a nice lassie.

As for Rab and Jean, with the problem of May Campbell solved for the time being, they grew more reckless with the turning year. In August, whenever they could arrange a meeting, they would wander through the woods at the back of Netherplace, or along the banks of the river at Coilsfield. The ditches were full of foxgloves, well past their best now, and creamy meadowsweet turning brown. By September, the leaves on the trees were just on the turn. Soon they'd be the colour of Rab's plaid, although it had suffered by being used as a blanket. Towards the end of the month, the apples in the orchards at Netherplace and Coilsfield were ripening, and even in the cottage gardens they would pass (and sometimes steal from) an old and hoary apple tree here and there: crisp, creamy Oslins mostly and Cambusnethan Pippins. There were other apple varieties that neither of them could name, for they were not gardeners, although Rab said his father would have known. There were also brambles aplenty, glossy and sweet, there for the taking in all the hedgerows, if you could brave their thorny stalks and the wasps that fed off them. He would pick them as they went and feed them to her. The sensation of his fingers against her lips, the scent and the sweetness of the berries, always made a tremor of desire pass through her body.

Sometimes, daringly, she would set off berrying in the daytime, taking advantage of the occasional golden afternoon when the harvest was all done, carrying a battered copper pan and heading out along the road to Mossgiel. He would slip away from the farm and meet her somewhere along the way, and they would fill the pan with luscious berries so that she would have something to take home to her mother. But from time to time, one or other of her sisters would tag along too, and then she would have to pass him by on the road, his dog lolloping at his heels, and pretend that the meeting was quite by chance, and pass the time of day with him as formally as she could. He would call her 'Miss Armour' and she would call him 'Mr Burns', with her sisters blushing and scolding her afterwards for talking to 'that man', well aware of his reputation for wickedness.

A few times they walked a little way down the road towards Auchinleck, towards Ballochmyle, avoiding prying eyes, listening for hoofbeats in the distance, always ready to take to the woods and fields on either side. They were still keeping their love secret, still hoping for a change in James and Mary Armour's feelings about Rab. One evening, they found themselves by the old Campbell tower of Kingencleuch, near the Lily Glen, where there was a trickle of a burn that joined with the River Ayr further down. It would be a pretty spot in springtime, full of flowers: woodruff, creeping jenny and bluebells, although now there were yellow tints of autumn everywhere. Rab seemed to have an unerring instinct for these places, and she thought he must have spent many hours roaming these woods and fields. It would be good to come back here next year, in May perhaps, when the whole place would be drenched in sweet scent and the purple flowers called baldeirie that were supposed to kindle love would be in vivid bloom. But perhaps love had been kindled already. There were steps cut into the rock down the side of the burn and a pool for bathing.

'I come here when it's warm and I'm weary,' he remarked. 'It's a very good place for bathing.'

She thought of him naked, sliding into the water, the whiteness of his body contrasted with the brown of his hands and his wiry forearms and his face, all of him that ever saw the sunshine.

He told her stories about the old tower of Kingencleuch, but chiefly how Mona was the daughter of the man who owned the place, a fearsome hunter called Cormac. The girl had fallen in love against her father's wishes with Percy Seton of Mauchline Castle. Cormac had forced his head huntsman to confront a wild boar in the woods above the River Ayr, and the man was gored to death, whereupon superstitious Cormac believed that the dead huntsman was haunting the vaults of his castle, seeking revenge. Percy took advantage of Cormac's credulity when, on the day of Mona's wedding to a man she despised, he had emerged, all covered in mud and sheep's blood, from the tunnel below the castle. His appearance had inspired terror in Cormac and his guests, terror in all of them except the bride. She had been warned in advance and was ready to leave, whereupon Percy carried her off to his own castle in Mauchline and married her there without further ado.

Rab's storytelling invariably made her laugh because he couldn't be serious for long, not at that time and not with her.

'Let that be a lesson to your father, Jeany!' he said. 'Let that be a grim warning. Who knows but there may be a tunnel running from Mossgiel to the Cowgate and that I might not emerge from it on some dark winter's evening and carry you off and marry you!'

The notion of marrying him both excited and alarmed her. He had mentioned once before that he was in want of a wife but not since. Was that the way his thoughts were going again? Was he so serious? Well, perhaps he was. If their regular meetings did not constitute courting, what did? And if they had done little more than kiss and cuddle and touch each other, lying together and working each other up into a fine lather of feelings, it was still something that both her parents and the kirk would see as reason enough for marriage, even though they might not like the idea very much.

In the woods to the east of the haunted tower they came across a mighty rock, a series of massive vertical boulders of red sandstone, laid on end, and carved all over with strange marks: rings and stars, squares and spirals and depressions in the stone.

'What is it? Who made these marks?' she asked.

'I don't know. I've been here before and I aye find myself wondering, but I've no idea. We're not the first to be here, though, Jeany. Look – somebody has carved the year 1751 up there.'

'So they have. But why would they make all these signs on the rock?'

'I think these are much older. Long, long ago, before Mauchline was even a town.'

'Do you think so? Do you think elves made them, Rab?'

When they were ploughing, the men would turn up all kinds of strange things, not least the beautifully carved heads of what looked like wee toty arrows, and they would call them 'elf shot', thinking that the sites marked some long ago battle among the fairy folk who had lived here long before men walked the land.

'I don't know about elves. My mother would think so. But then she believes in all kinds of ghosts and goblins and other strange folk. It is a sair trial to her, Jeany, for she's aye on the lookout for ill omens. But this looks like a map, or a plan of something, made in stone, and I don't think elves had need of such things. But nobody seems to ken what it is. I've asked folk and there are few who even know of its existence. Your father might know something. He's a stonemason after all. And he's built bridges round here.'

'That's true, he has.'

'But I darenae be the one to ask him, and you'd better not tell him you've seen it, or he'll wonder what you're doing wandering the braes of Ballochmyle and who you've been here with!'

'He's never once spoken of it.'

'You see more of it in the winter. The bushes hide it well in the summertime. Now that the leaves are falling and the grasses are dying, you can get a sight of it from further away. But nobody walks here, and they believe the old tower is haunted by the dead huntsman, so they stay away from it.'

She traced the shapes with her fingers, intrigued and puzzled by them. She had never seen anything like this before. 'Do you think it is a map of some sort?'

'I've seen such stones laid flat to the ground in one or two other places. But never in such quantity as this. Just the odd ring or spiral. Back when I was a lad, there was an old cousin of my mother's living with us. She told such tales! She said folk would pour milk into them as an offering to the fairies. But that's on big flagstones out on the moors. This is different.'

'I didn't even know it was here, Rab.'

'Few do. There's a kind of superstitious fear of the place in many folk. And look,' he pointed at one of the carvings. 'What about this? What do you think this might be? Do you not think it looks like a deer or a doe?'

'Aye, it does. Very like.'

'There are three of them. Maybe some man went hunting in these woods and carved these images as a kind of magic to call the creatures to him. Maybe I should carve an image of you, Jeany.'

She shivered. She wasn't sure she liked it. It didn't sound like something a good Christian body should be doing, gazing at a heathen thing in an unchancy, pagan place like this. There was a fey feeling to it, a puzzle to which they had no key.

She said, 'It's like writing that we cannae read.'

He ran his fingers over the carvings: spirals, cups, rings, whorls, squares, and stars. What could they all mean?

'It is so, Jeany. Just like writing. The feint a body can read it now. We've forgotten, if we ever had the skill, and the folk who made these marks, even if they were men and women just like us, they have left us no key to understanding any of it.'

'It's uncanny.'

'It might simply be a book in stone. A poem. A song if only we had the wit to understand it.'

She remembered the monstrous red stone with its strange symbols later that year when Rab's young brother John, who had been ailing for some time, died at Mossgiel. He died in late October, when the autumn storms were howling in from the west, and she found herself wondering if their visit to the stone had been unlucky, if the very fact that Rab had traced the heathen symbols with his fingers, back and forth, round and round, had somehow cursed him. But then she thought how foolish, what on earth would the minister say if she were to admit to such feelings, and wasn't it a daft thought that such ancient magic could have any power at all over a farmer like Rab and the daughter of a stonemason like herself?

Rab was sad and sorry about John. He was always sad and sorry about the onset of winter too. He told her that he liked the winter in some ways, liked to see the bare bones of the trees, and the bleakness of the landscape, but it was not his best time and it made him gloomy, fatigued beyond measure. And now they had lost John. It was always the way of it when somebody had been ill like that, every day a little worse. It was as though you got most of your grieving done first, before the inevitable end, so that when the sick individual died, there was a terrible sadness for sure, but a faint feeling of relief about it all the same. And a sense of guilt that you were relieved. It had happened often enough in Jean's family for her to know the feeling too and sympathise. And then there was the empty space in your life, one that you sought to fill with something else.

He had so often said to her in those last few months, when John had been failing more each day, 'I must get back for Johnnie,' or 'Johnnie's no weel and my mammy's that worried about him, but I'll take him some brambles or some blaeberries or some fresh hazelnuts. Perhaps they'll cheer him up.' All of these things he had said at one time or another, and now there was nobody to take anything to, and she could see that it pained him. She hated for

75

him to feel hurt, wanted more than anything to comfort him.

They grew closer, more affectionate than ever, and at the same time more comfortable in each other's company, in each other's arms. For weeks now they had been kissing and cuddling and more than that, until she was breathless at the very thought of him. She could not help but remember Betty Paton. He had fathered the wean, had been content to take his punishment by being singled out in the kirk on three successive Sundays, pay the fine for the benefit of the poor of the parish, and be declared a bachelor again. He had acknowledged the child and agreed to support her while there was breath in his body, but he had never promised Betty marriage and he never would. What would he do if she, Jean, gave herself to him and found herself in the same situation?

Increasingly, she was fearful of their meetings, of what might ensue. Sometimes it came to her – when she lay wakeful and worried in the early hours of the morning – that she should just do as she was told, make her mother and father happy, and consent to a betrothal with Rab Wilson the weaver. But he had gone to Paisley, and out of sight was very much out of mind. When she met with Rab Mossgiel, she was swept up in it all again, her heart racing, her mind clouded, and he would groan and say that she was a cruel, wanton lass, but he would be guided by her. Perhaps if he had been brutal rather than persuasive, if it had all happened too soon, too quickly, she would not have found herself loving him so dearly. But he waited and waited, until Jean herself could hardly bear to wait any longer. She was dizzy with desire for him, and those hours spent lying with him on a bed of moss, breast to breast, were exciting beyond measure. Illicit. Forbidden. Inadvisable. She knew all too well that they were rushing headlong towards something irrevocable. For sheer, wanton joy, for the sense of abandonment to and in another human being, nothing would ever match those first few months of her love for Rab Mossgiel.

Chapter Ten

The Room at Johnnie Dow's

But warily tent when ye come to court me,
And come nae unless the back-yett be a-jee;
Syne up the back-stile, and let naebody see,
And come as ye were na comin' to me.

In November of that same year, at Martinmas, May Campbell left Gavin Hamilton's house and went back to Coilsfield, back to working in the dairy there for a little while at least. The story in the town was that the baby was old enough not to need his nurse-maid, while May was needed at Coilsfield. Hamilton had engaged an older and more experienced woman as nurse for the children. Jean was sceptical. She knew little about dairying at that time, but she was well aware from conversations with Rab that the cold months were not the best for cheese making. After all, Gilbert and the rest of the family were excellent cheese makers. Although Coilsfield had a bigger herd and probably better fed and more productive cows, the dairy could probably have done well enough without May Campbell for the winter months. But the truth was that Alexander Hamilton was weaned, and May was no longer needed. Martinmas was as good a time as any for the change to be made.

'And besides,' said Rab, pulling a long face at once comical and serious, 'Jamie's come back.'

James Montgomerie was indeed back at Coilsfield. His atten-tion was, according to Rab, all on Eleanora Campbell and their young son, the 'merrie begotten wean' they called the child in the parish. Jean wondered if there had been much of merriment about his conception and doubted if there would be any merriment at all now, least of all for May. It was known that James regularly rode back and forth between his brother's house at Coilsfield and Riccarton outside Kilmarnock, where Eleanora had taken shelter from her husband. Jamie's attention was all taken up with the quarrel with Charles Maxwell and a prospective lawsuit for enticing the man's wife away from hearth and home and weans, but it seemed that May Campbell could not resist the attraction of being close to the man. She couldn't help herself.

Her absence from Mauchline was something of a relief to Jean. As close as she now was to Rab, possibly his chief confidante and companion, she was sure that he still had a fondness for the highlander, and she suspected that May herself harboured a lingering regard for Rab that had little to do with the sisterly affection he was in the habit of describing. Perhaps it was just that May seemed to be susceptible to any show of affection, all while preserving an appearance of virginal helplessness that didn't for one moment fool Jean, although she could well understand that most of the men of her acquaintance would be taken in by it.

Winter was upon them now, and there would be no more roaming the countryside, no more lying among flowers, or wandering along the lanes for berries. Or singing for him. Rab loved to hear her sing. Back in the summer and autumn, when they were in some quiet place in the woods or among the hills, he would make her sing this or that love song or ballad that she had learned from her mother. He would ask her to repeat the words and phrases over and over, so that he could remember them and write them down later on, perhaps with the aim of reworking them himself. He would ask her if she could remember when and where she had first heard a melody and what had been said about it and whether there were alternatives that she thought might be better suited to the words.

'Oh, Jeany,' he said to her one day, as he had that night at the rocking at Mossgiel. 'I was right. Naebody sings like you.'

It was a casual compliment, but she believed him. Her favourite at that time was the Bonnie Boy: '*Lady Mary Ann looked o'er the castle wall, and saw three bonnie boys, playing at the ball,*' with a melody that would wring your heart. But after Johnnie's death, the words '*my bonnie lad is young but he's growin yet*' made both of them sad, with its reflections on loss and the passage of time. Then winter came, practical considerations of wind and weather intervened and, for a short time, put an end to their assignations.

She thought she might die with wanting him.

This was a quiet time of the year on the farm, but Rab was intensely productive, or so he told her whenever they could contrive to meet. He was writing in his upstairs room for hours at a time, forgetful of cold, his nose moving closer and closer to the paper as the light failed, and as his fingers and his feet grew more icy and more stiff. He would only notice when he stopped, coming back into himself with a jolt of sensation, back into his own body when his mother or his sisters called him down to eat.

'They're aye fretting over me,' he said. 'Rubbing my fingers or making me sit beside the kitchen fire, or getting the cat to climb up onto my knees to warm me!'

'You should be glad they worry about you.'

She wished it was herself rubbing his fingers to warm them, embracing him, calling him down to eat with her.

'I'd rather have you, climbing up onto my knees to warm me!' he said, reading her thoughts.

Up in the gloomy garret room he shared with Gilbert, he liked to balance on the two back legs of his chair while he thought about the work, while he thought about the words. His mother was always telling him that she was going to remove the front legs of the chair because he only needed the back pair; she'd get Gilbert to saw them off and they could use them for firewood. He was acquiring books and paper that they could ill afford since the farm was struggling – but when was it not struggling? Stony ground would break your hands and your heart alike, but books came first for Rab, closely followed by paper and ink. He would beg or borrow books wherever he could, and whenever any of his Mauchline friends were travelling, he would give them lists of volumes he wanted, telling them to look out for second or third-hand copies wherever they might encounter them. If some gentleman with an extensive library could be persuaded to lend a few books to a poet, perhaps in exchange for a dedication to immortalise him in verse, then so much the better. He would return from visits to Gavin Hamilton's house with sheaves of paper and pockets full of quills, a tribute to Hamilton's admiration of his work. Once Hamilton even gave him an engraved ink bottle and a knife for sharpening quills that he said he 'no longer had any use for', although both items looked so new that Rab suspected they had been bought especially for him.

He told Jean that he would soon have enough work for a collection. That Hamilton and his other friends, especially the gentry, were beginning to urge him to publish the poems as a single volume, not circulate laborious paper copies as he had been wont to do until now, so that a select group of friends could read them. They thought it was time for a proper book.

'But how would you do that?' asked Jean. 'Isn't it very expensive? How do you go about making a book, Rab?'

'You have to take it to a printer. There's a man in Kilmarnock would do it for me. But you're right. It would cost a lot of money, and it's money I don't have. But if it was successful, it would make money as well. Only you never know if it will, or how much, till you've tried. It's a risk, to be sure.'

'So how would you go about it?'

'You have to invite subscriptions. You have to find out whether folk have faith in you, to the extent that they will put their hands in their pockets. That's very different from praising you for something that costs them nothing. It means that people who do have the money, people like Hamilton and Montgomerie and Mr Aiken, the lawyer in Ayr, they all have to agree to buy so many copies once the book is published, and they put some money into the pot.'

'Would they do that?'

'I'm told they would. Then that pays for a certain number of copies to be printed. If it works well, folk will set their names to more than one copy, and give them to friends. And they may subscribe to the next volume, if there is one, and so the whole venture progresses and is successful.'

She could not imagine why people wouldn't subscribe to his poems and go on supporting him, but he told her she was hardly impartial. He had been writing furiously, and – with the exception of some of his work that he said was for private rather than public dissemination – he had almost enough poems, long and short, to put together into a collection. They were a mixed bunch, and some of them were inflammatory, speaking as they did about the unfairness of life and circumstance. But what if the venture failed? The humiliation would be terrible. Could he risk it?

Because the nights were too dark and inclement for their previous meetings, he had taken to walking in to the Whitefoord Arms in the evening, through hail, rain or snow. There, he would pay a small sum for the use of one of the upstairs rooms, with a fireplace and a window that looked onto the alleyway between the hostelry and the Armour house. He told Johnnie Dow, reasonably enough, that he needed it for his writing, because the garret room at home was much too cold at this dead time of the year. But he would always gather a pocketful of pebbles along the way, and, once ensconced there, he would commence casting them across, one by one, at the side window of the room where Jean slept with her sisters. She was in the habit of retreating there when the kitchen was over noisy to do her needlework by the subtle gleam of a rushlight, for she was still seeing Catherine Govan now and then, still maintaining the not-quite-fiction of lessons in fine sewing. But she was anxiously waiting for springtime when she and Rab might walk out together again. The alleyway was narrow, and she would open the window, letting in a blast of damp November air, and they would converse across the space between. It was not like being beside him, but it was something. Absence seemed to have lent enchantment, for they were each longing for the other's embrace.

When he had been at the ploughing, they had turned up a mouse's nest, a common enough occurrence, but Rab had written a poem about it. He told her all about it, calling softly across the space between them. A lad, passing by below on some errand, looked up cheekily, craning his neck, trying to think of some clever comment to make, but there was not much to be seen in the darkness and what he heard was inexplicable. '*The best laid schemes o' mice an' men, gang aft agley...*'

What had mice to do with men, or men with mice for that matter, even though there was the devil to pay when they got into the meal chest? Rab Burns talking to Jeany Armour. That was something to be noticed and perhaps talked about. But then Rab Mossgiel was a wild man and a better friend than an enemy or so he had heard. A wicked tongue and a wicked pen when he chose. And as for James Armour – well, he was not so much wild as grim, but a fearsome kind of a body all the same. Nobody would want to cross either of those two. Not if he knew what was good for him. And so the lad passed on his way, whistling in the darkness. None of his business.

Eventually, Rab was unable to bear the separation any longer. Jean might still be able to get away to Catherine Govan's house at night, but where could they go after that? Catherine, quite willing to act as black fit and even to help Jean with her needlework, nevertheless drew the line at the couple using her house for secret assignations. The kirk session would be hard on her if it ever came out that she had encouraged fornication so blatantly. He therefore begged Jean to slip away when the house in the Cowgate was quiet, very late in the evening, and come up the back stair of the Whitefoord Arms when the inn too would be quiet. He had made arrangements for them to meet in private. She knew that this was a dangerous undertaking, but she couldn't help herself. She would go.

The family went early to bed in winter and were soon asleep. She could tell by the chorus of snoring. She tried to still her breathing, listening, hearing her own heartbeat in her ears, but there was no other sound, no movement in the house. She lay like that for perhaps half an hour, and then it came, a little ruckle of pebbles against the window. Would the other girls hear it and wake? She held her breath, but they slept on. In the dark, with just a thin shaft of moonlight to illuminate the room, she slid out of the bed she shared with her younger sisters, Helen and Mary. The chaff mattress rustled, but they didn't wake. She had kept on her stays and petticoats. She need only don the short woollen gown she habitually wore for everyday work, and a pair of leather shoes against the cold. Suddenly she wanted to laugh out loud. What on earth would she say if her father caught her? Or her mother for that matter? Well, she could always say that she was going to the outhouse to answer a call of nature in some degree of privacy. That was why she was going out the door and down the back stair, with a shawl instead of a cloak. That was the tale she had decided to tell, should she need to make excuses. The younger girls were fast asleep, used to three in a bed, used to their sleeping partners fidgeting in the night. They turned into the warm space she had vacated, luxuriating in it, tucking themselves further under the prickly blankets.

Holding her breath, she turned the cold, iron key, pulled the door open a crack and slid outside, going down the back stairs and finding herself on the flagstones, with the smell of damp leaves, mist and imminent frost in her nostrils. It was dark, but she knew the way well enough, and it had been so dark inside the house that it seemed lighter out here, with the moonlight and a few gleams of lamplight in the windows of the inn that loomed across the alleyway. She crossed the garden, a few ragged rows of kale all that was still growing at this time of year, and then she was out the side gate and pattering along through the mud to the back of the inn.

He was waiting for her in the doorway at the top of the stairs, beckoning her to come up. She climbed the stone steps, a wee thing hesitant. His arms slid around her, and he was tickling her, making her laugh.

They went inside. The servants sometimes used this back stair to service the upper rooms when there were guests. But there was nobody about at this time of night and in any case, the inn was quite quiet at this time of the year with only a few trades-people passing through on their way to Cumnock or north-east to Edinburgh. She found herself in a bedroom, both warm and comfortable, but rather plain. There was a cheerful fire in the grate, apple wood by the smell of it, since Johnnie Dow had taken down an old tree back in the spring. She saw a plate with bannocks and cheese, a flagon of wine, two glasses, nice ones with baluster stems. How had he done this? Had he paid Johnnie Dow? She shivered suddenly. He had planned all this so carefully.

There was a feather bed, a larch chair with curved arms, a small table with a flickering cruisie lamp, and that was all. An inadequate drape was pulled over the window, but she saw that this was the casement window from which he would lean out and throw pebbles across to attract her attention.

'How did you manage this?' she asked in wonderment.

'It's quite amazing what Johnnie Dow will do for a little money in his hand, Jeany. I've had the use of this room for a while, when they're quiet. I come here to work sometimes – and to speak to you across the way. But I haven't plucked up the courage to invite you here until now.'

'But he'll tell my father, will he no?'

'I don't think he will. He's a canny man. Why would he, when I'm happy to pay him? And when he thinks me a lad o' pairts. Thinks I may soon be richer than I am now. And already with friends among the gentry. While your father is very careful with his money.'

'That's true enough.'

'Take off your shawl and your shoes and make yourself at home.'

She did as he suggested, perching herself on the edge of the bed, for he had covered the chair with his plaid and his blue wool bonnet and a few books, leaving her no other option. Besides, the bed took up most of the space. He poured wine for her and for himself, sat down beside her and they drank.

'You have no notion how much I've missed you, Jeany.'

'And I you.'

She looked round, nervously, but he had closed the door and turned the key in the lock.

'You can go whenever you like. Never fear,' he said, reading her thoughts. 'But I don't want somebody mistaking this for their chamber and opening the door. My reputation is already lost beyond hope of redemption, but yours is more or less intact.'

He was right, of course. She wasn't afraid of being alone in there with him, only of being found out, of being discovered, her good name in tatters. But she saw that they would be left in peace, that nobody would come in to interrupt them.

'I'll let you out later, Jeany. Can you get back into your house the way you came out?'

'Aye. I don't see why not. They'll think the back door is locked and bolted. Everyone is indoors and sleeping. Nobody stirs in the night unless one of the weans is ill, and they're all well the night.'

He caught her in his arms and kissed her.

She was faintly ashamed of her legs, bare of stockings, the worn, woollen gown that she had thrown on over her petticoats because it was the first thing that came to hand. She had thought any other preparations would arouse suspicions if noticed. She had prettier clothes at home: a brightly printed Indian cotton that she wore in the summer, a cardinal red cloak for going to the kirk on Sundays. But she had come in whatever was to hand, too nervous to dress more carefully or search out her better clothes. It came to her suddenly that he didn't mind. She could have come to him in her shift and he wouldn't have minded. He would have been delighted with her.

She toppled onto the bed, the downy bed with its heaped pillows covered in cool linen, nothing like the oat straw bed at home. It enfolded her like a pair of soft arms: feathers, linen, smooth wool. And then he was enfolding her too, lying alongside her as they had done so often out of doors, breast to breast, sliding his arm under her, pulling her close. He had taken off his blue coat and his boots, loosened his shirt, pulled off her shawl. He untied her hair that fell in glossy curls, dark on the white pillow.

'You have bonnie hair,' he said, reminding her momentarily of her father, when she was a wee lass, when he was teaching her to read.

Rab was wearing a linen shirt and she thought, incongruously, that it must be of his mother's or perhaps his sisters' making. It was clean and fresh, deliberately so it seemed, a great deal of stuff and wide sleeves. His best shirt, his Sunday shirt. Just for her. The scent of him was very fine: a wee spice of sweat, earth, for he had been working, smoke from the fire at Mossgiel, oil of cloves on his breath and another scent, the sharp scent of desire.

It was different from being outside. It was the bed, the very domesticity of it. Like husband and wife. She could not get beyond the thought that they were like husband and wife. That there was no reason and no need to deny him. He was kissing her, his knee between her legs, his hand exploring, loosening her stays, straying to her petticoats. He still hesitated, questioning her, but she said 'yes' because when all was said and done, this was what she wanted. There was the sudden, surprising intrusion of him into her body. Not what she had expected at all. Very strange. And faintly uncomfortable.

'Wait, wait,' he said, touching her down there, touching himself inside her, and the sensation of pleasure, growing in intensity, surprised her.

No, not what she had expected at all.

Once, when she had first begun to bleed, her mother had told her that she was a woman now, and that she must be cautious in the company of men. She knew where the weans came from. Hadn't she seen childbirth often enough in the house where she was the eldest girl? Blushing but resolute, Mary Armour had gone on to talk about certain distasteful things, how the wean got *into* you in the first place. She had talked about what happened between the bull and his herd of cows. Jean knew what was what, but had never made the connection with mankind, could hardly believe it, and had spent weeks gazing at her father as he came and went about his business, all oblivious, in something approaching horror. It was impossible to live as a big family in such close proximity to one another without being aware of something going on, but James Armour was a restrained, religious man, not given to any great displays of passion. Moreover her mother had intimated that the whole process was deeply unpleasant, painful at worst, horrible at best, and that all a woman could do was lie back and bear it. It was the way things were. The way weans were made, and it was God's will.

Even that first time with Rab was neither revolting nor painful. Perhaps it was because she wanted him so much and because she was comfortable with him. Perhaps it was because she was a wicked lass, deep in her heart. She worried about getting a wean, right enough, but he told her he was being careful and it should be all right. She didn't know how it would be all right, but with one sweet wee daughter already, he clearly had no intention of getting another just yet. She had heard enough from the other lassies of the town to know that there was more to making weans than her mother supposed: this warmth, this closeness, this tenderness, for tenderness it seemed to be, and finally the things he did to her to make her cry out loud, at first with the shame but then with the raw, uncontrollable pleasure of it.

Afterwards, he put more peat on the fire and they sat together in the feather bed, pulling up the blankets for warmth, leaning against the pillows in the dim light, drinking wine, eating bannocks and cheese. She wished with all her heart that she could stay here with him the whole night long and wake up with him beside her in the morning.

She found herself saying to him, 'You ken, Rab, my father must be doing it wrong!'

He spluttered, spraying crumbs over the bed linen, choked, took a mouthful of wine, but couldn't stop laughing.

'In the name of the wee man, what maks ye say sic a thing, Jeany?'

'My mother told me it was horrible. Painful at worst, horrible at best. Those were her very words. And her with all these weans! So my father must be doing it wrong!'

'Aye, well, looking at James Armour, I think maybe he *is* doing it wrong. And him with so much practice.' He started laughing again. It was infectious and she found herself laughing too.

'Maybe there should be a school of fornication in the town. Lessons, like with the singing and the dancing. Maybe you could teach them all a thing or two, Rab.'

He pulled her close, kissed her with a sudden access of affection. 'Oh, my darling Jeany. I'd rather teach you a thing or two, so I would.'

Chapter Eleven

A Valentine's Gift

When heart-corroding care and grief
Deprive my soul of rest,
Her dear idea brings relief,
And solace to my breast.

After that, they contrived to meet in the inn every week, sometimes more than once a week. Heaven knew what Rab was paying
Johnnie Dow to secure the use of the room, but he seemed willing to carry on paying it, even if it meant going without some of
his precious books to see his Jeany alone, to make love to her and
then run down the back stairs to check that all was clear, that no
late night marauders were in the alleyway. Then she would slip on
her shoes and wrap her shawl around her. He would kiss her, and
sometimes that started things all over again. They couldn't help
themselves. He seemed to want to know every inch of her. But at
last, she would go back to her house, quietly closing and barring
the upper door behind her and sliding into bed without disturbing
her sisters too much. Hoping that nobody would notice the marks
of his lovemaking on her body.

For a while, this was enough, but she could see that he still worried about her, about his lack of acceptability in her parents' eyes.
Once or twice, very tentatively, she had broached the subject of
Rab Mossgiel with her father, only to see a stony look come over
his face.

'That skellum!' he would say. 'His name isn't fit to be mentioned in this house. Scandalous behaviour. And he's friends with
Gavin Hamilton who is not a good, God-fearing man in any way!'

Her mother would be frantically signalling to her behind his back, mouthing, 'Don't upset your father.'

She confessed herself at a loss as to what she might be able to do, or indeed what Rab himself might be able to do, to make her parents look more favourably on him.

'It's aye Rab Wilson this and Rab Wilson that with them,' she said, sadly. 'Rab's a kind man and a generous man and I'm sure he has fine prospects, but I don't want him. Not for a husband, anyway.'

'Maybe I should become a weaver instead of a farmer.'

'Maybe you should, but I don't think even that would change their minds. They have their heart set on the match.'

'And what about you, Jeany?'

'I'll be a disappointment to them, for sure. But I don't know what way we can change things.'

'I have a few ideas.'

'Such as?'

'I could go to Jamaica. Seek my fortune there.'

She gazed at him in dismay. 'Jamaica? Oh Rab, it's so far away and so dangerous.'

'And no place for a lass. Well, not immediately. But I've been making some enquiries and there would be work for me out there. Maybe I could make, well, if not my fortune, then a fair amount of money. Enough to make your father change his mind about me.'

'Maybe. But I wish you wouldn't.'

'Would you join me there, Jeany? If I went there and made a place for us?'

She realised that she had no image in her mind of Jamaica at all. She had heard about the ships that sailed for there from Scottish ports, picking up slaves along the way. She knew that many of the gentry who owned the big houses round about had made their fortunes from the slave trade. Her father, who knew about such things, had once remarked that slavery was built in with the very stones of the grand houses, and as far as she thought about it at all, she judged that it was a wicked business. Her father himself thought it was a wicked business, but he couldn't afford to turn down the building work whenever it came his way. He had a family to support, mouths to feed.

'The whole lot of them,' he would say, when he had taken too much to drink, 'built on tobacco and sugar and slaves.' Luckily, this wasn't very often, because it made him vastly incautious.

The way it worked was that goods would be sent from Port Glasgow to Nigeria where they would be exchanged for slaves who would then be sent on to the plantations of Jamaica: providing sugar for the punch that the gentry were so fond of.

'What about slavery?' she asked Rab. 'My father says it's a sinful trade, and I fancy he's right.'

'I fancy he is. There's no slavery in Scotland and a good thing too. Well, no proper slavery, although it feels that way when you're a tenant farmer.'

'Could you bear it, Rab? To work there? In Jamaica. In that trade?'

He frowned. 'I don't ken what to think about it, and that's the truth. But I must do something. I cannot carry on breaking my back for small reward here. This farm is no better than the last. I'm very fond of Gavin Hamilton and he of me, but the fact of the matter is that the gentry make use of us and our labour to improve their land. And when I'm out ploughing from dawn till dusk in that woeful sharp sleet that cuts into your face like a hundred knives, I find myself thinking that nothing could be worse, that it is a kind of slavery in itself. For where's the freedom in being tied to another man? I think that the Indies must be better. At least they say the place is warm, and flowers bloom there all year round.'

He didn't tell her that sickness bloomed there all year round as well, sickness and untold cruelty. And she was too young, too innocent at that time to know much about it.

'There must be something else,' she said. 'There must be some other way for you.'

91

She wanted to say 'for us', but she restrained herself. He had not offered her marriage yet, although it seemed to her that when he spoke of his future, he was always including her in the plans. But she was willing to wait for him. What else could she do?

'Well. There are my poems. I'm still thinking about that, still talking to folk who might be able to help me to get them published. And I'm still writing. The more I write, the better the book will be, if I ever succeed in publishing a whole volume.'

In January, he drew a sheaf of pages out of the pocket of his coat, and by the light of the fire, supplemented by the thin light of the lamp, he read her an 'Epistle' he had written to Davie Sillar. It was an old poem, written the previous year, but he had added more verses, he said, in honour of her, his 'darling Jean'.

'Am I really your darling?' she asked.

'I see no other Jean, do you?' he said, sliding his arm around her.

She was moved by it. Loved him all the more for it. But there was a nagging doubt at the back of her mind. Something was wrong, for sure. She didn't want to think about it, but something was very wrong.

He had told her that he would look after her, that he would be careful, that he was not wanting another wean just yet. So she had trusted herself to him, thinking that he must know what he was about. And at first, all had been well. But there had been no show of blood for her this month, no cramps, nothing. Days had gone by, and now a few weeks, and her body was beginning to feel very strange, a sense of dissolution that felt like an illness but wasn't, coupled with faint aches and pains and a tenderness in her breasts. She denied it even to herself, but soon she was forced to dissemble, pretending to her mother that she had already washed the bloody marks off her shift and her clouts, when really there had been no such thing. And now she was feeling sick and dizzy in the mornings, having to go to the outhouse where the sour smells made her feel even worse. What to do, she thought, wondering whether to tell him and how to tell him and what might be his response.

She thought of ways to soften the news, ways to tie him ever more closely to her. As Valentine's Day approached, she sought a gift for him, some token of her love that she might be able to give him before she was forced to give him another, less welcome piece of news.

* * *

Pocket watches were fashionable. Every ploughman, every farm servant even, wanted a watch at that time. The fashion had come in a few years earlier, and now any young man worth his salt would be able to draw a watch out of his waistcoat pocket, the more flamboyant the better. It mattered not how well the watch kept the time. They went by the sun for most practical purposes rather than the precise hours of the day, but still a watch was a fine thing to have. There was a clock and watchmaker in Mauchline called John Broun, Clockie Broun he was always called. He was a friend of Rab's and, as Rab's mother, Agnes Broun, was fond of saying, 'likely a cousin on my father's side', although she had never been able to be more exact than that. Had Agnes known about Clockie Broun's morals, which were something less than exemplary, she would never have claimed him for part of her family.

As well as making and mending clocks and watches, a skill that ran in his family, John Broun was also carrying on a lucrative trade in second-hand pocket watches. The gentry, as was only to be expected, liked to have things that were new whenever they could afford them. Some of them would go not just to Glasgow and Edinburgh, but to London, and while they were there they would purchase the newest and most fashionable timepieces, with highly decorative gold chains for those that could afford them. Then it was commonplace for them either to pass on their old pocket watches to favoured servants, or more likely, especially when they might have run up gambling debts, to sell them to Clockie for a modest sum. Sometimes, when the gambling debts were particularly pressing, they might be forced to sell almost new watches.

Clockie struck a hard bargain, but there were few alternatives. Clockie Broun knew when to hold his tongue and refrain from embarrassing a young gentleman by reporting back to his father; there had been a few occasions when father and son had paid discreet visits to Clockie at different times, neither knowing about the other. Then Clockie would sell the watches to the tenant farmers, the young tradesmen and even the ploughmen who worked on the farms nearby. You were of no consequence if you could not ostentatiously consult your watch from time to time, and if it was a large silver watch, with an obvious London provenance, so much the better for your standing in the town.

As a New Year gift to himself, Rab, who deemed himself a man of fashion, had asked Clockie, whom he knew from the Bachelors' Club of his Lochlea days, to find him a handsome pocket watch. Clockie, who secretly rather admired Rab, his daring and his evident self-love, agreed and soon came up with a watch worthy of a poet.

'I have just the thing,' said Clockie. 'And at a very good price indeed.'

It was rather more expensive than Rab would have wished, but it was a fine watch, and all the better in that it kept good time. It came from London, of course. A very bonnie watch, beautifully made, from a weel kent company of watchmakers down there, that had been bought when new by one of the young gentlemen. He had found himself in serious financial straits owing to an unfortunate fondness for good wine, fashionable ladies and gambling, and had been reluctantly forced to sell it. His father had not been at all disposed to settle his debts for him but was rather more inclined to teach him a lesson. Clockie kept his own counsel and never told the source of his stock.

Rab had carried it off triumphantly, and it had been much admired by his cronies. Jean admired it too. She would have dearly loved to have been able to buy a watch for him herself, but her stock of ready money was woefully small: a few pennies that her father gave her to buy necessities and the odd silver sixpence when he was feeling generous, when the business was doing well, and he would tell her to go and buy a new bonnet or ribbons for her hair. With the changing seasons, her mother would be given money to buy stuff for new clothes, as well as shawls and shoes, but Mary kept careful accounting of all that was spent. Whatever they could make at home, they did. James Armour was torn between a natural reserve where money was concerned ('miserliness' Jean's more indulged friends called it) and a desire to see his wife and his daughters well dressed, so that nobody could question his prosperity. It would be very bad for business if they looked as though they lived in penury. This was also why he was prepared to pay so much for the family pew in the kirk.

Whatever the reason, it was useful for Jean, who loved nice clothes and enjoyed showing them off on the Sabbath, but it did little to help her where access to ready money was concerned. Then, a peddler came to the town, his horse laden with necessities and desirables. Since it was early in February, he was carrying a stock of paper valentines, mostly pocket watch papers with designs already printed on them so that you could cut them out yourself and make them into a Valentine's gift for your loved one. All the lassies were buying them, and Jean was no exception. She chose a design with hearts and love birds and carried it home in triumph, folding the paper and cutting out the filigree pattern carefully with the sharp kitchen shears when there was nobody else in the house. It was difficult because the paper was small and the shears were clumsy, but she managed it and – finding pen and ink in her father's office next door – she wrote the initials R and J carefully in two of the hearts set on either side of a third, two hearts with love birds perched atop of them. Rab always called her his 'lintie' and told her that she had a fine 'wood-note wild', so it seemed singularly appropriate.

February was as changeable as always in this part of the world, and there would be the occasional soft day that was a harbinger of the spring to come. Through the continued good offices of Catherine Govan, they had arranged a Valentine's Day meeting, outdoors for once, in a secluded nook at the back of Netherplace, and were sitting together on his plaid that he had spread out against the seeping damp. There were already catkins on the hazels and silky buds on the willows while a watery sunlight was shining down on them. Jean felt in the pocket of her skirt and brought out the watch paper that she had carefully wrapped in a bit of silk, teasing it out from the folds of cloth. She made him put out his hand and laid it carefully on his palm.

'This is for your pocket watch. So that whenever you open it, you'll think of me.'

'I'm aye thinkin of you.' But his eyes were shining. 'This is fine!'

He took out his new watch. She saw that he had pricked out his name and the date, 1786, on it with some sharp instrument. He opened the case and slipped the watch paper inside. 'I'll wear it close to my heart, Jeany.'

She almost told him about the child that day. Almost told him about her fears, nay, her certainties, but she couldn't bring herself to do it. The day was too perfect, the sunlight of early spring warming them as they made love on the plaid with the lingering chill soaking through. She thought he might notice something different about her, but her belly had barely changed, and besides, her bunched up skirts meant that he saw little, even if they both felt plenty when his fingers slipped inside her, making her cry out with pleasure. Her predicament loomed at the back of her mind, huge and intractable, and she didn't know how he would respond, still didn't quite trust him. And so she waited another few weeks, and February passed by and Robert talked about his book.

* * *

In March, unable to ignore the evidence of her own body any longer, she plucked up the courage to tell him. It was hard to know the right words to say, and so she just came right out with it.

'Rab, I think I'm going to have your wean.'

She saw his face freeze, the small intimation of dismay, quickly followed by a kind of satisfaction, before he turned to her and embraced her.

'Are you sure?'

'I'm not sure and I can't ask anyone, can I? But I think so. I feel so strange. And I've been sick in the mornings, though not so much now. Are you angry?'

'Why would I be angry when it's nane of your doing?'

'Well, it's *some* of my doing, surely.'

'Aye, but it isn't possible to get a wean all by yourself, Jeany, even though some folk seem to think a lassie can.'

Jean knew exactly what he meant. 'She's got herself wi' a wean,' they would say in the town, disparagingly. Then the kirk session would have to step in because they didn't believe a lassie could get a wean all by herself either, and they would force the guilty lad to do the right thing and marry the lass. Jean didn't want to be forced into marriage, not with somebody who didn't want her, much as she loved him.

'What will we do, Rab?'

Nothing if not impulsive, he said, 'We'll marry of course! I'm not having Daddie Auld and Willie Fisher pursuing me and accusing me of scandalising the parish. We'll marry as soon as we can. It's always been my intention. I thought you knew that.'

'But how? How can we do that? My father...'

'James Armour will not be a happy man. But no matter! What can he say if we're legally wed?'

'He won't agree. He'll show you the door, and he'll be so angry with me.' So disappointed, she thought, but didn't say it.

'He would never be so foolish, Jean. Not if you're carrying my wean. I'll draw up an agreement, and we must both sign it and then that's us married, legally married, and nobody, not even your father can separate us.'

'Is that the truth?'

'As true as I'm sitting here.'

'But who would mak the papers for us?'

'Oh I can do that myself. I'm sure I can. I've signed enough agreements in the past aye, and drafted one or two myself. It's a simple enough thing to do. If I need any help I can ask Mr Hamilton. He'll keep his own counsel.'

'Can it be legal to do sic a thing, though?'

'Aye it is. I remember talking about it one evening at the Bachelor's Club in Tarbolton. It may not be usual, but it's legal for sure. I've known others do it when the young man in question had few resources but wanted to make the marriage legal and above board. Folk, couples like us, do it to prevent a lass from being forced into another marriage against her will. If I draw up the agreement, will you sign?'

'Of course I will. Gladly. But what about witnesses?'

'There's no need of witnesses, if we two can agree and put our names to the document. That's all that's needed. And then we'll be married and you can have your wean – our wean – in peace, without being summoned before the session for fornication, although we'll need to make it a regular marriage according to the kirk, sooner or later. But that's a small matter, and there'll be nothing James Armour can do about it.'

She quailed a little at the thought of her father's anger. She thought that Rab did not know the full extent of it. Could not conceive of such rage. But what else was to be done? She was certain she was carrying Rab's wean, he was offering to marry her without further ado, she loved him, he surely loved her, and what other solution was there?

A few days later, he came to Catherine Govan's house with the papers all carefully drawn up. They represented a simple but formal agreement of marriage, and Rab assured Jean that nobody could contest such an agreement if both of them signed their names under no duress. Catherine was present but would not sign as witness. She was as sympathetic as ever to the young people, but still very reluctant to be drawn into any future conflict between the Burns and Armour families, and she foresaw that nothing would turn out to be quite as easy as the young couple seemed to think. In this, she was quite right. Privately she wondered if Rab was being too impulsive. In her experience, three month weans were often lost, and perhaps there would be no need to go to the trouble of marrying the lass, but she would certainly not have said as much to Rab or pointed out the possibility to Jean. Besides, it was clear to her that the couple were as much in love as ever, and she was very reluctant to spoil their mutual fondness by warnings about a harsh future. They would find out all too soon that the words of the old song were right. Woeful want had a habit of dampening desire. A hungry care was indeed an unco care.

Chapter Twelve

The Curling Match

An' now Thou kens our waefu' case;
For Geordie's jurr we're in disgrace,
Because we stang'd her through the place,
An' hurt her spleuchan.

There was a cold spell in early March, and the shallow and roughly circular Loch Broun, not far from Mossgiel, froze over, as it so often did after New Year. The ice was deep enough for curling. Jean took her younger sisters to watch: Helen, just coming up to twelve years old and six year old Mary. It looked as though the whole town had turned out for what might be the last match of the season. Rab was there, of course, and he was out on the ice, taking part, but she doubted if they would be able to do more than smile at each other and even that was fraught with risk.

Jean found the walk out to the loch something of a trial. She could not catch her breath in the extreme cold, but mostly this was because she had begun to lace herself more tightly in an effort to disguise her condition. Her breasts and her belly were beginning to swell, and she was terrified that her sharp-eyed mother would notice. But Mary Armour was busy with a Robert of her own, the youngest in the family, wee Robbie Armour, who was two years old and up to all kinds of mischief, while four year old Janet, who was supposed to keep an eye on him for her mother, seldom did. Jean had offered to mind the older weans, and Mary had sent them on their way to Loch Broun to get the lassies out of her hair for a while, which had been Jean's intention all along. It alarmed her how easy it was becoming to dissemble, to twist the truth in her own interests. She supposed that this was how it must be, once you set your feet on the paths of sin, as Daddie Auld was always telling them in the kirk on Sundays. Damnation was easy. It was salvation that was hard.

The older lads were working, but Adam Armour, fifteen and full of his own importance, was hanging around the fringes of the curling with a gang of lads of his own age or a little older. Jean knew that she would have to be careful, lest he should carry tales back to his father or back to Willie Fisher with whom he seemed to be on remarkably friendly terms these days. She had a strong suspicion that Willie, the eyes and ears of the parish, was paying some of the young lads the odd sixpence for such information as needed to be brought before the kirk session, information about scandal, about illicit relationships, about assignations and affairs of the heart. There were spies everywhere and Jean realised that, if the truth were known, she would be seen as indulging in fornication with a man who was only a little better than the devil himself. Worse, she was actually married to the man. She had certainly signed a paper to that effect and so had he. What would any of them say if they knew? Soon, they would all know. Her condition would betray itself as surely as the sun rose in the morning and set at night. What would she do then?

For now, the cold weather helped, because she could tighten her stays and wrap herself in her cloak against the frosts. Rab, with a sharp eye and a strong arm, was good at the curling and was a popular participant, but Jean had to pretend to ignore him. Nevertheless, she would occasionally catch him staring at her and once or twice, daringly, he would wink at her and she would frown, shaking her head, trying hard not to laugh.

'Jeany, is that Rab Mossgiel looking at you?' asked Helen.

'No. I don't think so. Why would he?'

'Well I think he's very handsome, so I do,' said Helen. 'All the lassies do. I wonder why father hates him so much?'

'Hush. Don't look at him.'

'But he keeps looking this way. And I'm sure he winked at you just now.'

'How can you say such a thing, Nelly?'

'Because it's true.'

As usual at these gatherings, plenty of drink was taken: strong spirits and strong wine, anything that might drive away the chills for the spectators, and by the end of the day, there was a certain amount of drunken hilarity. The men in particular, young and old, were laughing in that loud, showy way they had when they had taken too much whisky, throwing their heads back and roaring like bulls. Whisky either made men daft – and she fancied that was the way Rab was, thank goodness – or it made them angry and ready to fight with their own shadows. The respectable women were taking themselves homewards and Jean was moving that way too, seeing that Rab was still playing and she would not be able to speak to him in such a public place with her sisters and brother watching her every move. The atmosphere was growing uneasily aggressive, there was something in the air, and she was aware of the need to shepherd the youngsters home before things became downright dangerous.

She got the girls safely home as the sun was setting and made them take off cloaks and shawls and shoes, chafing wee Mary's chilly toes to warm them. She settled them by the fire with their bowls of hot porridge and a little butter, cupped in their hands against the cold. The youngest were already asleep in the bed in the wall, which was a blessing, and her father had just come in and was taking his snuff and his ale.

'Where's Adam?' he asked. 'Was he not with you at the curling?'

'Aye, he was and I thought he was behind us on the road, but he isn't here yet.'

'Was he with the other lads?'

'He was, aye, a whole group of them. But he'll likely be home soon, when his belly is bothering him.'

James Armour said nothing, frowned, buried his face in his mug.

They heard the racket from some way off, like the sound of rough music coming through the town, although there was no music, just voices singing and shouting and whistling. They only found out exactly what had happened later, and Jean was very glad that she had shepherded her sisters home when she did. The previous year, one Agnes Wilson had turned up in the town, destitute and desperate, and been hired as maid at Poosie Nancy's that lay on the opposite corner of the Cowgate to the more respectable Whitefoord Arms. The hostelry was run by Geordie Gibson and his wife, Nancy. It was, so James Armour was fond of saying, a den of thieves, vagabonds and whores, but however Daddie Auld might thunder retribution from the pulpit on the Sabbath, nothing seemed to deter them. Rab had remarked to Jean that he had been in there once or twice out of curiosity and it was mostly the haunt of people who had fallen on hard times, but it might happen to the best of us, and the impecunious and impoverished must go somewhere, mustn't they? Nothing deterred Rab when he was in the mood to investigate something.

'Because Johnnie Dow wouldn't be wanting them in his respectable change house, after all, would he?' His stress on the word 'respectable' in the light of all that they had done in the upper room there made her blush.

Jean saw the truth of that, but found big black-bearded Geordie very frightening, disliking the way he gazed after her in the street, and the way his wife, who never seemed quite sober, would stand watching with folded arms, laughing at her discomfort. Geordie and Nancy had a grown-up daughter called Jess, fleet of foot but very childlike. It seemed to Jean that the girl had never really grown to maturity. She was a simple soul who would do any man's bidding for a few coins or even a drink or a piece of cake held in her hand. She would gladly do as she was told, whether it involved innocently running with a message or letting a man lie with her, although lie was perhaps not the right word, since most of these transactions were carried out standing up in the alleyway at the back of the inn or, scandalously, in the kirkyard by night. Knowing what she knew now, Jean doubted very much if there was so much as a kind word for Jess when the men had done their work. They called her Racer Jess in the town, setting her to run and making wagers with strangers as to who would win. It was always Jess, of course. No incomer would have guessed how fast she was. But although they made money out of her from time to time, the men despised her and the women might pity her, but did nothing to help her. Sometimes Mr Auld would come along and speak to the parents, solemnly berating them about the need for morality and sobriety, but they would nod and agree with him and then ignore him. Jean thought he pitied Jess, but was at a loss as to how he could help her.

If Jess was oddly innocent, Agnes Wilson was clearly no such thing. She was an older woman with a broad pink face that put you in mind of a ham, buxom, loud-mouthed and wanton. She had so much surplus flesh that it seemed to spill out of her too-tight clothes. She was no maid, they said, in any sense of that word, and although she was employed by Geordie to clean the rooms for the customers, it was common knowledge that she was employed to service them in other ways, with her employers taking their share of the proceeds and giving Agnes such money as they thought fit. 'Geordie's jurr' – Geordie's whore – they called her. While some of Jess's transactions might have a certain ingenuousness about them, just a wee feel up an alleyway by a lad who was too nervous to do much more, Agnes was more blatant about the whole thing. There had been complaints to the kirk elders that she was corrupting the morals of the youth and disturbing the peace. If there had been a local magistrate, they would have applied to have her removed, but there was none in the town.

And yet Rab refused to condemn her, even to Jean. Or not in so many words. He would avoid her, but he would not scorn her. 'She's a poor havrel body,' he said. 'She's older than Jess. Too old to be able to change her ways. And God help her, what else is she to do? Where is she to go? She would be destitute and cast on the mercy of the Parish, and I can't see any of them rushing to assist her, can you?'

Once again, Jean was forced to admit the truth of his words, even though the sight of Agnes with her breasts half exposed, arms folded to push them higher, and her skirts kilted up showing plump legs, disgusted her. She couldn't help it. She had been taught to fear and despise these women and, kindly as all her inclinations were, it was hard to change.

That March day, at the curling, Agnes Wilson had been moving through the crowd doing what she did best, taking a drink and disappearing for the odd ten minutes, hardly more than that, every now and then. Jean had seen her young brother and his cronies watching from the fringes of the crowd, at first nudging each other as though they were egging each other on to approach her, but then, aware that they were being watched by Jean and others, retreating.

Adam was small of stature. Jean's parents were not exactly tall, but at fifteen, Adam was still smaller than Jean herself, smaller even than twelve year old Nelly. It was a source of irritation to him. His friends were outstripping him, and he got up to all kinds of mischief to prove himself a man, to prove himself grown. His mother tried to comfort him by telling him tales of her own brothers who had suddenly stretched out by the time they were sixteen or seventeen.

He was also very drunk. That much became apparent later. They had been handing round a flagon of whisky, possibly illicit whisky from some hillside farm where there was a rough and ready still, brought down by another of the lads, and Adam had taken more than his fair share of the spirits, too much for a lad of his age and size. At some point on the way back to Mauchline, the group had come across Agnes Wilson, also somewhat the worse for drink. She had goaded them, swaggering along, 'Are you wantin to try me, lads? D'ye have the siller?' and Adam, seizing a wooden fence pole that was lying by the side of the track, had shouted 'Come on lads, let's stang the jurr and see how she likes it! Let's stang her through the toun!'

It took very little persuasion, none at all really, for the other lads to follow him, seize a suddenly bewildered and protesting Agnes, set her astride the rough wooden pole and, with a lad or two on either side of her holding her roughly in place, carry her, bouncing her up and down on the wood, through the town. They were mostly strong lads, a few ploughboys among them, and she could not fight back. You could hear the din of it from one side of the town to the other, the lads roaring and bawling, laughing and jeering, and poor Agnes, shrieking that she was bleeding, that the rough wood was cutting her down there, that there were – God help her – splinters in her spleuchan! She could be heard cursing them for all she was worth, in words that made James head for the door, telling Jean and her mother to 'get the lassies intae their beds for God's sake!'

It only stopped when James Armour and a few other men rushed out from neighbouring houses and dragged their sons away, while Geordie emerged from Poosie Nancy's throwing punches right, left and centre, unceremoniously pulling a weeping Agnes from the now bloody pole and hauling her into the inn. Adam was even fighting his father, while James was administering a series of resounding slaps to the young man's head, presumably in an effort to bring him to his senses, which at last it seemed to do. He fled out the back of the house and into the relative safety of the outhouse, banging the door behind him. James was heaving with rage.

'I really thought he might kill him,' Jean said to her mother afterwards, when the house was quiet.

'Well I thought so tae, if I'm honest,' said Mary, shaking her head. 'What are we tae dae with the lad? But after a', she is a whore, so she is. And you ken fine how seriously Adam taks his religion!'

Adam was a professed 'auld licht' believer at that time, a firm traditionalist. But Jean sometimes wondered if it might not be a belief of convenience, because he was so convinced that he was already saved. He was blessed and nothing he did or said in this life would change things. He could sin all he liked. It was a dangerous belief and doubly so for a daft young man like Adam. Rab despised such philosophies and, in her heart, she could not subscribe to them either. Jean's God was a merciful God, whenever she took the time and trouble to think about Him, and she thought it would be a poor deity who did not take into account our sorrows and sufferings here below.

It did not end there, however.

Two things happened after that, each of them alarming in its own way. Ever with an eye to the possibility of money, Geordie Gibson sought some kind of compensation for the injuries sustained by his 'maid', even going so far as to ride into Ayr to consult a lawyer. This meant that Adam and the other lads had to leave town for a few weeks until things cooled down, staying with friends in Riccarton or Tarbolton or wherever they might seek refuge from the forces of law. It was only when James Armour put a reluctant hand in his pocket and paid out some money to Geordie that the lad came home, his tail between his legs, not so much penitent for his outrageous behaviour, as worn down by the tongue lashing his father had given him for bringing the whole family into disrepute and losing them money into the bargain.

That was one thing, and it might all have died down, had Rab Mossgiel not written a long poem about it, copied it out several times and circulated it throughout the town. God help us, thought Jean, why did he have to do sic a thing and do it now when I am in this state and we are supposed to be married and I've told nobody?

She read it but didn't understand it. She thought at first he was sympathising with her brother, but if that was the case, why was he saying the lad was as *lang as a gude kail-whittle* – as tall as a kale stalk – which was true but hardly flattering, since he was well aware that Adam was ashamed of his small stature. He told her it was a satire, and when she asked him what that was, he said he was mocking Adam and his beliefs and his cruelty. She read it again and she thought maybe she understood something of it, but that made it even worse, and she knew her father would be wild when he saw it.

'Not as wild as Adam,' Rab remarked carelessly and coolly. 'Which is the whole point, lass.'

Actually, Adam was flattered, just at first, and Rab wasn't about to explain himself. She could see that he would always act first and maybe regret it later. He could not or would not think before he acted, but would do what seemed best to him on the spur of the moment. And that terrified her, especially now when she had been trying to bring herself to the point of telling her mother some of what they had done, and what the consequences had been and would be, later that year. All would be well because they were legally married. She had rehearsed the words in her head, but she could not force them from between her lips. And now this: '*As for the jurr – puir worthless body! She's got mischief enough already.*' As for the whore, poor worthless body...

So there they were, with half the town laughing at Adam Armour, for they perceived that the poem was not at all kind to him, and the other half outraged at the violence of the language. Rab was her lover, and her husband too though she still found it hard to believe in the truth of the marriage, but he dared to mock anything and everything. It was one thing to poke fun at Adam Armour, but he had mocked Willie Fisher too, and surely nobody was safe from the barbs of his wit, not even Daddie Auld. Her father was torn between anger at Adam for behaving so badly, and what he saw as justified rage at the perpetrator of the offending poem. But Addie was a lad and couldn't be expected to have the sense he was born with. The biggest sin of all in James Armour's book was for some man to make a fool of him, and whatever his wife or daughter might say to placate him, he blamed Rab Mossgiel more than he blamed his son.

Chapter Thirteen

Broken Promises

All you that are in love and cannot it remove,
I pity the pains you endure;
For experience makes me know that your hearts are full o' woe,
A woe that no mortal can cure.

With plans for his book well underway – Gavin Hamilton and others helping to gather subscribers – and Jean's belly swelling unmistakably, Rab urged her yet again to tell her parents about the baby and the marriage. Their future was uncertain, but as a last resort, he would take up a position in the Indies and try to make his fortune there. Or if not his fortune, then enough money to be able to provide Jean and the expected child with a more settled future.

'They may be shocked, but they need to know. And if they will agree to acknowledge the marriage, you could come to Mossgiel. We could be together. There's mair space since poor Johnnie died, and we could have the garret room to ourselves. Gilbert would willingly sleep down the stairs. Or perhaps we could take a room in Mauchline. I could scrape together the money for that, or maybe your father could give us something if he had a mind.'

She couldn't see her father 'having a mind' to anything where marriage to Rab Burns was concerned, but she didn't tell him that. Confession and, it was to be hoped, forgiveness, was becoming a matter of some urgency.

'Will I come to your house and tell him?' he persisted. 'Will I come, and then we can do it together? It might be easier that way and perhaps he would be less inclined to be angry with you.'

'And perhaps he would be even more inclined to be angry.'

'But I'm your husband. How many times must I tell you before you believe me? He could do nothing to you with your husband standing beside you!' He put his arm around her, pulled her close, felt her belly. 'And I fancy we'd better not wait much longer,' he added.

She had hoped to conceal the pregnancy for a few months longer, but it was rapidly becoming impossible.

'Och Jeany, Jeany,' said Catherine Govan thoughtlessly, seeing her coming in the door one day. 'Ye're getting that big, has naebody in your household noticed yet? Between that and your peely-wally face in the mornings, somebody must have seen something!'

The sickness had abated somewhat, but only the other night her little sister had said, 'You're getting awfy fat, Jeany. Have you been eating too much crowdie and cream?'

She had tried to laugh it off, but it was true. And not, sadly, down to crowdie and cream.

Later that week, Rab left the signed marriage agreement at Catherine Govan's for Jean to pick up, so that she would have a formal document to show her father. With it he left a note for Jean in his usual bold scrawl: 'You may have need of this. But it should be all you need to persuade him. Tell Mr Armour it is all legal and even if he wanted to, he could not contest it. If you fear for his response, then I should be with you, but if you want to speak to him yourself, you had better do it soon.'

* * *

She chose her moment carefully, when the house was reasonably quiet, the younger children in bed, the older lads away from home, although Adam Armour was pacing moodily about the kitchen. He was not allowed out in the evenings, not yet, although it was clear that his presence was more irritating to his father than his undisciplined absence would be. Adam had still not quite forgiven his father for shaming him, as he saw it, in front of his friends, although he would have been fearful of crossing the man in any more open manner. Mr Auld had spoken sternly to him, thunderously even, and he did not dare to contest the minister. So he contented himself with whistling a tune and grimacing behind his father's back, pulling faces occasionally and drumming his fingers on the table as a mark of his impatience. His mother frowned at him from her place beside the chimney.

'Sit at peace, can't you, Addie?'

The lad threw himself into a chair, but carried on drumming on the arm, jiggling his leg up and down. Jean thought that it was now or never. She didn't want to have to speak in front of her brother. She knew he was no friend to Rab just now, especially not after the circulation of that poem. Like Jean, he had thought it a testament to himself at first, and had swaggered a little upon reading it, until somebody had pointed out that there might be another meaning to it entirely, that Rab was not very fond of those of the 'auld licht' Presbyterian persuasion, and no great supporter of summary justice. Even Daddie Auld was no supporter of summary justice, and there were few points upon which the poet and the man of God agreed.

But there never seemed to be a time when there was complete privacy, when Jean could get her father on his own, or, preferably, her father and her mother and nobody else. She thought her mother might help to calm James's anger. He would no doubt be very angry indeed. But she was counting on the fact that what couldn't be cured must be endured. The child and the marriage lines were indisputable facts with which they would just have to come to terms. And perhaps they would be relieved that Rab had offered her marriage and made their union legitimate. What other recourse did she have now?

She waited until James was settled at the table and had eaten his fill, after a hard day's work. He was often out of temper when he was hungry. She waited until he had drunk just enough and then she reached across the table, took his hands and said, 'Father, I have something to tell you. There's something we need to speak about.'

She could feel her heart pounding. He looked up from the remains of his meal, frowning. 'What have you to tell me, Jeany?'

It was plain to her that he had no notion of what she was about to say.

'I have to tell you that I'm with child.'

She heard her mother's astonished gasp behind her.

'What are you saying?' Her father gazed at her in puzzlement. 'You cannae be. How can that be? What are you saying?'

'I'm with child.' Unconsciously, she patted her swollen stomach. 'Rab Burns in Mossgiel is the father. And he's asked me to marry him. Well – more than that. We're already married.' She had been clutching at the paper like a talisman and now she laid it on the table. 'You see? We have both signed our names to the agreement and he says it's legal, all legal and above board.' She tried to smile at him as though it were the most joyous thing in the world. 'We're married, so you needn't be alarmed on my account. I'm to have his wean and move to Mossgiel, and we're to be man and wife…'

Adam Armour started to laugh, a loud, high-pitched giggle. 'Good God, Jeany,' he said. 'What a foolish whore you are, to be sure! Maybe we should hae stang'd you through the toun instead o Nancy!'

She coloured up, but her father turned towards his son. 'And *you* can haud yer wheesht, ye wee blaggard. One more word out of *you* and you'll feel my belt across your backside whether you think you're grown or no!'

Adam subsided in his seat, somewhat cowed.

Slowly James turned to face Jean, lifted the paper, peered at it as though he could not read the words written there.

He half rose in his seat, clutched at his forehead, called out 'Mary!' and slid to the floor. It was as well there was a rag rug beneath him, or he might have cracked his head on the flagstones. As it was, Jean's mother set up a great wailing, and rushed over to help him, fearing that he might be having a seizure, but he came to himself almost immediately. He had only fainted.

'Give me something to drink!' he said hoarsely.

Mary fetched the bottle of her own cordial that sat by the fire: whisky, Jamaican sugar and aniseed. She poured out a generous measure. He drank it, begged another wordlessly, drank that too, still clutching the offending document.

His wife helped him up, and he sat down at the table again, brandishing the paper at his daughter. 'What is this nonsense?' he asked. 'What is this devil's work?'

'It isnae devil's work, father. It's legal. Mr Hamilton himself says it's legal.'

'Mr Hamilton, Mr Hamilton, whatever does he have to dae with this?'

'Well, nothing, save only that he is a friend of...'

'Of that rogue and vagabond frae Mossgiel. That fiend in human form. Immoral, irreverent, insolent...'

'I love him, and he loves me.'

'Nonsense! You're a wee lassie just. What would you ken of love?'

'Well, she kens something, clearly,' muttered Adam.

His father turned on him. 'And you can haud yer wheesht, I said. This is between me and Jeany. In fact away you go...'

'Where am I to go?'

'I care not so long as you are out of my sight. Here!' He put his hand in his pocket and flung a handful of coins at his son. 'Away to Johnnie Dow's for an hour till we sort this out. But say naething, do you hear? If I find out ye have been blabbin about oor Jean's pre-dicament, I won't be responsible for my actions. D'you hear me?'

'Aye, I hear.' Adam took the gifts the Gods provided, pocketed the coins and left. It would have been more than his life was worth to speak about anything but the quality of the ale on offer, and that was what he did, staying in the inn until the money was all spent.

In the kitchen, Jean stared at her father with some trepidation. He was silent for a few minutes, shaking his head, considering all his options. Her mother fussed about, pouring more cordial, glancing sidelong at her daughter. What was to be done?

'Jimmie,' she said at last, 'D'you no think marriage might be the best plan?'

'To Rab Mossgiel? I'll see him in hell first!' He shook the paper. 'This means naething. Marriage might be the best plan, you're right, Mary, but no to him. There's Rab Wilson, all set up in Paisley, a good God fearing man with prospects, fetching in three pounds a week so I hear, and he's aye had a fondness for oor Jean.'

'But not now, surely? Now that she's carrying another man's wean?'

'There's many a man has brought up another man's wean!'

'I don't love…' Jean began, but he silenced her.

'You – you'll do as you're tellt. Get up to your bed. I don't want to see your face any more the night. I'm ashamed of you. Tell me lass, did he tak advantage of you? Did he force you?'

'No!' It came out more loudly than she intended. 'No he did not. I consented. And I've consented to this marriage.'

'We'll see about that. I'll be away into Ayr first thing, Mary, to see Mr Aiken the lawyer with this … this paper. There must be something we can do. And as for you, Jean, you're going nowhere till I say so. I don't know what tissue of falsehood and lies has been going on behind my back. I thought you were better than this, Jeany, much better than this. Shame on you, lass. Shame on you.'

The following morning he set off for Ayr at first light. Jean attempted to come down, but Mary shooed her back upstairs, brought her barley bread and some tea, sent the other children out of the house to stay with a neighbour.

'Your father says you're to stay where ye are, and I daurna cross him, Jeany. He's right. You've been very foolish, and that Rab Mossgiel isnae a good man. He's a knotless thread and he will aye slip away frae you at time of need.'

Later on that morning, she heard a rapping on the door and voices raised, her mother's shrill remonstrations against Rab's angry tones. She went to the top of the stairs but didn't dare to descend. Soon there was the slamming of the door and an ominous silence. Her father was away the whole day. In the evening, she heard a shower of pebbles cast against the window and opened the casement to see Rab's head poking out of the window opposite, the window of the room that held such pleasant memories.

'What's going on, Jeany? Your mother sent me from your door!'

'I don't ken, Rab. My father's away into Ayr with the marriage paper, and my mother won't let me down the stairs, and that's all I ken.'

'Wee Addie was following me just now, throwing stones, pulling tongues.'

'He'll catch it if father sees him.'

'He almost caught it when I saw him. I'll wring his scrawny neck if I can lay hands on him. He and his cronies ran off. But, Jeany, can you slip out later?'

'I don't think so. I would try but I'm feart, Rab.'

'Was he very angry?'

'He fainted clean away at the news. My mother had to revive him with cordial!'

'Good God! Am I such a bad prospect as a husband?' He sounded half amused, but defiant too.

'I don't think so, but *he* does. He hates you like poison. I don't think I realised how deep it runs with him. And I'm feart of him right now. Let's leave it be. Let's leave it for a day or two till he calms down. The news came as sic a shock to him. Go back to Mossgiel, Rab. Wait there. I'll get word to you as soon as I can. I'll get word to Katy Govan and she can send you news with Willie.'

'Well, if you're sure.'

'Aye, I'm sure.'

The truth was that she was afraid, afraid of violence between her father and even her brothers and her lover, afraid of what they might do. Where injustice was concerned, Rab's temper could be fierce and uncompromising.

Although the days were already growing longer, it was fully dark before her father came back, before she heard the slamming of the door and his step in the kitchen. He came to the foot of the stairs and called to her to come down. She had been upstairs for most of the day. Mary had insisted on accompanying her to the outhouse to attend to her personal needs, and had brought food and drink to her. She comforted herself with the thought that they could hardly keep her a prisoner up here for long. As a fairly frequent visitor to the house, Mr Auld would certainly have something to say about that. James Armour had been riding hard, and his cheeks were flushed. He unwrapped his plaid, for the evening had been chilly.

'What did Mr Aiken say?' asked his wife, anxiously.

James frowned. 'It is a marriage document after a fashion, but only after a fashion. He told me, when pressed – for he counts himself a friend to Mossgiel – that Rab Burns could go to any court in the land and they would send him away with his tail between his legs like the worthless cur he is.'

Jean flinched again before his obvious hatred of Rab.

'Why do you dislike him so much?' she was moved to ask, but she already knew the answer. Jean was James's ewe lamb, and Rab was the wolf that had enticed her from the fold. James disapproved of everything about Rab, not least this attempt to force his hand, to force his agreement to the match.

'But, Jimmie…' Mary laid a hand on his arm. 'What about the wean? I mean you cannae deny the wean, can you? And neither can she! What are we to dae about that?'

'There's many a slip,' he muttered.

'I don't ken what you mean,' said Jean.

'And we cannae keep her locked in here, can we?' added Mary.

'Indeed we cannae. I need to go out again. You, Jeany, you'll not stray from this fireside, do you hear me? Not even if the good Lord himself came calling and told you it was the day of judgment. Mary, I hold you responsible.'

He drank a dram or two, ate sparingly and was gone again. Jean wept and pleaded with her mother to let her go out, to let her at least get some kind of message to Rab, but Mary was adamant. Her husband was right and Jean must do as she was told.

It was late in the evening before James came back, slightly the worse for drink, which was unusual for him. Jean was already in bed, but she could hear him stumbling about and Mary's soft tones as she tried to calm him. Nelly had pestered her to know what was going on, but she would say nothing to her younger sister, not while wee Mary was all ears.

She could not sleep and lay there listening to the owls calling in the old trees beside the kirk and the quiet breathing of her sisters, trying to think of some way in which she could get a message to Rab, terrified of what he might do, of what her father would do if they met. She got up and paced quietly to the window, gazing across at the inn opposite, at their window, but all was in darkness. What had she expected? That he would be there with a candle burning for her? No, she had told him to go back to Mossgiel and that was where he would be. At last, chilled to the bone, she crept back under the blankets, warming her feet against Nelly who squirmed away from her cold toes. She fell asleep, dreaming about her lover and waking up disappointed with tears on her face. She had slept late and they had let her lie, but when she went downstairs, they were waiting for her. Her father had, it seemed, already been up and doing very early that morning, making arrangements for her.

'Jean – you'd best mak yourself ready. Mary, you can help her pack up some of her things.'

'What for?' Jean had a sudden hope that he was sending her to Mossgiel, to Rab, but it was immediately dashed.

'You're off to Paisley, to the Sneddon. I've arranged for a place for you with the mail coach to Kilmarnock and thence to Paisley. You're to stay with the Purdies. I've already sent messages. I'm sure Elizabeth will come out to meet you on the way.'

Elizabeth was her aunt, her mother's sister, married to Andrew

Purdie who worked as a carpenter. They lived in the Sneddon district of Paisley, and although they occasionally visited Mauchline, Jean didn't know them very well. They were sending her among strangers.

'You mean I'm to go alone?' said Jean, aghast.

'One of the Wilson lads is going to stay with his brother for a while, and he'll look out for ye along the way. I'll have no arguments about this, Jean. You're going and that's that. Maybe you'll come to your senses if you're away from this place, from the malignant influence of that man.'

'But he's a good man!'

She had been going to repeat that she loved him, but James interrupted her, holding up his hand as though to physically block her words from reaching him.

'And meanwhile, I've sent a message to Rab Wilson, asking if he will be pleased to call on you when you're there, telling him you're on a family visit, just. And that's what we'll tell the folk here as well, if there are enquiries as to your whereabouts, as there are bound to be. Nothing the folk here like more than a good gossip!'

'Are you mad?' The words burst out of her. 'You may keep quiet about it all, and mother may do whatever you tell her. You may even force Addie to keep his mouth shut, but you have no power over Rab.'

'We'll just have to see about that, won't we?'

Chapter Fourteen

At the Sneddon

From ev'ry joy and pleasure torn,
Life's weary vale I'll wander thro';
And hopeless, comfortless, I'll mourn
A faithless woman's broken vow!

They sent her to Paisley to stay with the disapproving aunt and uncle she didn't know very well, in a town she neither knew nor liked very much when she got there. It seemed a bleak enough place in March, with its grim stone houses and the smoke of many small chimneys: weaving shops and sheds, and a few new manufactories as well. The town was clearly on the rise. The Purdies lived in a district called the Sneddon, in a chilly, stone-built two storey house that was as full of children as Jean's house in the Cowgate, fuller perhaps, with Andrew Purdie's single storey workshop next door. They were not far from the huge poorhouse, with its adjacent asylum, built some thirty years earlier, so her aunt told her, with a meaningful look. This was where you might end up, she seemed to be saying, if you became destitute. Especially if you became destitute with a bastard child to care for. When Jean tried to tell her Aunt Eliza that the coming child would not be a bastard (how she hated that word) because she was legally married to the father, her aunt simply pursed her lips and said, 'What proof do you have of that, Jeany?'

The words were ominous. A couple of weeks later, in the middle of April, her father came to Paisley, riding through the night, lingering only a few hours to rest the horse. She thought at first that he might be coming to bring her home. But a glance at his grim face let her see that he had other, less congenial business in hand.

He drew a battered paper out of the breast of his long coat and threw it down on the table in front of Jean and her aunt. 'There!' he said. 'There's your marriage paper, Jean. You may do what you like with it now and much good may it do you – or him for that matter.'

She unfolded it, not understanding at first. Then she saw that the names had been cut out of it. It was a document that confirmed the marriage between nobody at all.

'Who did this?' she asked.

'Mr Aiken, the lawyer. Who else?'

She faltered. 'But Mr Aiken is a friend of Rab's. He's helping him with his book.'

'His book! There'll be nae book, lass. It's all nonsense, just. Dreams and daydreams. Aiken may be a friend to any number of blaggards. He's a lawyer, and they must frequently sup with the devil. But he is also a business acquaintance of mine, and I told him in no uncertain terms that he must find a solution to your predicament. To *my* predicament. He hemmed and hawed as lawyers aye do, but my will prevailed and he followed my instructions and cut the names out. So there is nae proof of any marriage, however much you might wish there were, miss. And Robert Burns may burn in hell for all I care.'

'Does he know that you have done this?'

'Aye he does. I saw him in the town, on his way to visit that reprobate Gavin Hamilton, nae doubt, and I told him myself.'

'What did he say? What must he think of me?'

'I don't know and I don't care, Jean. He seemed somewhat taken aback, I declare.' He grinned, wolfishly. She hardly recognised him for the solemn but kindly father who had first taught her to read. Given her silver sixpences to buy ribbons for her hair. Where had that man gone? What had become of him? Was this all her fault?

'And I'll tell you something else. I took the greatest pleasure in telling him that you had denied him. I told him you had changed your mind, you were ready to do your family's bidding, as befitted a good Christian lass, and that since the names were all cut out of his foolish, unlucky document, and with your agreement, he could take himself off to Mossgiel and hang himself from the oak at his road end there for all I cared.'

James Armour went back to Mauchline the next day, taking the paper with him. She was glad of it. The holes there were like a blank space in her heart. Who could prove anything now? She missed Mauchline, she missed her friends, but most of all, she missed Rab. What would he be doing? He must be very angry with the whole family but with her most of all – and with Aiken too. Surely, Mr Aiken had professed to be his friend and supporter. He had always spoken well of the man in the past, told her that the lawyer was encouraging him to publish his poems, was seeking subscribers for him.

Had he found out where she had gone? Would he come and find her? It was a long journey, and his days were heavily circumscribed by farm work and family commitments, but she still found herself wondering, now that she was away from James Armour's house, why Rab would not come to her. Did he think her faithless? But then, perhaps he had believed her father. James could be very forceful when he chose. Perhaps he thought that she had rejected him because she had allowed herself to be spirited away to Paisley. But what other option did she have? Could she have escaped from the house in the Cowgate by night, tramped through the dark to Mossgiel and thrown herself on his and his family's mercy? Well, she supposed she might have done it, but it had seemed quite impossible at the time. They had even locked the back door and taken away the key. Now that she was in Paisley, she couldn't even think of making such a journey alone and unprotected, certainly not in her condition.

She had no resources, no money of her own, and she was watched, day and night. If she had thought she might be able to write to him from here, she was very much mistaken. This was a house where writing paper was a scarce commodity, apart from the few bills of sale that Andrew Purdie used. There was no sympathetic servant to help her. She thought of the novels she and the other Mauchline belles had read, and how in those, some faithful servant had always been happy to carry messages between the lovers. The only servants in this house were a sour faced and unapproachable maid who helped out with the children and the cooking, and a silent old man who hauled wood about in the workshop, staggering beneath the weight of the rough planks, on spindly legs. She had even asked her aunt if she might write to her friend Catherine Govan, but was told that she was not allowed any correspondence at all. Her father was a canny man, and presumably he had already realised that a black fit must have been involved. He would not make the same mistake twice.

* * *

To her extreme embarrassment, Rab Wilson came to visit her a few weeks after her arrival. Surprisingly – or perhaps not surprisingly at all in view of her family's plans for her – the Purdies left her alone with him for a while. He was a tall young man: grave, godly and diffident. He seemed to be trying hard to keep his eyes off her swelling belly, and not quite succeeding. It was little wonder, because it seemed to be growing bigger by the day, bigger than it should have been, she thought, worriedly.

He took her hand.

'Are you quite well, Miss Armour?'

'I am quite well, thank you.' She was smitten with a sudden terrible desire to laugh. Here was her old suitor paying court to her, while she was carrying another man's child. It seemed very strange. How had she ever found herself in this predicament?

She sat down and gestured to him to sit as well, which he did, shuffling uncomfortably in his seat, the chair too low for his long legs. They were in the closest thing the Purdies had to a parlour: a best room, with furniture made by her uncle, rag rugs on the floor and nice drapes at the windows, one of the benefits of living in a weaving town, no doubt. It was a chilly day in April and the grim maid had even come in and lit a fire for them, tut-tutting at the inconvenience. But the room had a cheerless air and the chimney smoked, suggesting that it was seldom used.

At last he plucked up the courage to speak.

'Miss Armour,' he said. 'I don't know what to say to you. They told me you were come to Paisley, and that I would be most welcome to visit you, but it seems to me that you were all unaware of this.'

She thought it was daft that they were being so very formal when they had known each other all their lives, more or less, or at least since she was toddling about the town and he was four years older, looking after her. She could remember him from the bleach green when their respective mothers would take them there and let them run about, playing chase and catch, while the women got on with spreading the linens.

'Oh Rab,' she said, 'I'm so sorry they've got you embroiled in all this. It's none of your fault and none of your doing, but to tell you the truth, I'm happy to see a friendly face.'

He seemed relieved. 'Well, I'm aye happy to see you, Jean. You ken that fine.'

'I do.'

'And whatever I can do for you, I will. But why don't you tell me about it? The whole sorry tale. I'll always be a good friend to you, and you can confide in me.'

She told him then, told him all about the other Rab, her Rab, and about the wean and the marriage lines and how her father had responded.

He was silent for a few moments, shaking his head, more in sorrow than in anger.

'But I think this means that you're legally married, Jean, whatever they may say or do.'

'I'm sure that's the case. Or I hoped so. And now you think so too. But what can I do? They've taken away my proof, and unless

Rab comes and takes me back to Mossgiel…'

'I'm not sure he could do that, Jeany. It would be such an extreme measure. The kirk would never forgive him for it.'

'You're right. Nobody would forgive him. Least of all my parents.'

'Perhaps you should just bide here, bide your time. I've heard from my family in Mauchline.'

'What do they say? What are they saying about me?'

He shook his head, frowned, sighed.

'Och, Rab. I thought you were my friend.'

'I am your friend. Your good friend. It's just … I don't know what to advise you for the best.'

'Just tell me what's happening in Mauchline.'

'They're saying that James Lamie went to see your mother last week, on behalf of the session. There had been gossip, talk, you ken what it's like there. If you're sick, they'll have you dead and buried.'

'They will.'

'Well, Lamie wanted to know if you were with child. But your mother said, no you weren't. You had gone to Paisley to stay with friends, and weren't you allowed to make a family visit without the kirk wanting to have a hand in the matter?'

'She'll be doing as she's told. Saying what my father told her to say.'

'Aye well, I don't know about the sense of it. When the wean comes, there'll be no gainsaying it.'

'Perhaps she thought I would be married to you by then, and that would be the end of the matter.'

'I would marry you if I thought it would do any good, if I thought it was what you wanted. You must know that, Jean. But you're married to somebody else, in the eyes of God and in the eyes of the law, and I think your husband might have something to say about it. Justifiably. Whatever your father hopes or fears.'

'You're right. But what about Rab Mossgiel. What's he saying?

What's he doing?'

He fidgeted in his chair again, screwed up his face in embarrassment.

'Come on, Rab. Just tell me.'

'Well, mind now, this is hearsay.'

'Aye.'

'He went to your house in the Cowgate and banged on the door and made a terrible fuss, once he knew that you had gone. They thought he would break it down.'

'That won't make my father like him any better.'

'No, it won't.'

'Gilbert had to come and drag him away, take him home again. Much the worse for drink, they're saying. It was all round the town. And he's been raving about your faithlessness ever since.'

'*My* faithlessness? *Mine*? What did he expect me to do?'

'He's not being reasonable. But then, neither is your father. And I don't know what the answer is, Jeany. Rab's no a...' He stopped. 'He's no what you would call a...'

'A steady man. Or like to be a good provider. No. He isn't. But I love him all the same.'

He shook his head. 'I'm that sorry, Jeany.'

'There's more, isn't there?'

'Well it's all a guddle, to be sure. Your father is threatening him with the kirk and the law, for fornication and for enticing his daughter away. He wants money your Rab doesn't have. And Rab's beginning to talk about going away to the Indies to seek his fortune.'

'Aye well, he was talking about going to the Indies before this.'

'But there's more.'

'What more?'

She felt a cold clutching at her heart. The child moved. It had moved before, but this time she felt a distinct ripple across her belly, one side to the other.

'What more?'

'He's been seen going about with May Campbell.'

'No.' She shook her head. It couldn't be.

'I don't ken if there's anything in it, really. He was trying to get her to meet with him in the old castle by Mr Hamilton's house, but she wouldn't have it.'

'How do you ken this?'

'He was complaining to Blane, his ploughman, that the lassie wouldnae meet him. But it might all be hearsay and gossip.'

'No. I'm sure she wouldnae meet him there, at any rate.'

'You sound as if you know something about her.'

'I do, worse luck. She wouldnae meet Rab Mossgiel there because she was in the habit of meeting another body there.'

'Are you talking about Jamie Montgomerie?'

'Aye, I am.'

'Is that still going on?'

'I've no notion. I've not seen much of May Campbell since she went back to work at Coilsfield, and that's the truth. But she was fond of Rab Mossgiel. Very fond of him. And Rab was sorry for her.'

'He has a warm heart where the lassies are concerned.'

'That's what you could call it, for sure.'

It hurt the heart of her. Here she was, in Paisley, carrying his child, the subject of so much gossip and censure, while he was in Mauchline carrying on with May Campbell of all people. It was like a deliberate slight, as though he knew what would be most calcu-lated to injure her. It was cruel, and she hadn't thought it of him. But perhaps she hadn't realised the depths of his hurt either. She wanted to cry, but thought that crying would do no good at all.

Rab Wilson took her hand, his face raw with concern.

'Jeany – are you all right?'

'I will be. I'm just disappointed in him.'

'Well, it pains me to admit it, but it seems to me that he is hit-ting upon precisely the worst thing he can do to you. I don't like it, but I do understand it. And you know May Campbell. She has this air of...'

'Helplessness. Aye. She has. Men like that kind of thing. Especially men like Rab Mossgiel.'

'He doesn't ken what's good for him. Has no idea how fine you are. What a treasure he has in you.'

She took a great sobbing breath, controlling herself with an effort. 'You're so kind to me. But you'd best go, or they'll be thinking I've agreed to marry *you*.' She smiled, tremulously. She saw that she could marry him, live here in Paisley, bear her child and then his children. He was not a man to bear grudges, a good man, kind, generous, a little solemn to be sure. It would not be a bad life. The temptation was very great, when she was so alone here, so very much without resources. But she couldn't do it. Somewhere deep inside her, a voice was telling her that she mustn't do it. It was not destined to be.

'Jean!' He had stood up and was preparing to take his leave. 'Do you have any money?'

'Nothing. They let me bring my clothes but that's all. They feed me here, and I help with the weans. They're not unkind, but I have nothing.'

He pulled a handful of silver coins out of his pocket. She would have refused them, backing away from him, but he seized her hand and folded her fingers over the money.

'Jeany, this is as much for me as for you. I should feel very sorry to think of you without the wherewithal to buy anything. Hide these away somewhere, or they may take them off you. At least it means that if the opportunity arises, or if you really can't bear to be here any longer, you'll have some means to go home without recourse to any of your relatives.'

'You're so kind to me.'

'I'm very fond of you. As who wouldnae be? And if you're agreeable, I'll come and visit you again.'

'I'll be glad to see you.'

'Listen – I won't speak to your aunt and uncle about what we've said today. Well, I won't speak in any great detail. This isn't because I'm trying to persuade you. But if they think...'

'That there is a chance ... aye ... they'll allow you to keep on visiting me.'

'Exactly.'

'And you'll bring me what news you can from Mauchline?'

He looked at her in some dismay. 'Do you *want* news from Mauchline?'

'I may not want it, but I surely need it.'

'Will you write to him, Jean? D'you think it would help?'

'I would have. I might even have asked you to take a letter for me if you would do it.'

'I'll do it if you want me to.'

She thought of pretty May Campbell with her fair hair and her sweet face. She thought of May and Rab, walking on the banks of the river Ayr, with spring coming on fast, the buds on all the trees, the bluebells scenting the woods. She thought of all the places where they had lain together, kissing and conversing, murmuring of love and liking, and kissing again.

'No. I won't write to him. I won't lower myself to plead with him. If he can forget me so soon, so quickly, then perhaps my mother and father are right. Perhaps I should try to forget him as well. Although I'm living with a constant reminder.' She patted her belly. 'But bring me what news you can from Mauchline, even if you think it'll hurt me to hear it. I can at least trust you not to make more of it than it is.'

'You can. And I will. Take care, Jean. And don't be too down-hearted. Maybe it'll all come right in the end.'

He took his leave of her, and she saw that her aunt and uncle were smiling as he left, thinking that the meeting had gone as well as could be expected, thinking that if there was any young man who could put Rab the poet out of their niece's mind, it would surely be Rab the weaver.

The next time he came, Rab Wilson brought another bundle of news from Mauchline. Her parents were trying hard to pretend that she was not with child, although since James was consulting lawyers and the holy beagles of the kirk were in full cry after Rab Mossgiel, this was getting harder by the day. The book of his poetry was going to be published in Kilmarnock, and there were already plenty of subscribers, including Mr Aiken himself, so the venture was likely to be a success. Nevertheless, he was still making plans to go to the Indies. Probably in October of that year. He had asked May Campbell to go with him, although that was only a rumour. Perhaps he had asked May Campbell if – were he to send for her – she would join him there. That was another rumour. Her friends at Coilsfield and in Mauchline were tight lipped about it all, Rab's friends less so. They said that one John Lees was acting as black fit between the two of them.

'Not Katy Govan, then?' asked Jean.

'No, not Katy Govan. Why?'

'Ach never mind. Don't mind me.'

'Well, there's more if you want to hear it.'

'I do want to hear it. I want to ken all about it.'

In an effort to convince Rab Mossgiel that May was not all she should be, some of his cronies had arranged to meet him in the wee tavern near the bleach green, the one they called The Elbow because of where it sat on a bend in the lane and the consequent shape of it. It was owned by a seaman who had given up the sea and, as so many of them did, had taken to selling drink to make a reasonably honest shilling. Old Tar, they called him. Rab, all unsuspecting, had joined the other lads there one light spring evening, in the middle room that was kitchen and snug in one, only to see a blushing May Campbell emerge from an inner room, where there was a convenient bed, in the very act of adjusting her gown. May had passed Rab by without a second glance, blushing at the jeers and catcalls of the other lads. There was a pause, and then James Montgomerie himself strode out, all unabashed. The door was open, the bed rumpled.

'But none of this seemed to persuade him,' said Rab Wilson, frowning. 'Your Robert, I mean. He just would not have it. I think she cannot be faithful to him, but it seems he doesn't care. Not where Montgomerie is concerned, anyway.'

Jean shook her head, sorry for May, sorry for her man too, in spite of herself. She thought of Rab Mossgiel arranging for a bedroom at the Whitefoord Arms, much as James must have arranged for the use of a room at the Elbow Tavern.

'The thing is, he kens fine that she loves Jamie.'

'He does?'

'Oh, aye, he does.'

She remembered that day last year, down by the banks of the Ayr, poor May Campbell rushing through the shrubs and bushes, her sad, tearstained face, Rab's concern for her. Nothing if not soft hearted.

'He kens all about it, and so do I for that matter. She's been in love with Jamie Montgomerie for years. Since ever she first went to work at Coilsfield, I fancy, and that was a few years ago now.'

She almost told him about the lost baby, almost told him the truth about May Campbell's summer spent working for Gavin Hamilton and the real reason for it, but she stopped herself just in time, biting her tongue. It was not her secret to tell and, much as she trusted Rab Wilson to keep his own counsel, these things had a habit of slipping out. It would never do.

'Then why is she planning to go away with Rab Burns?'

'Desperation? Resignation? She likes him well enough. There'll never be anything but the occasional snatched moment for her with Jamie Montgomerie and she knows it, but I think she cannot say no to him while they are living in the same house.'

Just as I couldn't say no to Rab Mossgiel, she thought, feeling again that suffocating sensation that she might die for lack of him. That perhaps she would rather die. How strong the desires of the body were, overriding all considerations of morality and propriety. And how very unwise. No wonder the Saviour had said, 'let him who is without sin cast the first stone.'

'You think they are both trying to make the best of it?'

'I think maybe they are.'

'Well, as far as I know, she has left Coilsfield now.'

'She has left?' Jean was very surprised. Leaving Coilsfield meant leaving Jamie Montgomerie.

'Aye. She left on Whitsunday, as was her right. Her friends seem to think that she is going home to Campbeltown to make whatever arrangements are needed with her family, and to wait for him, for Rab, to summon her. If he ever does.'

'You think it unlikely?' There was a certain amount of comfort in talking about it with somebody who knew and sympathised.

He shook his head. She thought how easy she was in his company these days. Like a brother. Like one of her grown up brothers. 'Not so much unlikely as – ach, I don't know. It's all hearsay and rumour, Jean. But if his book of poems is published and it is a success, as does seem likely from what I'm hearing, then...'

'Then poor May Campbell may wait a very long time for him to make up his mind about her and the Indies and all.'

'I think so.'

'Maybe my mother is right. Maybe he is a knotless thread!'

He smiled ruefully in her direction. 'And yet, you seem to love him still.'

'I do. I can't deny it. I can't help myself. He may change, but I will not.'

'They say he gave her a bible. They say he made her swear an oath to wait for him, some terrible and blasphemous oath, with quotes from here, there and everywhere within the holy book, to bind her. That's what one of the other dairymaids at Coilsfield said. My sister is friendly with the lass. She saw the bible afterwards. May was displaying it like a talisman. A piece of magic.'

It was clear to Jean that Rab Wilson did not approve of such treatment of any bible. He gazed at her with something like anguish in his candid eyes.

'So perhaps he is serious after all,' she said, slowly.

'But it seems a very odd thing to do. Don't you think so, Jean?

The oaths, I mean. The other lass thought it looked like the work of a madman, a lunatic, and said that she would not have put her name to it at any price.'

'Maybe he wants to be sure of her. Maybe he's still smarting from thinking that I broke my vows to him when I have done no such thing.'

'Aye, legally you're still his wife. Whatever your father may say or do to persuade you and the kirk otherwise. And I think Rab knows that in his heart, knows it full well, and is reluctant to commit himself completely to another woman. And he protests too much, protests to anyone who will listen that he has been wronged.'

'*He* has been wronged?'

'That's the way he sees it. But he seems so crazed about it that I fancy his affections may still lie with you.'

'Do you think that can be true?'

'Maybe so.'

'While poor May places all her trust in him.'

'I'm not sure she's even doing that. Last time I was home in Mauchline, my sister said May Campbell had asked her brother in Greenock to find out about respectable situations in Glasgow, to make enquiries about the prospects of working there as a nursemaid.'

'Glasgow?'

'Aye. Not so very far from here. I think she still doesn't know what she's going to do, doesn't know what might happen. If your Rab asks her to go with him to the Indies, for sure she will. Or maybe she'll just wait for him to send for her. If he doesn't, I don't think it'll be any great tragedy for her.'

'You mean her heart isn't set on it?'

'I think I mean that she has no great passion for him.' He blushed, even as he said the word. 'It seems to me that they are like two injured people, leaning on each other for support. Both with the means of healing themselves in their own hands should they choose to do it. Neither of them strong enough to see it through to the end. If I were advising her, I think I would tell her she should either stay in Campbeltown or go to Greenock if her brother is there, or even to Glasgow. She should make a new life for herself while she can. But whatever she does, she should not waste her life hankering after another woman's man with such foolish fondness.'

'But is that other woman's man Rab or Jamie?'

'Oh, Jamie for sure. I do not think that she loves your man at all, Jean! Not truly. Not the way you love him. Although I'm sure she cares for him very much, and is willing to seek such shelter as he can offer her.'

'I'm not so sure.'

'She would not last two weeks in the Indies.'

'Maybe not. And maybe neither would I. But she might be foolish enough to go with him, to try the experiment, if he asks her.'

The next time he came, Rab Wilson brought a parcel for her, a gift, he said. It was a shawl in fine silk, printed with flowers in vivid shades of pink and red, green and gold: roses, tulips, carnations, auriculas. Never had she been given such a gift. Not once in her life. Rab Mossgiel had certainly not thought to present her with such a luxury, although the practicalities of concealing it from her parents would have made it inadvisable anyway. She had given him the paper valentine back in February, and he had presented her with posies of wild flowers, sweetmeats sometimes, favours bought for a few pennies from a passing peddler. But that was all. This was handsome indeed. In fact, she blushed to realise that her family would almost certainly see it as the gift of a lover to his lass.

'I know what you're thinking,' he said. 'But take it as a gift of friendship. From one very old and good friend to another. I know that's all we'll ever be. I'm not heartbroken, Jeany, and I know fine you're not either. So can we not be the best of friends? Take it. I found it on a visit to Glasgow and thought of you. The flowers on it put me in mind of you, running about the bleach green in summer, when you were just a wee lass, with your curls flying out behind you.'

It would have been ungracious to refuse it, and she took it with thanks, kissing his cheek, folding it away, doubting if she would ever wear it in Paisley. Too many questions would be asked, too many of the wrong conclusions would be drawn.

Chapter Fifteen

Going Home

O had ye been a wooer leal,
We would hae met wi' hearts mair keen:
Hey how my Johnny lad,
Ye're no' sae kind's ye should hae been.

In the second week of June, Jean came back to Mauchline. She had grown quite fond of her uncle and aunt and her cousins in the weeks she had been staying in the house in Back Sneddon Street, and they seemed genuinely sad to see her go, but they had also accepted, reluctantly, that she and Rab Wilson were never going to make a match of it. That being the case, she had better go home to Mauchline and face the consequences of her unwise behaviour with Rab Mossgiel, letting the kirk in the person of the Reverend William Auld do whatever was needed to resolve the situation. Rab Wilson had escorted her part of the way, made sure she was safely on the coach from Kilmarnock to Mauchline, kissed her gently on both cheeks and bade her a safe journey and a good outcome to all her troubles.

'Have courage, Jeany,' he said. 'You never know. It may all come right in the end.'

She smiled at him and waved till he was out of sight, feeling forlorn. There were so few people wholly on her side. Not even Rab Mossgiel. Certainly not Rab Mossgiel from what she had heard. His resentment at what he saw as her faithlessness seemed to have grown with the baby inside her.

Her belly was swelling by the day. It was alarming how large it was growing. Was it going to be a boy, she wondered? A big boy who looked like his father? However it was, her condition was unmistakable and there was no denying it now. The kirk session already knew, she would be compeared to appear before them, would be asked about the father of her child, and there was nothing to be done but tell the truth. She saw all this in her mother's face when she met her from the coach and hurried her into the house in the Cowgate, bag and baggage.

For the first few weeks, they kept her quietly in the house. Jean found herself wondering if anyone knew of her arrival, surprised that the news had not filtered through the town. She would have no peace when word got out. The full might of the Kirk would be down on her and her condition. But to her astonishment, her first visitor was not the Reverend Auld, nor even James Lamie, come on the session's business, but Rab Mossgiel himself, hammering at the door, demanding to see her, as though all these weeks had not passed, as though he thought she would have heard nothing about his affair with May Campbell. She was upstairs, hearing Nelly read, using the family bible, when he came to the door. When she heard his voice, she flushed, crimson to the very roots of her hair.

'Is that Rab Burns?' whispered Nelly, seizing the chance to escape from the loathed lessons. 'He sounds awfy angry, Jean.'

The whole street would know all about it now. But then they would have known all about it already, would surely have been waiting for her return. Waiting to see how things developed. Her mother barred the door, would not let him come in, even though Jean came to the top of the stairs and, with Nelly pulling at her skirts, begged to be allowed to speak to him. She could see his blue coat, his black hair. Her heart pounded at the sight of him. But she realised that her parents were still obdurate. No good would come of letting the whole sorry situation be rekindled.

It seemed, quite suddenly, that Rab thought so too. One last try perhaps. She had heard that he had put on sackcloth and ashes, so to speak, and gone to the kirk the previous Sunday. It had been many years since any penitent had been forced to wear real sackcloth. The tailors of the town had long ago refused to provide it. More leeway still had been given, and Robert Burns had been permitted to stay in his own seat rather than perching on the cutty stool, only standing up to be admonished for his sins. She had not been there, but this coming Sunday, so her father said, she must stand up beside her partner in crime and take her punishment, so that the whole congregation might see the wages of sin. Three Sundays. They must be admonished for three Sundays, which meant that there would be one Sunday, the last, when she must stand up alone, knowing that Rab would already be a free man, free to marry May Campbell if he wished, while she ... what would she be in the eyes of the congregation, in the eyes of the town? She couldn't say what would be worse, what would be more humiliating: to stand up beside him or to stand up without him.

This visit was a last throw of the dice. He had steeled himself to come, and now he was very angry that they were again barring the door to him. He peered over Mary Armour's shoulder and caught a glimpse of Jean on the stairs, shouted her name.

'Will ye no even speak to me, Jeany?' he said. 'Good God, lass, you were content to lie in my arms and now you deny me in front of the whole town!'

'Shameful!' Mary exclaimed, her face red with mortification on her own and her daughter's behalf, aware that half the doors in the street were open, with folk listening behind them. Thoroughly alarmed, she tried to push him away and slam the door in his face, but he had put his booted foot on the step, angled into the doorway, and she couldn't close it. He was much stronger than she, and James was away. The youngest children, Janet and Robert, set up a great howling, frightened by the commotion and by the anger in his voice.

'You'd best do something, Jeany!' hissed Nelly. 'Will you no speak to him?'

Impelled by a little push from her sister, Jean came rushing down the stairs, or rushing as much as she could, given the tremendous burden she carried before her.

'You're frightening the weans!' she said, indignantly. She looked across at the infants on the hearthrug: Janet and wee Robert, red faced, tears running down their cheeks, chests heaving with sobs. 'And you two can haud yer wheesht. Can ye no see, it's only Rab Burns of Mossgiel, not auld Nick?'

She heard her mother muttering 'might as well be' under her breath and had a terrible desire to laugh. There was something comical about the situation that belied its seriousness. But perhaps it was her condition that was making her so flighty. Besides, it would never do. Her father would never forgive her for bringing such trouble to their door. And he would most certainly get to hear about it. If her mother didn't tell him, the neighbours would.

'Rab, this isnae helping. Ye need to gang awa hame.'

He stood his ground. 'So tell me, Jeany, what *will* help?'

'They say I'm to stand up beside you in the kirk this Sunday, and the Sunday following. Maybe then we'll have done with it all.'

'I don't want you beside me. I would be very well pleased not to have your company at all, even in the kirk.'

'Father says I must.'

'Then you must, since you seem to obey him in everything.'

'I don't want to either. I'm ashamed to do it in this condition.'

He seemed to have been fixed on her face, staring into her eyes, but now he lowered his gaze to her immense belly and was momentarily confounded, speechless. A rare thing for him. 'What can I do? ' he asked, more gently. 'Jeany, is there anything I can do? '

'Nothing. You're frightening my mother and the weans. Please, please, Rab – just go. Just away back to Mossgiel and leave us in peace.'

His look of absolute dismay confounded her.

'I'm warning you, if I go this day, I'll no be back in a hurry.'

'Go!' she said again, desperately. Anything to get him to leave, while her mother stood behind her, wringing her hands.

'You poor misguided wretch. What have they done to you? What have they done to my brave girl?'

Little Janet, more courageous than her brother, had come to stand beside her sister and was tugging at her skirts with one hand, gazing up at Rab with her thumb in her mouth.

Jean shook her head. 'Just go. Please!'

'All right. I'll go. But I'm warning you, this is the last time. Your last chance. I'll no be back!' he said as he left. Then, raising his voice so that the whole street could hear – and, thought Jean, the whole street would still be listening – 'Jean Armour, you've played me false in every way! You must think me a fool, but at least I am no knave. Well hell mend you. You can go to the devil for all I care!'

He was gone, storming off towards the Whitefoord Arms, there, no doubt, to drown his sorrows with Johnnie Dow's finest whisky.

She went indoors and sank down on the bottom step, weeping. Mary came and put her arms around her. 'Wheesht, Jeany! It's no very good for the wean, lass. Wheesht.'

'He'll never come back, will he? I've denied him and betrayed him. He'll never speak to me again.'

'Aye well, maybe that will be for the best.'

Soon after that, and while she was still very much shaken after her encounter with Rab, they gave her pen and ink and paper and her father told her what she must write.

'I am heartily sorry that I have given and must give your session trouble on my account. I acknowledge that I am with child and Robert Burns in Mossgiel is the father. I am with great respect your most humble servant, Jean Armour.'

The evening of that same day, having received her letter, Daddie Auld came to the house, creeping along the Cowgate, muffled in his coat. He didn't much care about gossip, but he did care about Jean, had known her since she was a baby and then as a lass, dancing about the green or sitting primly in the kirk, her hands folded in front of her. He thought a good deal of her. He liked to hear her sing. If anyone could be said to have the voice of an angel, it would be Jeany Armour. It was a voice that did your heart good, a gift from God that made even a dour old man like himself think the world not such a bad place after all. He had always thought her a sweet, sunny natured lass with a natural goodness about her, and he had seen no reason to change his mind, whatever temptation she might have succumbed to. Truth to tell, he sympathised with her somewhat. He was no friend to Rab Mossgiel, although the younger brother Gilbert was a different matter, and he had heard good and admirable things about their father, William. But in James's shoes, and given Jean's predicament, he thought that he might well have simply gone along with the marriage. Neither of them seemed averse to it. The signed paper was evidence of that. The couple would have muddled through. He had seen many a good marriage endure long after inauspicious beginnings. Usually his chief problem was in getting the young man to assume the responsibility of fatherhood. No lass should be left alone to carry such a burden. But it seemed that Rab Mossgiel was proud to be named as father, had been enthusiastic about marriage to Jean, equally enthusiastic about his weans. That was all too rare, and he had a strong suspicion that the good Lord to whom he prayed each day would encourage it. But James Armour seemed set against Rab as a son-in-law, and who was he to argue with the man? He must surely know his own daughter's wishes.

Auld sat down opposite her, sighed, asked her what she planned to do. He drew the session minutes book out of his pocket. The session clerk had copied the letter into it, so that there was a formal record of her guilt. Now, she must sign her name to it, which she did on the kitchen table, blurring the entry with tears. All that remained was for her to stand up in the kirk for the next three weeks and she would be a free woman again.

'Is that what you want, Jeany?' he asked. 'You can speak freely to me, lass.'

Tactfully, Mary left them alone, shooing the younger children out of the room and into the back kitchen and thence into the garden where she found something useful for them to do. Jean shook her head, confused. She didn't know. It seemed the wean's father hated her now. She would gladly have married him, but her father and mother disliked him so much. She had not been brave enough to fight her parents and all was lost. Or perhaps Rab had not fought hard enough for her, had not realised how difficult it would be for a young woman who was used to being a loving and obedient daughter to defy her parents. It came to her with a spark of hope that she would have to wait till the baby was born. Perhaps Rab would feel differently then. Everyone knew he was very fond of his daughter by Betty Paton. He had even written a poem for the child, loving, defiant. *Welcome my bonnie, sweet, wee daughter.* Perhaps he would find it in his heart to be equally fond of this other child, if and when it came safely into the world. But for now, she could only think that order must somehow be restored as soon and as decently as possible, and Mr Auld seemed to agree with her.

'Jean, I've decided I won't make you stand up in the kirk. Not in your condition, lass. You'll be called this Sunday, but you needn't be there. You just ca' canny and stay quietly at home.'

'My father says I must come.'

'And I say you mustn't!' She saw a flash of anger in his eyes and realised that it was not aimed at her, but at her father. Mr Auld was known to be a patient man, but you didn't cross him. Not if you were wise. 'And I think your father will be content to follow my advice in this, at least. Don't you?'

'That's very kind of you.' She was subdued but grateful. It would have been terrible to be admonished and shamed before the eyes of the whole congregation, with Willie Fisher and James Lamie glaring at her and staring at her belly as though they wished they had had the filling of it themselves. The very thought of it made her feel sick and dizzy. She put a hand to her head.

'Are you well, Jeany?'

'Aye. The heat doesn't help. I get a wee thing dizzy now and then.'

'Which is why I will not have you standing up in the kirk. No, no. The letter will do.' He patted the book. 'There'll be trouble about it, of course, and some of the elders will complain.' He gave her a wee grin, unexpectedly mischievous. 'But then they're aye complaining about something or other. It's a regular pastime for some of them. But they'll not cross me. You stay quietly at home. Let the lad take his punishment and take the blame too. I'm thinking it will do him no harm to be pulled up short by the recognition of the part he has played in all this. He feels hard done by the now, or so I've heard. He was not exactly a picture of penitence last Sunday, but at least he was there and acknowledging his fault. If he'll stand up in the kirk for another two Sundays, and give some money for the relief of the poor, then I'll give him the bachelor's certificate he seems to want and all will be well.'

'I don't think anything will ever be well again,' she said, dully.

'Jeany, oh my dear Jeany!' He patted her hand. 'These things have a habit of sorting themselves out in the end. I'm an old man and have seen a very great deal in my life so far. What's for you won't go by you. Let's wait and see, eh? Let's just wait and see.'

He was a man of great wisdom and a surprising kindliness, given his traditional views, so perhaps she should put her trust in him and the good Lord too. Perhaps that was all she could do.

* * *

If Jean was hoping for some respite in the weeks that followed, she was doomed to disappointment. Rab was still planning to go to the Indies. Jean had no idea what had become of May Campbell, or even whether they were still betrothed. Was she waiting for him? Was she in Campbeltown or was she in Greenock with her brother? There was no word in the town, no word at Coilsfield either, and Rab was saying nothing, although it seemed that his plans for the Indies were progressing. If he was writing to May about all this, nobody else seemed to know. Meanwhile, his book of poems was almost ready for publication, and another week or so would see its distribution to a great many subscribers. She was glad for him, wished forlornly that she might see a copy, wondered if any of the poems concerned her. She didn't think so. Not love poems, anyway. Although knowing what a malicious streak he possessed when his feelings were hurt, she wondered uneasily if he might have found some way of avenging what he saw as her lack of faith in him. Words could be weapons where Rab was concerned.

Worse, it was becoming clear that Mary and James Armour had begun to wonder whether there might be some way of wringing money as well as penitence out of Rab Mossgiel and all without relinquishing their daughter as a marriageable prospect. It had begun when one or two of James's drinking cronies had told him, to his utter astonishment and profound mortification, that the forthcoming book was likely to be a success, that Rab might even make some money out of it. It had never occurred to him that poetry might be lucrative, that Rab might become – God forbid – a rich man. Nobody made money out of poetry, did they? He had always despised the lad's bookishness, the way he aye had his nose in a book. Armour had thought him an idler who did little but read. His younger brother, he fancied, was the better farmer. In fact, he might even have entertained the more sober and cautious Gilbert as a suitor for Jeany instead of Rab Wilson, if that young man had shown the slightest interest in her or she in him.

If Jean did not want the weaver, or the weaver did not want her, then some other, more acceptable young man might do. But to that end, he had to secure a better dowry for his daughter since, barring unforeseen circumstances at the birth, she would have another man's child in tow, and although James was not a poor man, he still had a large family to provide for. He therefore cast about for some way of securing her future that did not involve spending too much of his own money. The farm at Mossgiel was not prosperous, for all Mr Hamilton's promises to the Burns family, and they were a large family too, but now it seemed that Rab might become wealthy. Well, there was no use in regretting his over-hasty dismissal of the poet as a prospective son-in-law. But perhaps something could be done. His wife was in agreement with him, and indeed the initial suggestion had come from her, once she had learned that there might be money in poetry after all.

He therefore went to Ayr to consult with another lawyer, not Aiken this time, since he thought it better if Mossgiel's friends knew nothing about the move until it was too late to counter it. Jean heard her parents talking about it very late one night, when they thought she was fast asleep in bed. But she was not sleeping well. The fine, warm spell continued. The room upstairs was unbearably stuffy and the baby seemed to be tossing and turning at inconvenient hours, quiet whenever she walked about, but waking and moving whenever she attempted to lie still. Her sisters complained that Jean's belly was forever kicking them in the back. She got up, sliding quietly out of bed, thinking about all those times she had slid out of bed to meet with Rab, thinking about the room in the Whitefoord Arms, the feather bed where he had loved her. Such a short time ago, too. She wanted to weep. She was forever dissolving into tears these days, and there was nobody to dry them, nobody to help her, not even her mother, who was too preoccupied with the rest of the family, too cowed by her husband's wrath to go against his wishes. And it was his chief wish that Jean be left alone to reflect upon her sinfulness. Then, once the baby was born, they would see if they could find some young man with better prospects 'willing to take her on.' Jean hated the way he said that, as though she would be an unwelcome burden for somebody. She had even thought about going to speak to Mr Auld again, but what could she say to him? That she wanted to see a kindly face, hear a kindly word? No. It couldn't be done. He would simply tell her to honour and obey her father as the commandment instructed.

She got up and tiptoed, barefoot, to the top of the stairs, glad of the coolness on the soles of her feet. She could hear the low murmur from below: her father laying down the law as he so often did these days. But she heard her own name mentioned and also Mossgiel, and that worried her. They always called Rab plain 'Mossgiel', never Mr Burns. She went as far as she dared, sat down and strained to listen. Her father was speaking and her mother was agreeing with him, as usual. It seemed that her parents were making plans, and she could hardly believe her ears. The idea had come from Mary, but James had found out how to put it into practice. He would be seeking a warrant to throw Rab in jail until he should find security for a truly enormous sum of money. Not that Rab possessed such a sum, of course. But that was immaterial. He had prospects. And if the book were to become successful…

She leaned her hot head against the wall, the tears running down her face, wondering how she could warn Rab about all that was being plotted against him.

Chapter Sixteen

Two Heartbeats

O, wha my babie-clouts will buy?
O, wha will tent me when I cry?
Wha will kiss me where I lie? –
The rantin dog, the daddie o't!

Not long after Jean came back from Paisley, one of the town midwives, Agnes Sloan, came to the house, summoned there by Mary Armour. Jean was so very big and Mary, with plenty of experience of childbirth, was worried. Her daughter had been adamant that the baby wasn't due until late August or early September, if she was counting the months correctly. Mary wondered whether she could be counting right. Perhaps the child had been conceived earlier than Jean was admitting. After all, she seemed to have been meeting up with Rab throughout the whole winter and seeing him during the preceding summer – for far longer, in fact, than she had ever admitted to her parents. Mary didn't want any unwelcome surprises. But there were preparations to be made, and since this was Jeany's first (and, it was devoutly to be hoped, last) baby until she was a safely married woman, Mary thought it prudent to summon the midwife to take a look at her daughter.

Agnes had delivered more babies than she could count, many safely, some disastrously, but then childbirth was a dangerous business and sometimes there was nothing you could do but pray for a good outcome. Jean looked like a strong young woman who would have little trouble in pushing an infant into the world, but you could never be sure.

She looked shrewdly at Jean, frowning. 'When d'you think

you're due, lass?'

'Late in August, maybe September. I cannae be certain.'

'As late as that? Your mammy's right. You're gey big.'

'I've been big all along.' Jean shifted uncomfortably. Agnes and her mother had made her perch on the box bed where Mary and James slept. She could smell the sour scent of her father's working clothes on the blankets.

'I would have thought late July, early August from the look of you.'

Jean was alarmed. 'So soon?'

'Maybe. Weans come when they're good and ready, and there's nothing we can do to help or hinder them. Well, no so very much anyway. There are ane or twa things to bring a baby on more quickly, but some are very inadvisable.'

She cast a quick glance at Mary. Mary's babies were sometimes late, and certain measures had been taken in the past: castor oil, one or two herbal preparations. Vigorous lovemaking also worked, if the husband and wife could be persuaded to it without too much embarrassment. But it looked to her as though Jean wouldn't need any such assistance, even though the father might have been willing, knowing his reputation in the town. She gazed at Jean's belly, drawing her brows together as though something had just occurred to her.

'Lie down, lass,' she said. 'Lie back and loosen your clothes.' She had brought a battered leather bag with her, the one she carried about the town whenever she was called to attend a birth, and now she drew a narrow wooden trumpet out of it, very neatly turned in beech wood. 'Does the wean move much?'

'Aye it does. Especially at night, but all the time, really. It only quietens when I'm walking, but my fingers and my ankles are swelling up that much and I cannae walk very far. The heat is driving me half daft, Mistress Sloan and that's the truth.'

The elderly woman placed the wider end of the trumpet on Jean's belly and bent down to put her ear over the narrower end, an expression of intense concentration on her face. Mary hovered anxiously in the background. Agnes moved the trumpet, listened again, and then again.

'Can you hear the heart beating?' asked Jean, afraid that something might be wrong. Agnes was still frowning. 'Wheesht,' she said. 'Let me listen.'

There was a moment's silence. Then her face cleared. She raised her head, put the trumpet away. She was smiling.

'Well,' she said, thoroughly enjoying her moment of triumph. 'Well, well, Jean Armour.'

'What?' asked Mary, alarmed.

'There's twa!'

'Twa?' Jean echoed her. 'What are you saying?'

'Twa heartbeats, and twa weans. That's why you're so big, lass. Your dates are likely right enough. And you'll get bigger yet. Twins. They say they run in families. But *you've* had nae twins, Mary, have ye?'

'No. I havenae.'

'Maybe the father then.' She turned to Jean with a wicked grin. Jean blushed. 'I don't ken.'

'Maybe you should ask him, eh?'

'Agnes Sloan, you ken fine well she cannae ask him,' Mary spoke, severely.

The midwife chuckled. 'I thought he might be happy about it. It's weel kent Rab Mossgiel is fond of his weans. He might appreciate twa at the one go. Mary, I'll tak a wee drappie of whatever you have in the house before I go.'

Jean wanted to see the back of the woman, but they had to keep her sweet. Otherwise the news that Jean Armour was expecting Rab Mossgiel's twins would soon be all over the town, and Rab would be among the first to be told. But there was small hope of buying the woman's silence with whisky or even the excellent cheese and bannocks that Mary set before her. Agnes ate and drank her fill and only went away when it was clear that no more whisky would be forthcoming.

'Your dates are probably right enough, Jean,' she said as her parting shot. 'I'll come in again and see you afore your time. Make sure you lie down in the day if you can, put your feet up when your ankles swell, if your mammy will let you. And try not to excite yourself. You have twa weans to think about now!'

Jean could have cried, but there seemed no point in weeping. A certain excitement was warring with the panic inside her, and again there came that unholy desire to laugh. What next, she wondered. In the name of God, what next?

They had been right not to trust to Agnes's silence. The news was soon all over the town.

'Jeany Armour's carrying twins. Have ye heard? Jeany Armour's carrying Rab Mossgiel's twins.'

It was far too good a tale not to be told again and again, in change houses and shops. Within half a day, it had spread to the four corners of the town and out as far as Mossgiel with Catherine Govan's nephew, Willie. His aunt had grown very fond of Jean, felt guilty about her own role in the affair, and was genuinely concerned that the father of the babies should be made aware of what was in store for him as soon as possible.

Even Rab was shocked into uncharacteristic silence, while his family crept about him, not knowing how to respond. Jean had her penitence before her, and he knew that the kirk session minutes would soon be amended to 'children' rather than child. Robert Burns's children. And then even the few people who might have remained in ignorance would be sure to know all about it.

* * *

She had to see him, to speak to him. But for a little while, she was at a loss as to how she could contrive a meeting. Then, one afternoon, Nelly and Betty Miller, daughters of the proprietor of the Sun Inn, came visiting. She remembered Rab's song about the Mauchline belles, in which he had described her as the jewel of them all. She doubted if she could be described as a jewel now. More like a ship in full sail. She noticed that both young women had that self-satisfied and faintly smug look of having escaped Jean's fate and done rather better for themselves. But their sympathy for her was genuine enough. James was away from home and Mary Armour saw no harm in allowing Jean some visitors, especially respectable young women like the Miller sisters. Somewhere at the back of her mind was the unsettling knowledge that Nelly had begun walking out with Dr John Mackenzie, and he was a friend of Rab Mossgiel. But if you couldn't trust a doctor, who else could you trust? And Jean needed some kind of diversion from the uncomfortable prospect of giving birth to twins without any husband to support her or any establishment of her own.

Of the two sisters, Betty was naturally more sympathetic, and perhaps more well disposed towards Rab too. Nelly had found him a handsome lad to be sure, but she could not stand what she thought of as his idleness, his bookishness and love of poetry. Give her a man of science like Dr Mackenzie any day of the week, aye, and a good provider too. Nelly had the uneasy feeling that if you were married to Rab Burns, books would come before anything else in the house, even food on the table. Books and lassies. Who would want to be married to a lad like that?

When her mother had occasion to go to the house next door, leaving them alone for a few minutes, Jean seized her chance, took hold of their hands and said, 'Nelly, Betty, will you do something for me?'

'What?'

'Can you see Rab for me?'

'We see him most days in the town.'

'No. I mean, will you speak to him for me? Tell him I must see him. Privately. Tonight, it must be tonight. The sooner the better. You must say that I *beg* him to speak to me. To find a way.'

'But why? We thought that was all by, Jeany.'

'It is all by, but there's something I must tell him. It's about my parents. It's for his own good, not mine. Not on my behalf at all.

You can tell him that, if it helps you to persuade him.'

Betty shook her head. 'But how is he to speak to you, Jeany? You are never out alone these days, and your mother would not let him near you. She would bar the door to him again. Besides, he's making plans to go to the Indies.'

Nelly nudged her sister.

'It's all right,' said Jean. 'I ken all about it. You mean that he's planning to go off with May Campbell.'

'Well, to be fair, nobody is very certain about Rab Mossgiel and May Campbell. We all ken fine it's Jamie Montgomerie she loves. They say Rab has been writing to her, but that's all they say.' Nelly looked from her sister to Jean. 'But Betty's right. How is he to speak to you?'

'Can you not give him a message from me?'

'A letter?'

'No. Not a letter. They keep all the paper in my father's desk in the house next door. It would be too dangerous. Just tell him … tell him the usual place. He'll ken fine what you mean. The place I might be able to get to. Tell him to wait for me. Tell him I'll be there if I can. And if I cannae, then he must find some other way himself. Tell him that he *must*. For his ain good. Tell him that it's for his ain sake, not mine.'

Jean was still clutching at Betty when they heard Mary Armour coming back in. She sat back, composed her features and began to talk about the latest fashion in bonnets. Taking their cue from her, Nelly and Betty joined in, until it was time to leave.

The sisters walked homewards through the sunny afternoon, nudging one another, giggling a little, enjoying the drama of it all, to be sure, but glad that they were on the outside looking in. They had caught something of Jeany's fervour, nevertheless, and they agreed that they must give Rab the message. They decided that Mossgiel itself might be the best place for seeing Rab alone. It was not late, and so they kilted up their skirts to keep them out of the mud, and walked out to the farmhouse. There they found Rab chopping wood, all by himself, looking sullen and handsome, so they were able to pass on the message in comparative privacy and with not a little excitement at the sight of him. He gazed at them for a moment, thanked them, asked them to say nothing of this to anyone else, and went back to his chopping with renewed vigour. They took a good deal of pleasure from the whole enterprise. The intrigue was exciting and they were caught up in it. It was like something from one of their novels. How could life ever be dull when Mauchline held Rab Burns and his affairs of the heart?

Chapter Seventeen

A Foolish
Hankering Fondness

Wha will crack to me my lane?
Wha will mak me fidgin' fain?
Wha will kiss me o'er again? —
The rantin' dog, the daddie o't!

She didn't know how or even if she was going to manage it. Not at her already massive size. But manage it she must. She didn't know if he would relent so far as to come to the Whitefoord Arms again, but she thought he might, if she knew him at all. And she didn't believe she could have been quite so mistaken in him. The truth was that she wasn't mistaken. He needed almost no persuasion, for the simple reason that he still had what he thought of as a 'foolish hankering fondness' for her, still loved her hopelessly and helplessly.

'Never man loved or rather adored a woman more than I did her,' he wrote plaintively and passionately to one of his friends.

She had stayed awake long into the night, afraid of falling asleep and missing him. It was not long after midsummer and the nights were very short. She found herself thinking back to that first outdoor tryst, this time last year, the meeting beside the old thorn tree and the walk towards Barskimming, the wild roses and bishop weed alongside the path, the intense love she had felt for him, still did feel for him, if the truth be told.

The light fading in the west would, within a couple of hours, be replaced by the gleam of light in the east. People kept late hours and woke often at this time of year. It had been a rainy evening after a fine day, but, as so often at night here, the weather faired away again from the west and the sky cleared to a deep, satisfying blue as the sun set. She was on pins all evening, anxiously waiting for her siblings to fall asleep. Of her grown-up brothers, John was already living next door and James was away from home, but she hoped against hope that Addie, with all his malicious curiosity, would not take it into his head to stay up late. As it happened, he had been working with his father all day and came in exhausted. He ate his supper, went through to the cottage next door and fell into bed without even bothering to wash the stone dust from his hands and face. Robbie, the youngest, had been fretful at bedtime. He had been bitten by something while he was playing in the garden, midges in all likelihood, or possibly clegs, the big horseflies that sucked your blood before you were aware of it, and raised painful weals in the process. He was complaining of sore, itchy skin. Mary wiped the little lad down with cool water and, because her husband had fallen asleep early, she took the child into their bed and he soon settled down. He still liked to sleep in between his parents when he could, and Mary liked the sensation of his warm body next to her, her last baby, although she knew that James would send him back to his own bed if he woke up and found him there. Janet, a placid child, slept soundly every night.

Nelly and Mary were used to their sister's restlessness by now and simply turned over as she shifted in the bed, glad to be relieved of the size of her belly that seemed to take up most of the mattress. She got up and went over to the window. She had deliberately left it open before climbing into bed, saying that the room was hot, which it invariably was at this time of year. Now she sat up in the arm chair, shifting her weight occasionally to ease the discomfort of her belly, the pressure that kept making her want to piss, even when she had nothing much to piss with. Once, she got up and relieved herself in the earthenware chamber pot, balancing with difficulty. The small noise sounded like a waterfall to her frightened ears, and she hoped it wouldn't wake the girls, but as she slid the pot back under the bed, they didn't stir. Then she resumed her vigil, sliding her feet into her shoes, staring across at the upper window of the Whitefoord Arms.

Time passed.

She dozed, never quite falling asleep. At the very darkest part of the night, the sudden springing up of lamplight and a little hail of pebbles against the window roused her. She got to her feet, peering through the window, and saw the light in the room opposite, could just make him out across the deserted alleyway. He was standing at the bottom of the stone stair, his face a white patch framed by black hair, ghostly against the darkness. He raised a tentative hand in greeting, and her heart thumped in her breast. Clutching her shawl around her shoulders, still in her nightdress, she opened the back door. At least they had given off locking it and taking away the key, but then they had never known about her night-time assignations at the Whitefoord Arms, thinking that all her meetings with Rab had been in the open air at Coilsfield or Netherplace, perhaps in a barn or in the depths of a haystack, in a fause-house somewhere or other.

She crept down the outside stair, her heart in her mouth. She was so ungainly, so very big. How could she go on like this for another month or more? She sidled out into the yard, slipping along the flagstones, still damp from the day's rain, out the back gate and into the alleyway where the mud was slippery, glad that she had thought to put on her shoes. It struck her that if she were to tumble over, she would be like a beetle on its back, one of the big May beetles that sometimes bumbled into the house to singe themselves against the flames, her legs in the air, unable to right herself. Again came that awful desire to laugh, to carry on laughing until she cried. She saw that his plaid was wrapped around him, although it wasn't a cold night. Perhaps he thought it gave him a certain anonymity. He stood aside and she laboured up the back-stairs with him behind her, quelling the desire to run. She couldn't have done it. Wordlessly, he held the door for her and she slid inside, turning slightly to accommodate the ungainly bulk of her belly. The inn was silent.

Inside the room, she sat on the bed, slipped off her shawl. A chill seeped through from her damp shoes to her feet. He pulled the curtains. The bed had not been made up this time. There was just the mattress and a thin blanket covering it. No fire, but a few cold ashes in the grate. A lamp that smelled faintly of fish oil. Nobody had been in here for some time. The room was seldom used. He closed the door and stood with his back to it, glaring at her. Then his gaze softened. He couldn't keep it up, this anger. It was much easier to resent her in her absence than in her much loved presence.

'What is this about, Jeany? The Miller lassies seemed to think it was urgent. I thought you never wanted to see me or speak to me again.'

'I never said that.'

'Well, that's what your mother told me, isn't it? And you sent me away. If you're missed over there, there'll be hell to pay. So maybe you should say what you came to say and go home as soon as may be.'

She felt tears starting in her eyes and rubbed at them with the sleeve of her nightdress. The gesture seemed to upset him. He half moved in her direction, and then controlled himself, planted himself firmly against the door again, folding his arms against his feelings.

'What?' he said. 'What is it?'

'My father. He has got a warrant to throw you in the jail.'

He raised his eyebrows. This was clearly news to him; whatever he might have been expecting, it wasn't this. 'What are you saying?'

'A warrant. And they say you'll have to find security for some enormous sum of money. I hardly ken what. It's terrible, Rab. They don't want you to find out about it till they arrest you, and I can't bear it. I don't want the father of my babies to be in jail when they're born.'

To her amazement, she saw that there was a faint smile playing about his lips. As though he too felt like laughing out loud at the daftness of the situation. Laughing till he cried. 'No, I can see that,' he said. 'And d'you ken, Jeany, I'm no just too happy about it myself.'

'I don't want any of this. I had to find a way to tell you, and I didn't trust anyone else to do it for me.'

He was pale as death in the lamplight but still faintly amused. To her relief, he pushed himself away from the door and came and sat beside her on the bed, shaking his head. 'Whose idea was this, I wonder?'

'I think it was my mother's at the start. I heard them talking about it when they thought I was asleep. Mr Auld, he had told my father to let it be, and I fancy he might have done that. He aye listens to Mr Auld. But my mother said she had heard you would soon make money from your poems. She had heard how successful your book was going to be, and she thought I should have a share of it. Believe me, Rab, I would never have done this to you, never.'

'The auld bitch!'

'Don't cry her that!'

'But she is, Jeany. She is. And this is what you've come to tell me?'

'I cannae bear it. I cannae bear for them to hurt you.'

She shifted on the bed, couldn't help groaning.

'Are you ill?'

'No. My back hurts, that's all. It's the way the weans are sitting. That's what Agnes Sloan says.'

He ran his hand gently up and down her back, his fingers on the bones of her spine. She shivered.

'And now that you know you're carrying twins? How have you been, Jeany?'

'I'm well enough. But I cannae say I'm no feart because I am.'

'When are they due?'

'The end of August. Or September. You'll likely be gone by then.'

'Maybe. Maybe not.'

'What will you do, Rab?'

'I'm not very sure myself just at this moment. I'm waiting to see what happens with my book. But this is worrying.'

'That's why I wanted to see you. I wonder what you can do. '

'I'll think of something. Take advice. Take legal advice. And possibly disappear for a while.'

'Where will you go?'

'To the devil?'

She put her hand on his arm, but he shrugged it off. He still seemed torn between anger and tenderness. 'Why should you care?'

'I do care about you though.'

'You've a strange way of showing it.'

She turned, found his eyes burning into hers, looked away again.

'But where *will* you go?'

'My aunty Jean lives at Old Rome, near Kilmarnock. Her and her man, James Allan. I'll likely go to them for a while. She's my mother's half-sister and a Maybole lassie, so nobody from Mauchline kens much about her. I doubt it anyway, unless you tell them.'

'I'll say nothing.'

'Close to my printer as well. I can handle my books and my subscriptions from there, and with a bit of luck they won't know where I've been till I'm gone to Jamaica.'

'You're still set on going to Jamaica then?'

'Aye. I'll go to ground there like an auld fox.'

'I'm sorry for it.'

'Are you?'

'And May Campbell? Will *she* be with you.'

'Why do you ask, Jean? Are you jealous of her?'

She nodded, always candid about her feelings. It was one of her many virtues. 'Aye. I am.'

'But you…' He couldn't continue, seemed exasperated rather than anything else. Sad too. His voice broke slightly. 'The truth is,

Jeany, I have no idea. I plan to go, but I doubt if the Indies would suit May. She's too frail. I've only booked a passage for me. Even though she said she would be willing to go with me or wait for me. Whichever I wanted.'

May Campbell had always been a compliant lass, much more so than Jean. But it was Jean's spirit that had appealed to him. Still did, if the truth be told.

'Are the rumours true that she is with child again?'

'If she is, I ken nothing about it.'

'Does she love you?'

'Love? She loves Jamie Montgomerie. After a fashion. But she would be happy enough to be my wife, I think. She has sworn as much, anyway. And I doubt if she will go back on her word.' The smallest stress on *she*.

'Where is she now?'

'She said she would go to Campbeltown to spend some time with her family, and from there to Greenock. If she won't come to the Indies, she'll have to find a situation of some sort. I believe she's staying with her brother. I've sent letters to her but heard nothing back from her.'

Jean found this obscurely comforting. She hesitated. But this might be her last chance to speak to him alone, to say what was in her heart. 'It was very quick, wasn't it, Rab?'

'Quick? What was quick?'

'May Campbell and you. I mean … I had barely gone to Paisley and…'

'Aye. You'd gone to Paisley. We were married, Jeany, legally married, but you rejected me for a better offer. For your weaver lad. And took yourself off, carrying my weans with you!'

'I didnae!' The injustice of this roused her to anger.

'You did. And you let your father cut our names out of the marriage lines. Ach, if you only knew how that tore the heart out of me when I heard about it!'

'I couldnae stop him. They sent me away.'

'Rab Wilson was courting you, so I heard.'

'He came to visit, just. There was no courting involved. He was a good friend to me when I was sorely in need of friendship, but that was all. Nothing happened, Rab. Nothing at all. While you...'

'Hush!' He leapt up, listened at the door. Their voices had been raised. But all was quiet below.

'Well, well,' he said, sitting down beside her again. 'It's all over and done with now and too late for repining. But listen, Jeany, whatever I do to stop them from persecuting me, whatever I do legally, I'll take care of the weans when they're born. Don't you worry about that. I'll leave instructions with Gilbert, and with Mr Hamilton too. You'll not be left destitute, no matter what happens at home. But you understand that I have to make some kind of deposition in favour of Gilbert and my wee Betsy. I have to take good care of her as well. And I can't let your father cast my mother and the others out of house and home on my account, can I? Which would be the result, if James succeeded in his plotting against me.'

'You must do as you think fit with what's yours. And they'll not cast me out on the streets, Rab, whatever you may think of them. So you must look after your own family.'

'I thought *you* were going to be my family.'

'So did I.'

There seemed nothing more to be said. She hauled herself to her feet.

'I need to get back home. It'll be light soon. They'll be waking up. As long as I'm in the back garden, they won't be suspicious. I can say I went to the outhouse. But if they find me in the lane...'

'Aye, aye – I'll come down with you. I may as well walk home to Mossgiel now. I have work to do, and I may as well make an early start.'

He extinguished the lamp and went ahead of her on the stairs.

'Mind yourself,' he whispered at the bend, where the stone was crumbling. 'Don't want you falling down, Jeany. Put your hand on my shoulder.'

She did so, leaning on him. He reached up and patted her hand, squeezed her fingers.

At the foot of the stairs they were thrown together again for an instant. He glanced left and right to make sure that the alleyway was empty.

'No lights anywhere,' he said. 'Take care, Jeany. I'll watch till you're safely in.'

She tried to squeeze past him.

'You too, Rab. Take care of yourself. I hope your poems go well. I'd like to read them some time.'

'Would you?'

'Aye. I would.'

'I'll make sure you get a copy. Maybe leave one with Katy Govan for you.'

'Would you do that?'

'Of course.'

He slid his arms around her, but the mound of her belly was in the way. The babies in there kicked out suddenly, as though aware of their mother's distress, their father's proximity. Could such things happen?

'Did you feel that?' she said.

'Aye. How could I not feel it? Oh, Jeany!' He leaned over the bump of her belly, took her face in his two hands and kissed her on the lips, then turned her gently towards the gate into the back garden of her house, gave her a little push, and watched while she went inside.

Nobody woke. Her feet in the leather brogues were icy. She climbed the stairs breathlessly, crawled into bed, elbowing her siblings gently aside, and lay staring into the grey light of a summer morning, with the babies turning and tumbling inside her. She had a vision of fish, swimming about the pool of her belly, like the fish you sometimes saw in the river pools, or like the skylarks, tumbling through the skies above Mossgiel.

Chapter Eighteen

Poems, Chiefly in the Scottish Dialect

Ye powers that smile on virtuous love,
O, sweetly smile on somebody!
Frae ilka danger keep him free,
And send me safe my somebody.

As the time for her confinement drew nearer, Jean couldn't help but wish that she was safely married to Rab, that she was living with him and giving birth at Mossgiel with her husband outside, pacing about and worrying and then coming in to comfort and congratulate her and hold the babies. But she despaired of any renewal of his offer to marry her. She believed that he would not risk it. The truth was that the warrant, the petition to seize his property, was still in existence, albeit trumped by Rab's own legal deposition of most of his possessions in favour of his brother Gilbert, and Betty Paton's daughter. It had gradually been borne in upon James Armour that Rab Mossgiel had friends in high places, not just Gavin Hamilton, who only counted as minor gentry in James's eyes, but the Montgomerie family and the Earl of Glencairn and others. The poetry book, with its mass of high-born subscribers, seemed to have made all the difference. Rab had supporters and admirers now, and whatever Mary Armour might say about wresting payment from the father of the weans, it was clearly becoming unwise to pursue the poet with the full might of the law. Besides, Jean had taken her courage in both hands and told her parents that she herself would be taking no further steps against Rab.

'I'll not do it,' she said. 'I'll say you forced me to sign. Which is the truth. You did. But I'll pursue him no more.'

'You'll do as you're tellt, lassie!' her father said, but Jean was obdurate and James seemed less forceful than he had once been. Perhaps he had an inkling that he had been wrong.

'I won't. He has done the right thing. I rejected *him*. I didn't want to, but you said I must. Now you seem to have changed your minds. Well, it's too late. He has told me he'll take care of our children and I believe him. He's a good man, and I'll do nothing without consulting him first.'

She was so resolute in the face of their threats and pleading, that they were forced to concede defeat, especially in view of her condition. Mr Auld came to see her, but it was not in his nature to threaten a lass, and she could see that he was half on her side, so the visit only strengthened her will. Against all her hopes and expectations, Rab came back from Old Rome, near Kilmarnock, and made up his mind to see her. He had not gone to Jamaica. Doubt had been cast on his travelling plans by some casual acquaintance, and he had seized on these misgivings like a drowning man on a piece of wood, thought Jean. But there were other vessels, other possibilities, and he assured anybody who would listen that it was only a postponement of his voyage.

On his first visit, her mother seemed inclined to bar the door to him again, but her father was there and grudgingly allowed him in, perhaps encouraged by Daddie Auld, and by tales of Rab's imminent success and his admirers among the gentry, who also happened to be his own longstanding customers. Business was business, after all. Country houses needed stonework, rivers needed bridges, and a living had to be made.

This first official visit was not, it has to be said, a great success. The young lovers – if lovers they could still be called, which was very doubtful – held a stilted and sorry conversation, with Rab standing warming his backside at the kitchen fire, although the day was a fine one. He was not invited to sit down, and he spent but a few moments enquiring after her health. Jean was so sore with the weight of the weans by that time that she could hardly raise herself to welcome him, on the verge of tears and with the sobs threatening to choke her. The second visit, at the end of August, went a little better. The sight of him did her heart good, and he seemed more cheerful. It was clear by now that the threat of litigation had been lifted. James was away from home and Mary, prompted by young Nelly, who had taken a great liking to Rab, relented to the extent that she left the couple to themselves for a short while, even though privacy was at such a premium in this house.

'I thought you'd be away to the Indies by now,' Jean said, rather forlornly. 'I thought I would never see you again.'

'I should have been. I fully expected to set sail aboard the *Nancy*, but I did not get enough warning. Time and tide. A scant two days' notice. I could not have wound up my affairs here and gone to Greenock in time, so I decided to postpone my voyage again.'

She refrained from mentioning May Campbell. Whatever had happened, she didn't want to know.

'When will you go now?'

'I'm to be a passenger aboard the *Bell* that sails at the end of next month.'

'Just yourself?'

'Just myself.'

'So you'll be here when the twins are born?'

'Aye. I expect I will.'

'Have you thought about names, Rab?'

'Let's see what happens first, eh? Are you still afraid, Jeany?'

'I am. A wee bit.'

'I'm sorry for it. I've been anxious about you, to tell you the honest truth.'

'Och, Rab. How did this … how did we find ourselves in this..?'

She halted, not knowing how to continue, hoping that he would speak for her. He said nothing, but just stood up and headed for the door.

'I must be away, Jeany. I have work to do, errands in the town. Farm business. I wanted to make sure that you were well, that's all, and it seems that you are.'

'Aye. I'm well enough.'

He halted at the door, put his hand inside the breast of his coat. 'I almost forgot. I brought you a copy of my book. You said you wanted to read it and here it is. I thought I would deliver it myself, rather than trusting it to Katy, especially since you'll not be able to leave the house for a while.'

He handed it to her. He had cut the pages for her himself. *Poems, Chiefly in the Scottish Dialect,* by Robert Burns. Printed by John Wilson in Kilmarnock.

'Will you put your name to it, for me?'

'Another time, perhaps.'

There seemed little more to be said, and it was clear that he was not going to help her any more than he already had. He was still unwilling to forgive what he saw as her perfidy, and now he was adamant that support for the children, once born, was as much as he would be able to give her. It was the very least he could do, but it was all he would do.

When he had gone, she turned the pages, curious about the work and, if the truth be told, very curious to see if she merited a mention there. She soon found a long poem called *The Holy Fair* and was amazed by his boldness. It had been quite early in their affair, when they had been meeting clandestinely and walking in the countryside around the town. They had sat together, the two of them, at the Holy Fair in Mauchline, the twice yearly religious festival supposed to prepare the townsfolk for communion to render their souls more pleasing to God. They were there for the good of their souls, to listen to the sermons. It was one of the few times when she and Rab had been out in public together, and she had behaved as though it were purely accidental, coming along a little late, finding no chair save one beside Rab Mossgiel. He had been casually resting his hand on it so as to discourage anyone else from sitting beside him. She had plumped herself down as though irritated by his unwelcome proximity. He had turned, nodded to her, tipped his blue bonnet to her very formally, and then deliberately turned away from her. She behaved as though she had nothing whatsoever to do with him and might sit where she chose. It had been so exciting. She had longed to touch him, to take his hand, but people might see. It felt as though something was pulling her relentlessly in his direction, as though every bit of her was inclining towards him. It was so strong, so undeniable, that she was sure the preacher, had he glanced her way, must have noticed it. She could remember the sensation of it as vividly as anything in her life so far. And it was only intensified when Rab edged closer, when his arm crept slowly around the back of her chair.

Wi' arm reposed on the chair-back, He sweetly does compose him; which by degrees flips round her neck, an's loof upon her bosom, unkend that day.

So he had written, describing exactly what had happened, So he had published for all to see. She was momentarily hot with embarrassment. The Holy Fair. Would anyone remember as she remembered? It was in the middle of that spring and summer courtship, but till that moment, he had been careful to behave well in public. There had been so much drink taken, and the hellfire preacher from Kilmarnock was attracting all eyes to him. Slowly but surely, Rab's hand had slid down under her shawl, inside her gown, worming its way between stays and skin, and onto her breast, finding the nipple. For a few moments she had done nothing about it, but sat very still in astonishment at his boldness, in alarm at the way her whole body responded to him, overriding all caution or propriety. She should have known then what the outcome would be if she persisted in allowing him so much freedom. At last, when she could bear it no longer, and when he seemed to be growing ever more daring in his caresses, she had resolutely moved away, and his hand had dropped to his side again. She heard him chuckle, felt his breath on her cheek.

'Och, Jeany,' he whispered. 'Was that no sweet?'

She couldn't look at him, but fixed her gaze firmly on the preacher, breathless with desire.

There's some are fou o love divine, and some are fou o brandy; an monie jobs that day begin, may end in houghmagandie some ither day.

Fornication. How true those words seemed now. It had all ended in *houghmagandie* and ill-begotten weans and tears and seemed like to continue to plague her. And yet he had been right. It had been sweet at the time. So very sweet that she couldn't possibly regret it.

When she heard her mother coming back in, she put the book in the dresser drawer, and later on managed to smuggle it upstairs to hide under the mattress. Although they seemed a little more well disposed towards her lover, she still didn't trust either of her parents not to put the book on the back of the fire were they to come across it by chance.

Later, she took a candle end upstairs and thumbed through the rest of the pages by its guttering flame, supplemented by the failing light at her window, when her sisters were asleep.

There was a poem about his muse, Coila, the embodiment of Kyle, where he was born: *a wildly-witty rustic grace shone full upon her*. Had she, Jean, such a *wildly-witty rustic grace*? Was that what he meant? *Halloween*: who would ever write a poem about Halloween and courting in the fause-house? Mr Auld would not be pleased. Nor would the kirk elders, James Lamie and Willie Fisher. Charms to summon a vision of a future lover. Charms to allow you to catch a glimpse of the man you would marry. She had worked these charms herself on Halloween, not in this house, for her father would not approve either, but with her friends elsewhere, heart in mouth, never seeing anything but imagining plenty in the dark.

Never once seeing Rab Mossgiel.

To a Mouse. That, she understood very well, because he had spoken to her about it. He was so soft hearted a man that he could sympathise with the creature whose winter home his plough had destroyed. So why could he not sympathise with her, with all her hopes destroyed? *But och, I backward cast my e'e, on prospects drear! An forward tho' I canna see, I guess an fear.* That had been last year, last November, when they had been seeing each other regularly. But perhaps he had already been worrying about his prospects as a husband, worrying that Jean's father would not look kindly on a poor tenant body as a son-in-law. And hadn't he been right all along?

It was when she came to a poem called *The Lament* that she was shocked rigid.

It was subtitled, pompously, *occasioned by the unfortunate issue of a friend's amour,* and for a little while she found herself trying to decide who among his many friends it might be, so many lads and so many affairs of the heart in and around the town that you could hardly keep track of them. But as she read, she saw that the title was misleading. The 'I' of the poem was surely Rab himself, and to her alarm, she saw that it was a poem aimed wholly at herself. *Encircled in her clasping arms, how have the raptur's moments flown! How have I wish'd for fortune's charms, for her dear sake, and hers alone!*

She read on, heart in mouth. How could he write like this, but more, how could he possibly publish it for all to read? It was so very private. Should have remained private. Would anybody, reading this, genuinely think that it was about some 'friend'? Or would they draw the same conclusions as she? How could she ever show her face in company again? Or in any company where she knew this book might have been read, the words shared? *From ev'ry joy and pleasure torn, Life's weary vale I'll wander thro, and hopeless, comfortless, I'll mourn a faithless woman's broken vow.*

A faithless woman's broken vow. That last verse made her cry out loud. Wee Mary slept on, but Nelly woke up and whispered, 'Are ye all right, Jean? Are the babies coming?'

'No, not yet. Just – my back's that sair.'

'You're greeting!'

'I am not!' She drew out a handkerchief and dabbed at her eyes. 'It's just I've been reading and there's no much light and it's hurting my eyes.'

'What are ye reading? Are ye reading your bible, Jeany?'

Jean smiled through her tears. It might have been better if she *was* reading her bible. 'Just a book. Just Rab's poems if you want to know.'

'Is that Rab's poetry?' The girl squirmed out of bed and came over to her, hanging over the back of her chair. 'Are they good? Folk are sayin they're very good and everyone's reading them. Did he give you that copy, Jeany? Did he?'

'Aye, he did. And don't you go telling our mammy, Nelly.'

'No. I willnae. But can I see it?'

'Later. Go back to sleep now.'

'Does he write about you, Jeany? I'd like it fine, so I would, if somebody would write a poem or a song about me.'

'Well maybe they will someday,' she said, thinking that it was not always a good thing for a man to write a poem about you.

'Are you coming back to bed?' persisted Nelly.

'Soon. Let me just sit up here for a wee while longer. My back's too bad to lie down properly. Go back to sleep, Nelly, there's a good lass. Go to sleep and leave me in peace.'

Nelly lay down, sighed, closed her eyes. 'A poem or a song,' she murmured. 'Maybe you could ask him for me, Jeany. Maybe you could ask him to write one for me. I wouldnae mind which.'

Jean sat on, the book open on her lap, open at the poem he had called *The Lament*. Even allowing for his tendency to make a tragedy out of the least little upset, the sadness in the poem made her feel sick with longing for him. That at least seemed true.

'*A faithless woman's broken vow.*' And if he became very famous, a weel kent writer throughout the land, would that be how she would always be known and remembered? A faithless woman who had broken her vow to him.

Oh, it was hard.

* * *

169

The twins were born on 3rd September: a boy and a girl. The pains started slowly, but when her waters broke, they intensified with appalling swiftness, to the point where she wanted to get down on all fours and howl like a dog. Jean hadn't imagined it could ever be so painful. She had seen her mother giving birth and had known about the pain, but knowing about it and experiencing it were two different things. Mary sent her husband off to work and all the children except Nelly out of the house to stay with a neighbour. Nelly, she sent for Agnes Sloan, who came scuttling importantly along the street carrying her leather bag, calling for hot water to wash away the blood, and threadbare linen sheets to cover the mattress. You wouldn't want to ruin the good linen. Nelly would have gone to join the other children, but her mother detained her.

'Time young Helen sees what's what,' said Agnes approvingly. 'It might make her think twice when the lads come calling! No that it made much difference wi Jean, eh?'

Jean's travail went on all day. They made sure she ate and drank to keep up her strength, and the babies were born in the evening, a big rosy boy and a smaller but still healthy girl. It seemed that she had carried Rab's twins for the full nine months, which was something of a rarity, said Agnes. In her experience, twins often came early. But not this time.

'All the same, best get them baptised quickly, just in case. You never know.'

When the babies were safely delivered, Jean's mother sent Adam Armour of all people out to Mossgiel with the news. Perhaps it was deliberate, another wee slight. But it seemed that Adam too was faintly impressed with Rab's growing celebrity. If he was not exactly a model of politeness, nor was he as rude as had been his wont a few short months ago. His demeanour was roguish rather than downright uncouth.

'It's a lad and a lass!' he called out excitedly, before he had even got in the door. 'My mammy says to tell you it's a fine boy and a girl too, and they're both weel and she wants to know what you're wanting to cry them. Have ye ony names in mind?'

Rab's mother invited him in, sat him down, gave him a drink. Never let it be said that she couldn't be hospitable, even to a wee gowk like Addie Armour.

'To wet the weans' heads,' she said.

'What about your sister?' asked Rab, suddenly anxious. So many women did not survive childbirth, and with twins it was doubly dangerous.

'Oh she's fine tae. The weans were crying fit to burst when I left, but she's feeding them. She's milk enough for the twa.'

'Tell her I'll come and see her first thing tomorrow. The baptism will be soon, likely?'

'Aye, father says no tomorrow, but maybe the day after. Mr Auld likes to have it done as soon as possible, ken.' He spoke knowingly, as though familiar with the ways of bairns and baptism.

'God bless the weans and God bless their mother. Be sure and tell her I said that, Addie, will you? There's a good lad!'

'For sure!' Adam finished his drink like a man of the world and got to his feet. 'How's the rhyming, Rab?'

'The rhyming goes very well, Addie. Very well indeed.'

'So we heard tell. My mammy says you're welcome to the house at ony time.'

'Does she now?'

'Aye she does. Be sure and tell him, she said. Between you and me…' he leaned in close and confidentially, 'I think she's a bit sorry she denied you the house that time. A wee bit sorry now that they ever forbade the marriage and cut the names out of the paper.'

'Did she say that?'

'Not to me. But I hear things, so I do. They had no idea books could bring in siller. That's what I heard them saying the other night. No idea at all.'

'Well, just between you and me, Addie, I wasn't so very sure of it myself.'

That night Rab wet the babies' heads with a few drams in the company of Gilbert and the other men about the farm. And in the morning, he brushed his coat well and took himself off to see Jean, with some silver in his pocket as a gift for the new baby boy and girl Burns.

She was very glad to see him. The weans were swaddled up, two neat bundles, the boy a good deal bigger than the girl, two wee faces with a look of their father about them. No denying their parenthood, had he been so inclined. As so often happened, in these early hours after the birth, the family resemblance was very strong, but seemed to flit and change about their faces, ghostly likenesses, now Jean, now Rab. He bent down and kissed them, the girl first, then the boy. He seemed very moved.

'What will we call them?' Jean asked. 'The firstborn boy should be named for your father. He should be William, and the girl for my mother, Mary.'

'We cannae do that, Jeany,' he said in a low voice. 'The truth is that I won't have this wee one called Mary, not after all I've suffered at your mother's hands. And my mammy might think shame to call the lad William.'

'It isn't his fault!'

'No, it isn't. But all the same…'

She had been thinking about this half the night, watching the two heads at her breast, one on each side. 'Then, let's name them for us twa that made them.'

'Robert and Jean?'

'Aye. Why not? They're good names.'

'Aye,' he said. 'Let's do that. Nobody can object to that, surely. Certainly not me. And I would like fine to have another wee Jeany in the family.'

So, the following day, the twins were baptised Robert and Jean for their father and mother, and their names were entered into the parish register.

For a while, Rab seemed so taken with the weans, so thoroughly enchanted with fatherhood all over again, that Jean had some hopes of redeeming the situation. People told her that he was proud of the twins, was never done with talking about them, except to her. He seemed to be avoiding her except when it was strictly necessary to make arrangements for the children. She had more than enough milk for the two of them, thank God, but they had settled matters between them that when both were weaned, the boy would go to Mossgiel and the girl would stay in Mauchline. Jean was far from happy about this. She thought it would break her heart to part with her son. But her father was only just beginning to accept the situation, and it might be easier for all concerned if there was only a single extra mouth to feed in the family. She would be able to look after her daughter, and she knew that Robert would be well cared for at Mossgiel. Agnes Broun was an indulgent mother, especially now that there was no stern husband to curb her, and Jean thought she would be a loving grandmother to the lad. Rab was tender to any who found themselves under his roof or in need of protection. But more than that, Mossgiel was not so very far away. It would be spring before the twins were well weaned. She pushed aside all thoughts of Rab going away to the Indies. She pictured herself taking the wee girl wrapped up in her shawl and walking out to the farm to see her son. Rab would be there too. They would be a family, after a fashion. She had a vague idea that if the lad was at Mossgiel, there was more of a chance that they might be together again as man and wife.

Chapter Nineteen

Events in Greenock

O plight me your faith, my Mary,
And plight me your lily-white hand;
O plight me your faith, my Mary,
Before I leave Scotia's strand.

He postponed his voyage yet again. He was not aboard the *Bell* when it left at the end of September. He still spoke about the Indies as though he would soon be going. But he did not go. His poems were becoming wildly successful. Everyone from dairymaids and stable lads to noblemen and their ladies sought a copy. The original subscribers were enthusiastic. Word of the ploughman poet had spread like a summer fire on a dry heath. They called him 'heaven taught' although he remarked drily that heaven had very little to do with it. Any learning he had acquired was mostly down to his father, followed by his first teacher, John Murdoch, who had always had a higher opinion of Gilbert's lively imagination, finding Rab too grave, too tender-hearted for true scholarship, or poetry for that matter. But once he had been able to read, a whole world of learning had opened up to him, when he could get the books.

Jean kept her precious volume of his poems openly on display now in the house in the Cowgate, although she suspected that her still-disapproving parents had not yet ventured to read it and would not notice the poem called *The Lament*, even if they did. They were not great readers. Not great scholars either. James was a practical man, skilled with his hands. Her mother knew songs and stories, but they were all in her head, not on paper. Jean had never thought herself a reader either, but this was different.

In October, with the twins still with Jean in Mauchline, Rab told her that he had spoken to his printer about a second edition of his poems, but nothing had yet come of it. His friends were telling him that he ought to go to Edinburgh, where his fame had gone before him and where he would be well received by men of letters, the nobility, wealthy men and women. But he had an inkling, he said, that they were dazzled by his poetic prowess only as one might be amazed by a dog that could stand upright and walk on its hind legs: not that the skill was such a great thing in itself, but that a dog was doing it. A lowly tenant farmer who ploughed his own furrow could also make verses. He would be a species of curiosity. Like a prodigiously ugly fish. Or an armadillo.

'I expect they'll put me in a cabinet and gaze at me only to make mock of me.'

He made her laugh – she could never help herself. When he was not making her weep, he could always make her laugh. Not just her, either, but most women, young and old. It was one of the reasons why they were so charmed by him.

He must, so Jean thought, be writing to poor May Campbell all this time, keeping her informed of what was going on, although perhaps not all of it. Perhaps he had not seen fit to mention Jean and the twins, although others would almost certainly have told her. But if he had written to her, he hadn't said anything to Jean about it. She didn't even know whether her rival was still in Campbeltown with her family or at Greenock. May Campbell's father, Archibald, was a sea captain and it would be an easy matter for her to take passage with him on his sloop as far as the herring quay in Greenock, there to wait for her lover. Or one of them. It had struck Jean that Jamie Montgomerie might also be in Glasgow from time to time. With or without Eleanora. But Rab scarcely mentioned the girl, certainly not to Jean. Perhaps the tug of his children, here in Mauchline, meant that he could no longer contemplate leaving Scotland's shores with any ease.

She knew that he was a man for whom the life of his mind, what he sometimes referred to as his 'bardship', was more vivid than the everyday world of this small town with all its preoccupations, its rules and prohibitions, or the world of his stony, sour, difficult farm. He was a dreamer who could persuade himself that his dreams were real. He would easily imagine himself in love with two or more women at the same time. He may well have made promises to May Campbell, and now he would believe that he had to keep them. Perhaps he had offered to console her for whatever she had lost with Jamie Montgomerie. Perhaps he thought she would be a fitting substitute for the wife he had lost in Jean. More biddable, at least. And perhaps he really had loved her, loved her still, in his way. Jean was generous enough to acknowledge that. He was a man who would dream of love, write about it, make it real.

For a time.

But now he was in two minds, his capricious heart pulled in two directions, and she sensed that her prior claim on him was stronger, with all the weight of their twins behind it. With all the weight of his natural affection for her. May Campbell might be the sweet spring flower, ripe for the plucking. She was like the pale may of her namesake in the hedgerows, flowers that powerfully scented the air for a few weeks and were as suddenly gone. What did that mean? That Jean was like the roots beneath, the tangle of handsome, vigorous life that kept the banks of the river in place. Or the striking but elusive purple orchid of Ayrshire: the baldeirie. But the truth was that she was sure of none of this. She could not fathom him and she doubted if he fully understood her, either.

Quietly, carefully, she suggested that a trip to Edinburgh might be no bad thing, even if they did think him a curiosity and come to gape at him. He would certainly be welcomed there. It would be good for him to be celebrated. And it was by no means so far or so dangerous as the Indies. He would be able to come back and visit his children as often as he liked. She was careful not to say that he would be able to come back and visit their mother, as well. If she felt a pang of conscience for May Campbell, she put it firmly to the back of her mind. She had more than herself to consider now. She had the other Jean and Robert. They mattered more.

* * *

In very early November, Jean was shocked to find Mauchline buzzing with the news that May Campbell, Highland Mary, dairymaid at Coilsfield, nursemaid to Gavin Hamilton's baby son and Jamie Montgomerie's 'friend', had died at Greenock on the Clyde, after a short illness. Jean had pieced the sorry tale together from Rab, or as much as he could or would tell her, which was little enough, and from Gilbert, who had learned what he could. It seemed that May's father, Archie Campbell, had been as delighted by his daughter's attachment to Rab Burns as James and Mary Armour had been about Jean; that is, he was horrified that a good, God fearing lass should have promised herself to a young man notorious for his irreligious verses and his bastard weans. The man was nothing but a rake, whatever the Edinburgh lords and ladies might say of him. Her mother was more encouraging, more inclined to forgive. And May herself – who knew what May felt?

The young woman had spent some weeks happily visiting relatives in and around Campbeltown. She had also, seemingly, procured a new position in Glasgow, in the respectable household of one Colonel McIvor, so it was clear that she had not been expecting to go to the Indies with Rab. Not at that time, anyway. It had so happened that May's elder brother was going to Greenock to take up an apprenticeship as a carpenter in that town in October. May had planned to be there some weeks earlier, in September, supposedly in order to be in plenty of time to take up her new situation. But the term date wasn't until Martinmas, in November. That was when her new position would start. Jean found herself wondering if poor May had hoped or even planned to meet with Robert Burns before he left for the Indies. Was that why she had tried to go to Greenock early? Had Rab suggested it? Even Jean knew that he had been planning to sail aboard the Bell at the end of September. But whatever he might have said to his *Highland Mary* about *going to the Indies and leaving old Scotia's shore,* he had not gone. Something, or some combination of events, had changed his mind.

As it turned out, there had been delays with Archibald's vessel, and May and her brother had not set out until October. Had Archie planned it, Jean wondered, in hopes that the poet would already have left the port? Had he arranged the delays himself as a means of keeping his daughter safely at home in Campbeltown? Or was it simply down to the seasonal hazards of wind and weather? In the event, the sloop had a very rough passage through October winds and high seas, and Archibald must have found himself regretting the delay. May was very sick on the crossing and still very poorly when she disembarked at Greenock and took up lodgings along with her brother.

Not long after their arrival, May's brother had attended a ceremony to mark the start of his carpentry apprenticeship, had supped far from wisely and had become very unwell. May attended to him as best she could, but she soon fell ill herself, although whether she was already sickening after the sea voyage, nobody could say for sure. The fever was of a type that seemed to spread within a building, perhaps even, uncannily, from bed to bed. Her brother recovered as May sickened. It was typhus, rife in Greenock at that time, especially in the cramped lodging houses where they were staying. May would have been better off in breezy Campbeltown. How her father must have regretted the voyage afterwards.

Some members of the family thought she had been infected with the 'evil eye', that somebody had cursed her, which gave Jean a momentary pang of guilt when first she heard of it. Had she ever really wished ill to May Campbell? Well, perhaps not, but she had not wished her well either. Rab was hers. May didn't love him, not as she, Jean, did, so what was she doing promising herself to him? May's friends and relatives in Greenock had taken seven smooth stones from a channel where two rivers crossed, bathed them in milk and then given her the milk to drink, but the remedy had no effect. Her brother lived and thrived, but Highland Mary sickened, her mind confused, her frail body burning up like a torch and dwindling to nothing. She had called for water, but they would not give it to her. Water was thought to be deadly for those suffering from such fevers as this. She had whispered, through cracked lips, that if it was God's will, she would be happy to recover and be Robert Burns's wife, but she knew that she was dying and was equally happy to go to her God.

When she heard this story, Jean thought fiercely that she would certainly not have been equally happy to go to her God. How like daft May Campbell frae Dunoon, she thought, and then felt ashamed of herself for her lack of charity. The news of the girl's death had come to Rab himself, late one November afternoon, in a letter brought up to Mossgiel. He had taken it to the window to catch the last of the light in order to read it, and had then gone out into the wintry twilight and the rain, walking about for hours, overwhelmed by grief. The poor lass was dead and he blamed himself. Perhaps he blamed himself even more, felt even more guilty, because it came as the solution to a terrible dilemma for him. Jean had noticed how grief over a death seemed to increase in proportion to the guilt of the mourner. How family members who had not spoken for years and had not even liked each other very much might be stricken with regret upon hearing that the object of their derision had passed away.

The news spread throughout the town, of course. And the story was embellished with each telling. The girl had been waiting at Greenock for Rab Burns to join her, marry her and take her to the Indies. Or marry her, take a room for her, but leave her behind, while he went to seek his fortune. Or make her his mistress and abandon her. The story varied according to who was telling it and how much they approved or disapproved of the poet. Also, she may or may not have been carrying Mossgiel's child. Or Montgomerie's child. Or no child at all – (Jean thought the last was probably closer to the truth.) She had died of the fever. Or the plague. She had died in childbirth. Who knew? Who could be sure? One thing was certain. Poor May Campbell was dead and gone, and whether Rab Mossgiel or Jamie Montgomerie or some noxious fever was to blame, she would never be coming back to Mauchline again.

Not long after the news of her death came to Mauchline, Jean had a vivid dream about May, with her soft, pretty face, her fair hair, and air of vulnerability. She was running in desperation through the shrubs and bushes and long grasses towards the sandstone cliff beside the River Ayr. Jean saw the pain on her face, felt the warmth of her between them, she and Rab, as they walked with her to the dairy at Coilsfield.

She woke with a start, and a pang of real regret for the waste of such a life, thinking, who among us has not loved unwisely and lived to regret it afterwards?

Chapter Twenty

Letters and Visits

Thy sons, Edina, social, kind,
With open arms the stranger hail;
Their views enlarg'd, their liberal mind,
Above the narrow, rural vale.

Late in November, and while still keeping his option of sailing to the New World open, Rab went to Edinburgh, and Jean stayed at home in the Cowgate with the twins. During his time in Edinburgh and when he was elsewhere, travelling about the country, he wrote to her. He wrote infrequently, but she treasured his letters. There was talk of another edition of his poems, three thousand copies, to be published in April. There was talk of a position in the excise. There was still debate about Jamaica, but he did not think he would go at all now. (Jean's heart could not help but leap for joy at that piece of news.) He was feeling unwell and the city did not suit him. In the next letter, he was feeling much better, excited and happier than he had been for some time. The city had its dark side, but a great deal of elegance.

As he had suspected, he was something of a curiosity. He was invited out a good deal so that people could gaze in wonder at the captive Ayrshire Bard. 'Like the armadillo!' he wrote. The Duchess of Gordon had taken him under her wing. There was talk of a portrait or more than one. The food was very fancy, but he did not like all these tarts and pastries. Give him a good haggis or simple Scotch collops any day. Would Jean like to have a cookery book? He had seen a cookery book here and thought he might get it for her one day. He craved a plate of bannocks and his brother's sweet milk cheese and a mug of his mother's ale. He had been very drunk and could not well keep to the line when he was writing. (That was true, she thought, looking at the note he had scrawled.) He was not drinking much at all and was as sober as she could wish him to be. The ladies seemed to like the idea of a ploughman poet. The girls who flocked to see him, to hear him read his verses and to pay him compliments were pretty, but they were not Jean.

He admitted that he was missing her.

'I dreamed of you last night,' he wrote, once. 'And felt a miserable blank in my heart when I awoke.'

She knew that this was an unthinking compliment, thrown in at the end of the latest letter because he could never resist charming her, but she hugged it close for all that. Edinburgh had certainly taken the Ayrshire Bard to her heart. It seemed to Jean, reading the short letters he found the time to write, that he was flying, like one of those daring aeronauts she had heard about who went up in balloons full of hot air, high, high above them all. She wondered when and where he might come back down to earth.

In the next letter, in the spring of 1787, he gave her some inkling. He was thinking about another farm, about renting a place in Dumfriesshire from one Patrick Miller of Dalswinton. He intended to travel there and look it over, although he had no great hopes of the land being in any better condition than Mossgiel, and that was poor enough. He might see her and the children as he was passing through Mauchline on his way back.

When she could no longer pretend that the twins were not weaned, Robbie went to Mossgiel. He was growing by the day, eating heartily of whatever porridge or milky mess they placed before him, a sturdy little lad, and he had a look of Rab about him: no denying *his* father, they said in the town. Jean was smaller, finer and the image of her mother. Jean could not bear to let Robbie go, but her parents said she must, it had all been agreed between the two families, and she could see no other option. Rab's mother and sisters were kinder and more understanding.

The baby wept bitterly at first when she tried to leave him, the tears rolling down his chubby cheeks, and she wept even more bitterly all the road home, but he was soon installed as a small prince in the Mossgiel household, everyone's favourite. They told her to come and see him as often as she pleased, which she did, whenever the weather was clement, wrapping Jean up close to her in her shawl and carrying the one twin out to spend time with the other.

Robbie grew happy and placid at Mossgiel, accepting his mother's and his sister's sudden appearances in his life and their subsequent absences with equanimity. Jean did not want her two children to grow apart from one another, not if she could help it, and she still had the faint but diminishing hope that Rab might come back and ask her again to marry him. She would lie in bed at nights, going over it all in her head, wondering how she could have done things differently. To her shame and mortification, she realised that her parents had changed their tune completely. Word of Rab's Edinburgh fame had spread to Ayrshire, and James was forced to admit that they had made a mistake. Jean had been right to go against their wishes. In fact, he wished that she had been firmer in the face of their opposition. Mary was indignant at first, but then persuaded to agree with him. All unexpectedly, Rab Mossgiel was a success. There might have been a prosperous future for their daughter. But after all, the fact of the twins' existence was undeniable. He had never sought to deny his fatherhood. Perhaps they could persuade him that the marriage had been legitimate after all, that in the eyes of the law and the Lord, he was still married to Jean. Dismayed by the hypocrisy rather than the change of heart, Jean refused to discuss it. When they tried to broach the subject with her, she pretended that she didn't understand them. She would not demean herself so far as to beg Rab to come back to her. If he was destined to come back, perhaps he would, but she would not be a party to any more duplicity.

He came back to Mauchline, but only briefly.

He had written that he planned to visit Mossgiel, where he was anxious to see his son. Besides that, he planned to enjoy the company of a few old friends including Gavin Hamilton. But he also wished to see his 'twa Jeanies.' He planned to spend the first night of his visit at Johnnie Dow's before going on to pass a few days at Mossgiel. Could he come over and see his daughter first thing in the morning? There was no invitation for Jean to slip across the alleyway. No invitation to an assignation at the back door of the Whitefoord Arms, she noticed, and she had too much pride to ask him. But perhaps he thought there was no more need of secrecy, and he was right. He could come over to see his daughter, and welcome. So said her parents when she cautiously enquired if Rab might visit.

* * *

Jean dressed in her best: a new cotton gown, printed with red and blue flowers. Her waist had almost resumed its girlish proportions and it fitted her, although she thought the stays might suffocate her. Mary offered to help her with her hair, but Jean was having none of it, although she allowed Nelly to comb her curls for her and thread a scrap of blue ribbon through them. She splashed cold water on her face, scrubbed at her cheeks until they were pink, bit at her lips to plump them up. When he came to the door, just a little late, her mother welcomed him in. James had made himself scarce, taking the boys with him. Rab seemed curiously formal to her, his boots well polished, his hair tied back and a silver headed stick in his hand. He looked like a gentleman. Like Mr Hamilton. But more handsome. She was holding baby Jean in her arms so that he couldn't help but see the resemblance, dark curls, two bonnie lassies together. Jeany was ten months old and almost walking now, hauling herself up on this or that piece of furniture whenever she was allowed. She squirmed and fidgeted, trying to get out of her mother's arms. When she screwed up her face and frowned at the strange man, he tickled her and she started to laugh instead.

'D'you ken your daddy, my bonnie lamb?' he said, and she stretched out her chubby arms to him.

Mary Armour, satisfied with this welcome, shooed the other children out of the room, and followed them, leaving the couple alone with the child between them.

'You'll have plenty to talk about, son!' she said.

Jean rolled her eyes behind her mother's dignified, departing back and Rab gazed after her in disbelief.

'Am I mishearing, Jeany? Did your mammy just call me "son" or have my months in the city affected my ears?'

Jean shook her head. 'No. You didn't mishear. And believe me, I'm black affronted by her. By both of them. I'm so ashamed, Rab. They have changed their tune where you are concerned.'

'As has half of Mauchline, so it seems.'

'What do you mean?'

'My fame and fortune – if fortune it can be called which I very much doubt – seems to have gone before me. Folk who would once have viewed me as a bad influence, a fornicator for sure, now seem to be fawning over me. It sickens me somewhat, I'll admit.'

'No just my mother and father then?'

'Och, no just them. All kinds of unexpected folk. I'll tell you, Jeany, here's something that will amaze you. I passed James Lamie as I rode into the toun and would you believe, he tipped his Kilmarnock bonnet to me and gave me a kind of a bow. A grudging acknowledgment, with his face tripping him, but an acknowledgment all the same. I almost fell off my horse. All that remains is for Holy Willie Fisher to welcome me into his home for a dram or two, and I'll consider myself to be in a perpetual dream!'

'There has been a lot of talk about you.'

'But not from you, Jeany?'

'You ken fine I say naething about you, and they keep silent about you where I am concerned. They have no idea in the least what I think.'

'And what *do* you think?'

'You know what I think of you. Very much what I have aye thought of you, Rab.'

'You mean no very much. That's what you said to me on the bleach green.'

'You ken fine what I mean. And how much I love you still.'

He coloured, but didn't respond.

The child began squirming again, and Jean set her daughter down on the rug where she amused herself by picking at the corners of rags of which it was made. Then she crawled over to her father with amazing rapidity and hauled herself up on his knees, smiling at him all the while. 'Dada,' she said, although whether it was a real word or a babble of sound, they couldn't have said. Rab seemed delighted enough with it and with her. He put his hand into his pocket and pulled out a coral teether with a silver top.

'I found this in Edinburgh. I had to buy two though: one for Jeany and one for Robbie. It's an expensive business producing twins!'

The child grasped the toy and put the wrong end in her mouth. He picked her up, turned the teether round so that she could gnaw on the coral, and dandled her. She didn't object.

'She seems fine and healthy.'

'She is. But she's a handful. You never ken what she'll be into next.'

'And what about you, Jeany?'

'Och, I'm fine and healthy too. Have you seen Robbie yet? At Mossgiel?'

'I'm going there after this. They tell me he's the image of me, while this wee one is more like her mammy.'

'That's the truth.'

He stayed for an hour, drank a glass of wine bought in specially for his visit, and played with the baby, who seemed very taken with him and with her new toy. Mary Armour had left the good glasses out for them. When he rose to leave, he picked up his daughter again and kissed her on both cheeks. She gurgled happily in his arms, batting at his head with her hands.

'Have you all you need for her?' he asked, before he left.

'Aye, I have.'

'You'll send me word if you need money? You mustn't worry. I'll look after the weans.'

'There's no need of money. We can look after her. And your mother will need help with Robbie, surely.'

'Listen, Jean, I've ordered some silk for gowns for my mother and my sisters. But there will be enough for you. In fact...' he hesitated. 'In fact, I made sure I ordered enough for you. Black lutestring silk for Sundays. I'll get them to send a length of cloth down for you as soon as it comes.'

'That's very kind of you, but you didn't need to. You mustn't feel beholden, Rab. It's enough that you support the weans.'

'Well, your father pays for the best seat in the kirk, so you may as well dress for the occasion. I'll not have the Mauchline matrons and worthies remarking that Rab Burns is ungenerous in providing for the mother of his children.'

So that was all she was to be. The mother of his weans. But the gift was a generous one. James Armour had never bought the very best lutestring silk for the women of his family. In fact silk was at a premium altogether. Before Rab left, he leaned across the child and kissed her on the cheek.

'My twa Jeanies,' he said. 'I'll come again when next I'm in the town.'

'When might that be do you think?'

'I'm going back to Edinburgh after this, and then I'm minded to go on a tour of the Highlands. If I'm to write about my country, I want to see more of it. But perhaps after that. Perhaps in July. I'll write to you and let you know.'

As soon as he left, her mother emerged to enquire after him. Did he have any plans? She meant where Jean was concerned, of course, rather than any more general query as to what Rab might be going to do next. But Jean could tell her nothing, beyond the bare facts that his poems were going well, the Edinburgh folk were making much of him, he seemed pleased to see her and the weans, and that there would be a length of fine lutestring silk arriving from Mossgiel, a gift from Rab, for a new Sunday dress.

Chapter Twenty-one

On the Banks of Ayr

Louis, what reck I by thee,
Or Geordie on his ocean?
Dyvor, beggar louns to me,
I reign in Jeanie's bosom!

By early July, Rab was back in Mauchline, but this time he stayed out at Mossgiel and came to the house in the Cowgate in the early evening. His appearance was somewhat alarming. He was as bruised as though he had been in a fight, with a cut across his forehead, and he was limping into the bargain. He looked so unwell, so battered, that Mary Armour pursed her lips in disapproval at the sight of him, but he hastened to reassure her, albeit with less than his usual airy self-confidence.

'I was not brawling, even though it might look that way. It was a riding accident, Mistress Armour. My horse bolted and threw me when I was riding along the shores of Loch Lomond. It was a lucky thing I wasn't tipped head first into the water! But I lived to tell the tale as you see.'

When he had kissed and played with his daughter, and perhaps because the house was busy and there was little privacy to be had at this time of the evening, he suggested that Jean might like to walk out with him for a while, if her parents were agreeable and if her mother would put the child to bed for her.

The evening was a fine one, and he observed that Jean was looking pale, although in truth, he looked in rather worse health than she did. All the same, when he suggested that perhaps she needed a breath of air and that a walk around the town would do her no harm, she agreed readily enough.

'Aye,' said James. 'You must go, Jean. You go and tak a turn about the town. Your mother will see the wee lass into her bed, won't you, Mary? I'm sure you and Mr Burns have things to say to each other.'

Jean could hardly believe her father's acquiescence, and she caught a glimpse of Rab's expression, still torn between surprise at their change of heart and disgust at how a modicum of success, a whiff of celebrity and the acquisition of a certain amount of wealth, might do wonders for his reputation. They welcomed him, where before there had been only disapproval. Nevertheless, she was ready to seize any opportunity to be alone with him, so she agreed. Whatever good sense she might resolve to cultivate in his absence always seemed to desert her in his presence. Her mother took the complaining child in her arms. Wee Jean was at that stage where she hated to see her mother leave the house and always wanted to go too, but Mary distracted her while Jean fetched a shawl, and they slipped out together. Rab offered her his arm and soon, instead of taking the promised turn around the town, they were walking out along the Barskimming Road, away from the prying eyes of the Mauchline folk, and towards the River Ayr.

'Just like old times,' he remarked. But their conversation was stilted and overly polite at first, as though they hardly knew where to begin.

'So what really happened?' she asked, when they were well away from the town. 'I mean your cuts and bruises, Rab. Did your horse bolt, after all? Was it really a riding accident? My mother thought you must have been in a fight somewhere. Was that what it was? Were you brawling? You can tell me the truth at least.'

He laughed. 'There was no fight, but there was a battle of sorts!'

'What do you mean?'

'Ach it was nothing at all. Well, not so very much. It was at Loch Lomond. Three of us. We had been a merry party and we had been at the dancing with the ladies of the house where we were staying.'

'And at the drinking too?'

'Just a wee bit. We stayed awake the whole night and saw the sun rise over Ben Lomond.'

'And then?'

'Ah weel.' He looked sheepish. 'Then we rode on towards Dumbarton, with only a few hours of sleep between us. We dined half way down the Loch, and I'm sorry to say we pushed the bottle there as well. And we were no that fou, but ... we were a wee thing merry. So then we rode on soberly enough...'

'Soberly?' she laughed. '*Soberly*?'

He grinned. 'Aye, soberly enough by then. And all would have been well if we had not come upon a Highlandman at the gallop. A big red headed fellow. No saddle or bridle, had he, nothing but a woollen blanket and a hair halter, though I'll allow it was a tolerably good horse. I was mounted on Jenny Geddes in the usual way. But we scorned to let a Highlander pass us, good horse or no, so off we went with whip and spur. My companions soon fell behind, but you ken Jenny. She won't be beaten.'

'Aye, just like her master!'

'She set up a great pace along the road, and we would surely have beaten our rival fair and square except that just as we were passing him, did the fellow not turn, wheeling his horse in front of me to stop me, when he knew the race was all but lost?'

'Which it no doubt did – stop you, I mean!'

'Aye, it did. But himself first and worst, I fear. He went head first into a clipped hedge, with his bare arse showing and great oaths, I suppose, coming out of his mouth, although I could not understand one word of them since they were in his ain tongue.'

'What about you?'

'That's just the pity of it. Down came Jenny Geddes over the Highlander's horse, and down came your Rab, in between the twa of them.'

'Good God, Rab!'

'Ah but she did not trample me, not Jenny. She's a fine beast for all that she's no longer young. And the Highlandman and his horse lived to tell the tale and all.'

'You could have been killed!'

He stopped, looked down at her, her arm tucked through his. 'Which I sometimes think would not have been such a bad outcome after all. What do you think yourself, Jeany?'

She almost thought him serious. Perhaps he was.

'I should have been very sad indeed to hear of it,' she said, primly.

'Should you? Well, that's something at any rate. But it could have been much worse. All I had for my sins were the few cuts and bruises your mother noticed and a certain stiffness here and there, and a wee bit lameness which seems to be dissipating even as we walk. Well, the lameness more than the... the *stiffness*, right at this moment, Jeany.' He looked down at her, chuckled. 'But that's your fault, lass. Oh, and a firm resolution to remain sober for the future and not to indulge in any more racing with wild Highlanders. You'll be glad to hear that I shall be the very pattern of sobriety from now on.'

'Will you?'

'Mostly.'

She was thinking how he had said 'your Rab', thoughtlessly. Was he, she wondered, still *her Rab* even after all that had passed between them, even after her parents had behaved so unkindly to him? Was she still his Jean?

* * *

They walked arm in arm, along the all too familiar Barskimming Road and towards the river. There seemed an inevitability about it, a foolish inevitability. She should have known what would happen. Perhaps she *had* known what would happen all along. Maybe they were both aware of it and by a sort of mutual but unspoken agreement did nothing to stop it. They had no caution, no care. There was a magic about the evening, with the low sun throwing everything into sharp relief. There was a tangle of honeysuckle: pink and cream and deep yellow in all the hedges or clambering through the trees, and the scent of it was as sweet as wine. You could breathe it in and feel light-headed on it.

At some point on the long walk, he took her hand, as though it were the most natural thing in the world, and he threaded his fingers through hers, swinging her arm alongside his. His palm was warm and dry.

'Where are we going?' she asked

'I don't ken. Where should we go? To the banks of the Ayr, maybe?'

'Aye – why not? I havenae walked there for a long while, Rab. And I think the last time I was with you.'

It was true. She couldn't bear to walk there without him, even with her sisters for company.

As soon as they found the river, he was complaining of the pain in his leg from the fall, where he had jarred it and bruised it, like a wean that wants to be kissed better, she thought. They must needs sit down for a rest before going back. It was a warm evening after a dry spell, dryer than usual anyway, and the river was very low and moving sluggishly between flat stones. They stopped in a dell where the grass was long and lush, a hollow fringed with meadow-sweet and the last of the marching lines of summer foxgloves, so many soldiers in pink uniform, standing to attention round about, as though guarding it. It overlooked a deep weel, a pool that hardly seemed to move at all. In winter, the river would come tumbling down with a froth of peat from the hills, but now it was quiet, reflective. The midges were beginning their nightly dance over the water.

'They'll be nipping us, soon enough,' he said. But for the time being, the midges were too intent on the water and the swallows came swooping and diving over them, picking them off, their sharp cries filling the air. From time to time, they could see a trout leaping up to a fly, sometimes right out of the water, with the ripples spreading out as it fell back.

'I should have brought my rod!' he said.

You couldn't help but gaze and keep gazing, waiting for the next silvery splash as a fish broke the surface, shedding droplets, coins of light and water.

Somewhere in the thicket behind them came the notes of a thrush, the mavis at her evening song. They fell silent to listen, and then he turned to her and embraced her, and when he did, it seemed as though there was nothing else to be done between the two of them, nothing but this. When they came together it was as natural as breathing. She had never lost her desire for him, had only buried it for a while and, presumably, he felt the same, since there seemed no need even to speak about it. No questions asked, and no replies needed. It was as though everything had been aimed at this one moment. As though some decision had already been made without recourse to either of them. When he was not with her, she thought she might die of wanting him. It was that simple. She had no thought for the future, no memory of the past.

He was gentle, quite tentative, although she had long since healed after the birth of the twins. When he was inside her, she still thought she might die with the pleasure of it. It was a home-coming, the scent of him, the sensation of him.

'How I've missed my wee whaup's nest,' he said. 'My Jean's downy nest. And no just so wee as it once was, but gey sweet all the same.'

She opened her eyes and saw a luminous sky, and dark leaves above her, felt soft grass beneath her. She could hear the piercing cries of the swallows out over the water, and their own more sub-dued cries, momentarily silencing the birds.

Afterwards, he held her close and she rested against him for a while, but it was growing darker. A small wind had risen and the midges, driven off the water, were nipping at them, at any areas of exposed flesh. He slapped at his legs. She did the same, and thought there would be tell-tale blotches on places where they had no business to be, places that had no business to be exposed to the air, and to the midges either. They laughed over it, but it was a serious matter.

'What will your mother say, if she sees?'

'She willnae see. I sleep with my sisters. And with wee Jeany beside me. Naebody will see.'

'Best not be scratching at them then. More scandal,' he said, and she glanced around as though half expecting to see Willie Fisher or James Lamie hiding behind a tree, peering out disapprovingly at them.

'Do you think we've done wrong?' she asked, anxiously. 'Do you think this was wise?'

'Not wise at all, my love, but when have I ever been wise where you are concerned?'

They dressed, and then they walked home together through the twilight, his arm around her waist. When they grew closer to the town, they walked more decorously, her arm in his, like a respectable courting couple. But she could feel his body inclining towards her, the warmth of him. As soon as they were in the Cowgate, he hurried her along the alleyway and, glancing around to make sure that there were no observers, pulled her into the shelter of the back stairs at the Whitefoord Arms and kissed her on the lips. She thought her heart would break when he moved away from her, and she reached out to touch his bruised face. He seized her hand, walked her to the back gate of her house and through into the garden. But he didn't come in. He said he didn't want to disturb the household. She could see that the lamps were burning indoors, that her mother and perhaps her father too had waited up, possibly expecting developments of some kind. A formal offer of marriage maybe. She could hardly tell them that marriage was not the kind of offer that had been made. That an offer of an entirely different kind had been made and accepted and enjoyed between the two of them. But not marriage. She hoped none of it was written on her face, as it was surely written on her body, midge bites and all.

He said he would have come in, wished her parents good night, but it was late and he must be getting back to Mossgiel now. They were expecting him there, and he didn't see them so very often. They missed him, his family, when he was away.

'I miss you too,' she said.

He sighed. 'I wish...' he said, and then hesitated, unwilling to finish.

'What do you wish?'

'I don't ken. I don't rightly ken, Jeany, and that's the truth. But I must go. I'll write to you, though. I'll write from Edinburgh.'

He walked quickly away, turning into the Cowgate, heading in the direction of Mossgiel. He would be another half hour on the road to get there, even if he went at a fast pace, and she could see that he was limping more painfully now from the riding accident. They shouldn't have walked so far. She climbed the back stairs, put her hand on the latch, took a deep breath and went indoors.

There were grass stains on her skirts. She was sore, beneath her petticoats, damp, sticky, raw from the unaccustomed lovemaking. But she couldn't find it in herself to regret even a moment of it.

The regrets would all come later.

Chapter Twenty-two

A Girl out of Pocket

Thou'll break my heart, thou warbling bird,
That wantons thro' the flowering thorn:
Thou minds me o' departed joys,
Departed never to return.

She didn't see him again for some time, either in the town or at her house. He left Mossgiel in August and journeyed back to Edinburgh where, as far as Jean could tell from the infrequent news of him that reached her, he was either morosely drinking all by himself, or travelling in company with his difficult, prickly and ill tempered friend, William Nicol. Word of him mostly came via his family at Mossgiel, where she would go to visit Robbie. His letters were infrequent now, and she wondered why. But they told her at the farm that he was on another tour of the Highlands, his appetite having been whetted by the first, notwithstanding races with bare arsed Highlandmen and tumbles into hedges. Jean sensed that Nicol liked to bask in the reflected glow of Rab's success, but like so many people who are all too ready to give offence, he himself was remarkably easily offended.

They had met Niel Gow, the fiddler, on their travels, and Rab was thinking about song writing and song collecting. He loved the old songs of Scotland and wanted to find some way of preserving them. Did he miss her singing, she wondered. He returned to Edinburgh via Fife, where Jean's mother had relatives, ostensibly visiting the people who had subscribed to his books. He was also picking up traditional songs along the way, tinkering with them, making them even more beautiful. This was the way the tradition worked. Nothing was ever set in stone. The songs of the people grew and changed shape all the time. But he was becoming a master of the art. He wrote a song about his love being *like a red, red rose* and sent it to the family in Mossgiel. Jean recognised bits of it, phrases, images that she had sung to him herself, parts of other old songs. Rab's sister, Isabella, told Jean that he had written that Jean might like this, might like to sing it because it would very much suit her voice.

'He said to be sure and tell you. He was most particular about it,' added Isabella.

It was to be sung to a new tune by Niel Gow, called *Major Graham of Inchbrakie's Strathspey,* and he would play it over to them some time on the fiddle. Jean wondered if the celebrated fiddler had played it to Rab when they had met. But it would only be later that she learned the melody for herself and saw how it suited her voice, in particular, what Rab called the 'wild irregularity' of it, those soaring and dipping notes of which she was so eminently capable. *O my luve's like a red red rose, that's newly sprung in June, and my love's like the melodie, that's sweetly played in tune. As fair art thou, my bonnie lass, sae deep in luve am I, and I will luve thee still, my dear, till a' the sea's gang dry.* Did he love her still, or was it just for the sake of the song? He would profess to almost anything for the sake of a poem or a song.

She had never liked October much, hating the storms that would rampage in from the west, the storms that had proved so troublesome for May Campbell on her last sea voyage. The end of summer brought a settled sadness in its wake. She often thought that she would fly away with the birds, if she could.

The daft thing was that she had wanted to take the wee girl with her. Wanted to take her out to Mossgiel. She had promised to go and visit Robbie, but it was a foul day, one of the first real days of winter, for all that it was only October, wet and windy with clouds like bruises filling the sky and the road ankle deep in mud. She liked to keep her promises, so she said she would go for an hour or two, at any rate. But her mother had persuaded her to leave Jeany behind, persuaded her that she would be much better off in the house. She wouldn't want the child to catch a chill, would she? So she had kissed her little daughter, wrapped herself in a cloak and set off for Mossgiel. Had there been an inkling of disaster? A premonition? She didn't think so. She had been cold and wet enough by the time she got there, but they had made her welcome as usual, drying her muddy shoes and her cloak by the fire, making tea, probably brought by Rab from Edinburgh, and a slice of tart made with that autumn's apples and a few late brambles to go with it. Rab was well, they said, and was speaking of coming to visit. He had moved to the New Town, and he had rented a very nice room there. She thought it would be a good thing that he was coming home, because she needed to see him – she had news for him, something she must tell him as soon as possible, although she had said nothing to anyone else about it. Not yet.

And then Willie Patrick was hammering on the door, panting for breath, having run all the way from Mauchline where he had been sent on an errand earlier that day, saying, 'Jeany, Jeany, you're to come home wi me the now. Something's happened. Something terrible!'

Nobody could say for certain how it had happened. The wean was walking well, only a scant two months after her first birthday, up on her feet and toddling about. But unsteady for all that. Not quite sure footed enough yet but quick in her movements and curious. Very curious. The fire in the kitchen grate fascinated her, but she couldn't reach it with any ease, and they kept an eye on her, kept her away from it. But Mary Armour had been putting more coals on the fire that was smoking wretchedly because of the way the wind was blowing. She had left a big black pot of hot water hanging on the swee, swung out to one side while she did it. And wee Jeany had been able to reach that all right, had toddled over in an instant, reached up and pulled the whole of it over on top of herself. Afterwards, Jean was glad she had not heard the screams, because she would never have been rid of them, all the days that remained to her. Sometimes she fancied she could hear them in her mind although she had not been there. Willie Patrick's father, the cobbler, came rushing along the street to help. They summoned Doctor Mackenzie and he did what he could, which was little enough. The pains seemed to subside after a while, but the child died a few days later, her skin so red and raw and peeling that Jean couldn't even hold her in her arms until after she was dead.

Word had already reached Rab. Jean could barely speak, let alone write, too shocked and sad even to cry. Mary blamed herself and wept ceaselessly in between busying herself with her own young children, while poor James, who had loved his little granddaughter most sincerely, took himself to the kirk and stayed there, praying, night and day. And when that didn't help, he crossed the road to the Whitefoord Arms and drank. But Daddie Auld came and took him back to the kirk after a while and spoke to him, and then he came home and went back to work. There were other mouths to feed. However you felt in yourself, the living were more important than the dead. The house was quiet, the atmosphere heavy with mourning. Children died all the time. Mary and James had lost children. But this was different. They all knew that this shouldn't have happened, that it could have been prevented. They all feared Rab, if the truth be told. He would be so angry. Toweringly angry. Mackenzie took it upon himself to write to him, explaining what had happened as clearly and sympathetically as he could. How it was an accident. He had seen this happen on other occasions too. Most doctors had. The house could be a dangerous place for toddling weans. Jean was certainly not to blame. She hadn't even been there. She had been visiting Robbie. And as for Mary ... there had been a moment's inattention. A moment's distraction. That was all it took. If she could call the moment back, she would.

But the damage was done, and in more ways than one.

If Rab had been only intermittently concerned for Jean before, he seemed doubly indifferent now, although he had written to another friend that he was a 'girl out of pocket and by careless, murdering mischance too,' the casual phrases disguising the cold rage that lay underneath. Mackenzie spoke to Jean about it, gravely, cautiously. He had heard something similar from Robert, loved the man like a brother and was worried about him.

'This is how Rab responds, you see. When something goes too deep. I'm very alarmed for him. He suffers in winter you know, and this won't help him. I wish he were back here. I could wish, Jeany, that you and he were safely married. I think that would be best for him, you know, even now. Even with this tragedy hanging over the two of you.'

She had not wept properly, not even at the dreadful funeral, with the tiny coffin, and the disapproving or sympathetic murmurs of the few members of the congregation who could bring themselves to attend. Daddie Auld had been as kind to her as he could be. There had been unaccustomed tears in his eyes. But even he seemed to be appalled by the magnitude of what had happened. Nobody wanted to talk about it because nobody knew what to say about it. And all of them were wondering what Rab might say or do when he came back from Edinburgh, Rab who was aye fond of his weans, the fondest of fathers. It was as though they had tried to bury it all with the child. Even Rab seemed to have done that. Because if he allowed himself to dwell on it too closely, it would overwhelm him with grief and fury and he might drown.

'I could wish it too,' said Jean. 'Could wish that we were safely married. And for more than one reason.'

Mackenzie gazed at her, wondering what she meant, and then quite suddenly realising the significance of it. She had come to his house in the Back Causeway opposite Nance Tinnock's change house. Needing to tell somebody, and who but a doctor? A doctor Rab had once – in fun to be sure – named 'Common Sense.' But she couldn't speak to him at home so she had come here.

'What other reason would there be?' he asked, frowning. And then, 'Oh Jean, you're not are you?'

'I may well be.'

She had tried to ignore the signs all over again, tried to put them to the back of her mind. She knew it was foolish but she couldn't help herself. After the twins were born and while she was feeding them, her body had taken some time to return to its normal monthly rhythm. So she hadn't thought about it much. But she hadn't been feeding any infant for months now, and she could fool herself no longer. The signs, the feelings, the sickness – so hard to hide from her mother – the changes in her body were unmistakable. She was carrying Rab Mossgiel's child again.

'How could this happen?' He broke into her thoughts.

'In the usual way, Doctor Mackenzie. You should ken that, a man of your profession. What other way would there be?'

He shook his head. 'When did it happen? He's hardly been here!'

He seemed faintly exasperated, but she thought it was with his friend, rather than with her. He didn't once doubt her, knew exactly who the father must be.

'In July I think. Well, I know full well. It must have been very late in July. I had not been alone with him before that, and I have not seen him since. It was just the once.'

'That's all it takes, Jean. Just the once.'

'He came home and he came to see me, and to see my poor wee Jeany.' Her breath caught in a sob. 'And he was very kind to me back then.'

'But he didn't come back when your girl died. Even though I wrote to him. And I'm certain others must have written to him as well.'

She shuddered, shook her head. 'No. I think he would not. He was so angry. I'm sure he was so angry that he kept away for fear he would hurt somebody. He blamed my mother and my father. Still does, I think.'

'But not you, I hope. You were not even there.'

'I don't ken. Maybe he does blame me. Maybe I am to blame.'

'You mustn't think that way, Jean. Does anyone else know about this? Has anyone else noticed that you're with child?' He was wondering how on earth he could help her.

'I don't think so. Not my parents. Too much has been going on in our house. My mother can barely look at me in any case, for fear that she sees accusation in my face. But she's not to blame. It could have happened even if I'd been there.'

'You're a good girl, Jeany. A good, kindly girl. And I could wish your man ... ah well, let's leave that aside for the moment. What about the kirk session? They were interested in your condition soon enough last time, weren't they?'

'They were, but they have noticed nothing. They suspect nothing. Why should they? As far as they ken, Rab's been gone for months and there's been no other man. Good God! Once it's kent in the parish they'll think me little better than a whore. I've no proof that he's the father, even though he is. If he denies it, I'll be no better than Racer Jess in their eyes!'

He put an arm around her shoulders. 'You're moving too far ahead. Rab is not a man to deny his own child. You of all people must know that.'

'I would have said that before, but now? I think he hates me.'

'Let's worry about all that later on. For the present, it's the session that must concern us. And keeping your situation a secret while we make plans.'

'The session kens nothing about it. Not even Willie Fisher. So much else has been happening and besides, they've been quarrelling with Mr Hamilton, haven't they?'

'Oh, aye!' His lips twitched suddenly. 'The small matter of the tatties.'

The kirk session had been in dispute with Rab's friend, Gavin Hamilton, Mackenzie's friend too if it came to that, about the sin of Sabbath breaking. Hamilton had been walking in his garden, not far from where they were now sitting, when his children had asked for a boiling of new potatoes. He had summoned one of his servants and asked the man to dig a few schaws. The man had complied, but somebody had noticed and reported Hamilton to the session for breaking the sanctity of the Sabbath day. He was compeared to appear before them, but he had been leading them a merry dance ever since, and would continue to do so. He had explained that his children had tasted no new potatoes that year and had begged him for them. Who could refuse his own children when they made such a request? The session officers had questioned some of his household servants and learned that there had been new potatoes in the kitchen the week before, so Hamilton had lied. It was exactly the kind of dispute that would make Rab smile. He would love the intricacies of it all, the way in which Hamilton was clearly tying the session, in the shape of Willie Fisher and James Lamie, in knots. And Common Sense, in the person of Doctor Mackenzie, would be equally amused, but faintly shocked too. In other circumstances.

'You know,' Mackenzie observed mildly, 'all this nonsense could have been avoided if Gavin had simply dug his own tatties.'

'What do you mean?'

'Well, do you not think that it was the very act of making another man break the Sabbath that has upset them all so much?'

'I suppose so.' She was momentarily distracted from her own troubles, vast as they were in comparison to the matter of the tatties. And perhaps that had been the good doctor's intention. She said, 'But he wouldn't have done that, would he? I doubt if Gavin Hamilton has ever lifted a graip in his life!'

'Aye well, you're right there. He wouldn't know one end of a tattie fork from the other. So perhaps he and his children should have gone without tatties till Monday. Ach, it'll go no further, you know. No further than here in Mauchline, I mean. Once the Ayr Presbytery are involved, it will all be stopped. Hamilton has influential friends in plenty. Fisher and Lamie seem to think he's small fry, and vulnerable to their censure, but he isn't. And they'll find it out soon enough.'

'I'm only glad it has distracted them from noticing me.'

'And perhaps it will continue to do so for a few weeks yet.' He was doing brief calculations. 'Very late July you said – so the baby is due at the end of April?'

'Do you think it could be babies again?'

'What? Ah God, Jean, do *you* think so?'

'For some reason, I have it in my mind that it might be twins again. There's just something. I mind how I felt the first time.'

'Oh Jean!'

'Could you listen? Agnes listened the last time, and she could tell. But it was later. How soon could you tell? I don't want to tell Agnes Sloan. If I do it'll be all over the town. I don't want my parents to find out, no just yet at any rate.'

'I don't rightly know. It might be a bit soon. But I can try. And what about Rab? Have you written to him? Have you told him?'

She shook her head, mutely. How could she tell Rab in the light of their daughter's death?

He made sure that none of his servants were nearby. God knows what they would think he might be up to with Jeany Armour, and her with a reputation for scandal too. He took the slender wooden listening trumpet from the press where he kept all his medical things and made her perch on a high stool, smoothing her dress down over the swelling mound of her belly, still not very noticeable, fortunately. He set his ear to it and listened, moving it about from time to time. She could hear his breathing and hers and the ticking of the clock on the mantel.

Then he stood upright and sighed. 'I can't be sure and that's the truth. It could be two heartbeats. Or possibly not. It might just be the one. We'll need to wait a while. But what are you going to do? Will you tell Rab?'

'Should I?'

'I think you must. Jean, I have to ask this, even though I already know the answer. So don't be angry with me. There's been nobody else?'

'No. There's never been anybody else for me.'

He looked at her candid eyes, her open face, pinched with sorrow and worry, and he believed her. He thought that Rab would believe her too, if only he was here to see her at this moment. But Rab was in Edinburgh, where he had met a young woman and would-be poetess called Nancy McLehose. Nancy was not a widow, but she might as well have been. Her husband was away in the Indies, but the word was that she was well rid of him, since he had been a notoriously violent man. Rab was clearly very taken with her and she with him, and Mackenzie had grave misgivings about the friendship, about Rab's propensity for falling madly in love and just as precipitately falling out of it again. He couldn't tell Jean any of this. She would find out soon enough.

'Well, you can write to him from here if you like. Just a note. I'll send the letter for you and put in something of my own.'

'Would you do that for me?'

He sighed, looked mildly irritated, although she could see that it was irritation with his friend rather than with herself.

'Sit yourself down at my desk. Write to him now, today. I'll make sure he gets it. And, Jean, even if you let nobody else know about this for now, you need to take care of yourself and the baby. Eat properly. Get plenty of fresh air. Rest if you can.'

Chapter Twenty-three

Willie's Mill

Your rosy cheeks are turn'd sae wan,
Ye're greener than the grass, lassie.
Your coatie's shorter by a span
Yet deil an inch the less, lassie.

Rab was dallying with pretty Nancy McLehose in Edinburgh. While the letters were flying back and forth between them, sometimes on an hourly basis, while the poems, gifts and trysts were coming thick and fast, Rab was trying very hard indeed to forget about Jean and not to worry too much about whether people were speaking of her in any way. Jean herself, meanwhile, was struggling to keep her condition hidden from those closest to her.

Extraordinarily, she managed to keep the pregnancy a secret until the following February. Around New Year, Doctor Mackenzie confirmed that he could hear two heartbeats. She was expecting twins again. He asked her if she had had any word of support from Rab, to which she could only reply that she hadn't. Not a word of encouragement or even pity for the plight in which she found herself. Perhaps he was hoping that Jean would lose the child, leaving him free to pursue his *amours* in Edinburgh. Then he would be able to resolve not to make the same mistake three times over. But he didn't know that it was twins again. Mackenzie said that he would try writing a longer letter to his friend, telling him the true state of affairs.

Ever since the death of her daughter, Jean's appetite had deserted her. Although her belly was swelling inexorably, her face had grown thin, and if it was not easy, then it was certainly possible to disguise her condition, what Rab pleased to call her 'appearance', especially in winter. She told everyone that she was feeling the cold all the time, which was true, and she huddled herself into shawls as well as lacing her stays ever tighter, desperately hoping that she was not injuring the babies inside her.

The blow, when it came, fell suddenly. Early in February, not long before Valentine's Day, her mother came into the room all unexpectedly when she was dressing herself, and screamed, 'Oh dear God, Jeany, what have you gone and done now?'

She had, as she could not help but admit, 'got herself with child' all over again. And by the same man as well.

'Thank heavens your father's away at his work,' was all Mary could say at first. 'But this'll be the death of him, Jeany!'

Jean thought it might be the death of her too, but what was she to do? After a good deal of fretting and fussing, Mary hustled her errant daughter round to Doctor Mackenzie's house, having wrung from Jean the unwelcome admission that he, at least, had been aware of her condition for some time, and had promised to send the news to Rab in Edinburgh.

'And have *you* had any word from the fornicating skellum?' Mary demanded, as soon as they were inside, driven to treating the innocent Mackenzie with a discourtesy that made Jean hang her head in shame.

Mackenzie was embarrassed that he should be placed in this position, that much was clear. He seemed furious with his friend for abandoning Jean, but anxious that she should not fall to the censure of her parents and the kirk session all over again.

'Heaven help us when Jeany's father finds out!' Mary took hold of her daughter's arm and shook her in exasperation. 'D'you no have the sense you were born with?'

Jean began to weep, not loudly, but with the tears simply streaming down her face. Mackenzie glanced at her and felt fit to burst out crying himself, from pure sympathy.

'I confess I have no idea what to do next!' he told the women, handing Jean his handkerchief. 'But you'd best dry your eyes, lass. Mistress Armour, will you leave her here for the moment? If anyone asks about her, tell them that she is unwell and is seeking some physic from me. But is there nowhere she could go so that she would be away from the town and the gossips for a while? Have you no friends or relatives who might take pity on her?' He was still a single man, and it would be very inadvisable for him to take her in without the protection of the weans' father, with so much scandal clinging to her name, even though there were a couple of female servants in the house. He had his own professional and personal reputation to consider.

Eventually, Mary went back to the Cowgate and Mackenzie left Jean alternately dozing and weeping in front of his study fire while he rode out to Mossgiel to consult with the Burns family there. Gilbert had grown very fond of Jean. The news surprised and shocked him, but he, at least, was deeply concerned.

'I'll confess, I'm heartily ashamed of my brother,' he said. 'I would hardly credit it, but how can I question Jean's honesty?'

'No. The lassie's telling the truth, that much is clear.' Mackenzie thought that Gilbert seemed more like the elder of the two brothers himself in point of sense and responsibility. 'The obvious solution would be for you to take Jean in here at Mossgiel, but I can see you're short of space,' he said.

'Aye, we are. And I think my mother is very reluctant to go against Rab's wishes in his absence.'

'What are his wishes?' Mackenzie asked.

'Who kens? Not me, that's for sure. These days, his talk is all of Nancy, or his letters are, anyway. He calls her his Clarinda, would you believe, and she cries him Sylvander.'

It was clear that the assumed names disgusted Gilbert even more, perhaps, than the relationship, the affair or whatever it was. Privately, Gilbert thought that Nancy was like a minor fever in his brother's blood, virulent and dangerous while it lasted, but soon over. He couldn't say as much to Mackenzie, or to Jean, in case he was proved wrong. You never could tell with Rab.

Eventually, they settled between them that they would beg shelter for her with kindly Willie Muir and his wife at the mill, beside Tarbolton. Willie was a trusted acquaintance from the Burns family's Lochlea days, a crony of Rab and Gilbert's father, rather than the lads themselves. James Armour was a business acquaintance as well, and Jean had visited the Muirs with her mother from time to time. Mary packed up some of Jean's belongings and sent one of the lads to carry the box across to Mackenzie's house, as soon as darkness was falling over the town, giving them a measure of privacy. Then Mackenzie himself took Jean the five miles to Willie's Mill in a borrowed gig. If anyone enquired too closely as to her whereabouts, they would be told that Jean had gone on a visit to old friends, much as they had fended off inquisitive neighbours when Jean was in Paisley.

'But what will your father say?' Mary repeated. 'And how am I going to tell him?'

James Armour didn't faint this time. If anything he seemed more sad and disappointed than angry. A day or two later, he sent word to Willie's Mill that Jean was not, under any circumstances, to show her face in the Cowgate again, or not until Mossgiel had agreed to shoulder his responsibilities. The shame would be too much for James and his wife to bear, and would damage the reputation of the whole family.

The Muirs, husband and wife, told Jean that she was very welcome to stay with them throughout her whole confinement if need be. Mackenzie offered to pay them for her bed and board, but they refused indignantly. They owed it to the family in memory of Rab's father, if nothing else. The two men had been friends and Willie had admired William Burness tremendously. Once the babies were born, Willie and his wife hoped that Rab would be more inclined to come round to the idea of marriage again, although Jean did not seem very hopeful.

'This isn't like Rab,' said Willie to Dr Mackenzie. 'Not the good-hearted lad I thought him. Not his father's son at all. Why has he abandoned her?'

He liked Rab and he liked Jean and he couldn't understand why they didn't simply make a match of it. It was clear to anyone with eyes to see and ears to hear that they were meant for each other. This would not have happened, he thought, if Rab had not gone off to the wicked town of Edinburgh and been puffed and praised out of all proportion to his deserts.

'The Bard!' he said to his wife, with a certain amount of scorn. 'They're calling him the Bard. But I'm thinking his Bardship needs to take some responsibility for his ain human failings.'

Even when a man was flying high, celebrated, made much of, he needed a good steadfast woman at home, a wife to bring him back down to earth. That's what Willie thought. He was reminded, so he told Jean, in an attempt to cheer her, of the ballad of Tam Lin and his lass, Janet, who had borne his child and then bravely rescued Tam from the Queen of Faery. Perhaps Rab needed a woman brave enough to rescue him.

Perhaps Willie was more right than he knew.

At any rate, it was at Willie's Mill that Rab found his erstwhile jewel towards the end of the month. He was riding from a visit to Ellisland, the farm he was considering renting in Dumfriesshire, and on his way home to Mossgiel. When Rab came to the mill, Willie was not reassured, not at first. Willie thought that he had changed, and not for the better either. The young man strode into the house with an air of condescension. Strutted in. Cock of the walk. That's how Willie would have described it, and how his wife did describe it later, full of indignation, voicing both their concerns.

'Would you credit it? Would you credit the pride of the man in his fine clothes? And poor Jeany Armour carrying his weans all over again!'

Maybe he was tired after his long journey, and maybe he was worried and unhappy about Jean. Well, of course he was unhappy about Jean. But she was his responsibility now and yet he seemed reluctant to admit his guilt, reluctant even to engage in conversation with her. To her dismay, Jean sensed something close to revulsion in him at the sight of her swollen belly and ankles, her blotchy, tearstained face. Her vulnerability seemed to inspire a kind of cruelty in him, rather than the kindness Willie and his wife had anticipated, the support Jean had hoped for. She saw it in his face. Everything about her irritated him. Last time, she had been defiant. Now, she could not hide either her desperation or her desire to please him, and he seemed to think her fawning, vulgar, insipid. She was no fool, and she could tell that he was comparing her in his mind's eye to somebody else. At the time, she didn't know who it might be. She had heard rumours of some Edinburgh lady with whom he was enamoured, but whenever she tried to question them, Rab's friends, even Doctor Mackenzie, would clam up, claiming not to know what he was up to. Later, she realised he must have been thinking about Nancy McLehose, and wishing that she was as polished, as ladylike, as proper and pretty and clever. He did not acquit himself at all well, seemed reluctant even to take her hand, never mind embrace her. He stared at her as coldly as though she had been a stranger and said, 'What in the name of God have you done now, Miss Armour?' and she rushed out of the room in tears again.

Willie, watching all this, could hardly contain his wrath. He was disgusted with his young friend.

'Rab, Rab, could you not have found it in you to behave more kindly to the lass?'

Still the lad persisted with his lordly manners, his condescension.

'She exasperates me. Heaven help me, she has no pride and no dignity. Did you see the way she fawned over me? Willie, she does not have the sense she was born with!'

The older man's dismay spilled over into fury.

'Aye, and you have some sense, I suppose! But no pity? No humanity? Ken, lad, I'm surprised you can find a hat big enough for that head of yours, but I suppose there are many wonders to be had in Edinburgh! Where is this coming from?' continued Willie, when Rab didn't rise to the bait. 'She must have been good enough for you at one time. More than one time, evidently. What would your father have said? Or have you grown too grand for honest Ayrshire folk like us? For kindly folk like your friends and family?'

Rab had the grace to blush although he maintained his truculent manner. 'No. No, you ken fine I haven't, Willie. But maybe there are some things I have outgrown, and I haven't the least idea what I am to do with her.'

'You seemed to have ideas in plenty about that a few short months ago!' Willie took a deep breath to steady himself. 'Listen, lad. She's welcome to stay on here until you make up your mind. She's a good girl and no trouble to us at all. But if you are genuinely asking me what you should do, I'll tell you.'

'Go on.'

'If you don't intend to marry her, you need to acknowledge that her predicament is your responsibility at least. And to do it publicly. Find her a room in town, close to her mother, if her mother will not take her in. Mary Armour should at least forgive her enough to help her with her confinement. And James should not object.'

'She says her mother will not have her back or help her in any way. And I suppose I am the culprit.'

'Well, you are, are you no? It taks twa to mak a wean, Rab. She will need some help when the babies are born, and I doubt if you intend to be by her side for long. You'll be awa back to that Edinburgh. So you'll need to find her some shelter, a room and a bed, and you must give her some support. You owe her that much at least. And if you don't find her *ladylike* enough for your fine city tastes now, just ask yourself if you have treated *her* like a lady, the lady she most surely is, in our eyes, anyway.'

Rab was silent for a moment. 'Where should she go?'

'That's for you to decide. Dr Mackenzie says he has a room you could tak for her. Not in his house but next door, in the same building. The tenant left recently, and he has not let it yet. She will need furniture, chiefly a bed. And who else to supply it but the father of her weans?'

'You don't think much of me, do you?' Rab said, in a low voice.

'Not just at this moment, son, no. I do not. And I can tell you this much. Your father would have been black affronted, so he would. He would have been most profoundly ashamed of you. And so am I. So are we all that used to love you.'

The observation hit home, as it was meant to do.

'You're right, of course.' Rab was suddenly subdued. 'But I can't help the way I feel, can I? All the same, I'll make my peace with her as far as I can. I'll ride back into Mauchline and see what I can do. If I send a message, once the room is ready, do you have a gig you could bring her in?'

'Aye, I'll see she gets there safely, for the lass cannae walk or even ride, that's for sure, not in her condition.'

* * *

He took the room for her. Her parents were reluctant to furnish it, so he found her a good mahogany bed and Willie Patrick carried a chaff mattress across from the house in the Cowgate. Mary had allowed that, or at least James had pleaded and Mary had conceded. It was a nine days' wonder in the town, and the change houses were alive with the scandal of it. Jean Armour was expecting twins all over again, and Rab Mossgiel had come home from Edinburgh to assist her in her friendless state. The kirk session kept unduly quiet on this occasion which was, so Jean found out later, almost entirely down to Daddie Auld, who had decided that she had suffered enough. He seemed to think that it might be better if the kirk kept well out of it for the time being and let things take their course, however it might end. Rab purchased some few pieces of furniture for her, borrowing the rest from Mackenzie and from Nance Tinnock over the way, bringing one or two home comforts from Mossgiel, things that his mother and sisters had wished to send for her. They pitied her, even while they were reluctant to challenge Rab.

In fact, his mother had said, 'You'll be marrying the lass now, likely?' but he had raised dark eyebrows and said, 'What gars you think that, when she has no claim on me? She had her chance and she rejected me. She has no claim that I ken! My affections lie elsewhere now. I'll support the weans when they come, but that's all.'

Agnes knew that when her son was in this truculent frame of mind there was no arguing with him, so she kept quiet, hoping for the best. Gilbert too counselled caution. Rab could be stubborn when he chose but these moods seldom lasted long. His natural good nature always reasserted itself.

Willie Muir brought Jean and her few possessions into town. By the time they got there, she was feeling very sick. The rutted road, the cold, damp evening and the stench of the horse didn't help. He could see that Rab was waiting for her, so he thought it best to leave the two of them alone together, hoping that they might finally make their peace with one another. He deposited her, bag and baggage, beside the stable where Mackenzie kept his horse, and turned right around to get home to the mill before daylight failed entirely.

'Good luck to you, my dear Jeany!' he said, as he left. 'And mind, if you need us, we're just along the road. You're welcome back any time. It's been a pleasure having you in the house, lass.'

The stable was empty, Mackenzie having been summoned to the bedside of a sick patient, and Rab pulled her inside where the twilight hardly reached.

'This is very good of you. Good of you to find a place for me.'

But if she had hoped for a change of heart, she was wrong. He had been drinking, that much was clear, perhaps in Nance Tinnock's over the way. His breath smelled of whisky. He pulled her close to him, or as close as her belly would allow, and he muttered in her ear, 'Don't think this means ought, Jeany.'

'No. I don't.' She rallied, momentarily. 'Although they *are* your weans, Rab.'

'How can I be sure?'

It was what she had feared he might say all along, but it still felt as though he had stabbed her through the heart.

'They *are* yours. You ken fine they're yours. There's been naebody but you.'

'Maybe so. But you have nae claim on me.' His voice was thick. It didn't sound like Rab at all. 'Let me hear you say it!'

'I have nae claim on you.'

It wasn't true though, was it? Even as she said the words, she knew that she had every claim on him. But he seemed to be very angry, almost to the point of tears. Once, she had seen a neighbour's dog corner a big rat near the outhouse at the back of their house in the Cowgate. The rat had bared its teeth, backed against the wall. The image came into her mind now.

He persisted, 'I don't care what advice you've been given by Willie Muir or Mackenzie. You have nae claim on me, neither in life nor in death. I would have been glad to marry you. I *did* marry you but you rejected me. You broke your word. Now you want what you cannae have, but I've moved on, Jeany, onwards and upwards. I'm the Bard now. Folk know my name. Beyond a room and a bed, you have nae claim on me whatsoever!'

'Then you should have left me at Willlie's Mill,' she said, moving away from him, sobbing, rubbing her eyes. The dust from the road had gathered on her cheeks and now the tears left smudges there. Inside her the babies moved convulsively, disturbed by her anguish. 'I wish you had left me there. At least there folk were kind and cared what became of me. I wish I were dead. I'd be better off dead!'

'I *do* care what becomes of you.'

'Well you have a strange way of showing it.'

'What do you want from me?'

'Naething. Except maybe a glimpse of the old Rab. The Rab who loved me and was kind to me.'

Really, she thought, she wanted her father to embrace her and call her his wee Jeany. She didn't want anything to do with this strange, cruel man who looked like Rab but sounded and behaved nothing like him.

He seemed momentarily confused. He turned away, his hand over his eyes.

'You have found me a room, and you have found me a bed. You'd best leave me to lie on it, Rab, and get back to your fine Edinburgh ladies.'

She tried to push past him, to find her own way into the house, but he restrained her.

'My fine Edinburgh ladies?' he said. 'Who cares about Edinburgh ladies?'

He pulled her close. The very scent of him was familiar to her, the warmth of him. If he didn't speak, she might pretend he was the same old Rab.

Knowing that he wasn't. Not at this moment.

There was a confused jumble of sensations. He kissed her fiercely, and she responded to him although there was a part of her that wanted only to find her room and her bed, lie down and sleep. She was sick and dizzy. The walls of the stable went spinning around her. She was aware of sinking slowly down onto dried horse litter, not falling, so he must have caught her, eased her down gently, like a ewe onto its back. There were cold flagstones beneath her, the dark stable with its pungent smell of horse, the cool air on her legs. He groaned. 'Jeany!' he said. She didn't want him very much at all, at that moment. But obscurely, stupidly, she didn't want to hurt his feelings either. She lay still, beneath him. Letting him do what he wanted. At first she thought it would be all right, but suddenly he was too forceful, too vigorous. It felt as though he was punishing her and the weans inside her, and she cried out in pain.

Somewhere in the village, a dog howled, a long, mournful sound. It seemed to bring him to his senses.

He muttered, 'I'm sorry, I'm so sorry,' and withdrew, abruptly. 'What am I thinking?'

He was muttering to himself rather than to her, but she knew what he was saying.

'A standing cock has nae conscience.'

He scrambled to his feet, doing up his breeches, fumbling a little. 'Dear God, Jeany, what am I doing to you?'

She found herself apologising to *him*. Thinking of all the times she had lain in bed, wanting him. Wondering at her own revulsion. She had wanted him for sure, just not like this. Not in this way. Not now.

He helped her to stand up, brushed her down, brushed the straw and the dry horse litter from her skirts. She felt very strange, even more dizzy, almost fell against him. He put one arm around her, picked up her bag with the other, and lead her into the house. The room was warm. Somebody had lit a fire. Somebody had made the bed. Why had he used the horse litter in the stable when there was a perfectly good bed? She came as close to hating him at that moment as she ever would. He sat her down, took off her cloak, took off her shoes and gently rubbed her feet, gazing into her face. He was white as his linen.

'You're so cold,' he said. 'Oh, my dear.'

He had brought tea from Mossgiel. Fresh milk, cheese, oat bread, all packed in a basket. From his mother, he said. She wanted him to go away and leave her in peace. She wanted to do nothing more than lie down and go to sleep. Eventually she curled up on the chaff mattress that rustled under her. He pulled the blankets over her, tucking her in.

'I don't know what to do,' he said. 'I have to go back to Mossgiel. Will you manage here, if I leave you?'

'Yes.' She was already drifting into sleep. 'I'll manage. Go away, Rab. Leave me be.'

'Mackenzie will look in on you. And Nance Tinnock. She'll fetch you anything you want.' He seemed anxious about her welfare, but not anxious enough to stay. Or maybe it was just that he was too ashamed of himself to stay.

Just before he left, he bent down, brushed the hair away from her cheek, planted a little kiss there. Not a lover's kiss at all. But she was already drifting into sleep.

'I'm sorry,' he said. 'I'm so sorry for all this, Jeany.'

Chapter Twenty-four

Husband and Wife

I hae a wife of my ain,
I'll partake wi' naebody;
I'll take Cuckold frae nane,
I'll gie Cuckold to naebody.

Only a few days later, her waters broke and the twin girls came, much too soon. The birth was surprisingly easy. Her mother relented to the extent that she came over from the Cowgate to help her daughter. And Doctor Mackenzie came in as well. They were born quite quickly, but they were too tiny to survive for long. Too small and frail for the world. But perfect: fingers, toes, tiny rosebud mouths, perfect in every way. Rab paid a brief visit, leant over the crib, touching their waxy cheeks. Jean turned her face to the wall and would not look at him. If she had, she might have seen tears in his eyes but he could hardly bring himself to speak to her. He left some money for her though, to pay for necessities, and went back to Mossgiel. If anything, the money made her feel even worse. She put it in a drawer, knowing that she would be forced to use it sooner or later.

One of the babies survived only a few days. The other lingered on for some twelve days more. In the intervening period, Mackenzie came in to check up on Jean's health and that of the surviving twin. But as Jean improved, the baby failed. It was as though the wee mite was anxious to rejoin her sister, thought Mackenzie. The good doctor brought with him the unwelcome news that Rab had gone back to Edinburgh. He had decided to take the lease of Ellisland in Dumfriesshire, and he needed to see his new landlord, Mr Miller, who was in the city at that time. Besides that, he was looking for money from his Edinburgh publisher, and he was also seeking to enter the excise service. This surprised Jean and Mackenzie both. Ellisland would be a last throw of the dice as far as farming was concerned. It seemed that the excise, however unsuited to his natural inclinations – Rab had never been a great one for submitting to authority – might be a more secure way of earning a living than farming, if all did not go well in Dumfriesshire.

'But all of these things,' the doctor said, 'seem to indicate that he is planning a more settled way of life, although you never can tell where our Rab is concerned.'

Mackenzie was trying to offer her some hope, although he was far from hopeful himself. If Rab was happy to travel between Mauchline and Edinburgh, he could easily travel between Ellisland and Edinburgh too. 'I can't see Rab as an enthusiastic exciseman,' he continued. 'Can you, Jeany?'

'No, not him.'

'He's as changeable as the weather.'

'He is that.'

Gloom had descended on her and nothing could shift it.

Had he said anything to Jean about this excise plan? He had not. Then perhaps he had somebody else in mind for a wife. They were both thinking it, both reluctant to voice it for fear that saying it aloud might make it real. Mackenzie had heard something about Nancy McLehose, but he was not nicknamed 'Common Sense' for nothing, and he could see how thoroughly impractical such an attachment would be. He was confident that Jean knew very little about Nancy at that time, even if she seemed to be fretting about the fine Edinburgh ladies she imagined throwing themselves at the Bard, and he was not going to be the one to enlighten her. Besides, Nancy was still a married woman, even though Rab had judiciously termed her a widow in his letters to his friends. She was also a religious woman with influential friends who kept a stern eye on her behaviour.

Altogether, John Mackenzie thought Nancy too might be in the nature of a last throw of the dice for Rab. The threat to Jean's happiness, if she still wanted Rab, which seemed doubtful, might be imaginary rather than real. He knew that Rab never could resist a love affair. Never could resist spinning dreams and daydreams out of desire. The feeling was no less intense for its ephemeral nature. But the tension between his passion for Nancy and his affection for his old love was clearly making him exceedingly miserable. Anyone with an ounce of wit could see it, and it was there in all his letters, although few among his friends and relatives were brave enough to tell him so. Mackenzie sincerely hoped that Rab would come to his senses and do so without delay.

The babies were written up as unbaptised and unnamed in the parish register, but Daddie Auld gave instructions that they were to be buried inside the kirkyard, in consecrated ground. Perhaps he knew that Jean had splashed warm water on their tiny heads, knowing full well that they were too small to live, that their breathing was laboured, that they were not feeding properly. Blessing them in the name of the father and of the son. Wishing with all her heart that she could follow them into the grave.

Yet all unexpectedly, before the end of that month, Rab was back in Mauchline. Early one morning, with all the birds of spring in full song, he came knocking at Jean's door. She opened it to find him standing there, somewhat sheepishly, hat in hand and with the most extraordinary expression of pained penitence on his face, as though he had arranged his features before knocking. It was so unlike him that she could only gape at him in amazement.

'Can I come in, Jeany?' he asked, solemnly. 'I have something to say to you.'

'Aye. Aye, of course. After all, you're paying the rent, Rab. You're my landlord, if nothing else.'

She held the door open for him, glancing up and down the street, but it was early and there were no prying eyes. He seemed taken aback by the bitterness in her tone, but said nothing until he was inside, still maintaining his almost comical expression of contrition. She followed him in. She was still in her night clothes. There seemed to be little point in getting up and dressed these days, although she had promised to go out to Mossgiel to see Robbie later. It was all she lived for. But she was suddenly ashamed of her dishevelled appearance. He looked so smart in his well brushed coat, his plaid just so, his shiny boots. He looked even more like a gentleman, albeit a remorseful one.

'You should have sent word, Rab. I would have been up and dressed for you at least.'

She had stirred the fire into life, and there was hot water in the iron kettle on the swee. The kettle had come with the room, and she had been very glad of it. Hot water was such a comfort. She still had the tea he had brought from Mossgiel, and she offered to make some for him. Nance Tinnock had given her two pretty cups, with birds and flowers on them.

'I ken fine you like to have nice things about you,' Nance had said. 'Bonnie delft for a bonnie lass.'

Jean had been moved to tears by the older woman's kindness, but then it didn't take much to make her cry these days. She had been ashamed of her weakness, wondering what had become of the lighthearted lass who had sung and danced so confidently. Now, her father, her God and her lover all seemed to have forsaken her. Her girl children were dead, and even her son had been taken from her.

It was a chilly morning, and she wrapped a shawl around her, the first to come to hand. It was the silk shawl that Rab Wilson had given her in Paisley.

'Where did you get that?' her visitor asked.

So he still noticed such things about her, still noticed her clothes. And he was suspicious. Quite possibly jealous too. Like the dog in the manger in the old book of fables they had read at the school when she was a girl. If he didn't want her, he didn't want any other body to have her either.

'It was a gift from a friend,' she said, with something of her old spirit. He really was impossible. An impossible man.

'What friend would that be?'

'And what would it have to do with you, anyway, Rab Burns? I have nae claim on you, remember?'

'Everything about you has to do with me, Jeany. D'you not ken that yet?'

He sounded very subdued. Sad too. His face had resumed its normal aspect.

'Well, you've a very strange way of showing it.'

'Let's not quarrel, eh?'

'I'm trying hard not to, Rab. I'd like it fine if we could be friends, for the sake of Robbie, at least.'

'I'd like it fine too. And I meant nothing by it. I was just curious. I'm allowed to be curious. So who gave you the shawl?'

'Rab Wilson if you must know.'

'Recently?'

'No. Don't be daft! He's in Paisley. I haven't seen him for a long while. He gave it to me at the Sneddon that time, when I had nothing and nobody and he was the only friend I had.'

'Ah. I thought...'

'Well, you ken what thought did?'

'Aye. Followed a muck cart and thought it was a wedding.'

She found herself giving him a watery smile.

'So you thought that he had maybe been back courting me again? Small chance of that, Rab. Small chance of any lad courting me now.'

'Just as well!' he said, with a touch of the old braggart.

'Why?' She could hardly believe it, the cheek of the man.

'Because you're still legally married to me. The God's honest truth is that you've never *not* been married to me, ever since we signed that paper and whatever your father and mother might have thought. Whatever they might have done to mutilate it.'

'But you said…'

'Och, never mind what I said. Or did, Jeany. I was a wee thing daft for a while. Willie Muir was right all along. I think the Edinburgh air must have gone to my head.'

'I think it must.'

'Listen…' He sat down on the bed and pulled her down beside him, capturing her hand in both of his. 'Listen to me. Can you ever find it in your heart to forgive me?'

'For what?'

'For being so unkind. And more than unkind. Cruel. Especially that time in the stable.'

'It wasnae that I didnae want you. I've aye wanted you. But it wasnae like you.'

'No. It wasnae. I've hated myself for it ever since.'

'I wanted you. Just no like that.'

'No. No like that. And in sic a place.' He shook his head. 'Can you ever forgive me?'

'Why are you here, Rab?'

'I've been making plans.'

'What plans?'

He took a deep breath, squeezing her hand. 'I've signed the lease of a farm down in Dumfriesshire. There's no house to speak of on the land, nothing but a lightless but 'n ben, so there'll need to be a new house built. I'll need a wife who kens a bit about dairying, so I thought you might like to go out to Mossgiel this summer and learn. My mother and my sisters will teach you all you need to ken, and you can see Robbie at the same time. He's aye fretting for his mammy, or so they tell me.'

'Am I hearing this right?'

He rushed on. She thought about him chasing the Highlandman, even at the risk of toppling off Jenny Geddes. An impulsive man.

'I'll be coming to and fro once the building work starts. You ken the builders won't work properly with nobody to supervise them. They'll come and sit on their cart, drinking their ale, eating their bread and cheese and saying that's what they aye do before they begin. And besides, I'll need to start working on the farm as soon as may be. But I'm going to be in training for the excise with Mr Findlay in Tarbolton first. Six weeks training before I go to Ellisland.'

'Aye. I heard.'

'But in the midst of all this, Jean, I'm sorely in want of a wife, and I wondered if you could forgive me enough to apply for the position. Well, the truth of the matter is, it's a position you already have. Just never taken it up right. But it's yours if you still want it. Till a the seas gang dry.'

He recited all this as though he had learned it off by heart beforehand. As perhaps he had. She could hardly believe her ears.

'I thought you said...'

He interrupted her. 'Aye, well. I did say. I said a lot of things I now regret. To my lasting shame. But whatever I may or may not have said, I've made up my mind now. I can't think of anyone else who would make a better wife to me than you, Jeany. You ken me better than most. Perhaps better than anyone.' He turned to face her. 'I'm a poet. It's my brag and my failing. I might be able to *imagine* sic a wife, to fancy her, in the same way that I can *imagine* the angels in heaven, or auld Nick in shape o' beast, but I have never seen or met anyone to match you. I've never met anyone who loves me like you do. And I'd be plain daft to discard sic a treasure, once found. The honest truth is that you have my hand and my heart. You've aye had it. But I don't ken if you still want to be married to me after all. Do you?'

She found herself nodding. He took this for consent and raced on.

'Well, what we could do is this. We could walk over to Gavin Hamilton's house. We could go later on today if you like, when you're dressed and ready, and we could sign a fresh paper. He has told me he'll be happy to witness it, and then nobody, not even James Armour or Daddie Auld himself can say that we arenae man and wife.'

She gazed at him in utter amazement. 'Why?' she said after a while. 'Why have you changed your mind?'

'I don't rightly ken. Well I do. I ken all too well. The truth is that I never *did* change my mind. It was aye you, Jeany. From the moment I first clapped eyes on you.'

She thought that for once he had told her the absolute truth. The poet in him always would be able to imagine something better, more heavenly, more perfect in every way. But when it came to the demands of his ordinary, every day life, she was the person uppermost in his mind. It was a very strange proposal. She wondered, in passing, if there could be another woman in the whole of Ayrshire, in the whole of Scotland even, who would assent to such an offer of marriage.

But she found herself nodding again. 'Aye,' she said.

'You agree?'

'I think so. But I'll need to get dressed, first.'

'Are you still sore from the weans?' he asked, gazing at her, a spark of the old desire kindling in his eyes.

'Aye, I am,' she said firmly.

'That's a pity.'

'Well I'm sorry for you. But I'm sore in my body and my heart tae, Rab. You'll just have to wait till I feel a wee bit better.'

'I'll wait till you're good and ready then.'

'Aye. You will so.'

* * *

She dressed in the best she had, wrapped Rab Wilson's shawl about her, and they walked arm in arm to Gavin Hamilton's house where, in a small back room, they pledged to be faithful to one another.

'Do you, Jean Armour, take this man to be your married husband?' said Mr Hamilton, and she replied, 'I do, before God and these witnesses.'

When Rab had repeated the same form of words, they both signed a paper that Hamilton had drawn up to that effect. He said that he would be keeping it in the safe in his house, where he kept his own official papers, so that nobody could get their hands on it and mutilate it in any way.

'What about the kirk?' asked Jean. 'What about Daddie Auld? Will the kirk recognise the marriage?'

'Let's wait until they come to us, Jeany. I'm not inclined to go cap in hand to them, and I think Mr Hamilton would agree with me.'

After this very quiet ceremony, Mr and Mrs Hamilton toasted the couple with a glass of wine and a simple meal, and Rab gave Jean and Mrs Hamilton their 'favours': pairs of very pretty gloves: cream kid leather, stitched with blue silk for Mrs Hamilton and with pink roses for Jean. Rab had bought them in Edinburgh, he told her later, so he had perhaps been planning the wedding for a while, counting on her agreement. Then, rousing the local gossips to a frenzy of wild speculation, they walked about the town arm in arm – and in the afternoon – went to Mossgiel to tell the family the good news.

The sudden change in her fortunes left Jean feeling very odd. It was going to be hard to adjust to it. She felt like a woman in a song or story, who had fallen asleep for a hundred years and woken to find everything changed about her. Was this a mistake? A dream? Would she wake up tomorrow morning to the same miserable sensation of loss? Would there be nothing in her bed but a few dried leaves, crumbling to dust when she touched them? But when she woke up the following morning to find his arms around her, his whole body curved gently around her back and his warm breath on her hair as he slept, she knew that it was real. A different story altogether.

'Tam Lin,' she said, half to herself.

'What?' He hugged her more tightly to him, not quite awake, his hand cupping her breast, sighing at the softness.

'Never mind. It was a song I had in my mind just. An old song. I'm that glad to have you back, Rab.'

A few days later, he told her that he had ordered a new shawl for her from his old Mauchline friend and hers, James Smith, who had gone to Linlithgow to set up a calico printing business there. He had asked for the best that young man had in stock. He would always like to see Jean well dressed. For her part, she had always loved pretty things. She liked to keep the house clean and fresh, and even to bring flowers indoors from the fields and hedgerows when she could. But although she loved Rab Wilson's silk shawl, she parcelled it up and sent it back to his family, with a note saying that since she was now married to Robert Burns, was now Mistress Burns rather than Miss Armour, it might be best if the gift was returned to Mr Wilson, in case he should be able to find another use for it. She couldn't have said quite why she did this. Rab had certainly not requested it. But it seemed like a promise, a confirmation of something between the two of them. Whether Rab would ever be as assiduous in holding to the vows they had made, she very much doubted. But she could hope and pray.

∗ ∗ ∗

There followed perhaps the happiest period of her whole life. She shed years and cares over the following months. Saunders Tait, the wretched tailor in Tarbolton, was still making mocking poems about the couple, but who cared when she had Rab and he had her and when they seemed to be making each other so content? Tait's jealousy didn't trouble them. In fact the more he wrote ridiculous and paltry verse about her dress and Rab's concern for it, the more Rab seemed to delight in spending money on the finest printed cotton or silk for best gowns, on new shawls and bonnets, silk stockings, leather shoes, kid gloves.

In the middle of June, having finished his excise training, he moved to Ellisland on the River Nith to commence farming there and to oversee the building of the new house. Rab did not much enjoy living alone at Ellisland, and he had already confessed to Jean that the farm itself might not turn out to be quite the bargain he had supposed. But the new farmhouse was coming along, and he was beginning to make acquaintances in the locality, not least Robert Riddell, at the big house called Friar's Carse, who seemed delighted to have the celebrated poet for a neighbour and a friend.

Rab rode back and forth between Ellisland and Mauchline as often as he could, and she would generally walk out along the road to meet him. She was alone in the room in the Back Causeway at that time. Wee Robbie was still at Mossgiel, but she would see him most days when she walked out to the farm to learn about dairying and how to make the sweet milk cheese that was Gilbert's speciality. Each day's milk had to be curdled, mixed with salt and the curds broken up by hand. Then they had to be covered with a cloth and pressed in a frame under a heavy stone before being laid up to dry. The product itself was hard but mild with a very pleasant taste, and Robbie availed himself of the ready supply at Mossgiel. He was talking now and toddling, rushing to meet her in the mornings. He never seemed to be without a piece of cheese in his hand and was growing into a sturdy little lad in consequence. She delighted to see him clutching his bannock, his cheese, his wedge of rosy apple, holding it out to her, wanting to share it with her. He was the image of his daddy.

'Mammy, mammy!' he would call, with a grin splitting his face.

They had decided to leave him where he was, at the farm, until they could all move south together. There seemed to be no point in upsetting the arrangements, and the lad was better off at Mossgiel where there were plenty of people to look after him and where his mother spent most of her days. But she had loved the feeling of his warm body in her arms, his chubby hands in her hair, the scent of him. She missed him at night as much as she missed her husband. All the same, it meant that there was nothing to keep her in Mauchline, no child to mind. It was like being free again. Like that first summer before the children came. But now the year was toppling slowly into autumn, and still the house was not ready.

They were in love and in lust. The honeymoon, he called it, but it went on for months. Rab would always say that when he had a sight of Corsincon Hill at Cumnock, he knew he would soon be home. Jean would come out along the road to meet him whenever she could. She would sometimes go barefoot with the dust between her toes. One day, the cadger passed her on his way from Mauchline to Cumnock, and he reined in his horse.

'Will ye jump up on the cart, Mistress Burns?' he called with a sly grin, but she shook her head, not trusting him at all, believing that he would think her a light-skirts and have a wee feel. Her reputation was uncertain at best. There had been so much gossip. So much scandal. He shrugged as much as to say, 'Your loss, Mistress,' and clicked to his horse, soon leaving her far behind.

At home, she had made the bed all fresh, washing the ticking and filling it up with sweet oat chaff from the harvest. How it would rustle and squeak beneath their combined weight! Before the babies were born, Willie Patrick had come staggering over from the Cowgate with the mattress balanced precariously on his narrow shoulders, because at that time, the time of her shame, her mother wouldn't let her brothers lift a finger to help her and her father had been reluctant to intervene. But things were much better now. Slowly but surely the Armours were accepting their new son-in-law, her father more quickly than her mother.

She heard the hoofbeats on the road before she saw him. The sun was sinking in the west but there was enough light, and there he was on Jenny Geddes. He dismounted, left the placid mare to crop the long grass, and they went away from the road, away from prying eyes, lay down together on a grassy slope behind the hedge. They could hardly ever wait for long enough to get back to the chaff mattress and besides, they were husband and wife, and could do what they pleased. They did plenty, and when they were finished, he would pull her up in front of him, his arms clasped close around her, and she would turn her cheek into the scratchy wool of his coat. Every time, without exception, he would run his fingers under her skirts, caressing her knee and then moving higher, until she was warm and wet and wanting him all over again.

In August, their idyll was interrupted by a stern visit from Daddie Auld, who had been expecting Rab to confirm the marriage in the kirk and had now run out of patience. Truth to tell, Rab had been expecting the visit too and only a certain devilry had kept him away. Jean apologised to the minister and immediately upon Rab's next visit to Mauchline took him along to the session meeting which both of them had been compeared to attend. There, they acknowledged their 'irregular' marriage and their sorrow for that irregularity, about which Jean's contrition, at least, was genuine. They desired that the session would take such steps as might seem to them proper in order for the solemn confirmation of the said marriage. The session rebuked them formally for the irregularity and engaged them to adhere faithfully to one another as husband and wife all the days of their life. The elders agreed, furthermore, to refer to Mr Burns, his own generosity, and absolved both parties from any scandal.

And so it was done.

Rab gave a generous guinea 'for the behoof of the poor' and they could not have been more legitimately married. To their surprise, Rab's even more than Jean's, James Armour gave them a magnificent punch bowl in Inveraray marble, of his own making, as a wedding gift, and Rab's friend and patron, Mrs Frances Dunlop, sent a fine heifer, and another friend a plough. Rab celebrated the marriage all over again that night, whispering in her ear that she was his muse, the only one he would ever need, and most certainly the lassie he loved best.

Chapter Twenty-five

Ellisland

Of a' the airts the wind can blaw,
I dearly like the west,
For there the bonnie lassie lives,
The lassie I lo'e best:

There was no doubt about it: Ellisland was beautiful. In spring and summer it seemed picturesque beyond measure. The new house was going to be quite spacious for the home of a simple tenant farmer, so large that its shadow would fall across the River Nith onto the field opposite. There was a good spring to supply fresh water for the household; there was a garden a little way from the new house, and an old orchard, planted some years earlier, with a few still-productive apple trees. There was a riverbank walk, with lush grass and a view of trout and salmon rising to flies in season. A private path led to the folly known as the Hermitage at Friar's Carse. Rab had soon begged permission from Robert Riddell to go there and write in the peace and quiet of the stone-built den. He and Riddell got on very well, their mutual love of books and reading making them instant friends. Ellisland was a poet's farm, sure enough, but even as Jean could appreciate the surroundings and their appeal for Rab, she found herself wondering if that would be enough, if it would be a farmer's farm as well. Of course, she would be supervising the cheese making, and there was the excise work too, which would be reasonably well paid. But he would have to cover a large area, and it would involve a very great deal of riding about the county for Rab, summer and winter alike, while the fields would have to be worked at the same time. She had the occasional twinge of misgiving about it all, about how difficult it might be to keep things going once they were installed here. Nevertheless, she could hardly wait to move.

The room in Mauchline had been a welcome place of shelter for Jean. She was endlessly grateful to Doctor Mackenzie for helping her in her hour of need, and she had come to appreciate it as somewhere to call home, the first establishment of her own she had ever known as a legitimately married woman, but it had never really been more than a stop-gap until she could join her husband in Dumfriesshire.

At first, Rab took shelter with an elderly couple, Davy and Nance Cullie, who lived on the edge of his new farm. Their cottage, if it could even be dignified with that name, was a cold, old, smoky hovel that he could not think of bringing his young wife to live in, never mind his growing son. The floor was of clay, the rafters were all black with soot, for the smoke found its way out as best it could rather than via any serviceable chimney. When the doors and windows were open, the sunlight trickled in as the smoke trickled out, making a sort of misty twilight of the interior. He wrote to Jean that 'every blast that blows and every shower that falls gets in, and I am only preserved from being chilled to death by being suffocated by constant smoke.' He coughed all the time. Davy and Nance coughed too, but they saw nothing unusual about that. Rab fancied they were preserved by the smoke, like a pair of herring. He would sit inside and interview labourers, and he had set up a desk where he could work on a poem or a song when he could find the time, but it was not a place to house his small family.

No wonder, then, that he was glad to ride back to Mauchline and his wife as often as he could, spending about half his time there, reading, writing and otherwise dallying with Jean, playing with Robbie and Betsy Paton's Bess, or visiting friends and relatives. But he had to be in Dumfriesshire to get the farm up and running, clearing stones, sowing grass seed, trying hard to set in train some improvement of the land. He also had to supervise the building of his new house, often lending a hand when a big stone had to be lifted, for he had not lost the strength of his youth, the muscles acquired when he had, as he described it, worked like a galley-slave at Mount Oliphant and then at Lochlea.

Even so, the work progressed slowly. He had called down a blessing on the foundation stone himself, placing a pair of worn leather brogues beneath it for luck. He had ordered the necessary wood from Dumfries. To his embarrassment and secret delight, he had learned that some twenty-four carpenters had gathered around to see the signature of the famous poet on the order. Alexander Crombie was the stonemason chosen to undertake the project. He came highly recommended by James Armour, and he was making a good job of it. Jean would even have her parlour in which to receive visitors, wearing her fine silk gowns and caps, her pretty shawls.

There were other necessities to be ordered and procured, and Jean was excited by the novelty of it all: table and bed linens, better and cheaper bought by the yard and made up at home, so they were advised; cutlery and crockery and a cookery book for Jean – who was not a bad cook – but was anxious to improve, Hannah Glasse's *Art of Cookery Made Plain and Easy*. There were recipes for sweetmeats, for preserving gooseberries and cucumbers, for making haggis and even lip salve. Rab declared that he preferred good plain meat dishes, but Jean was anxious to try new things and Rab – as he had promised so many months ago – had procured a second-hand copy from Edinburgh for her when he was ordering books for himself. He was always keen to extend his own library, even when they couldn't really afford the additional expense.

Alongside all this frantic activity, he was collecting, writing and rewriting songs and always coming home to Mauchline with a budget of new songs that he wanted his 'sweet muse', as he had taken to calling her, to sing for him, so that he could change them or modify them to suit himself. Then he would get down his fiddle and she would sing, and between the two of them they would try this or that melody and this or that version of a song, and she found the whole process vastly entertaining. He never left off praising her voice.

In October, with the weather deteriorating, Rab thought that he couldn't bear to stay in the hovel much longer. If doors and windows had to be kept closed, the air inside would become intolerable. But the house at Ellisland was nowhere near finished. Fortunately, a Dumfries lawyer named Newall came to his rescue, on the recommendation of Robert Riddell, and he was offered a furnished house called The Isle, situated nearby. Although it was a big, chilly place, a house that the Newalls only used during the summer months when they wanted to bring their children out of the fetid town, Jean said that he should take it and she would come and join him. Privately, she thought that if Rab didn't need to spend quite so much time travelling back and forth between Dumfriesshire and Mauchline, unable to resist the attraction of Jeany's warm bed and warm body, the building work might go more quickly, and she was right. Her father had said as much, and he knew all about stonemasons and carpenters and what might happen if they were left unsupervised for any length of time.

Besides, being a clever and capable young woman, she had learned all that they could teach her about dairying at Mossgiel, and she wanted to be off to Dumfries, and living properly with her husband. By December of that year, she had given up the tenancy of the snug room in Mauchline, with all its memories, sad and joyful. Taking wee Robbie with her, her own dear lad at last, she travelled down to Nithsdale. She brought with her her mother's young cousin, Elizabeth Smith, to help about the house, as well as a couple of farm servants from Ayrshire, chosen by Rab and his brother Gilbert. Fanny and William Burness, who were Rab's orphaned cousins, would also be living with them. William was waiting to take up an apprenticeship as a stonemason with James Armour and had offered to help out on the new venture over the winter until the position became available in the spring.

Jean brought some furniture and furnishings with her, packed and roped into a cart, to be stored in the Newall's house until they could be put in the new house: wooden tables and chairs that had been made in Mauchline, the mahogany bed, a long cased clock ordered specially from Clockie Broun, a copper kettle and some kitchen essentials. The family stayed at the chilly Newall house until June of the following year when they took official possession of Ellisland, walking the short distance to the new house in procession, wearing their very best clothes, with Elizabeth Smith in front carrying the family bible and a bowl of salt. Traditionally, a maiden must take possession of a newly built house, and Eliza's father had been so worried about his daughter's innocence and her moral welfare that before he had allowed her to go to Dumfriesshire, he had taken Rab to one side (Rab, of all people! thought Jean) and begged him to keep an eye on her and to hear her catechism regularly. To give Rab his due, he had scrupulously complied with the father's wishes. Perhaps it was a novelty for him to be trusted like this.

Jean herself was very noticeably with child again. Her move from Mauchline to the Newall House had been almost instantly productive, since the chilly old building had meant long nights in the Newall's big feather bed, with Eliza minding Robbie in another room. Sometimes Jean thought that she and Rab had only to look at each other for her to conceive. But she didn't think it was twins again, and this was something of a relief to her, if only in that it might ensure a healthy child.

In the new house, a piece of oatcake was broken over Jean's head, showering her dark curls with crumbs, to the delight of Robbie, who chuckled and tangled his fingers in her hair to pick them out. They drank to the success of the new house and the new venture and, in the evening, there was music and dancing. In honour of the move, Frances Dunlop had sent the very generous gift of a four poster bed with a new mattress, well stuffed with feathers, so the old mahogany and chaff bed could be used elsewhere, for visitors or for their growing family.

It wasn't long before there were other arrivals and departures. Rab's young brother William passed through on his way to learn saddlery in Newcastle. Rab's cousin went back to Mauchline to take up his apprenticeship with James Armour, but his elder brother John came in his stead. There were some ewes, four working horses and nine or ten cows on the farm, including four of the new brown and white Ayrshires that gave such good milk and that Rab had brought with him from Mossgiel, the first to be introduced into Dumfries. And in early September of 1789, there was a new baby to bless the house as well, when Jean gave birth to Francis Wallace, a big, healthy boy, not shy of making himself heard when he was hungry or cold.

By December of that year, and in spite of the comfort of the new house, Rab was ill with a chill and a persistent headache. To Jean's anxious eyes, he always seemed unable to shake off these illnesses, especially in winter, and the dark days did not help him at all. He needed warmth and sunlight. They all did, but Rab more than most. He seemed wretchedly downhearted for no very obvious reason, and nothing seemed to bring him ease, although he seldom lost patience either with his children or with his workers, his natural good nature always asserting itself.

He would have had good reason to be cross.

Wee Frank was howling a great deal, his mouth afire with thrush which he had communicated to his mother, or rather to her breasts, and she could have riven them apart with the miserable itching and the shooting pains whenever he suckled. Rab brought a bottle of wine vinegar back from Friar's Carse, saying that the nursemaid there had suggested it might help, if diluted with water. Jean bathed her nipples and the baby's mouth with a small quantity of it in warm water, and although he screwed up his rosebud lips at the taste, it helped.

In January, Rab was saying that the farm was a 'ruinous affair', but Jean didn't know how else to help. She was already doing so much, while Rab concentrated on furthering his career with the excise, which she supposed made a kind of sense. If the farm failed, they would be reliant on his other work and they wouldn't starve. But between running the house, organising the servants, cooking and cleaning, taking care of the two children, making sure everyone was well fed, and working in the dairy into the bargain, she was as exhausted as her husband. Perhaps more so.

'But I think we must give it another year, at least, don't you?' he said.

'Aye, I think we must. The house is so fine, even if the farm is not. I wish there was some way you could get more money for your work, though, Rab. You seem to spend so much time on it, and folk are always telling me what a great writer you are, what a credit to Scotland, so why does nobody pay you very much?'

'I don't want to be paid for the songs, Jean. I'm proud to do it, and I have a kind of feeling that they're not mine at all, that they belong to everyone. It would be like you laying claim to every song you have ever sung while bouncing one of the weans on your knee.'

'But I'm not sure you can keep working at this pace, between the farm and the excise.'

'No. The riding half kills me in winter, and as soon as I'm recovered from that in some measure, I have the farm again. But we'll give it another year and see what happens. I love it here, love the house, love its situation. I just can't fathom how we can even begin to make it pay for itself.'

Chapter Twenty-six

The Sailor

Then come, sweet Muse, inspire my lay!
For a' the lee-lang simmer's day
I couldna sing, I couldna say,
How much, how dear, I love thee.

Rab was coming up thirty one, Jean only twenty five, with three lost children and two living and cherished, one of them only a babe in arms. That winter and through the early spring of 1790, they gave shelter to a sailor who had come begging to their house door. Jean was working in the kitchen and Rab was reading and writing, balancing on two legs of his chair as he still did, saying it helped him to think, while Jean echoed his mother in threatening to saw off the spare legs with the big kitchen knife, when there was a knock at the door. When Jean opened it, a man in a ragged oilskin coat almost fell onto the flags, and righted himself by clinging on to the wooden press just in time. He stood in the doorway, swaying, his face grey. They could smell the unwashed stench of his clothes and his body, and hear the wheezing in his chest from several feet away. He was asking only for some bread and fresh water, but Rab whispered to her that if they turned him away they would probably find him dead in a ditch by morning.

'But what about the weans? Who knows what sickness he may be carrying?'

Rab acknowledged the truth of this, so he and one of the ploughmen oxtered the stranger into an outbuilding, and they made him up a bed of sorts, covering a heap of straw with a couple of old blankets. Jean did not want his lice in her house, but nor did she want to be responsible for his death. They gave him barley bread, cheese and ale, and that night, Rab took him a bowl of Jean's broth and a measure of good French brandy as well, one of the perks of his job. The traveller kept apologising for the inconvenience. He said his name was Hugh Kennedy and he was trying to get to Liverpool, where he had left a wife and several children some years previously to go on a long voyage in search of his fortune, or at least some money for security in their old age. But upon his return, with no fortune to show for his years away, he had been decanted at Greenock on the Clyde and no ship would take him in his current state of health, even as far as Liverpool, so he must needs walk. Once he was feeling better, he regaled them with tales of the strange sights he had seen in foreign parts, the monstrous whales and other sea creatures, the scented flowers on islands where the sun shone all the time but where dreadful fevers claimed the lives of many men.

Jean found herself thinking about May Campbell, but said nothing. Rab remarked that he himself had once 'planned a trip to the Indies', and the sailor shook his head.

'You would not have liked their ways, sir. From what I have seen of you and your lady and your household, you would not have liked the buying and selling of men and women at all. It is a hard life aboard an ordinary ship, but it is as a paradise compared to the slave ships.'

He stayed with them for six weeks or so, doing odds and ends of work for them as his strength increased, rope work in particular which seemed to be his real skill. He could splice two ends of a rope together so that it was as good as new; you couldn't even see the join, and he said it would last for years. Besides that, he carved a couple of butter moulds for Jean, with flowers, primroses that he remembered from when he was just a lad living in the countryside near Glasgow, and he also made a tiny model of a ship for Robbie, with thread for rigging and sails made of scraps of linen. Later that year, the child took it down to the shallow pools in the

Nith and sailed it there, proudly watched by his mother and father. With the spring, though, the sailor went on his way, calling down blessings on the whole family, promising to send them word of his arrival in Liverpool, but they never heard anything more of him. Jean often wondered if he had found his wife and his children all grown up and changed after the years he had been away, or if some ill had befallen him along the way.

Rab had resumed his correspondence with Nancy McLehose in Edinburgh, after a fashion. Jean hadn't known about it until later, because he hadn't told her until she found it out for herself, coming across the letters as she was attempting to tidy his desk. To be fair, the letters were few and far between. As always when he was low in spirits – and he was very low in spirits and very unwell too, that winter – he sought solace in the admiration of some amenable woman and continued to seek it throughout that year and the next too. Nancy, in her assumed persona of Clarinda, fitted the role admirably, without ever being a real threat to his home life at Ellisland.

In the summer of 1790, feeling better, feeling more like himself again, he composed the long poem he called *Tam o' Shanter*. He told Jean that he had been thinking about it, or something very like it, for some time, ever since he had been a lad staying in Kirkoswald, learning mathematics. He had visited the Carrick shore with a friend; they had been out on the sea in a wee coble, and Rab had been as sick as a dog.

'Douglas Graham lived at nearby Shanter Farm, and he invited us in to recover from the *mal de mer*, handing out drams with great generosity.'

'Did the drams help?'

'Oh aye. They did. But I'll never make a sailor, Jeany. Douglas was very fond of his dram, but he had a fearsome wife. On market days, on more than one occasion, he drank away most of the profits at Ayr. Then, of course, he had to resort to making up stories about being pursued by witches and warlocks to explain his lateness, his dishevelled appearance, his utter lack of siller money!'

'I'm surprised you haven't resorted to that yourself, Rab!'

'Aye, well now that you mention it…' He began to chuckle. 'But I've never forgotten him or his wife!'

He had been mulling over the story for some weeks, but it was as he walked up and down the green lane beside the Nith that the whole tale came together in his mind. As usual with him, he was saying the lines aloud and laughing at his own words. Willie Clark, one of the Ellisland farm labourers, saw him striding up and down, declaiming, gesticulating and almost weeping with laughter.

'He's like ane demented, Mistress Burns,' the man said, rushing into the kitchen to tell Jean about it. 'Are ye wantin me to rin and fetch the doctor fae Auldgirth?'

Jean began to laugh too, but she could see that the man was genuinely alarmed. 'No, no, Willie. Just you leave him be. That's how he writes. He'll have been thinking it all out in his head for days now, and then when the time is right, it will all just come tumbling out of him and he'll be writing it down the whole night long. But he aye has to say it aloud first.'

Later that afternoon, though, it began to rain heavily and she thought that she had better go and fetch him in, because he was quite capable of staying out there until he was half drowned. She took his big umbrella out to him. He opened it over their two heads and they walked up to the house together with the thundery rain bouncing off the cloth.

'Willie tells me you've been reciting a new poem.'

'Oh, I have, I have and this is the best yet!'

He was still bubbling over with laughter when he said, '*Now Tam, O Tam! Had they been queans, A' plump and strapping in their teens! Their sarks instead o' creeshie flainen, Been snaw white seventeen hunder linen.*'

The next evening, once he had it all written down and fixed on the page, as well as in his head, he recited the whole thing for the household, standing up and suiting the actions to the words or sitting astride a kitchen chair and practically bouncing up and down, as though he were Tam himself, the *blethering, blustering, drunken blellum*, riding home from Ayr astride his faithful grey mare Meg, the very model of Jenny Geddes, and encountering more than he bargained for. Jean thought he could have been an actor, but then it struck her that he so often *was* an actor. The more time she spent with him, the more she saw that he showed different faces to different folk. You couldn't pin him down. They had often used that expression as an insult. 'Two faced,' the lassies in Mauchline had said, speaking of this or that lad, one you couldn't trust. A knotless thread who would slide away from you at time of need. But this was different. It wasn't that he deliberately dissembled. It was more that for a brief time, he really was these different people in his own mind. Whatever face he presented to the world was the true one for that time. He believed it himself. It was all too real for him.

When his father reached the climax of the story, young Robbie crawled under the table in fright, seeking comfort from the soft fur and cold noses of the dogs. He would probably have nightmares about the dance of witches in Alloway's auld haunted kirk with *Auld Nick, in shape o' beast*, playing the pipes, and Tam calling out '*weel done, Cutty-sark!*' to the youngest and bonniest of the witches, only just escaping with his life when the whole pack of them pursued him. But at least there was a happy ending of sorts. At least poor Meg *brought off her master hale*, leaping over the running water of the River Doon, even if she did leave behind her *ain grey tail*, pulled off by the youngest of the pursuing witches, Nanny, buxom and fair, in her cutty-sark, her short shift.

They held a dance at their house that summer, to celebrate a visit from Rab's great friend, Robert Ainslie. Jean thought she was expecting again, although it was early days. They were seriously considering giving up the farm when the following year's harvest was done, so in view of Jean's condition and the fact that there would be another new baby in the house next summer, they also thought to take advantage of the season and the long, light nights for a small celebration. They engaged a fiddler, but Rab played the fiddle too, and Jean was still fleet of foot enough to make the best of it, although her waist was not as neat as it had once been. There was no doubt about it, having babies did things to your figure that could not be remedied, not even by tight lacing.

All the same, it was like being back in Mauchline, like the old days at Morton's Ballroom, and Jean enjoyed the occasion very much. She had baked a great store of pies and tarts and cakes on the recommendation and the recipes of Hannah Glasse. Rab invited the innkeeper and his wife from the Globe Inn, in Dumfries, their landlord's gardener, the farm labourers, one or two clerks and their wives, and all to meet Rab's particular friend Mr Ainslie. Jean wondered what Ainslie made of Ellisland and its tenants. He seemed to look down his long nose at her all the time, and she had a feeling he despised her. Ainslie had an estate near Kirkcudbright and an office in Edinburgh, so he would visit them from time to time, whenever he was in the area. Rab loved him like a brother, more so perhaps, so there was nothing to be done about it, nothing Jean could say that wouldn't be misunderstood.

Perhaps he thought that Rab could have done better for himself. Perhaps he believed that Rab should be issuing invitations to his landlord and his gentry neighbours instead of common innkeepers and gardeners. He sat himself down in a corner, refusing to dance, eating and drinking noisily, gazing at the assembled company with a scornful smirk on his face. And yet Rab's own father had been a gardener before he was a farmer. When two of the young farm-hands became loud and argumentative on unaccustomed strong drink, Rab pulled them apart.

'Haud yer wheesht, lads,' he said, 'Get to your beds, or you'll find that I'll skewer you in verse in the morning!'

It was a threat he was well capable of carrying out, and they knew it. He turned from the suddenly subdued lads to grin at Ainslie in his corner.

'Beware of the Bard, eh?' he said, and Ainslie winked and grinned back at him.

Jean sang, when requested, as she always did, and there was enthusiastic applause. Her voice was as clear and pure as ever, and she caught Rab gazing at her as she sang, with that faintly bemused, loving expression her voice always seemed to engender in him. She would have enjoyed it more if Ainslie had not been visiting. There was something about him that she could not like much. It was in the way he looked at her, as though he was privy to some secret information about her, but she couldn't tell what that might be. She sometimes wondered if Rab had told him more about their private affairs than was advisable or even loyal. He was inclined to lose his head where his men friends were concerned and write letters to them late at night, particularly if he had taken a bit too much to drink, and then he would send them in the morning without reading them over first.

But Ainslie was wrong, she thought, when the dance was over and he had gone back to Kirkcudbright: wrong about Rab and wrong about her. There was no doubt about it. Rab was contented when he was fishing in the Nith, wearing his precious fox-skin cap that made him look like a Galloway gypsy and his shabby great-coat belted around him, not caring a whistle who saw him. She had never seen Rab happier than when he was seated at his own fireside, the gentleman farmer, his dram beside him, his children playing on the rug. He never minded the noise the weans made, hardly seemed to hear it. There he would sit with one of the dogs sighing and resting its chin on his knee. More often than not, there would be a book in his hand, something that he could read by the light of a blazing fire. And she herself would be sitting opposite him with a bit of sewing or even some fine needlework, practising what Catherine Govan had managed to teach her on those few occasions when she had not been roaming across the countryside with Rab, making weans.

Chapter Twenty-seven

Golden Locks

Yestreen I had a pint o' wine,
A place where body saw na;
Yestreen lay on this breist o mine
The gowden locks of Anna.

Rab's masonic connections served him well within the excise, and he was promoted in July, just around the time that his poor younger brother, William, died of a fever in London. He had moved there from his position in Newcastle, but they didn't hear about the death until September. The news took a very long time to come north. Jean wished the lad had stayed with them at Ellisland, but he had been determined to move on, determined to better himself. And fevers could strike at any time, wherever you were living. Rab himself was far from healthy. He seemed to be ill with some unnamed sickness or other every winter now, taking longer to get over it each year.

The promotion meant a lot less riding, because he was more or less based in Dumfries, which was a mercy. But this also meant that he had to go back and forth between Ellisland and the town, and sometimes he would stay in the Globe Inn, where there was a congenial host and several good, clean, letting bedrooms. Jean was pregnant, but so, it seemed, was Ann Park, the barmaid at the Globe Inn. Ann was twenty years old, sonsie and easygoing, and didn't seem to mind whether a man was married or not if that man was a famous poet with a wicked eye and a persuasive tongue. The words of the poem *had they been queans, all plump and strapping in their teens* seemed to take on a whole new significance for

Jean. Ann named Robert Burns in Ellisland as the father of her ill-begotten wean, and Rab did not contest the accusation. Somewhat sheepishly, he admitted to Jean that Ann Park had been warming his bed at the Globe from time to time while he was still making love to his wife at Ellisland.

In January of the following year, Rab took a tumble off his horse and broke his right arm, and Jean found it very hard to sympathise with him. She was heavily pregnant now and out of all patience with him, although she mostly held her tongue for the sake of peace and quiet. If she had once started to tell him what she thought of his behaviour at that time, there would have been all out war, and she didn't want to disturb the children in or out of the womb. Besides, the broken arm gave her a good excuse, if one were needed, to leave him alone in the feather bed and sleep with the children on the old mahogany bed. By the end of March, when the arm was healing, news came that Ann Park had given birth to Rab's daughter, Elizabeth, over in Leith. She had gone to stay with her parents there for her confinement.

'Another Betty,' Jean wrote to her sister in Mauchline in exasperation, wondering what on earth was to become of the infant.

Rab had even written a poem about Ann Park: *Yestreen lay on this breist o' mine, the gowden locks o' Anna.* Jean had found it, although he had done little to conceal it. Perhaps he thought she wouldn't even make the connection. She had been angrily ferreting about among his papers when he was out of the house, noticing how he had changed plain Ann to poetic Anna. How like him, she thought, in no very complimentary way.

'Do you really think me so foolish?' she demanded, indignantly. 'Do you think I'm not able to read, Rab? That I don't find it hurtful when you talk about another woman in this way?'

He coloured up, but refused to argue with her. 'It's a poem, just,' he said, shrugging, as though it meant nothing, as though there had been no warm bedroom at the Globe, no child.

Nine days later, Jean herself gave birth to a son, William Nicol, another fine strong boy. It had been a long winter, and she was weary of carrying weans, weary of coping with the farm and the expectations of everyone round about her that she, Jean, would bear all of it as staunchly, as uncomplaining as the Ayrshire cows she milked in the dairy. She was weary of Rab and his propensity for falling in and out of love, his assumption that she would always forgive him, although she could practically hear her mother saying, 'What did we tell you? But you've made your bed, lass, and now you had better lie on it.'

'I *am* lying on it, mother,' she said aloud, as though Mary Armour might be able to hear her, up in Mauchline. She was vigorously plumping up the feathers in their pillows. 'But I don't get to lie on it in peace for very long!' she added. 'I do not, that's for sure!'

The kitchen cat had wandered in. It sat on Jean's nursing stool and watched her complacently through half closed eyes.

'And you can away and catch a few mice!' she said, but the cat only began to wash her face, lazily.

They were planning to give up the farm that autumn and move to Dumfries so that Rab could concentrate on his excise work and his poetry, although he had done nothing, as yet, about finding new accommodation for them. She had a presentiment that nothing they could afford or find in that town would be as spacious, as comfortable, as the house they were relinquishing, although a house in Dumfries would mean few if any nights in the Globe Inn for Rab. A settled gloom descended on her even as her strength returned. Rab didn't seem to notice. He had been writing a letter to his distinguished friend, Frances Dunlop, and – very much pleased with his own turn of phrase – was declaiming to anyone who would listen, but chiefly his wife, how good it was for a man to find a female partner with *rustic grace, unaffected modesty and unsullied purity*, with whom he could share his life.

'After all,' he said, regarding his chosen female partner steadily, a gleam of something very like mischief in his eye, 'we cannot hope for that polished mind, that delicacy of soul that is to be found in the more elevated stations in life, can we, dearest?'

He was feeling hard done by. She had still not returned to his bed.

Jean looked about her. She had the new baby at her breast, and her nipples were inflamed and raw again. The house was a mess, the bed linen was grubby and his shirts were all soiled, or so he had informed her that morning, wondering why no washing had been done. The older children, Robbie and Frank, were squabbling and quarrelling about who owned a small wooden horse with only three legs, and a couple of dogs were growling over a bone beneath the table. The baby had soiled himself again, and was now posseting all over the shoulder of her only reasonably clean gown.

'Delicacy?' she said. 'Oh aye, you're wanting delicacy, are you? Oh my, but your coat's hangin on a very shoogly peg, Rab Burns. Maybe you should tak yourself off to Edinburgh and see if you can get some *delicacy* frae your old friend Nancy McLehose. Or maybe find your way to *Anna of the gowden locks*, down in Leith while you're there, eh? Maybe she'll give you what you're looking for!'

The children howled, the dogs – roused by the anger in her tone – commenced rushing about, snarling. The kitchen cat had leapt up onto the top of the press, claws extended, fur on end. Exasperated beyond all measure, Jean seized a ladle and laid about her 'as lustily as a reaper from the corn ridge' said Rab, later, half admiring, half appalled at the tempest that he seemed to have unleashed. He hadn't realised that she knew so much about Nancy as well as Ann Park. But then he never hid any of his correspondence, so what did he expect? Jean burst into angry tears and rushed off to the bedroom, still holding the baby, who had relinquished the breast, screwing up his face in alarm at his mother's unaccustomed rage.

'Don't *you* start now,' she told him, putting him to the inflamed nipple rather more firmly than usual.

William Nicol looked up at her, then began to suckle again,

sighing with contentment. Feeding him calmed her, in spite of the pain, but she surprised herself by her constant recourse to weeping these days. She knew that it was commonplace after childbirth, but it had not happened with the other weans, or not for so very long, anyway. A day or two later, one of Mistress Dunlop's protégées, a rustic poetess called Janet Little, came to see Rab, bringing a sheaf of her poems to show him. He was away from home and instead, she found Jean, practically drowned in tears. Janet was a tall young woman of somewhat plain appearance, like a kindly horse, thought Jean, at first sight of her. She was dismayed to find Rab's *bonnie Jean* in this state. It was not at all what she had expected. Perhaps she had been anticipating a sort of bardic domestic bliss. To give her her due, she set down her poems, took the baby onto her lap, lent Jean a handkerchief and watched with benign concern while the jewel of them all tried to calm herself sufficiently to offer her visitor the usual hospitality. Once the sobs had subsided and Jean had recovered her equanimity for long enough to feed the baby, the two women drank tea together and ate pretty much the whole of a fruit cake that Mistress Dunlop had sent particularly for Rab.

'He'll never miss what he doesn't know about, will he?' said Janet Little, comfortably.

She must have reported back to Frances Dunlop, for by return came a big parcel containing a new shawl, a beautifully trimmed bonnet and a length of very fine printed calico 'for a summer gown, for bonnie Jean.' None of which solved the problem of Rab's tendency to fall in love with any tolerably pretty woman he met, but they certainly made his wife feel a little better.

* * *

In August of that year, Rab sold his last crops as a farmer, but Jean took herself to Mauchline to show off the new baby and the new bonnet to her family. She did not want to be at Ellisland for the sale, and she was still less than happy with Rab, although the harvest had gone well and they got as good a price as any for the crops that year. Afterwards there was the usual celebration, which Jean had also wanted to avoid at all costs. Those attending became very drunk and started to fight, some thirty of them, brawling over small slights and imagined injuries. Some were very sick, not just outside, but inside the house too, with the dogs becoming drunk and incapable on the vomit they were lapping up from the stone floors. Since it was impossible to stop the brawlers without incurring injuries, Rab thought he might as well leave them to fight themselves to a standstill and a stupor, and assess the damages later on. He found it quite amusing, Jean less so when she heard about it. But he had the good grace to clean up, or at least to help the farm labourers and lassies to restore order and cleanliness before the mistress of the house got back from Mauchline.

When she came home from the Cowgate, it was to the thoroughly unwelcome news that Ann Park could not or would not look after her daughter. Her parents did not want to give shelter to the child and had indignantly suggested that the infant should go to her father. Perhaps they would have felt differently about a son. Sometimes, these days, Jean would lie awake and think of how it might have been if she had stayed in Paisley and married Rab Wilson. He was a kind man and she had no reason to think he would have changed. In fact, from what she heard of him, she knew that he had not changed, but he was very happily married. The twins would still have been born, and Rab Burns might well have wanted to keep Robbie. Sons were generally more valued than daughters. They would have argued about it, and he might have won. But she would have kept baby Jean, and the child would not have been in Mauchline, might have lived and grown. She thought, 'if wishes were horses, beggars would ride' and she still couldn't quite picture herself married to Rab Wilson, couldn't picture the everyday reality of it. But she could dimly imagine that she might have been contented with him as she was seldom contented with her husband these days.

'What will we do, Jeany?' Rab asked. He was unusually contrite. 'I ken fine it's an imposition. A burden on you. And I'm very sorry for it. But I can't see my wean destitute, can I?'

Jean couldn't see any wean destitute either. Was that a virtue or a failing? She didn't know; only knew what she felt in her heart was the right thing to do. As soon as arrangements could be made, she travelled all the way to Leith to bring the infant back with her. She had plenty to say about it though, most of it wrathful. She was reminded of Tam o' Shanter's wife, *nursing her wrath to keep it warm*. She could not help but think about the three girls she had lost: Jean, and then the twins. The coincidence of the birthdates of William Nicol and Ann Park's Betty, so close, both Rab's children, was very hurtful. At first, she vowed that Betty should be kept separate from her own children, should spend all her time in the kitchen and not mix with the others, and Rab agreed. He would have agreed to almost anything at that time, in an effort to keep the peace. The very air of the house seemed poisonous, with his wife scolding him constantly and his own guilt eating into him.

When Mistress Dunlop praised her for her preternatural Christian forbearance in the face of her husband's impossible behaviour, Jean only said, 'Oor Rab should hae had twa wives,' in her broadest Mauchline. It might have been impolite, but it was true. He *should* have had two wives, or even a whole harem of them, like an Eastern potentate. Then he might have been happy, albeit exhausted, and she wouldn't have had so much cleaning and washing and cooking to do.

With the time for leaving Ellisland rapidly approaching, he had managed to secure them a first floor tenement in the Wee Vennel, not for nothing known as the 'stinking vennel' in Dumfries. It stank because an open sewer ran right down the middle of the street and into the river. There were three rooms, of which only two were of decent size.

'It's temporary,' he said, noting the disappointment on her face at her first sight of the place, its cramped rooms and unhappy situation. There was a bawdy house at the river end of the street, and the river flooded all too frequently in the autumn and winter months, bursting its banks, bringing disease with it, although on the upper floor they should be safe enough.

'This is no place for the weans,' she said, and he agreed.

'But once we're here, Jean, we can surely look for somewhere better.'

Dumfries had its attractions. It was a prosperous town, larger than Mauchline, with inns, banks, wealthy town houses, a new theatre, the assembly rooms where balls were held, attractions in plenty for those who could afford them; pretty walks beside the river for those who could not. And there was plenty of work for an exciseman.

She consented. What else could she do?

At least their household was smaller than it had been at Ellisland. The farm servants had found other positions. To their surprise, Fanny Burness had agreed to marry Jean's brother, Addie, having met him while she was visiting her own brother in Mauchline. Both Rab and Jean were forced to admit that the affair had been good for Addie who seemed to have grown in stature and good sense on account of it. He had become a much pleasanter young man than either of them might have anticipated, and Fanny had moved to Mauchline to be close to him.

The excise position would ease their financial worries, there was money from the sale of their stock, and reasonably bright prospects for the future. Rab promised that he would soon find them somewhere much nicer to live. Meanwhile, in the November of 1791, they moved into the Wee Vennel: Jean, Rab, Robbie, Francis, and babies William and Betty, squeezing in as best they could, trying to make the most of it. And at least it would be warm through the worst of the winter. Jean did not want Rab in her bed, but there was nowhere else for him to go, so she turned her back on him and put the big bolster between them.

'You'll drive me mad, Jeany,' he said. 'I cannae even touch you, let alone make love to you.'

'Good enough. Besides, what else can you expect? This is a terrible lodging. We were better off in the Back Causeway, in Mauchline.'

In December, Rab was relieved to be in Edinburgh on song-writing business, leaving Jean alone with the four children. While he was there, he met Nancy McLehose again. Clarinda, as he was still calling her, fondly gave him a lock of her hair, which he sent to a jeweller's on Princes Street to have set into a ring. Upon his return, Jean, who knew something of his previous dalliance now, came across the ring where he had left it incautiously on his desk. She recognised the hair for what and whose it might be, not because she knew for sure, but because she was no fool and it only served to confirm her suspicions. He was so open about it all, not even bothering to dissemble.

She threw it at him. He caught it. He couldn't help himself, although it might have been better to let it lie.

'Ken, Rab, if I see it in the house again, I'll put it on the back of the fire. And I have to say, I wadnae be at all unhappy to see you follow it, just at this moment!'

His utter lack of propriety, of regard for her, appalled her. What on earth would people think? The notion of an Edinburgh jeweller recognising Rab – as the man was bound to do – placing the hair in its setting, greeting him with a smile of complicity, angered her as nothing in her marriage, so far, had. Not even Ann Park and her baby. She had been deeply hurt by his behaviour. Now, pure, unadulterated rage possessed her.

'Get rid of it, Rab, before I dae!' she added, slamming plates onto the table, ladling his stew onto one of them, slicing bread vigorously with the largest of the kitchen knives.

He put the ring in his pocket, ate his meal without comment, stealing a glance at her every now and then.

Apparently he believed her, or perhaps the kitchen knife persuaded him, for she never saw the ring about his person again, although she assumed that he carried it close to his heart for a little while at least. Nothing, she thought wretchedly, was ever close to his heart for very long at any one time, although she found Nancy more of a threat than May Campbell or Ann Park had ever been. Or was it simply that forbidden fruits were the sweetest? The fact that the affair had never been properly consummated – if Rab was to be believed – left him free to imagine what might have been, what might yet be. As long as it remained so, he would still fancy himself in love with Nancy, after a fashion.

She took the children and went to Mauchline, where her mother and her sisters pointed out that she, Jean, was the only one he had loved enough to marry, which was true. But was it enough? She was not quite so blinded by her love for him as to think his lack of faith, his broken promises, excusable. In fact, she loathed his behaviour, could not excuse it. But having made her bed, she knew that she must lie on it. There were no alternatives. She was forced to admit that *Ae Fond Kiss*, so unashamedly written for Nancy, was a very beautiful song, one that, had it been written for anyone else, she might have been happy to sing for him. But if she had not been sure that he had several copies and knew it by heart, that might have gone on the back of the fire as well.

She returned to Dumfries where he seemed very pleased to see her.

'I thought you might be gone for good, Jeany,' he said to her.

In January came news that Nancy had embarked for the Indies in pursuit of her errant husband, James McLehose, leaving her children with his married cousin Elizabeth at Kittochside, near Glasgow. Jean was elated. Rab was faintly despondent, but not quite as low as might have been expected. His wife had removed the bolster but was still giving him the cold shoulder, turning her back on him at night. If there had been space and another room, she might have stayed out of the marital bed altogether. He delayed looking for anywhere else to live, partly out of his natural tendency to postpone things, partly from hopes of a reconciliation that seemed more likely when they were forced into such proximity. It is hard to maintain a quarrel with your spouse when you are lying spooned together, night after night, especially in winter. Especially when your desire for one another has not quite faded and perhaps never will.

He could have forced himself on her. It would have been a very easy matter. Many men would have done it, and she could hardly have objected. Wives did not object. But he still remembered that time in the stable: the horse litter, the early arrival of the twins, and the shame and sorrow that had overwhelmed him afterwards, the uncertainty, even while he was bragging about it to his friends, refashioning her pain into enjoyment. He would not do it again. If she had fallen out of liking with him, he must wait until she forgave him. He couldn't promise never to fall in love with another woman. Or if he did, it would be a lie, and he seldom lied to her, although he often omitted to tell her the truth and pretended that it was a kind of honesty. He could not write a love song without being well and truly in love. Often he would manufacture that love expressly for the purposes of the song or the poem, but the feeling was real enough. It was just that for him, at any rate, there was a distinction between loving and being in love. Whenever he fancied himself in love with yet another woman, it was nothing like the abiding affection he felt for Jean, that much was certain.

Sometimes it struck her that she ran, like any and all of the rivers or the burns that had inspired him, sure and true beneath everything he did or said or made: poems, songs, especially the songs. He swam in her cool waters, and if he rose occasionally when some mayfly enticed him out of his natural surroundings, what of it? She could understand it well enough, but it didn't mean she had to like it. She didn't like it at all. She had once thought she would always surrender to him, to his desires, thought that she could not resist him, but with the passage of time, she sensed a certain obstinacy deep inside her. It could so easily change into dislike, or – worse – indifference. But not yet. Not quite.

And certainly not where Betty Burns was concerned.

Betty, Ann Park's daughter, was impossible to dislike, and Jean was never one to blame a child for the accident of its parentage. Roly poly Betty was almost toddling now, pulling herself up on pieces of furniture, reminding her inexorably of her lost Jean. She even fancied a resemblance, although Jeany had been the image of her mother and Betty was very fair, like Ann. It was both a pleasure and an agony to her. She watched the fire, the pots and pans, minutely and anxiously, got Rab to cobble together a wooden pen so that the two smallest children could play together and amuse each other, well out of harm's way. And at last she succumbed to the love that was bubbling up inside her. Who could resist chubby cheeks, a smiling face? When the little girl first called her 'mammy', she was lost. It was one of Jean's chief virtues, one that Rab had certainly recognised in her and perhaps even exploited, that she could not bear a grudge for more than five minutes together. It was not in her nature to do it. Soon, Betty Burns was part of the family, and would remain so, Jean's darling, for the rest of her life.

Chapter Twenty-eight

The Deil and
the Exciseman

We'll mak our maut, and we'll brew our drink,
We'll laugh, sing, and rejoice, man,
And mony braw thanks to the meikle black deil,
That danc'd awa wi the Exciseman.

They stayed in the tenement in the Wee Vennel for some eighteen months. To Jean's profound relief, Rab had become friends with Maria Riddell. Maria was Robert Riddell's sister-in-law: young, pretty, talented with words, but well and truly married. He could fall in love with her with impunity. Jean saw that Maria would write to him, entertain him, even flirt with him and generally keep his mind off Nancy. But there would be no love affair, no matter how much he might yearn for one. Maria and her husband, Walter Riddell, were living at Woodley Park, some three miles out of town, but visited the other Riddells at Friar's Carse regularly. She even carried Rab off on a visit to the lead mines at Wanlockhead, a long and rather perilous expedition that fascinated her but thoroughly alarmed Rab. He told Jean later that Maria had been careless of damp and darkness, ruining a pair of gloves on the rough rock surfaces, and surprising even the miners by her bravery. On the other hand, he, Rab, had been almost overcome with the hideous gloom of the place that reminded him of nothing so much as a tomb.

'I was imagining rock falls, and being trapped there, unable to claw my way out, Jeany,' he said. He had had to head for the surface with all speed, and Maria had mocked him about it all the way home.

Maria was clearly fascinated by Rab, as captivated by him as women so often were. Jean admired her wit, her vivid conversation, but could not like her very much. She found the younger woman almost too concerned for her wellbeing, too condescendingly friendly whenever they met, which was seldom. Jean suspected that privately, Maria rather despised her, thought her too simple and poorly educated to be the life's partner of a poet like Rab. Fully aware of her own worth, Maria would never let herself be led into an unwise love affair with Robert Burns, and that was a blessing. She would invariably keep him at arm's length, although she would be very happy to be the focus of his attentions for as long as he was pleased to fancy himself in love with her.

In February of 1792, not long after the Wanlockhead adventure, Rab was involved in a real adventure, when the excise officers had to apprehend a schooner on the Solway. The *Rosamond* of Plymouth, suspected of being employed in smuggling ventures, was lying on the River Esk at the foot of the Sark Burn. The suspicions about smuggling proved to be all too true when the sailors fired on the approaching excisemen and accompanying dragoons, and all while gangs of local people did everything they could to assist the smugglers and hinder the troops. Eventually, the smugglers tried to scuttle the ship themselves by firing one of their own guns down through her side. Then they abandoned their vessel along with most of its contents, and fled as best they could, wading through shallow waters, running over dry sand, struggling through wet sand and quicksands, escaping to the English side of the Firth, leaving the schooner in the hands of the excise: a rich prize indeed.

Rab came home and told Jean all about it, equally full of excitement and illicit French brandy.

'But you could have been killed!' she said, appalled at the idea. 'I never thought the excise would be such a dangerous profession! What would we do without you?'

'There was little likelihood of anything happening to me. In fact we were more in danger from the villagers and tenant farmers who thought we were spoiling their smuggling operations than from the seamen!'

'Aye, well, so much of their livelihood on the Solway depends upon smuggled goods, doesn't it?'

'It does indeed so you can't really blame them. Or the smuggler lads for trying. They were firing almost blind, poor souls. The closer the troops got, the harder they found it to fire down at them and that left the soldiers and us free to board them.'

He had enjoyed the whole experience, that much was clear. It had been more of an adventure for him than the trip to Wanlockhead, and he felt he had acquitted himself well.

'Ach, Jeany, it made me feel like a lad again!' he said suddenly. 'You know that time when you think that nothing can touch you, when you're invincible. You don't think of the future, you just do what has to be done!'

'Aye, I do,' she said. 'I do know what you mean. And I remember.'

That night, she did not turn away from him in bed but moved into his arms, roused by some combination of thankfulness that he was safe, admiration for his bravery and his daring, but mostly in acknowledgement of the affection she felt for him, always would feel for him, no matter what. It was married love, kindly, comforting, immensely pleasurable. And not long after that, another child, a daughter this time, was conceived.

When the Rosamond was mended, refloated and brought to Dumfries, its cargo was sold for a profit of more than £100, some of which went to the excisemen involved. Incautiously, Rab bid for and bought four of the ship's guns and sent them to France, to assist the revolutionaries there: a very foolish move for an exciseman in the employment of the crown. But he was a great one for acting first and thinking about the consequences later. He always had been, and she supposed he always would be.

Elizabeth Burns was born in November of that year. If it

seemed odd to have two Elizabeths in the house, Rab didn't seem to think so and Jean didn't mind. As far as she was concerned, Betty was the name Ann Park had chosen, while Eliza was Rab's choice, and if there was a certain mad defiance about it, she didn't choose to quarrel with him over it. Betty and Eliza they would be. Nevertheless, he remarked that he did not feel at all equal to the task of raising girls. A girl must and should have a fortune of some sort, and they would always be too poor.

'You took me without a fortune,' Jean said.

'Aye, but you were special, Jeany,' he said, meaning it. 'You were my fortune, all and entire in yourself. My precious jewel.'

Who could not love such a man? she thought.

She never ceased loving him, even when she didn't like him much at all.

Rab was writing songs. He wrote *'The Deil cam fiddlin thro' the town and danced awa wi' th' Exciseman, and ilka wife cries "Auld Mahoun, I wish ye luck o' the prize man."'*

And what other *exciseman* to trade could write a song like this? Jean wondered, singing it for him, laughing at it while Rab played the fiddle.

'I expect,' he said, 'that there have been times this past year or twa when you could have seen a *muckle black deil* dancing away with your exciseman, Jeany. Is that not right?'

'Aye, maybe so.'

'I'm sorry. I'm very sorry. I don't ken what gets into me.'

'Oh I think you dae, Rab,' she said. 'I think you ken all too well.'

For a while, at least, Rab behaved himself.

But just when it seemed that they might be settling into a more peaceful family life, his impulsive nature would get the better of him and he would suddenly feel the need to do something extreme and all too often public. Writing songs about devils and excisemen and singing them at official excise dinners was the very least of it. He would be sending carronades to the French government, singing seditious songs in the new Dumfries theatre, being a 'man

262

o independent mind' as he would have termed it. Sometimes he got himself into trouble, all unnecessarily. Perhaps if there had been more schooners full of smuggled goods to tackle, he would have been less inclined to manufacture excitement. Jean alternated between worrying about him and the effects his indiscretions might have on the family, and losing all patience with him. But the wild side of his nature was, when all was said and done, one of the things she had most loved about him, and he was never going to change.

Acquiring French gloves for Maria Riddell on the sly from his excise work was a minor transgression, and Jean turned a blind eye to it, even though gloves were a notoriously intimate gift, one generally given and received by lovers or, as she knew all too well, as wedding favours. He assuaged her indignation by acquiring French gloves for his wife, too, very fine and soft in white kid this time, with insertions of knotted silk in blue. He brought home the occasional piece of lace, a Valenciennes lappet, a length of Alençon trim. His taste in such things was immaculate. It surprised her sometimes that a man like Rab could unerringly put himself into the mind of what a woman such as his wife might appreciate. He still liked her to look pretty and fashionable, to have nice things, even when she had a house and a string of children to tend to, not to mention a demanding husband. He bought her a length of the new gingham fabric for a gown, a rarity in the town and much too expensive, but she couldn't find it in her to protest. How could she censure his generosity towards her? She was uncomfortably aware that he was drinking more than he should these days, because alongside the French lace and the gloves, he had access to the occasional barrel of French brandy. Or was it that he could no longer carry his drink as he once did? Any over-indulgence made him suffer from headaches and unexpected chills interspersed with night sweats so severe that he often had to get up and change into a fresh shirt.

Winter came round again, bringing his usual low spirits. He

would be stricken with bouts of something that seemed a kind of panic. He often shook her awake in the night, beads of sweat covering his brow, asking her if he was dying. She could see no physical cause for it, nothing constitutional, and would try to calm him down, chafing his cold hands, trying to soothe him, pouring brandy for him. When she asked him what he felt like, he could only tell her that he felt very unwell.

'When I look in a mirror, Jeany, it's as though I don't even recognise the person I see there. It's as though I'm a stranger to myself, and then I fall into a panic.'

He had experienced this from time to time throughout his life, but it had come upon him with renewed intensity, and much more frequently, over the past year. Only a measure of the brandy soothed him. Sent him to sleep for a while at least.

In December, he took it into his head to write to Nancy's friend, Mary Peacock, for news of Nancy, wondering how she had fared in the Indies, wondering if she had had the proposed reconciliation with her husband. Mary replied with the news that Nancy had come back to Edinburgh, but the letter arrived when Rab was away from home. Jean broke the seal, read it, resealed it carefully with wax and a taper and then let it slide behind the heavy wooden press where they kept their linen, conveniently forgetting to tell Rab anything about it. It was only discovered in May of the following year, when they moved to a much bigger and better house in the Mill Hole Brae. The men who had come in to help with the removal shifted the big press, and there it was, all dusty, covered in cobwebs and the mysterious balls of grey fluff that collect behind cupboards and beneath beds, no matter how often you take a broom to them.

Mary Armour had been in the habit of quoting the Bible. 'Are you making a man under there, Jeany?' she had said. 'Remember man that thou art dust...'

When the letter came to light at last, Jean feigned surprise and contrition. 'I wondered what had become of that, Rab, but I thought you had seen it and taken it.'

'No. I wasn't aware of it.' He seemed very put out, but what could he say?

'I left it for you. It came while you were away on excise business and I was taking the weans to Mauchline for a week or two. I balanced it on a pile of books, so that you would see it. I thought it might be something to do with your songs or your poems. Perhaps from one of your friends in Edinburgh.'

She looked directly at him, a little smile on her lips. 'I do hope it isn't anything important. I should be sorry if that were the case, Rab. But perhaps it's something that you can mend now?'

He pocketed the letter. 'It's of no great importance, Jeany. You're right. Just a missive from a friend.'

'That's good then,' she said, steadily, surprised at how easy it was to dissemble. Perhaps she should do it more often.

He wrote to Nancy, Jean could hardly imagine with what passion, although she had an inkling, but he visited Maria Riddell too, to discuss life and liberty.

Which was reassuring.

After the three-roomed tenement, the house in the Mill Hole Brae was a model of comfort, a two storey dwelling with room for the growing family and with a modicum of privacy for husband and wife too. There was a good sized room downstairs, two bedrooms upstairs and even a small study for Rab, which was just as well, because when he was not working for the excise, he was collecting and reworking songs for publication by Mr George Thomson in Edinburgh, and to Jean's irritation, refusing all payment for the work. She understood his reluctance, but couldn't approve of it. They badly needed the money.

Willie Muir of the mill had died a little while ago, and soon after they moved into the new house, Muir's widow wrote to Rab to tell him that she was having some legal problems and to ask for his advice. With so many friends who were lawyers, Rab went out of his way to help her.

'They were so very kind to me,' said Jean, who would herself have urged him to help, had he not already been set on it. 'They gave me so much support at a time when I most needed it.'

'Willie was more than kind to me,' he observed. 'He made me see sense. He went out of his way to remind me of your worth. That you were beyond price. Besides which, he taught me that I was my father's son. And I still am, I think.'

'Are you, Rab?'

She was suddenly transported back to that little room in Mauchline, just the two of them, all in all to each other, making the chaff bed rustle and shift beneath their weight, making the chaff bed sing with their passion.

'Oh aye. At least, I am in every way that matters, Jeany. And your Rab, of course. All the rest is meaningless.'

Chapter Twenty-nine

Wood-Notes Wild

Waefu' want and hunger fley me,
Glowrin' by the hallan en';
Sair I fecht them at the door,
But aye I'm eerie they come ben.

In 1793, late in the same year that they had moved to the Mill Hole Brae, Rab had a quarrel with the whole Riddell family, but with Maria in particular. Jean had never been able to wring all the sorry details out of him, but she had drawn her own conclusions. He had been invited out to Friar's Carse to dine, but Jean was never extended the same courtesy. They always used the excuse of the children. Mistress Burns may find it difficult to attend, they wrote, because of the children. And in truth, it was not unusual for a husband and wife to dine out separately. Most of the gentry did it. But she knew full well that they did not want her, not then. They only wanted the literary lion, the performing dog, her husband.

Later, when her situation was different, when she was the distinguished widow of the famous poet, things changed. It amused her that she had become not just acceptable but desirable. Back then she was still the country mouse, the simple Mauchline lass. She was no fool. She knew how to behave in company, when to speak and when to hold her tongue, perhaps more than her husband. But still they did not invite her. Even Rab seemed to think that she would be out of her depths and never demurred about her exclusion. There was a part of her that was relieved, not out of any diffidence or lack of confidence in her own good manners, but because she did not much like these people. She didn't like their superficial polish, their dissembling, their pretensions, their condescension, even to her husband who, she was still firmly convinced and in spite of her occasional fury at his behaviour, was worth ten of them, each and every one. But he couldn't see it, and she couldn't persuade him of it. He must have his heroes. Perhaps all men must. She could only wait for his disillusionment, which she was certain must come.

That night at Friar's Carse, they had got very drunk. Once the ladies had left them, the other men of the party had proceeded to fire each other up to drink a woeful quantity of strong port wine. For some of them, it was habitual and they could hold their drink. Rab was an intermittent drinker and tended to stop just before he became incapable, although he had more than once, over the past year or so, alarmed Jean by his determination to drink rather more than a dram or two, making himself very ill in the process. But she remained convinced that some of the party had acted out of malice, had intended to shame him: the ploughman poet who was getting above himself. One of their number, or perhaps more than one, had suggested a re-enactment of the *Rape of the Sabine Women*.

'What's that when it's at home?' Jean asked him bluntly, afterwards, and he explained about the ancient Romans seizing wives for themselves, and she said, 'Just how many wives does a man need, Rab?'

But it was no laughing matter. They had urged Rab to go first. He had seized hold of his hostess, Maria's prim sister-in-law, Elizabeth, and planted wet kisses on her cheeks and lips. Well, he did not admit to kissing her on the lips, but Jean had her suspicions. The men had found it amusing, the women of the party less so. Jean was exasperated with him. How could he let himself be so patronised by these men and women who seemed to lack the most common courtesy, the good manners that would be found in any tenant farmer's parlour? They had deliberately made a fool of him. Didn't he understand that there was some part of them, however much they professed to admire him, that still thought of him as the curiosity, the dog that walked on its hind legs, the prodigiously ugly fish that should be kept in a cabinet to be taken out and stared at every so often?

He wrote a grovelling and apologetic letter, which Maria and her sister-in-law ignored. When Maria met him in the town, she ignored him, sweeping past him with her nose in the air. Jean had some suspicions that at least part of her anger might be because Rab had chosen to kiss Elizabeth and not her. Perhaps she would have been more ready to forgive the transgression if she herself had been the recipient of the supposed assault. Who knew?

Rab was sad, then hurt, then very angry. He wrote a handful of insulting verses about his one time friend. Jean was forced to admit that it was not like him to be quite so vicious where a friend, and a female friend at that, was concerned. But his pride was wounded. Besides, she could see that he missed Maria, missed her carefree company, their conversations, their shared enthusiasms. And word of the incident had got about the town. He was being ignored by more than the Riddells. When he walked along the street, men who had once been glad to greet him, the minor gentry who had their town houses here, would stride past, heads in the air, refusing to acknowledge him in any way at all. This was Dumfries, not Edinburgh, and transgressions were not easily forgiven or forgotten.

When Robert Riddell died, some four months later, Rab was smitten with useless regret. Why could the quarrel not have been made up? He cared not a jot for the widow who had always rather disapproved of him and his friendship with her husband, but he had cared deeply for Robert as well as Maria. He remembered his time at Ellisland, those woodland walks to the Hermitage, their conversations about books and poems, with great affection. He was sad and sorry. Jean pointed out that perhaps Robert Riddell's incipient illness had something to do with the ongoing quarrel.

'Sick men can make mountains out of molehills,' she said. 'The Robert Riddell you once knew would never have let himself be persuaded to abandon an old friend altogether. Certainly not an old friend like you, Rab.'

He saw the truth of this, agreed with her, but was still down-hearted about it.

To distract him, Jean suggested that he might like to design a seal for himself. He wrote so many letters, so he should have something that signified himself and his work. To her surprise, he set about the task with enthusiasm. It was a new thing for him, to be working with pictures rather than words. He decided that he wanted an image of a shepherd's horn and stock, with a woodlark and a green bay tree. He wanted the stock and horn to look real and took some trouble over it, describing how the instrument he had often heard played, over all his years of farming, was a strange creation, impossible to imagine without first seeing it. But where might he acquire one? He sent letters out in all directions.

At long last, after many enquiries from country dwelling friends and much searching through their cupboards and outhouses, he managed to find one. It was composed of the 'stock', the hollow thigh bone of a sheep, with several holes cut into it, like a flute, and a common cow's horn, cut off at the smaller end, so that the stock could be pushed up through it to magnify the sound. Then an oaten reed was cut and notched into a whistle, just like those he had made as a lad, and still did make for his children, whenever the corn stems were full grown. The instrument was played by holding the reed between the lips, putting it loosely into the smaller end of the stock, holding onto the horn, which hung somewhat bawdily down in front, and blowing, while covering and uncovering the holes in the stock to make the notes. That was the general idea, although the only sounds he could produce from this strange contraption were, as Jean said, 'like a sick ewe,' rather than anything more musical. They were choked with laughter. Rab almost burst his waistcoat buttons, and the children joined in, clamouring for a go and all of them equally useless at producing anything more melodic than a faint, eerie moan.

'Ah dear God, Rab,' said Jean, wiping her eyes on the corner of her apron. 'There's never a dull moment with you in the house.'

But she was touched to see his insistence on the woodlark as part of his seal, and when he told her that as well as '*better a wee bush than no bield,'* he wanted the motto '*wood-notes wild*' at the very top, she couldn't help but shed a tear.

'It's aye you, Jeany,' was all he said, squeezing her hand.

* * *

Jean was expecting again. She wrote to Mauchline now and then, although she had little time for letter writing. She invited her parents to visit, to see the new house. Mary elected to stay at home, which was something of a relief to Rab. He had never quite managed to get over his dislike of Jean's mother, blaming her, in large part, for the mutilation of the marriage lines, Jean's banishment to Paisley and his own suffering. Jean protested that it had been as much James's doing as Mary's, but Rab was not persuaded. James came on his own, seemed delighted with his daughter, with her comfortable little house, with his grandchildren, even with Betty Burns, who was no blood relation, but who had her father's warmth and charm when she chose and who seemed content to add a new grandfather to the circle of her family. He had overcome all his earlier dislike of Rab, and the two men had forged a kind of friendship over the years. If there had been any residual ill feeling between James and his most precious daughter, there was none now. In fact he seemed anxious to maintain the contact between the two households, anxious that his Jeany should never forget about her Mauchline family, her Mauchline connections.

In August of that year, James Glencairn Burns was born, but as the new baby grew and thrived, wee Eliza, their much loved youngest daughter, and the apple of her father's eye, was not as well as she should have been. There was nothing definite, nothing for the doctors to treat, just a failure to thrive, a listlessness, an inclination to fevers and a falling away, no matter what they might do to improve matters.

Ill health seemed to be dogging them, and Jean was doing her best to dismiss an ominous feeling that all was not well. She had always been the chief imposer of discipline among the children, the lawmaker and keeper, the magistrate in the house. Rab was too soft, endlessly kind. As long as they were not cruel to one another or to others, human or animal, he could tolerate all kinds of 'witty wickedness and manful mischief', as he called it. She would keep them in line, within reason, because all her own inclinations were towards kindliness too. But he was ill and – for him at least – inexplicably irritable. She tried to put it down to the weather, the winter that always seemed to make Rab unwell. It had been a snowy year, and there were dreadful blizzards, even in Dumfries where snow was something of a rarity. Rab was away on excise business and became stranded in Ecclefechan because of the wretched weather. When he did get home at last, he took to his bed, complaining of pains and general debilitation. She had never seen him looking so lean, not even when she had first known him, when he had been a young man. Back then, he had been wiry and strong. Now he looked increasingly frail to her worried eyes.

They needed more money than was coming into the house. The political situation was affecting Rab's excise work. England was at war with France, towing Scotland along in its wake, and his income was greatly reduced. Whatever Jean could do to alleviate matters, however well she managed her meagre household budget, it was becoming harder and harder to pay the essential bills and to put food on the table for their growing family. She tried to persuade him to ask for payment for his songs, for all the work he was doing for what she saw as a less than grateful nation, but he would have none of it, and instead, he borrowed money, robbing Peter to pay Paul. She wrote to her father. He helped out. She sang *a hungry care's an unco care* and tried hard to inject no trace of irony into the words.

In the spring of 1795, Rab was more often unwell than not, and the care of the house, the children and her husband, all on a diminishing income, fell fair and square on Jean's shoulders. He had resumed his friendship with Maria Riddell, at first tentatively, but then with something of his old gusto, knowing that he was forgiven. Jean was glad of it. At least it seemed to raise his spirits, albeit temporarily. All good health and good spirits seemed temporary with him these days. He got the toothache, a vastly swollen jaw, an abscess which eventually burst, flooding his mouth with sickening blood and poison. For some days, he could barely lift his head from the pillow. He had the tooth pulled in Dumfries, but the process was agonising, in spite of the half pint of French brandy he had drunk beforehand to dull the pain.

'Jeany, my heart was racing so much that I think I fainted for a few moments,' he said. 'They had to bring me round with more brandy.'

For some time he couldn't even shave, and Jean was treated to the sight of her husband with the dark stubble of a fresh beard, 'like a Galloway gypsy,' he remarked, gazing at himself in his shaving mirror. His face seemed much too thin, pale and attenuated. When they were living in Mauchline, he had written a poem about the toothache, a poem about the hell of all diseases, but this time, he was in far too much pain even for poetry.

His little Eliza, not yet three years old, was failing too. They had done everything possible: consulted with a doctor, who said that he could find nothing constitutionally wrong with her, but that her food did not seem to be suiting her. The child had almost no appetite and would pick at things from her father's plate. She was deeply attached to Rab, more so even than to her mother. She would follow him around, big eyes in a thin face, like some small animal, and whenever he sat down, she would clamber up onto his knee, often falling asleep there with her silky head resting on his chest, her hand clutching his thumb or finger, comforted by the contact with her beloved father.

In the summer of that year and in some desperation, Jean took the little lass to Mauchline, to see if country air and fresh food could do what love could not, but Eliza declined very quickly after that, and died there in September. Rab was too ill even to attend her funeral, but her death threw him into a long period of misery. Jean could do little to comfort him. She would wake in the night with tears on her cheeks and with a sense of something spiralling slowly but surely out of control, an unravelling that, however much she prayed and fretted, she could do nothing to halt.

Chapter Thirty

Flying Gout

O wert thou in the cauld blast,
On yonder lea, on yonder lea,
My plaidie to the angry airt,
I'd shelter thee, I'd shelter thee.

In December of 1795, Rab took to his bed with a fever and dreadful pains that seemed to spread through his whole body. He stayed there, more or less bedridden, until the end of January of the new year. Worried and frightened, Jean sent for the doctor to attend him, even though he said, with some truth, that they could ill afford it. Doctor Maxwell came, diagnosed rheumatism, prescribed a cordial, told him that he must rest and trust to God. He seemed to be suffering from utter exhaustion, coupled with intense pain whether he moved or not. He forgot things from one hour to the next. Sometimes, when he tried to write, he said that even the words would not come. For weeks, he hardly set foot out of doors, only moving between the bed and the fireside, with Jean dividing her time between her house, her husband and the children. Fortunately, she had some help in the shape of a young neighbour called Jessie Lewars, the sister of a fellow excise officer of Rab's. Greatly to her alarm, Jean realised that she was again with child, sickening in the mornings, better as the day went on. It was as though her body had assumed some relentless rhythm and every two years, without fail, however inadvisable, however infrequent their lovemaking, it must produce an infant. She didn't tell Rab, not at that time. She couldn't bear to worry him, sick as he was, and fretting all the time about not being able to take care of the family he already had.

Conditions outside the house seemed to reflect the misery within. The previous summer had seen dreadful weather following on from a harsh winter, and the harvest had been very bad. Now, in the dead of winter, there was little grain to be had in the town, people were going hungry and riots were threatened.

'What a good thing we got out of farming in time,' he said. 'That's something to be thankful for, at any rate.'

She agreed with him, in spite of her regrets about the house at Ellisland, but privately thought that they might have been safer in the countryside, might have found it easier to procure food. It was better when you could grow things for the table, keep a few hens. But nobody could prosper in these conditions. The excise work was equally uncertain, and the rheumatism – the sort of pains that usually afflicted a much older man – seemed to be dogging him inexorably, sometimes better, sometimes worse, but never quite going away.

They muddled through.

With the advent of spring, he seemed to rally, claiming that he felt better in mind and body alike. He still could not work full time, so his pay had been reduced accordingly, but they managed. Essentially, it was Jean who managed, penny pinching here, making do there, and receiving the odd unsolicited donation from her father in Mauchline, about which she told Rab nothing whatsoever, and which James even kept a secret from his wife. For a little while, she hoped that Rab's health would improve significantly, but a fool could have seen that the flesh was falling off him. She would have said that he looked consumptive, although he did not have the cough, the high colour of that disease. And he was still in so much pain.

Again he consulted Maxwell, who asked a colleague for a second opinion. This time they diagnosed the 'flying gout' which seemed only to be a way of describing the sudden and intense pains that moved over his whole body, flitting from one place to another, so acute that they took the breath from him. His very bones seemed to ache, and sometimes he could hardly find the strength to walk from one side of the room to the other. Riding about on excise business was unthinkable. Brandy gave him intermittent relief but inflamed his stomach. At last he settled on milk and a little port wine mixed together, which seemed to soothe him, temporarily at least.

Early in June, Maria Riddell, who apparently did not realise the seriousness of his condition, sent a message to him, asking him to attend an event she was holding to celebrate the King's birthday that coming Saturday. He replied that he could not come, he was too racked with rheumatism even to stand, never mind walk about an assembly room. And no, he told her, he was not even writing.

If he was not writing, things must be serious indeed, and Jean admitted to herself that he was failing day by day, edging towards some terrible precipice. The thought sent her into a panic. She was desperately worried about him, loving him more the more anxious she became, regretting the times when she had been impatient and angry with him. She could not bear to see him suffer. She would lie beside him in the night, in despair, listening to him as he tossed and turned, groaning with the pain of even the smallest movement. An anxious neighbour brought in some goose grease, and she rubbed it into his arms and legs and his white feet, but even the touch of her fingers seemed to hurt him now, and the ointment did little good.

She had managed to acquire a new feather bed to ease the pain of his poor limbs. Their old friend from their Ellisland days, Miss Newall, the lawyer's sister, had begged it from her brother. This, with fine linen sheets and a couple of soft blankets, helped the discomfort, but not much. Sometimes Miss Newall would invite Jean out to tea, leaving Jessie to mind the poet and the weans for an hour or two, but Jean could hardly settle away from the house. Rab knew about the baby now, and the knowledge had thrown him into a dreadful panic. He worried about Jean, he worried about his family, he worried about his poems and his papers.

'There are peddlers, even now, while I live, hawking songs and ballads with my name on them about the streets of Dumfries,' he wailed. 'And they are paltry verses, things that I would be ashamed to set my name to. But what can I do to stop them? And besides, my papers are in such a mess! Jeany, there are poems and songs not fit to be seen. If ought should happen to me, see that they are placed in Gilbert's hands. He'll ken what to do.'

Jean did her best to calm him, told him that all would yet be well. If they could find a cure for what ailed him, he might have plenty of years left to set things in order.

'You're a young man! And didn't your father live for many years beyond the age you are now? Isn't your mother living still?'

But even his voice had lost its timbre, seemed to her worried ears like the querulous tones of a much older man.

The doctors, gravely worried about him, and with some inkling that Scotland's greatest poet was sick unto death, began to suggest other possible cures, even if they were counsels of despair. The water cure was fashionable at that time, spas were becoming popular, but Rab was too sick to travel very far. However, there was a small chalybeate spring down at the Brow Well on the Solway, and they suggested that he might be able to go there. Jean, in the last weeks of her pregnancy, would have to stay in Dumfries. Before he left, as though with a premonition of what was to come, he spoke to the children one by one, patting them on the head, telling them to be good, to behave for their mother while he was away.

* * *

Maria Riddell herself – at last aware of the seriousness of his condition – had arranged for lodgings for him in a cottage close by the well and had even sent her carriage to Dumfries to bring him there. The Brow was a kind of tank into which a spring containing iron salts trickled. He drank the water two or three times a day from the iron cup that hung by a chain near the steps. It was close to the shore, and Rab had to struggle and stagger through dying thrift, the blossoms dry and pinky brown, rustling in the wind like a chaff bed, and then across acres of flat sand, into the water. He was supposed to go in up to his waist, and he was determined to do it, but the waters were very cold, even in summer. When she later visited the place to see it for herself, Jean wondered that he had not died on the spot, his body carried away on the tides of the Solway, like the little freshwater burns that ran into the wider salt waters beyond and left patterns on the surface of the sea. And maybe that would have been better, she thought. Maybe that would have been a fitting end for Burns the Bard, who sang of so many rivers and streams.

Maria, not at all well herself at that time, again sent her carriage to fetch him for a dinner neither of them could eat, and said afterwards that she saw only death in his face. On another afternoon, he visited the manse at nearby Ruthwell, where the ladies tried to pull the curtains to shade his eyes from the rays of the setting sun, but he shook his head and said, 'Please leave them. I fear that he will not shine long for me.'

He ran out of ready money and offered his landlady his precious seal in exchange for a bottle of port wine. He could swallow little else. He said the 'muckle black deil had got into his wallet' but perhaps his seal would do instead. She would not take it, but she filled his bottle anyway. They spoke of flounders. As a lass, the woman had kilted up her skirts and gone flounder trampling on the Solway. Rab said he would have given a good deal to have seen her. She spoke lightly of life in the face of death. Afterwards, she told Jean all about it, and Jean was grateful to her for her kindness, her determined good cheer in the face of tragedy.

He learned that a haberdasher, suspecting that he was dying, had taken out a writ against him for an unpaid bill. It was a relatively small sum, and the bill would certainly have been paid by any number of the poet's friends or relatives, but the news threw him into a panic. Jean wondered uneasily if the threat had cast his mind, confused by sickness, back to those months when her parents had conspired to have him thrown in jail. His illness meant that his salary would be reduced, would hardly be enough to support his family. And he was aware that Jean's confinement was imminent.

He wrote desperately to James Armour, 'For Heaven's sake and as you value the welfare of your daughter and my wife, do, my dearest Sir, write to Fife to Mistress Armour, to come, if possible.'

He sent a flurry of terrible, panic stricken letters: to James, to an unresponsive Frances Dunlop, to Gilbert, to his cousin in Montrose, James Burness, asking for money to pay the haberdasher. He wrote to Mr Thomson in Edinburgh with the same plea. Both Thomson and Burness readily arranged for money to be forwarded, said later that they had had no idea how ill he really was, but it all came much too late. Although he had been ailing for some time, the slide into acute illness happened so quickly that it seemed to take all of them except those closest to him by surprise. He wrote to Jean, in Dumfries. He said that the sea bathing had eased his pains but he could eat nothing. He told her he was glad that Jessie was beside her, helping her.

He called her his dearest love.

He had to borrow a gig to bring him home, like Jean herself when Doctor Mackenzie had taken her to Willie's Mill in disgrace. There was a farmer in Locharwoods, John Clark, who lent him his gig, with a fine gentry horse to pull it, and a man to drive it. He could not have ridden by himself. His landlady, she of the flounder trampling, had persuaded the farmer that it would be a good thing to do and that he would be remembered afterwards for his kindness to the great poet in his last days.

Rab could barely step down from the gig when he arrived home. He was all wrapped up in his plaid, although it was high summer. They had to stop at the bottom of the Mill Vennel that was much too steep for the horse. There had been a shower of rain, and the cobbles were slippery. His face was grey from the pain of the journey. He couldn't stand upright and Jessie, the lass who was helping Jean in the house, had to go out and oxter him in. He was muttering that he was worried about his papers, his poems. He still fretted that he had left indifferent pieces behind and they would be thrust upon the world when he was gone, with all their imperfections still upon them.

They were shocked by the deterioration in him, but Jean most of all. She gazed at him and thought that her heart would break. He looked skeletal, shook and shivered, and seemed in even more pain than when he had left. They put him to bed, and there he stayed, slipping in and out of sleep, or delirium, or both, it was hard to tell, and whenever he slept, they feared that he would never wake again.

Once, he came to himself abruptly and said, 'Don't let the Awkward Squad fire over me!' to Jessie's brother, John Lewars, who was watching at his bedside.

He meant the Dumfries volunteers, of course, few of them very efficient or soldierly. And John reassured him that they would not, but of course, they did.

Jean nursed him as best she could, determined to see her man out of the world, if it was God's will that he should go. But she would not have been able to do it without Jessie's help. Jean could and did sing to him, quietly, as she had sung to all their children, and her voice seemed to soothe him.

Very early on the morning of 21st July, she had been dozing in a chair, so far advanced in her pregnancy that she could not comfortably fall asleep. The child was kicking and tumbling inside her, as it did whenever she rested. Jessie had come in with his medicine and tried to hold the cup to his chapped lips, tried to rouse him a little, but he pushed it away. His face was so thin now that he looked all unlike himself. Even his nose seemed to have become finer, sharper.

Jean got up, steadying herself on the arm of the chair, and took the cup from Jessie. 'Rab, my dear, you need to take your medicine. It'll do you some good, ease the pain, if you can only try to swallow it.'

She sat on the edge of the bed, stroked his forehead gently, stroked the dark hair, shot through with grey. Suddenly, she had the strangest feeling, as though this was all unreal, as though there might be some magical place where she could turn back time, make it all different, if only she could get to it, if only she could reach it. There, he would be as she had known him at first: her strong, young lover, her husband, her man.

He woke at the sound of her voice, or perhaps her familiar touch, gazed at her, raised his head and drank a mouthful of the cordial, coughing at the bitter taste of it. He tried to say her name, recognition in his eyes for an instant, reached out his arms to her and then fell back on the bed.

'Oh Jeany,' said Jessie Lewars. 'Oh dear Jeany, I think he's gone.'

She was right.

Chapter Thirty-one

And Fare thee Weel

Till a' the seas gang dry, my dear,
And the rocks melt wi' the sun;
And I will luve thee still, my dear,
While the sands o' life shall run.

Jean and Jessie laid out the body, washing it lovingly. It was the very last time Jean could touch him, stroke his skin, plant a kiss on his cold cheek. But it only served to underline the profound difference between life and death. Even when he had lain at death's door, there had been something of the old Rab, the man she had loved so deeply, inhabiting this ravaged body. Now, nothing of him remained at all. Not in this sad shell, anyway. She was too exhausted, too shocked for tears, although there was plenty of weeping later. Weeping and worrying. What was she to do? How were they to live? But since the demands of the present were paramount, Jessie took the children out into the countryside round about Dumfries, to gather herbs and flowers to strew in the coffin: late roses, honeysuckle, creamy meadowsweet, gowans. It kept them busy, kept them from worrying about their mother and mourning their father too keenly. Jean watched with the body, only dozing in the chair until they came to lay him in his coffin.

She had wanted to go to the funeral. She had wanted to walk in procession behind the bier, however difficult, however scandalous for a woman, especially one in her advanced state of pregnancy. Gilbert had come from Mauchline and had promised to escort her, even though he disapproved of her decision. The funeral invitations had been sent out in young Robbie's name, as was only fitting. Whether Jean liked it or not, it was going to be a very grand occasion. The night before was showery, but as though in celebration of a poet who had loved nature in all her guises, the day turned fine and sunny just in time for the procession. The showers had washed the streets clean. The town smelled unusually fresh and sweet.

On the morning of the funeral, before she could even dress, her pains began. It was clear that she could not leave the house. An hour after they had come to carry Rab away, her waters broke, streaming onto the stone floor. She went into labour and gave birth to his last son, Maxwell, on the same day. Few people perceived or even cared how terrible that was for her: to be in such pain and distress at that time. Jessie, perhaps, although Jessie had no weans of her own yet. Mary Armour might have offered her some comfort, but Mary was in Fife and word had only just reached her. Rab's heartbroken mother would know what she was feeling. Nobody else. No man would have fully understood the darkness that engulfed her during the hours that she laboured for love of him on such a day.

Jean told only a few people that the night after the funeral, as she lay in their bed, wrapped up in blankets, aching for the warmth of her husband's body beside her, with the shape of his head in the pillow still and a few dark hairs attached to it, he had come to her. The whole house was quiet, Maxwell swaddled in her arms. She had been singing to the new wean until he slept, and she saw Rab coming into the room. He was as bold and clear as though he had still been in life and, she thought, rather more healthy than the last time she had laid eyes on him, a gleam in his eye and a flush of sunlight on his cheek.

She was not afraid.

When had she ever been afraid of him except just that one time, in the stable, in the Back Causeway? Rather she felt the wee bubble of laughter that she had so often felt with him, laughter, even in the most serious of situations, at the general absurdity of everything, even the very worst of things. She looked up at him while he gazed down at her and, in particular she thought, at the baby. Well, why not? He had aye loved the weans best, loved the curve of their cheeks, the soft, vulnerable place at the back of the neck, their perfect wee fingers and toes. Then he shook his head sadly, as though regretting that he could not stay, and disappeared, so suddenly that it seemed like a snowflake, melting away in your hand.

* * *

Afterwards, she was relieved that she hadn't been able to attend the funeral. According to Gilbert, who was in tears, and had to be comforted with Rab's best French brandy, they all came scuttling out of the woodwork like beetles or spiders, to show how much they thought of Rab. There was a procession to St Michael's kirk, not far away from their house. The ill rehearsed band played the Dead March from Saul, with many a squeak and shriek and false note. All those people who had cut him a couple of years earlier, after the quarrel with the Riddell family, turned out to mourn Scotland's Bard, and the Awkward Squad fired numerous volleys over his grave. He would have laughed long and loud to hear them, even though he had begged Lewars not to let them do it.

After a scarcely decent interval, they came about his widow like wasps from a byke, seeking anything that they might acquire or make use of: his poems, rough drafts and finished, his letters, his books, his very clothes if she had allowed them, which she did not. They all wanted something, anything, to remind them of the man they had too often shunned or patronised or underestimated while he was in life. But he was safely dead now and could neither discomfort them nor embarrass them with his challenging presence, and so they were free to worship him or denigrate him, or judge him as they saw fit. She understood it well enough because they had patronised and underestimated her too, still did in many ways.

They were forever telling her that he had promised them this or that poem, but anything would do: papers with his writing on, scraps, handkerchiefs even, anything. She had to conceal his clothes and lock the cupboard doors. She thought they would have taken the very feathers and splinters of wood from their bed, if she had allowed it. She caught one of them, a very respectable Dumfries merchant, actually making off with her husband's big umbrella. The man pretended he had thought it was his own, but not a drop of rain had fallen that day. The sun was shining and nobody was carrying an umbrella. She sometimes felt that if they could have anatomised *her* and taken parts of her away with them, they would have done it without a moment's hesitation.

They told her that her husband had been a great man, which she knew, but with some faults, which she also knew all too well, but which she would never admit now, fiercely loyal to him in death as in life. Somebody wrote in a local newspaper that 'His extraordinary endowments were accompanied by frailties which rendered them useless to himself and his family.' The words were burned into her head and her heart. She could never forget or forgive them. He had been provoking, impulsive and often unwise, but he had never been useless to her, never lacking in affection. And if he could be scornful of hypocrisy, he was also one of the kindest men she had ever known. A good heart, she thought. He had such a good, warm heart. She wished they would all go away and leave her in peace. All except Jessie. Jessie did not desert Jean. She stayed to help with the children. She told Jean, shyly, how Rab would talk to her about her various suitors, for she was a clever lass, telling her that one of them had 'not as much brains as a midge could lean its elbow on!'

'And d'you know, Jean, he was right!' she said, laughing and weeping at the same time. It was good to talk about him. It brought him back into their minds, as though he might walk through the door at any moment.

Jean coped, managed as she always had done. She had no money from her husband's estate until October, but she got a pension of twelve pounds a year as the widow of an excise officer. She had that at least. A benefactor came forward, she didn't know who, but it could be any one of Rab's old friends. She wondered if it might be Dr Mackenzie, but he never admitted it. Whoever it was paid her rent for the house in Mill Hole Brae, and carried on paying it until her financial situation was more settled, so she was secure there. This was a great relief to her. She had always known how to make do with little, but she would have hated to leave the house now, not least because it sometimes seemed to her as though her husband lingered there.

She never saw him again, only that one time after Maxwell was born, and she didn't expect to. She was no great believer in ghosts. But there were times when she felt as though if she were to turn around, he would be there, and times when she woke in the night with the distinct feeling that he was beside her in bed. She could sense the warmth of him, as though he were about to slide his arms around her, or she could feel his breath on her neck, raising the hairs there. She would have been very reluctant to lose these small but welcome visitations. They faded over time, but never entirely left her. Occasionally, she would wake with her whole body remembering him, like a broken fiddle that somehow remembers the notes that once brought it to life. And with that memory always, every single time, came a longing so deep, so strong, that it brought tears to her eyes, a memory of youth and life coursing through her, undeniable, irresistible, the necessity that excuses and explains almost everything about the love between a man and a woman.

After the burial, in a quiet corner of the kirkyard in Dumfries, Jean had her husband's grave covered with a simple slab. It was pleasing to her, and the children could take posies of flowers to place on it, which they did for many years, the flowers he had once loved. When they came visiting, William and Dorothy Wordsworth complained that they could not even find the grave, but Jean didn't much care.

'Those closest to him ken fine where he is,' she said.

Later, a trust fund was set up to support her and her children, and after some deliberation she gave most of Rab's papers to one James Currie, a Dumfriesshire man, a scholar and biographer who had promised to handle them with care. A few had gone missing, snatched by those early predators when she was at her most vulnerable, most grief stricken, but John Lewars had come to her rescue then and sent them packing. She knew that Rab had been worried about his remaining work, distressed that none of it had been set in order, and Mr Currie seemed to be a thoughtful and intelligent man. Gilbert advised her what to do, telling her that nothing would be lost, he would not allow it to be lost, although it might be better if some of it were to be edited. That was the word he used. 'Edited.' She had not quite known what that meant. She could only make whatever decisions seemed best and most sensible at the time and move on. Mr Currie never gave the papers back to her, never even considered that she might want them,

But she had hidden away a slender packet of all the letters that Rab had ever written to her, from Edinburgh and at other times too, snippets of news for her and enquiries about the weans, the odd intimate word of love, the occasional bawdy verse to make her laugh, had hidden them away at the very back of the press, wrapped in a bit of silk and folded into a linen pillowslip. Why should she let anyone else have them? They were hers and hers alone, and in case of illness and death, she had left strict instructions about them and their disposal.

She had not left word with her sons. She loved them dearly, but they couldn't be trusted not to put the demands of their father's sacred memory above the requests of their mother. It was only natural. Nor had she consulted any of his surviving men friends. Instead, she had spoken to a few carefully chosen women friends. They knew what had to be done. These letters, along with his watch with the valentine inside, she kept secret and close to her. She had not told anyone else about the existence of the letters, and so they assumed, foolishly confident, that such letters did not exist. She suspected that some of them did not even know that she had the skill of reading and writing, thought her a fond, foolish country lass, nothing more. She still unfolded them and reread them from time to time, obscurely comforted by his bold hand, by the very ink on the page. After he died, she wore his watch close to her heart for a long time, comforted by its steady tick tock, like a living creature that held some remembrance of the man who had once worn it, who had opened it and glanced from time to time at the hearts and the birds and the initials, R and J, that she had written there.

Maxwell did not live to see his third birthday. Like his sister, Elizabeth, before him, he dwindled before their eyes. In the April of the year when he should have been three, he died as quietly as he had lived. She buried him, and when the minister said that he gave him into the care of his loving father, it was Rab she saw, not the Lord God Almighty. But she knew it wasn't blasphemy. Maxwell was so small, had become so frail before he died, that she felt he might be afraid of God, but he would never be feart of his father and all would be well if his father could be waiting for him, ready to embrace him. Jean's God was kindly but strict, with something of Daddie Auld about him. If she imagined heaven at all, she saw a riverbank, with Rab and Maxwell and Eliza and maybe wee Jean as well, seated there together. Luath too, of course, and he of the footprints on the linen, with his pink tongue and his comical ears. The twins were harder to picture, but perhaps they *were* there, grown somewhat and playing a little way off.

They were in some dell, on the banks of the Ayr or the Doon or the Nith, somewhere among the long grasses, with the flowers blooming and the birds singing in the trees. No midges. She hoped there would be no midges in heaven, or if there were, perhaps they would be content to dance above the water, without feeling the need to nip every other living thing; without, as Rab once remarked, eating the tops off your stockings. And when she pictured this scene, she saw Rab whittling a wooden boat or a toy pistol like the one he made for Robbie, sternly telling him that he must not kill defenceless animals when he was old enough for real guns; making a whistle out of a reed, showing the children how to cut it this way and that, and then putting it to his lips and blowing. Or making them laugh until they ached, with the sick sheep sound of his stock and horn.

A few years later, Francis died of the putrid throat that seemed to infect so many young people. Again, she had a very vivid sense that she was giving him into the hands of his loving father, with whom he would be quite safe, until she could see all of them again.

Chapter Thirty-two

Mr Moir's Portrait

How lang and dreary is the night
When I am frae my dearie;
I restless lie frae e'en to morn
Though I were ne'er sae weary.

It was a crisp autumn morning in Edinburgh, and Jean was staying with Rab's friend, the song collector George Thomson and his family. She was about to sit for a portrait. Mr John Moir, the fashionable Aberdeen artist, was coming to Mr Thomson's house to paint her picture, a great honour. The night before, she had been disturbed to find herself dreaming about her husband again. It was fully sixteen years since she had lost him, and she still had nightmares where he was somewhere else, sick and dying, and she was grappling with some monstrous burden that pinned her down. She was desperate to find him before it was too late. These nightmares came infrequently now, usually when she was worried about one of the children. But this had been more like one of the sweet dreams she used to have when they were separated by place rather than by death, although even those had changed after he died.

There had been so much loving talk about him the previous evening. Perhaps that had inspired her sleeping visions. In the dream, she was riding with him instead of waiting for him, heading towards Mauchline. She could feel the warmth of his body behind her, and the movement of the horse beneath her. She looked up and she could see the sweet curve of Corsincon in the distance and she said, 'Not long now. We're almost home.' But at the same time she knew it couldn't be true, the hill was further away, near

Cumnock, and they would only see it if they were coming all the way from Ellisland. Inexplicably, this distressed her. She thought about the child. In the dream, she remembered that she had lost a child, she had lost more than one, and what would he say about that? She was beset by a sensation of panic. She must stop, change things, do things differently. There was still time. She felt a sob rising in her breast, and perhaps he felt it too.

'It's all right, Jeany!' he said. 'It's all right, my dearest love.'

His hand was on her knee, caressing her, moving higher.

It was so real, so vivid for a brief moment, that when a log settled down in the grate, she woke with a start, calling out, leaning back into the space where he was not, desperate to return to sleep. For a few years after his death, this dream, or something very like it, seemed to come to her almost weekly: always with the mare, Jenny Geddes, always the sensation of being held by him, encompassed by his arms, always the sorrow and the worry about a lost child or lost children and the moment of reassurance. She couldn't have said whether the sensation of him holding her was worth the disappointment of waking, the feeling of loss and panic that was a part of it all, that inevitably accompanied it.

The city was disturbing for all kinds of reasons: noisy, stinking, busy, although the new street where she was staying was quiet and respectable. Thomson was a kindly man, and he and his wife had been very welcoming. He played the fiddle and encouraged her to sing, praising her voice, 'Rab's muse' he called her and she was grateful for that, because the men of letters seldom acknowledged it. Some years after her husband's death, the great and the good had put up a statue of some strange marble woman who appeared to be flying over her husband, and they had called it his muse. She had noticed that the plough was bigger than almost anything else about the memorial, as though the plough counted for more than he or she or any of them. She thought that they should have made him with a book: a wee book in his hand instead of this strange female, striking a preposterous pose. He had never been without a book, even at meals or on horseback. Besides, she knew with absolute certainty, that *she* had been his muse, real flesh and blood, warm and yielding, not this cold marble woman with her smooth, impossibly white skin.

They were very mindful of her comfort in Mr Thomson's house. The bed was almost too soft, a big feather bed that enveloped her like a cloud. Mistress Thomson's little dog had taken a fancy to her and managed to inveigle himself into the room. He jumped up on the bed and cooried in and she couldn't find it in her heart to push him away. The warmth of him was comforting, and she lay with the creature nestled close, glad of the company in the unfamiliar bed. Laughter drifted up from the street outside. Hoofbeats came and went. The silky dog was snoring in her arms. She couldn't help but smile that she should have come to this: fine clothes, a feather bed in a rather grand house, her portrait about to be painted, and a wee dog in her arms.

The following morning, Katherine Thomson's maid helped her to dress in the clothes that she and Mistress Thomson had chosen together: a fine undergarment with a black silk gown over it, lutestring silk, of course. There was a lacy bonnet to soften her face and a grey silk shawl.

Mr Moir, the artist, was excited, curious, engaging. She could see that he was positively bursting with all the questions he was too polite to ask. She suspected that if only he could, he would have painted her husband. That she was second best for him. Everyone who came to her house in Dumfries, knocking on her door at all hours of the day and night, from spring through to autumn and even in the depths of a dreich West of Scotland winter, would rather be meeting her husband. Failing that, she would have to do. Nothing would change that now. If anything, the feeling grew more intense with each passing year, as though they clung to her as she aged, a living relict of something precious that they had scarcely known how to appreciate at the time. She was a focus for their regret as much as anything else.

John Moir was ready for her, showed her how to sit just slightly facing him, making sure that she was comfortable. He told her that he doubted if he would be able to finish the portrait before she had to go home to Dumfries, but he thought that he could make plenty of sketches and then he'd be able to complete it in her absence, whenever he could find the time. While he sketched, he asked her questions. At first she was afraid to answer, for fear of spoiling the picture, but he told her that it was fine to speak and he'd be happy to listen. It helped him to know about her, so that he could paint her as she truly was, and he would tell her if she needed to be still for a while. Sometimes they would stop for tea, with platters of petticoat tail shortbread biscuits, sweet and melting, a speciality of the house. Sometimes he would tell her to get up, move about.

He asked her about herself.

She was so surprised by this, just at first, that she was embarrassed by the question. People sometimes asked about her children, but they seldom asked her about herself. Folk only really wanted to know about her husband, and their real reason for speaking to her was her intimate, nay her embarrassing knowledge of the poet. There was always the smallest edge of prurience to their enquiries. She knew exactly what they wanted to know, and yet propriety demanded that they ask only harmless questions. That may have been why there had been so many offers of marriage: dreadful offers from wholly unsuitable people, most of them. There had been unimaginable proposals from elderly widowers with avarice in their eyes. Not for money, because she was not a rich woman. But for stories and secrets. For wanting to go where the poet had been. *My tocher's the jewel*, she thought. Her tocher, her dowry, was her memory. They wanted the answers to the questions they dare not ask, but she met them all with the same blandly courteous rejection.

Mr Moir was different.

'Tell me a little about yourself, Mistress Burns,' he said. She flushed. What could she tell this young man that wouldn't seem either foolish or scandalous? But a certain amount of scandal had been attached to his own name, or so Katherine Thomson had told her while she was dressing. He said, 'No, no, nothing about your husband. I'd rather know more about you. Tell me about your childhood. Tell me about when you were just a girl.'

And that seemed perfectly possible. Afterwards, when it was all finished, she could hardly remember what she had spoken about and what remained locked inside, because the words and the lines of John Moir's sketches had all flowed together into a single story, like all the tributary burns running into the rivers, leaving their patterns on the landscape of her life.

That night, she lay awake again in the comfortable room with the dog asleep at her feet. He stood up, turned around three times and lay down again, sighing heavily and resting his chin across her ankles. She could feel the warmth of him through the blankets that smelled nicely of lavender. Her mind was busy with the past, images and conversations swarming like bees in there. Another sitting tomorrow, and if she didn't get to sleep soon, she'd likely shame herself by dozing while Mr Moir was sketching.

She thought about that time at Paisley with Rab Wilson visiting her each week and bringing her tentative news from his family in Mauchline, but nothing from Rab Mossgiel. Since her husband's death, she had read some of Rab's letters to other people from that time: letters about her. Gilbert had begged her, with as much intensity as he ever displayed, to ignore Rab's correspondence from the time of their separation, but she had read it anyway. She had thought she knew everything about Rab, but they had amazed her, those letters. She had been shocked by the raw passion in them. The letters had brought it all back and more besides, had told her things she had never known or even guessed about the depths of his feelings for her. Some of those letters seemed to be the correspondence of a madman.

She saw that he might have made a hundred defiant decisions and resolutions, renouncing her for ever, telling himself that he had replaced her in his affections, falling in love, falling out of love, even going so far as to tell other women how much he despised her, but these all seemed to fall flat in the face of his compulsion to see her, to touch her, simply to be with her. There would always be that foolish, hankering fondness, that miserable blank in his heart for lack of her. She did not know why it should have been so, any more than she could explain her fixed attachment to him in the face of her family's disapproval and his bad behaviour.

'Never man loved or rather adored a woman more than I did her. And I do still love her to distraction after all, tho I won't tell her so, tho I see her, which I don't want to do.'

So he had written. He had been as mad as a hare in March. But he had loved her and desired her hopelessly and helplessly. There had been nothing she could do or say to change that essential fact. He had written to one of his friends, amid a tissue of nonsense such as she had never read the like of in her life before, and would scarcely have believed possible if she hadn't seen the words on the page, that he was 'nine parts and nine tenths, out of ten, stark staring mad.'

She had been retrospectively anguished to read it. If she had known this, she might have responded differently, might have moved heaven and earth to write to him, once it became possible, via Rab Wilson, to reassure him that she was being faithful to him, had been faithful to him all the time. But he had written to everyone but her. She wondered if he had given a single thought to her and her predicament at that time, so absorbed was he in his own injuries. I, me, myself. His letters were so completely self absorbed that there seemed to be no room for anyone else, not even Jean. Couldn't May Campbell have seen it? Well, maybe she had seen it, and maybe she too had been clutching at straws of hope, struggling to find a way out of her infatuation with James Montgomerie, who was undoubtedly head over ears in love with somebody else. Maybe just as Jean herself had thought, 'why *not* Rab Wilson?' before coming up with a dozen reasons why not,

May Campbell had been thinking, 'why not Rab Burns as well as any other man?' but had been incapable of imagining the reasons why it would never do.

* * *

The following day, the tea was served with buttered scones and cheesecakes. She couldn't have made better herself. They chatted of this and that, mostly how Mr Moir's work was going and his new studio, of which he was very proud, and his forthcoming exhibitions, of which he had high hopes. People always confided in her. Her children said that it was her own fault, she had a face that invited confidences, a kindly manner. Mr Moir had endured some problems with his family in Aberdeen. They were not happy about his career as an artist. They had disapproved of his trip to Italy in particular.

'I went there to learn all about life drawing, with real human models. Oh, Mistress Burns, you can have no notion of how much that alarmed my mother!'

'Naked models!' his mother had said, with something approaching horror. 'But what could you expect from a Papist country?' she had added, *sotto voce*. Mr Moir was laughing as he told the tale, and Jean chuckled with him, but she could see that he had been hurt by his family's response and still was, hurt by their lack of understanding of what drove him, what he loved to do above all other things.

'Parents don't always understand,' she said, mildly. 'But they often come round in the end. You have to give them time.'

'You wouldn't have been shocked, would you, Mistress Burns?' he said, putting down his cup and preparing to resume his work.

'No. Perhaps not. Although I can remember a time when I might have been. When I was very young and knew little about the ways of the world.'

'But you know more of the world now?'

She could see that he was teasing her and, to be sure, she mustn't look very worldly-wise to such a well-travelled man: a matronly woman whose only concerns involved her home and her children.

'Mr Moir, it's true that I'm leading a very quiet life. Or trying to. But even now, the world beats a path to my door, I'm afraid, in all its greed and all its indifference and its insatiable curiosity. I thought it might have died down, and it has, a little. Better in some ways, worse in others.'

'People can be very cruel,' he said.

'Unthinking,' she said. 'But yes, cruel too. A few months before my husband died, they would cross the street in Dumfries to avoid him, those fashionable people for whom he had become something of an embarrassment. He knew it, you know, he knew it himself. And that still hurts me on his behalf. He knew that it was all over, the adulation, the praise. The solution was obviously death, whereupon they realised what they had lost and they wanted him all over again, just when they couldn't have him.'

'You sound very angry about it.'

'I *am* angry about it still. I don't think that anyone could have saved him. He was a very sick man. Sick unto death. You could see it in his face. There's no denying that look. I've seen it even in the weans I've lost. You try to deny it at first, but then it becomes impossible. But they could have made things easier for him, could have given him a wee bit more...' she searched for the right word, 'affection. I think I mean simple, commonplace affection. They could have given him a wee bit more affection in his last year.'

'Then you do right to be angry, Mistress Burns.'

'Do I? I don't know. Bitterness is seldom useful. I had to find a way of accommodating it all and living my life as cheerfully as possible at the same time. For the sake of our children, if nothing else. But it's been hard, I'll allow.'

'I can see that you've succeeded.'

'I think I have. But it's a weary business. And now ... now they are shaping his image to suit themselves. Making a God of him. He was a fine man, an exceptional man, but when all's said and done, he was a man, just.'

Moir resumed his sketching, and Jean fell silent. Those words resonated in her mind. 'Bitterness is seldom useful.'

She thought again of May Campbell. She could put the thought of that lassie out of her mind for years on end, but back it would come and she couldn't say why, when there had been others, much harder to forgive. Perhaps it was that May had been a victim, a sacrificial lamb in more ways than one. Even though the girl had been dead for so many years, even when Jean knew the truth of it all and could easily guess what she didn't know for certain, she found it hard to forgive Highland Mary who was not Mary at all, but May frae Dunoon with her soft voice that sounded so sweet and so foreign. Her winsome ways. Her spurious innocence. Well, perhaps it had been real innocence after all, and not assumed. Who could ever know? There were people who had judged Jean just as harshly, and more of them perhaps. She felt the flush rising to her cheeks at the remembrance, and Mr Moir looked at her anxiously.

'Are you well, Mistress Armour? We can stop soon. There's always tomorrow.'

'No, no. I'm quite happy to sit here. Just you carry on.'

'Well, if you're certain?'

'I am, Mr Moir, I am.'

Chapter Thirty-three

Nancy

I'll ne'er blame my partial fancy,
Naething could resist my Nancy;
But to see her was to love her;
Love but her, and love for ever.

She was on her last sitting for Mr Moir. He had said that he didn't
know when he might finish the portrait, because he had other,
more pressing commissions, and she had to go home to Dumfries,
but he would complete it when he could, and exhibit it when it
was finished. That night, there was going to be a gathering of some
sort to which she was bidden with her host and his family: people
who had once known her husband. She was anticipating it with
some trepidation. But she had been told that James Hogg might be
there, and she was very fond of Mr Hogg.

Hogg, who wrote poems and novels, was a plain-speaking man
who seemed to have a genuine regard for her. He had visited her in
Dumfries, ostensibly to speak to her about her late husband whom
he professed to admire above all other poets, all writers. They had
become friends, and it had struck her more than once that there
was a softness in his eye when he looked at her, even though he
was some five years younger than she. He played the fiddle, like
Rab, better than Rab if the truth be told, and he liked to hear her
sing, admired her voice that could still carry a tune as well as ever.
Once or twice, he had played the fiddle and asked her to sing her
husband's songs. His particular favourites were hers too: *O Were
I on Parnassus Hill* and *Red Red Rose*. She could still reach those
impossibly high, soaring notes. He always finished with *The Deil's*

Awa' with the Exciseman, playing with what her old singing teacher used to call *brio*. It recalled Rab so vividly to her mind that she hardly knew whether to be glad or sorry about it. But she had spent one or two very happy evenings in Mr Hogg's company.

She had been told that he was living in Edinburgh now, pursuing a literary career, and that he had two daughters by two different women, which Jean could not find it in her heart to censure. She had been looking forward to meeting him again, but her visit to the city was almost over and this would be her last opportunity for a little while. She sincerely hoped Mr Hogg, with his kindly face, his shock of dark hair and his abrupt, countryman ways, would be at tonight's gathering. She was always careful not to overstep any boundaries of propriety where he was concerned, perhaps the more so since her liking for him was genuine. She felt at ease with him.

At the gathering that night, Jean was made to sit on a sofa in solitary splendour, on display, so to speak: the Bard's widow. It was an unenviable position for a shy woman, but she was reminded of her husband saying that he was like a dog on its hind legs, or an armadillo. People were brought to be introduced to her. This was what royalty must feel like, she thought, nodding and extending her hand and saying a few kind words. And once again she felt inappropriate laughter bubbling up inside her. It was like being bitten to death by midges. They nipped at her constantly. Sucking at her blood, hoping that some of it still had a little of the essence of the Bard left. Which, of course, it did.

Mr Hogg was there and he, at least, was a friendly face. She was relieved to see him. But then, they were bringing somebody else over to meet her, a small woman, something around her own age or perhaps just a little older. She was stylishly, almost fussily dressed, too much lace, a curly wig, a bonnet that looked somewhat too big and too fancy for her birdlike features, dwarfing them. Too much rouge, thought Jean. The woman was smiling at her, a fixed grin, extending hands like tiny talons. The scent of roses, faintly cloying, overwhelmed her.

'Mistress Burns, may I present Mistress Agnes McLehose,' said her host, and Jean was aware that Hogg was hovering in the background with a ludicrous expression, something between outright horror and barely concealed amusement on his face. And she did what she had always done, behaved kindly, extended her hand, said, 'I'm very pleased to meet you' and motioned to the woman to sit down beside her.

Nancy McLehose. Clarinda to his Sylvander, all those years ago. The fragile shepherdess and the handsome shepherd. Poor Nancy had not had an easy life. Jean knew all about her: the husband who had charmed her, married her against her family's wishes, treated her cruelly and who then abandoned her, going off to the Indies. James McLehose had managed to win over his reluctant bride by the simple but effective expedient of booking all the seats on a coach between Glasgow and Edinburgh so that he was alone with innocent Agnes Craig for the whole long journey, by the end of which time they were engaged. Her family had disapproved of him, and her family had been right.

A good woman.

Rab had always stressed what a good woman she was. So pious, in fact, that she had resisted most but not quite all of Rab's advances. And Jean knew just how difficult that must have been. Once, in Dumfries, she had coaxed it out of him. He had been unwell, and a wee thing fuzzy and compliant with medicinal drink, and they had been cooried up in bed together. Jean had asked him exactly what had gone on with Nancy in that room in the Potterow during his time in Edinburgh.

But he had hesitated, even then. 'You don't want to know, do you?'

'Aye, I do. There's been so much talk. I want to know the truth of it. You owe me that, at least, Rab.'

He had paused, then whispered, so as not to wake the children, 'No very much, Jeany, if I'm honest, if the truth be told. No very much at all. A kiss and a cuddle. Well, more than one. We made ourselves very hot and very happy. She thought it was a great sin to sit on my lap and let me kiss her and fondle her, even though I knew fine she was enjoying it. But she held back. And I darena push it, darena tak it any further, for I kent fine in the morning she would regret it bitterly, and that would have been the end of our meetings and the end of our correspondence. At that time, when I thought you had forsaken me, it seemed to be all that stood between me and madness.'

He had meant, of course, that it would have been the end of the affair that he was inventing and shaping, playing Nancy like a fish on the end of his line, working on her as he might work on a poem. But he had been no match for Nancy's religion, for her piety and her stern friends admonishing her for her bad behaviour: the scandal of a married woman, even one separated from her husband by distance and inclination, dallying with a ploughman poet. Jean wondered if Nancy had ever regretted her resistance.

'Nancy McLehose has been dining out on her supposed love affair with your husband for years,' Hogg had once told her, not without a certain amount of indignation. 'She cherishes his memory far more than that of her own husband, and no wonder.'

Had Nancy hoped and prayed that James McLehose would fall victim to one of those fatal foreign fevers, Jean wondered. The same sickness she herself had feared might strike Rab, if ever he had gone to the Indies. Had Mistress McLehose hoped for a convenient widowhood while Rab was still available? While he was still fulminating against Jean, vowing that he would never marry her now, not even if she came crawling to him in her shift. But then what sensible person could ever picture Nancy in the dairy at Ellisland, milking the cows and making sweet milk cheese?

'She went to the Indies, you know,' Hogg had continued. 'I suppose it was a last attempt to reunite with James McLehose, because her friends had persuaded her that it was the right thing to do, but of course she found that he had taken a mistress.'

Jean had known a bit about this, but not the whole of it, until

Hogg told her.

The mistress in question had been a slave who had borne him a daughter. Nancy was shocked, but even more revolted by his cruelty to the enslaved workers. He was a violent man in all possible ways. And a drunkard. Coming to her senses, she had turned around and sailed straight back to Scotland on the same ship, complaining of the heat and the insects rather than her husband's appalling behaviour.

Gazing at this plump little bird of a woman, Jean could see that the flutterings that must once have seemed deeply attractive in a young woman, the uncertainty, the studied vulnerability, had become habitual. Nancy could not help herself, her garrulous manner, but these ways did not sit very well on a woman of fifty, just as the too-youthful dress, cut low over an ample bosom, did not sit well on her either. Even so, it was quite impossible to dislike her. There was a warmth, an enterprise and a good nature about her that was irresistible. And a woman who could travel alone, all the way to the Indies where Rab had never dared to go, find her man in bed with another woman, turn on her heel and sail home again to pick up the threads of her life in Edinburgh, must have a certain strength of character. Jean was never done with admiring the unexpected strength of women.

So she summoned all her natural generosity of spirit and asked Nancy how she was and how her family was and even, heaven forgive her, found herself saying that her late husband had often spoken of Mistress McLehose with affection, reminiscing about their friendship in Edinburgh and how much he had valued it and how much of a support he had found it at a time when he was sorely in need of companionship. She could see Nancy blossoming under the attention, but also looking at her with something like disbelief, wondering if Jean could really be so foolish, so simple, so ignorant of those passionately loving letters, the poems, the gifts, the songs. And realising almost immediately, that it wasn't possible. That Jean may once have been a simple country lass, but no longer.

What made Jean so kind?

They gazed at each other and a sudden flash of understanding passed between the two of them, two women who had loved the same man, in different ways, loved him, known him, and been disappointed in him. Two women with an inkling that in some sense, they were heroines. That he had known how heroic they were and praised them at least in song.

Her prentice hand, she tried on man, and then she made the lassies-o.

Nancy pressed Jean's hand again. 'You're very kind,' she said and meant it.

Jean smiled, a little enigmatically to be sure. 'I have had to learn to be kind over the years.'

'No. I think you always were kind and good and better than...'

Nancy had almost been going to say, 'Better than he deserved.' But she stopped herself just in time. The thought, unspoken but obvious, lay in the air between them.

'All we can do is be kind to one another. Isn't that the truth?' said Jean.

'It is. For sure.'

When Nancy took her leave not long after, she asked Jean if perhaps they might take tea together. If Mistress Burns came to Edinburgh again, perhaps they might meet up and take a cup of tea and Jean agreed. Why not? They had at least something in common. Quite a lot in common. The folly of loving the same man not wisely but too well, the chief of it.

Later, Hogg said, 'I'm truly astonished by your forbearance,' but there had been no forbearance involved at all. Perhaps if things had been different in the end, she could have found it in her heart to hate Nancy. She doubted if they could ever become close friends. But why shatter somebody else's dreams? Why not leave Nancy to the harmless enjoyment of a passion that seemed to have outlasted everything else in her life, a vivid dream from which this woman never quite seemed to have awakened.

Chapter Thirty-four

The Drizzler

O, were I on Parnassus hill,
Or had o' Helicon my fill,
That I might catch poetic skill,
To sing how dear I love thee.

Some two years after Jean had sat for Mr Moir in Edinburgh, and
when the new monument was complete, they exhumed the body
of the poet and of his two sons, Maxwell and Francis. The monument had been funded by subscription, and the Prince Regent
himself had subscribed to the project. Jean could almost hear Rab
laughing uproariously.

'Good God, the Prince Regent paying for my tomb! How we
are come up in the world, my Jeany!'

Nobody had asked her opinion, of course. They had told her,
expecting her to be proud and pleased. If they had asked her permission, she might have wished, demanded even, although she had
never been in the habit of demanding, that they leave his poor
bones in peace. And the boys too: Francis and wee ailing Maxwell.
Why couldn't they let them rest where they were? What did it
matter whether there was a monument or not? What did it matter how much it cost to build? Her friends and neighbours were
indignant on her behalf, but she had given up being resentful years
earlier. Save your breath to cool your porridge, as her father used
to say, and her father had been right.

She heard later that they had done the deed at midnight, like
the ghouls they were. That was her first thought, and although
she knew it was ungenerous, unworthy of her, she couldn't help

it. Later still, somebody had told her that when they opened his coffin, his face and figure seemed momentarily as they had once been. But it was a brief, ghostly illusion, shattered by the movement of the coffin, so that the image collapsed into its component parts: bones and dust and hair. She was very glad that she hadn't been there to see it.

* * *

The other children lived and thrived. Some of Rab's old friends wanted to send the boys to the grammar school in Ayr, but Jean wouldn't have it and stubbornly refused their kind offers of help. She wanted to keep her children by her and to stay in Dumfries. Robbie was a clever lad, telling anyone who would listen that his father had been no rustic ploughman poet, but an educated man, which was nothing less than the truth. He went to Edinburgh University, then to Glasgow, and thence to a position in the Stamp Office in London, which did not suit him so well. He wrote poems, but more out of a sense of duty to his late father than from any real inclination. William and James became soldiers, joined the Indian Army and did very well for themselves. James married out there in India, but two of his children died young and his wife followed them while giving birth to a third child, a daughter named Sarah. When she was old enough to travel, this little girl was sent to Scotland to stay with Jean.

In 1828, an artist called Samuel Mackenzie painted a portrait of the two of them, grandmother and granddaughter together. Mr Mackenzie was by no means as congenial as Mr Moir and the portrait, competent rather than sympathetic, depicted Jean with only the remnants, a faint shadow, of the prettiness that John Moir had seen in her face some sixteen years earlier. She looked her age: plump and handsome still, but with a face somewhat marked by sorrow and suffering. Even while they were sitting for the portrait, with Sarah fidgeting and anxious to be gone, Jean wondered what had become of Mr Moir's portrait and why he had not yet finished it.

For this new picture, she wore a smart bonnet under which her iron-grey hair curls still softened her face, a fine shawl and a good silk gown. Rab would have been pleased to see her so well dressed. Sarah perched beside her, the very image of youth and health, an elfin face over a white muslin gown, the height of fashion, with puffed sleeves, ribbons and lace, and pretty pantalettes beneath, as befitted her girlhood. She loved that dress and could hardly be persuaded to take it off at night. Only the promise of an equally pretty nightgown comforted her. Her hair was as short as a boy's, and one arm was propped around her grandmother's shoulders. The other hand held a tiny bloom, picked only a few moments before and twirled between her starfish fingers: a dandelion head, with the seeds just ready to be blown away, telling time. The artist asked Jean to hold her spectacles, and placed a heavy book beside her, which he seemed to think signified her husband in some way, clever men being fond of weighty correspondences, although as soon as they were done sitting, Jean was blowing on the dandelion and making her granddaughter laugh. Which was precisely what Rab would have been doing as well.

A few years after Mr Mackenzie's harsher depiction, and quite unexpectedly, John Moir came to show Jean his finished portrait. He felt guilty at the tremendous delay. He couldn't explain it, save to say that the years had galloped by – 'So they have,' she said – and he had been busy with many other pressing commissions. She suspected that he had become aware of her advancing age and frailty, and had decided that he really must finish her portrait before she joined her husband.

It was a very beautiful picture.

It reminded her of a time when she was still a desirable woman, bonnie and buxom, a reasonably wealthy widow. She had not been lacking in suitors over the years, but she had turned all of them down. How could she ever be sure that any of them liked her for herself alone and not as a living mausoleum to her husband? How terrible to creep into bed with a man who wanted you for your secrets and memories rather than for yourself. Besides, she had wanted no other man. She knew that it was perfectly possible to love more than once. She had friends and relatives who had married two or even three times. But it was not for her. She had always told Rab that he was the only man for her, and it was the plain truth. It would have been all the same, whether he had been Scotland's Bard or a tenant farmer. It would have made no difference to her enduring love for him.

If there had been one surprise, it had been this happiness, this unanticipated contentment. Over almost all the years of her widowhood, she had been as happy as it was possible for a woman to be, and she had seen no reason whatsoever to change that, to give any other man power over her. She had made a great many faithful female friends and enjoyed their companionship enormously. They walked along the Nith in spring and summer, took tea together, listened to music. She was very well respected in the town, increasingly so with every year that passed. She had many visitors to the house in the Mill Hole Vennel, and she treated them all with the same courtesy and kindness, showing them the poet's chair, the poet's bed that was also her bed, the poet's toddy ladle and his painted china punch bowl. They gawped and asked foolish questions and begged for souvenirs, things to take away with them, but she refused them all.

'Everything that could be given away has been given,' she said, politely. 'This my home now and these are my possessions.'

She kept fresh flowers in the windows in spring and summer, and was amused to find that some visitors surreptitiously plucked the blossoms from them, perhaps to press between the leaves of a book. But apart from her official role as widow to the great poet, there had been plenty to keep her busy over the years: visits to Mauchline, to Gilbert and his family now living in East Lothian, to Ann Park's Betty, to Mr and Mrs Thomson in Edinburgh.

She even, on one visit to the capital, kept her promise to take tea with Nancy McLehose. They drank out of fine china cups and ate exceedingly fancy cakes together and discovered that they got on rather well. They had more in common than they could ever have supposed, including a liking for pretty clothes, jewellery and pictures. They spoke of silk scarves and embroidered stockings and the very latest fashions in shawls and gloves.

But there was more to be said, and at last, they came to it.

Back in 1802, Jean knew that a volume of her husband's intimate 'Letters Addressed to Clarinda' had been published, but almost immediately suppressed. She asked Nancy about it.

Nancy blushed, rested her little hand on her breast. 'Oh my dear Mistress Burns, it was a great betrayal! A friend of a friend, John Findlay, asked if he could borrow them from me, and I very foolishly agreed.'

'Oh aye. They love to *borrow* from us, don't they? But their understanding of the term is not the same as mine. When I borrow, I generally intend to give back.'

'We are far too trusting. Why do we ever trust men? I trusted Mr Findlay. But he handed them over to a certain Mr Stewart, in Glasgow, telling him that he had my permission, and he saw fit to publish them. I was mortified, I assure you. But I had influential friends back then, and the letters were returned to me, the books mostly destroyed. I suppose a few copies are still in existence. Findlay told me that I could have made some money from the publication, but I simply could not do it.'

'Which is greatly to your credit,' said Jean. 'I know something of your story, and things must have been hard for you during those years.'

'They were. But then, you yourself have never lived in the lap of luxury, have you? And yet here we are, we two, surviving!'

'Here we are indeed.'

Nancy even confessed, to Jean's utter astonishment, that on a few occasions, when funds had been sorely lacking, she had sat in the theatre behind some well dressed man, or sidled up beside him in some crowded assembly, and had taken the liberty of snipping a small amount of gold trim off his costume. Jean had heard of such things but had never known anyone who had actually dared to do it.

'You mean you were a *drizzler*,' she whispered, and Nancy put her finger to her lips and giggled like a girl.

'I suppose I was! But is it any worse, I wonder, than picking and poking and prying at the memory of a great and wonderful man?'

It was a serious crime, but Nancy had never been caught. She showed Jean the tiny scissors she used to keep in her pocket, and now kept in her reticule for more legitimate purposes, scissors in the shape of a bird with a needle sharp beak.

'You know, if you wear a deep lace frill at your wrist, they never notice the blades in your palm!' she said. 'They're too busy with their eyes on your breast. Or they were, back then. My figure is not what it was. But rich men are such easy prey. Picots were good. Dangling spangles were simple. Such rich pickings, Mistress Burns. I used to conceal the bits and pieces in my sleeves, once cut, and then transfer them to my pocket. And do you remember there was a fashion for gilded acorn trims one year?'

'I do. I thought them very fine.'

'So quick to snip. Fringes too. There was one young buck who wore medallions of beaten gold with cupids. I had two of them. Well, to tell the truth, I have them still. I could not bear to send such wee cherubs for melting.'

'What did you do with the rest?' Jean asked, intrigued.

'Took them home and teased the gold from the silken thread. There is a skill in that too. Most of the men were none the wiser. I'm sure they thought that their embellishments had fallen off. Blamed the poor seamstress.'

Jean had heard that there were women in Edinburgh to whom you could take all these bits of gold, once you had amassed enough of them. It was very much a woman's trade. The scraps would be weighed and cash would be paid, with the gold eventually being melted down and put to other uses. New trims, perhaps. The money had, so Nancy confessed, helped her to escape absolute penury on more than one occasion.

'But you don't do it now, do you?' Jean pressed her.

'No.' She shook her head, sadly. 'I think I would not risk it. I'm too old to be able to distract them. They do not like to gaze at me as they once did, and my fingers are not as nimble as they once were.'

'Oh, Mistress McLehose!' said Jean, torn between disapproval and a sneaking admiration at the woman's enterprise.

'Well,' said Nancy, licking her finger and picking up the last crumbs of her cake. 'Men so often deserve it, don't you think? Some of them, anyway. Peacocks. Strutting about in all their finery! Expecting us to fall in with their plans and schemes. Expecting us to agree with them and worship them and love them in spite of everything.'

'I suppose so. But it depends a good deal on the man, you know.'

'Och, you're right, Mistress Burns, it does, to be sure.'

'I'm very much afraid I could never say no to Rab.'

'Oh *I* could,' said Nancy. 'More's the pity.'

She looked at Jean, biting her lip, wondering if she had gone too far.

And then they laughed until the tears ran down their cheeks, and called for more tea and perhaps just another slice or two of that delicious cake.

It was true though. Jean could never have said no to Rab. Very few women could say no to Rab. In fact, she rather admired Nancy McLehose for her strength of character or possibly her piety, very much belied by the drizzling. But perhaps she had simply been fearful of the consequences where Rab was concerned. Jean had almost no regrets. One or two. She regretted that she had not been stronger. She regretted the names cut out of the paper. Still wondered if, had they been safely married and living at Mossgiel, wee Jeany might have lived.

Ah but her memories were rich, rich beyond imagining.

She still found herself dreaming of her husband from time to time, his blue coat, his plaid tied just so, not like the others, a fact which had so annoyed her poor father at first, his bonnie black hair curling down on his collar, his fine dark eyes, glowing with life and merriment, his smile, his way of making you laugh even when you thought you might be going to cry. His gentle hands that knew how to give you so much pleasure. His nose in a book. His poems. His songs. Especially his songs.

'Sing to me, Jeany,' he would say.

That night, in her dream, she sang:

Tho' I were doom'd to wander on,
Beyond the sea, beyond the sun,
Till my last weary sand was run;
Till then — and then I love thee!

And she woke, with his song on her lips.

Historical Note

In 1996 I was commissioned to write a radio play about the creation of Robert Burns's epic poem 'Tam O' Shanter'. This was followed some years later by a stage play called *Burns on the Solway*, about the last weeks of the poet's life. Both plays turned out to be as much about Jean Armour as they were about her famous husband, and that realisation prompted me to tackle a full-length novel. There is a vast amount of information about Robert out there but considerably less (and perhaps even more misinformation) about his wife. Too many Victorian scholars seem to have been content to maintain the fiction that in marrying Jean, a reasonably prosperous stonemason's daughter, the poet was somehow marrying beneath him. Even Catherine Carswell in her controversial but supposedly ground-breaking 1930 *Life of Robert Burns* is content to describe Jean as a 'young heifer', while making invidious comparisons between Jean's 'homely and hearty willingness' and Highland Mary's 'delicacy of spirit and a capacity for sacrifice to which Jean would always be a stranger.' From a twenty-first-century perspective, and with all the benefit of detailed research focusing on Jean herself, it is clear that nothing could have been further from the truth.

The couple's mutual attraction must have owed at least something to Jean's superb singing voice, coupled with her intimate knowledge of the traditional songs of her country, handed down to her by her mother and her grandmother. Many of them were songs dealing with women's preoccupations and predicaments, their joys and sorrows. Her husband said several times that she had the 'finest wood-note wild' in the country. When the poet came to design his personal seal, perched over all is a lark with 'wood-note wild' written above that, a motto which seems to refer to his abiding love for his wife. She supplied many of the traditional versions and even the melodies for some of her husband's finest songs, magically reworked by a master of the art.

Put this together with the poet's good humour and his willingness to empathise with the opposite sex (even when his behaviour didn't match his apparent understanding) and you have the basis for an attachment that seems perfectly reasonable. Such an ability was a rare gift in an eighteenth-century man, especially one as rakish and charming, as essentially *laddish* as Rab, and goes some way towards explaining his singular charisma. If I could still feel the warm blast of it, more than two hundred years later, there was no hope for Jean, but there is every indication that the abiding affection was mutual.

For anyone who wants to take the subject of Robert and Jean further, to tease out the facts from the fiction, I have included a select bibliography. The field of 'Burns Studies' is vast and complicated, including many meticulously researched biographies and research papers. It is easy for the casual enquirer to grow weary of dry facts, *chiels that winna ding*, in Rab's own words, lads that won't be beaten, forgetting that we are talking about a fine and frequently emotional poet with a personal story so romantic that, were it to be invented by a novelist such as myself, it might well prove utterly incredible. From the time they first met, Jean was never absent from that story for very long.

In imagining late eighteenth-century Mauchline in particular, I owe a great deal to another fine writer, John Galt, in his beautifully crafted and occasionally hilarious early novel about rural Ayrshire life: *Annals of the Parish,* and to Professor Alan Riach for bringing Galt so vividly to life. Biographies of Burns are legion, and most are well researched and interesting, but for a readable, thought-provoking and scholarly exploration of Rab's life, it would be hard to beat Robert Crawford's *The Bard*. Nor is the author shy of expressing his opinion that Jean was better than her husband realised, or possibly even deserved. His account of the women in Rab's life was particularly helpful to me. James Barke wrote an excellent and well informed series of novels about the life and times of Burns, but it is also worth seeking out his forthright and intelligent essay on Burns's bawdry in his 1959 edition of *The Merry Muses of Caledonia*, now updated by Valentina Bold.

Many old accounts of Burns's life and times are available in digitised form, online or as print on demand volumes, including a fascinating account of Robert Burns at Mossgiel, with reminiscences of the poet, and incidentally of Jean, by his herd boy, Willie Patrick, published in 1881, but collected by William Jolly some years earlier. The best sources are, as ever, primary sources, the poet's own work in particular. You should read the poems and songs, as well as Burns's notes on them, for as vivid a depiction of eighteenth-century Ayrshire and Dumfriesshire – and the milieu in which Rab and Jean lived – as you will find anywhere. The poet's letters are entertaining, intelligent, mercurial and occasionally explicit. Also worth consulting is the *First Statistical Account for Mauchline for 1791–1799*, written by the Reverend William 'Daddie' Auld himself. Extracts from the kirk session minutes of the 1780s are available online, and the Ayrshire History website (www.ayrshire-history.com) is an excellent resource, with the Mauchline section containing a wealth of evocative old photographs that – with only a little imagination – allow the viewer to recreate the town as Rab and Jean must have known it.

With regard to Highland Mary Campbell, whom the Victorians in particular seemed to wish to idealise as the poet's one true love, their liaison was surprisingly short-lived. There is, in fact, no proof that she was engaged as 'wet nurse' to Gavin Hamilton's son, as she is in the novel, although it is true that she was employed as nursemaid in the Hamilton household for a scant few months, in between spells as dairymaid at Coilsfield. There is, however, a certain amount of evidence that she was conducting an illicit affair with Hugh Montgomerie's younger brother James, who was definitely involved with Eleanora Maxwell Campbell at the same time.

There are a great many recordings of the poems and songs of Burns, and preference will be a matter of personal taste. I listened to the late Jean Redpath's extensive collection of the *Songs of Robert Burns*, which includes the beautiful and the bawdy, and everything in between, all sung in a pure, no-nonsense voice that seems to evoke Jean Armour, and with helpful notes about the history and background of each song. But there are many recordings and all are well worth exploring. Andy M Stewart's available recordings of Burns's songs are some of the best interpretations I have ever heard.

Little of Jean's own correspondence survives, although it's clear that she was literate. We have a scant handful of letters from the poet to his wife, touchingly domestic, extraordinarily loving. In fact, it seems very odd to me that so many commentators have been blind to just how much and how deeply he loved her, and was willing to tell her so.

The life stories of Rab and Jean's surviving children are only peripherally a part of the novel, but are well worth investigating. I was particularly intrigued by Jean's grand-daughter, Sarah, who lived with her grandmother for a while as a little girl. Extraordinarily, Sarah would live to see another new century and only died at the age of eighty-seven, in 1907. She and her husband lived in some splendour in Cheltenham. Throughout her long and distinguished life, Sarah remained indignant, furious even, at the treatment of her grandfather and her much-loved grandmother at the hands of all the men of letters who flocked around Jean after the poet's death. She was particularly angry that the letters and papers that should by rights have belonged to Jean and the Burns family were never returned. She was passionately defensive of her grandfather, feeling that his memory had been tarnished by faint praise and by an over-emphasis on his failings at the expense of his many virtues. This is a judgement with which Jean herself would have been in complete agreement.

There are, of course, various museums associated with Burns and all are worth visiting. The Robert Burns Birthplace Museum in Alloway and the nearby cottage that William Burness built for himself and his wife, and where Robert was born, are an excellent starting point for an overview of the poet's life and times, with a number of engaging artefacts, many of them associated with Jean herself. The rooms in the superb Burns House Museum in Mauchline, where the couple began their married life, are also deeply atmospheric, as is the Globe Inn in Dumfries and the Robert Burns House, now a museum, in the same town. Ellisland itself, little changed, is magical, and if you are going to see the ghosts of Rab and Jean anywhere, I fancy it will be there. The Ayrshire and Dumfriesshire countryside, the fields and woodlands, rivers and streams the poet and his wife knew and loved are, in essence, not much changed, and there are plenty of places for daydreaming, plenty of quietly beautiful corners where the past seems very close indeed.

My aim in this novel has been as much accuracy as is consistent with a fictional account. Everything either happened, or could have happened. The casual reader might be surprised by what is documented fact and how little is invention, but if he or she finds it hard to distinguish between the two, I will be very well pleased.

Catherine Czerkawska

Glossary

agley awry

airt direction, especially wind

ajee ajar

auld licht traditional presbyterian

Auld Nick the devil

aye I'm eerie they come ben I'm afraid they'll come in

babie-clouts baby clothes, sometimes swaddling clothes

back-style back stair, outdoor staircase leading to upper floor

back-yett back gate

baldeirie (sometimes beldairy) the green winged orchis with aphrodisiac properties

bannock large flat bread, often made from oats or barley

bawbee small coin

beastie small creature, often but not always an insect

bield shelter

birl whirl, spin

bishop weed ground elder

black affronted very embarrassed

black fit go-between, matchmaker

blaeberries bilberries

blaggard scoundrel

bletherin, blusterin, drunken blellum a chattering, blustering, drunken idler (from 'Tam o' Shanter')

braggart boaster

brambles blackberries

braw pleasing

brogues leather shoes

burr prickly seed head

but 'n ben single storey two-roomed cottage

ca' canny work slowly

chaff husks of corn (or oats in Scotland) used to fill mattresses where feathers could not be procured.

change house tavern

chuckie stone small pebble

clappin caressing

clegs horseflies

clouts often (but not exclusively) menstrual rags

coatie short coat

collops sliced meat

compeared summoned

coo cow

coorie snuggle

crack to me my lane talk to me alone

creeshie flannen dirty flannel

cronies friends

crowdie cream cheese

cruisie oil lamp with rush wick

cuckold husband of adulteress

cutty sark short linen shirt or shift, commonly worn by women, next to the skin.

daffin foolish behaviour or behaving foolishly

delft pottery

dram measure of whisky

drappie drop

dreich dreary and bleak, mostly of weather

drystane dry stone, as in walls

dyvor rogue, good-for-nothing

faither father

fause house false house, specifically, space within a corn stack

feart afraid

fidgin fain sexually aroused

fley frighten

for the behoof of on behalf of

fou full, drunk

gang go

gar make

gey very

glowrin glowering

gowan daisy

gowden golden

graip large fork (often for digging potatoes)

guid good

hair halter halter of woven hair, low-quality harness

hale sound

hallan en a kind of porch

haud yer wheesht be quiet

havrel halfwit

houghmagandie fornication

ilka every

interlowper incomer

jurr skivvy

kale kind of cabbage

ken/kent know/ knew

knotless thread feckless man

lad o' pairts young man with prospects

laverock sky lark

leal loyal

lintie linnet, songbird

loofs lies

loun lad

lutestring silk high quality, glossy silk

maut malt

mavis thrush

meikle black deil big black devil

midge or midgie the tiny but vicious mosquito-like insect of Scotland

nabbery gentry, colloquial Ayrshire

ne'er do weel vagabond, rogue

oslin old variety of dessert apple

oxtered took by the elbow

peely wally pale and ill

plaid or plaidie long and heavy woollen wrap, worn by men.
  Lowland plaids were often black and white check or in Burns's
  case, a fashionable autumn tint called feuille morte, or dead leaf.

prentice apprentice

pulling tongues sticking your tongue out at somebody, pulling
  faces.

quean young woman

reck heed

reticule small handbag

sair sore

schaws potato stems, including the section lying in the ground

seventeen hunner unit denoting quality of the weave in textile

shift woman's loose-fitting undergarment, worn under the stays,
  for comfort

siller silver, usually money

skellum rogue

sonsie jolly, plump and pleasant (originally meaning lucky)

span old measure, hand's width

spleuchan female pudendum, literally small pouch

stang to wound, in this case to carry astride a wooden pole

stumpie drugget short and made of coarse linen

swee swinging cast iron arm upon which a cooking pot could be
  hung over a fire

syne since

tent pay attention

the feint a (the devil a) emphatic negative

thole suffer, bear

toddy whisky, lemon and sugar

toun town

unco remarkable

unkend unknown

waeful want woeful poverty

wanton wander carelessly

wark work

wean child, especially in Ayrshire, although bairn is also used

weel well

weel (wael) a deep river pool

whaup curlew (**a whaup's in the nest** expecting a baby)

whin gorse

your coat's hangin on a shoogly peg (literally, your coat is hanging on a wobbly peg) you are on shaky ground

Bibliography

Jean Aitchison. 2001. *Servants in Ayrshire, 1750 – 1914*. Ayrshire Archaeological and Natural History Society.

AANHS Collections. 1959. *Ayrshire at the Time of Burns*. Ayrshire Archaeological and Natural History Society.

James Barke. 1959. *Bonnie Jean*. Collins.

W F Blair. 1922. *An Octogenarian's Reminiscences*. Kilmarnock Standard.

Alan Bold. 1992. *Robert Burns*. A Pitkin Guide.

A M Boyle. 1985. *The Ayrshire Book of Burns-Lore*. Alloway Publishing.

Nancy Bradfield. 1968. *Costume in Detail*. George G Harrap & Co Ltd.

Robert Burns. Henry Arthur Bright. 1874. *Some Account of the Glenriddell Manuscripts of Burns's Poems*. Kessinger Legacy Reprints.

Robert Burns. 1786. *Poems Chiefly in the Scottish Dialect*. Facsimile Kilmarnock Ed. printed by John Smith and Son, Glasgow Ltd, 1927.

Robert Burns. 1815. *The Works of Robert Burns with an Account of His Life*. Gale and Fenner, London.

Robert Burns. 1991. *The Complete Illustrated Poems, Songs and Ballads*. Lomond Books.

Robert Burns. 2013. *Complete Works, Ultimate Collection*, Everlasting Flames Publishing on Kindle.

David Kerr Cameron. 1978. *The Ballad and the Plough*. Victor Gollancz.

Catherine Carswell. 1990. *The Life of Robert Burns*. Canongate Classics.

Robert Crawford. 2010. *The Bard, Robert Burns, a Biography*. Pimlico.

R H Cromek. 1808. *Reliques of Robert Burns*. T Cadell & W Davies.

D C Cuthbertson. 1933. *Carrick Days*. Grant and Murray.

Charles S Dougall. 1911. *The Burns Country*. Adam and Charles Black.

Robert Fitzhugh and DeLancey Ferguson (ed). 1943. *Robert Burns, his Associates and Contemporaries*. The University of North Carolina Press.

John Galt. 1911. *The Annals of the Parish*. T N Foulis, Edinburgh.

George Gilfillan (ed). C1890. *The National Burns including the Airs of all the Songs*. William Mackenzie.

Hannah Glasse. 1747. This edition 1997. *The Art of Cookery Made Plain and Easy*. Applewood Books.

William Jolly. 1881. *Robert Burns at Mossgiel, with reminiscences of the poet by his herd boy*. Kessinger Legacy Reprints.

Maurine Lindsay (intro) 1981. *In the Land o' Burns*. Richard Drew Publishing.

James Mackay. 1987. *The Complete Letters of Robert Burns*. Alloway Publishing Ltd.

James Mackay. 2004. *Burns. A Biography*. Alloway Publishing Ltd.

Ian McIntyre. 2009. *Robert Burns, a Life*. Constable.

David McClure. 1994. *Tolls and Tacksmen*. Ayrshire Archaeological and Natural History Society.

Rosalind K Marshall. 1984. *Wet Nursing in Scotland 1500 – 1800*. Review of Scottish Culture.

Mauchline Burns Club. (Compiled by) 1986. *Mauchline in Times Past*. Chamberlain Publishing Ltd.

Mauchline Burns Club. 1996. *Mauchline Memories of Robert Burns*. Ayrshire Archaeological and Natural History Society.

Stuart Maxwell and Robin Hutchison. 1958. *Scottish Costume, 1550 – 1850*. Adam and Charles Black.

John D Ross. (Ed) *1894. Highland Mary: Interesting Papers on an Interesting Subject*. www.archive.org or Kessinger Legacy Reprints.

Gavin Sprott. 1990. *Robert Burns, Farmer*. National Museums of Scotland.

Maisie Steven. 1995. *Parish Life in 18th Century Scotland*. Scottish Cultural Press.

J B Stevenson. 1993. *Cup and Ring Markings at Ballochmyle, Ayrshire*. Edinburgh University Publishing.

Philip Sulley. 1896. *Robert Burns and Dumfries*. 1796 – 1896. Thos Hunter and Co. Dumfries.

Peter J Westwood. 2001. *Jean Armour, My Life and Times with Robert Burns*. Creedon Publications.

Acknowledgements

The list of people and institutions that have been helpful to me, generous with advice and support in all kinds of ways, is a long one, and I must apologise in advance for leaving anyone out. They include: Creative Scotland for financial support; the National Trust for Scotland; the beautiful Burns Birthplace Museum and Burns Cottage (with special thanks to Rebecca McCallum Stapley and Nat Edwards); the excellent Burns House Museum in Mauchline; the equally atmospheric and excellent Ellisland Farm with its uniquely knowledgeable curator, Les Byers; Friar's Carse Hotel, where the Riddells once lived; Robert Burns House in Dumfries; the Globe Inn, also in Dumfries (and especially Jane Brown); Scotland's People; Aberdeen University Library for helpful information about John Moir; the School of Scottish Studies at Edinburgh University; members of the Ayrshire Association of Businesswomen; the National Library of Scotland; and the Carnegie Library in Ayr.

Individual friends and acquaintances who have made the project much easier than it might otherwise have been include: the Rev David Albon and Hugh Brown of the Church of Scotland in Mauchline; the Rev Gerald Jones in Kirkmichael; Professor Alan Riach; Dr Valentina Bold; Nigel Deacon; Elinor Clark at Rozelle for kindly showing me the Moir portrait and the shawls; Elizabeth Kwasnik; old friends and dedicated Burns fans John and Brenda Kevan; the Royal College of Physicians and Surgeons in Glasgow; and Dr Sarah Learmonth for information about endocarditis and oral infection.

Thanks are due to Liam Brennan and Gerda Stevenson for 'being Rab and Jean' in my play *Tam o' Shanter*, for BBC Radio 4, and to Liam for reciting the poem in exactly the right accent; also to Donald Pirie, who was an utterly convincing Rab on stage at the Òran Mór, and to Clare Waugh, for being my definitive Jeany.

The project would have been much harder to complete without Alison Bell's inspirational and comforting chats over coffee and scones. Thanks too, to long-time friend and advice-giver Oenone Grant, to Valerie Laws and Chris Longmuir of Authors Electric, Carol Speirs of Many Thanks in Mauchline, writer friends Helena Sheridan, Fiona Atchison, Lesley Deschner and Janice Johnston, and all my many other Ayrshire friends and colleagues.

Huge thanks must go to my publisher, Sara Hunt, to Jenny Hamrick and Heather McDaid for editorial and proofreading, and to all at Saraband for support, inspiration and patience.

Finally, love, as ever, to my long-suffering husband Alan Lees, my son Charles and my dear late mum and dad who patiently and enthusiastically endured a great many weekends trekking and driving about Ayrshire and Dumfries with a poet-obsessed daughter.

This novel is dedicated, with love and respect, to the real Jean, with whom I seem to have lived and worked intensively for so many years.

By night, by day, a-field, at hame,
The thoughts o' thee, my breast inflame
And aye I muse and sing thy name —
I only live to love thee.

About the Author

Catherine Czerkawska, author of *The Physic Garden,* is a Scottish-based novelist and playwright. She graduated from Edinburgh University with a degree in Mediaeval Studies, followed by a Masters in Folk Life Studies from the University of Leeds. She has written many plays for the stage and for BBC Radio and for television, and has published nine novels, historical and contemporary. Her short stories have been published in many literary magazines and anthologies and as ebook collections, most recently by Hearst Magazines UK. She has also written non-fiction in the form of articles and books and has reviewed professionally for newspapers and magazines. *Wormwood*, her play about the Chernobyl disaster, was produced at Edinburgh's Traverse Theatre to critical acclaim in 1997, while her novel *The Curiosity Cabinet* was shortlisted for the Dundee Book Prize in 2005.

Catherine has taught creative writing for the Arvon Foundation and spent four years as Royal Literary Fund Writing Fellow at the University of the West of Scotland as well as serving on the committee of the Society of Authors in Scotland. When not writing, she collects and deals in the antique textiles that often find their way into her fiction.